UNDER THE SKIN

SUSANNA ROGERS

Print ISBN: 978-1-917705-03-5

Chapter One

A pub, loud music, the smell of stale beer. Perfect.

I leave my Corona on the bar while I knock back a shooter, quickly so as to cut down the burn at the back of my mouth. I don't even like vodka but I'm going to need it tonight. I'd order another, except the bloke next to me is chatting up the bartender, as if a pretty young thing like her is going to be interested in a middle-aged guy with a beer gut, not to mention a wedding ring.

It's been a while since I've worn mine, not since I searched out the first one-night stand after Charlie. The next day, I ripped the ring from my finger and sobbed my guts out because it felt like I was losing him all over again. And losing myself while I was at it.

I turn away and sip my beer, thinking about another vodka, wishing for oblivion.

"Well, hi there."

Oh God, he's talking to me.

"Hi," I say.

"Did you know you look just like Halle Berry?"

In my dreams maybe. My skin colour and crazy curly hair

come from my dad's Mauritian side of the family but I'm definitely no movie star.

"Um, no," I say, trying to avoid spluttering my beer.

"She's got the same big, brown eyes as you. She's very talented too."

Am I supposed to tell him I have special talents and play the game? I let him off easy, tell him I'm meeting someone, and he leaves.

Who am I kidding? That's exactly why I'm here. To find a man. To have sex. To get the burning that's been building inside me out of my system so that maybe, just maybe, I can feel normal again.

A band is setting up on the stage. There's a pool table on the far side of the room, a small dance floor, high tables with cowhide bar-stools, and neon signs for Buds and Becks. Makes me wonder what it'd be like to be a different person, to come here with friends to listen to the band, to drink and dance the night away, only it's not dancing I'm thinking of tonight.

Someone cuts through the crowd, waving at me. Ryan Moretti, my new next-door neighbour. Olive skin, some serious salt and pepper in his hair, quite a looker, only I shouldn't be looking or feeling anything for him. Hell, I can't possibly hook-up with someone I know. I made that mistake once before, a big mistake I'm never making again.

"Hi, Kate." Ryan edges closer. "I didn't know you liked rockabilly."

"Sorry?"

He nods towards the stage. "The band."

"Oh yeah, I love rockabilly." I shout to be heard, hoping he can't read my mind and that I don't sound like too much of a dork.

"I like a bit of fifties rock 'n' roll," he says, which explains the hairstyle. "How are you enjoying the house?"

A subject close to my heart. "It's awesome."

I'm housesitting for a year while the owner, Joel, is overseas. He wanted someone to take care of his cat and keep his house in its current state of immaculateness and not have huge gatherings. That's me. I am so not a party person.

And Ryan designed the place.

"You don't have to say that," he says.

I smile. "It's true. I'm lucky to be living there."

And the timing couldn't have been better. I wasn't coping in Melbourne and decided to come back to Perth for a fresh start. The hunky neighbour was merely an added bonus.

Ryan glances around. "I didn't expect to see you here."

"I'm catching up with a friend."

"We're meeting some people too. That's where we're off to next." He points to a guy behind him, hands in his pockets. "I'm keeping Sam company. Bad break-up."

I nod. "I guess he needs you then."

"You can join us if you like, Kate. You can always text your friend so they can come along too."

"Thanks." I force a smile, my heart sinking and swelling at the same time. "But not tonight."

A pause. "You've got my number if you change your mind."

So thoughtful of him, he gave it to me the day I moved in – in case something happened at night and I wanted him to check it out for me. The pull inside me is strong. Push and pull. Desire and deliberation.

Ryan and his friend leave. I let out a long sigh. It's tempting to have another vodka but I need to keep my wits about me and so far I'm not doing very well in the wits department.

A group of girls walk past. Heels, short skirts, strappy tops, as if it's not really winter out there. They look gorgeous but that's not me. I don't do skimpy, and don't like to wear anything less than long sleeves even in summer.

Maybe they're looking to meet someone too. I sure as hell

never thought in a hundred years that I'd end up trying to pick up a guy at a bar like this. Occasionally a friend would talk about hooking up with some guy she'd met and I'd giggle with the other girls, but I never wished that was me. For a start, you were putting your personal safety at risk going home with someone you didn't know, whether it was his place or yours, a concern I raised only once.

"It wasn't *his* place," Amy said at the time, deadpan. "It was the fire escape behind the club."

The other girls howled with laughter. I did too.

Part of me thinks I should be more careful but I've still got to live and God knows I don't want to hang around here all night.

I make my beer last as long as I can while leaning against the bar, trying to look natural. I'm surrounded by people who are happy, drinking, telling stories, laughing. You'd think this was the happiest place in the world. A group of people to my right burst out laughing after one of them says something. The guy is smiling, not laughing, looking at me. It's all about making a connection. Still, I lower my gaze, unable to keep it up.

He comes over, orders a Buffalo Trace and asks if he can get me something.

"You don't have to buy me a drink to talk to me." I don't even know if that's the right thing to say.

He smiles, white teeth gleaming against his dark skin. Turns out I'm doing fine because that's a friendly smile if I've ever seen one. He might be around my age, thirty-one, not too young and not too old. I'm like Goldilocks, who's found the bed that's just right.

"I'm Will." He shakes my hand. Polite.

"Nice to meet you. I'm Asher."

"Asher, that's a pretty name."

Much better than the Halle Berry line. I like this guy already.

"You here on your own?" he asks.

I sip my beer. "Got stood up by a girlfriend who had a better offer. Pretty sad really."

"Doesn't have to be sad. Things might work out for you anyway."

I smile over the rim of my glass.

Turns out I'm not so bad at flirting after all. And neither is he. I tell him a bit about myself and ask all about him. I smile and laugh at his jokes and get along with him just fine. He offers to buy me a drink again but I say I've had enough and he knocks back his bourbon without ordering another one. He suggests a game of pool. The guy is a hoot. Pool? Why not?

It happens quickly after that. He suggests his place. Fine by me, because there's no way I'm taking him back to mine so he knows where I live. I tell him my car is up the street, which is super-convenient because he didn't drive tonight.

Outside the bar, I'm overcome by a strange feeling as if we're being followed so I look around but there's nothing odd. I'm always imagining things.

Will pulls me close for a gentle kiss, then a not-so-gentle one, and I know this guy is going to hit the spot. My hand slides down to his butt while we walk to the car. Then when we get there, he says he likes the Mini, that it's cute like me. This guy is too much, a great arse and a great kisser, everything I could want right now.

My stomach is doing backflips as I drive through the suburbs, so maybe I'm not as good at this as I think. I park across the street from his place, thinking it's dark and the council should fork out for better lighting. Will takes my hand and slides his arm around my waist as we get out of the Mini. I stop thinking.

He turns on the hall light inside the house and nods towards the living room on the left. I shake my head, wait for him to get the message. It doesn't take long. He pulls me further into the house, pushes open another door, the bedroom. Neat and tidy, it's all the invitation I need. If the place was a mess or he'd left dirty underwear on the carpet, I'd probably leave.

He turns the light on. I turn it off. Not for a moment do I forget my scars. He can touch but I don't want him to see me. I wander in ahead of him, pull my shirt over my head and toss it on the floor. He wraps his arms around me and unclasps my bra in one swift move.

His fingertips brush my nipples. Electricity. I sigh. His hands cover my breasts. A power surge. I moan.

"Is that okay?" he asks.

I smile. "Very okay."

My boobs are on fire, burning at the slightest touch, aching as he kneads them in a way that's too much and not enough, my need desperate.

I want it gentle. I want it hard. I want it now.

Will gives me everything I want.

He's asleep as I search for my clothes scattered across the room and put them on as quietly as I can in the dark.

Will sits up, rubs his eyes. "What are you doing?"

"I'm going home. It's late."

"You don't have to go."

I give him a quick kiss on the cheek and step back.

"Asher, wait."

A pang of guilt shoots through me at the name I gave him. I'd forgotten.

He reaches across to turn on the bedside lamp, throws the covers off and slings his legs over the bed. "Hey, it doesn't have to be like this. Next time we can grab something to eat and go on a proper date. Or meet up for coffee. Get to know each other."

Everything is different now. It doesn't feel right to be looking at him sitting naked on the bed even though we've spent the last hour devouring each other. I feel more human now, less like a wild animal ready to pounce. Best we leave it here.

I step towards the door. "You're a lovely guy, Will."

"Do you really want to go… like this?"

"Yeah."

I feel bad for him. This would've been easier if all he wanted was a bit of fun, if he'd been less caring or if he was a bit of an arsehole. Turns out I picked a guy who's interested in a relationship when that's the last thing I want.

He slides off the bed and pulls on his jeans, the denim darker than the brown of his stomach and chest. "At least let me walk you to your car."

"Why?"

"To make sure you're safe."

I howl with laughter. Maybe it's the stress. Somehow this is the funniest thing I've ever heard. I've been training for years, first kickboxing, then Krav Maga, which is less martial artsy and where the rules don't matter. I loved everything about it, the cardio hit, the exhilaration, the feeling of power even if I knew violence was never simple, but that was in a different life.

Will doesn't know who he's talking to. But he's right. Bad shit can happen anywhere. Predators choose the time and place. It's a dangerous world out there.

Don't think about that night. Don't think about Charlie. My breath catches in my throat but the remnants of my laughter mask the fear.

"What's so funny?" Will asks.

I pull myself together. "You've gone to all the trouble of putting pants on. It'd be lovely if you walked me outside."

He adjusts himself as he steps closer. "This is kind of uncomfortable."

Fresh air hits me as soon as we walk out the door. It's dark out and I don't know the neighbourhood so maybe Will was right in wanting to walk with me. A gentleman. I hope he finds the right girl.

We reach the front of the Mini and I give Will a hug. Quick, this has to be quick.

He steps away, hesitates. "Bye, Asher."

The night air amplifies the sound of a car engine starting up, the rest of the street quiet. I wander to the driver's side of the Mini while he lingers in the middle of the road, watching me.

"Goodnight, Will," I say.

The low hum of the car engine becomes a roar. A vehicle comes speeding down the street. Dark. No lights. Will turns his head.

"Move!" I yell.

Will runs off the road onto the front verge outside his house. The four-wheel-drive veers, mounts the footpath, heading straight for him.

"Noooo!" I scream.

A god-awful thump fills the air. I watch in horror as the car crashes into Will, the bumper smashing into his legs, his body rolling over the bonnet onto the far side. Another thump as he lands on the grass.

The car screeches off into the distance.

Chapter Two

Paramedics. Police. Uniforms everywhere. The neighbours come out onto the street. Ambulance. Hospital. Doctors. Nurses. I tell them I'm fine, just shaken. I'm not the one who got hit.

Later, the police station. A statement. I know the drill. They don't do major interviews in hospital corridors.

Though it's two in the morning, I call Laura on the way to the station, thankful she still has a landline in case one of the kids needs to reach her at some terrible hour. A call this late can only be bad news so I apologise for scaring her and tell her what's happened. She meets me at the station.

She's been my lifesaver so many times it's not funny. Before I moved back here, it didn't matter that she lived on the other side of the country in a different time zone, she used to call or message in the morning to get me out of bed. It was a godsend in the first month or two when I was full of dread and couldn't face the day; until I got my act together, that is, relatively speaking. It's never mattered that she's fifteen years older than me and at a different stage in life, not after we got to know each other. It always felt like we were meant to be friends, especially since Charlie was best mates with her brother.

A young cop, Alex Sheridan, introduces himself then leads us to a small waiting room with white walls and pale-grey padded vinyl chairs. Some old magazines and a pristine copy of the Police Department *Annual Report* sit on top of a melamine coffee table.

Laura ushers me towards a seat. She's pulled her brown hair into a ponytail and looks unassuming, as always, but her face transforms when she speaks and gives you her full attention. And somehow, miracle of miracles, she doesn't look like she's half asleep.

The officer stands in the doorway. He must be in his twenties but has the soft skin of a teenager, so pale and smooth it's almost translucent.

He clears his throat. "Are you Kate's lawyer?"

"Laura Bentley." She turns to him. "I'm a solicitor. I'm also her friend, and I think Kate needs to talk to a friend for starters."

"Sure. I'll give you some time." The officer leaves.

Laura sits down beside me, her hand on my shoulder. "Tell me everything."

So I do. She nods, asks the occasional question. She listens.

Laura has told me lots of stories. She works part-time for Legal Aid, spends most of her time defending young offenders, kids who are out on the streets at night and who haven't had a chance in life, the ones other people have given up on. Many of them have committed crimes and inflicted terrible damage on other people, she's aware of that. She's also seen the police treat kids unfairly and fail to investigate properly. Worse things than that too.

In my experience, the police have only ever been polite and professional. In Laura's world, it's different. But I trust her.

Besides, something feels off tonight, other than the obvious fact that an innocent man is in hospital with serious injuries. This doesn't feel like it was a case of wrong place, wrong time. It feels plain wrong.

I stare at the carpet, an exciting shade of dark grey to contrast with the walls and furniture. Wouldn't want too much colour.

"I didn't do anything bad," I say.

"I know."

Laura has primed me about the way the law works and how it isn't about right or wrong or fair or just. *The law is only about the law.* It's certainly not about the truth, though that's probably the most valuable thing of all, the one thing that will help us survive and thrive.

"I'm glad you called me first," she says. "You did the right thing."

Still, I can't look at her. "I know it seems terrible. Charlie has only been gone a year. And here I am hooking up with some guy I met at the pub. I'm so into personal safety and security. It doesn't even make sense."

"I don't think you did anything stupid, Kate. I'm not judging you and it's none of my business anyway. I can see what you're going through." She squeezes my hand. "You still miss him."

My lower lip trembles.

"I wish you'd get yourself into therapy and get some professional help," Laura says.

Something she's said before. Tried that and it didn't work.

The young cop knocks on the door. "There's a room free now if you're ready."

We follow Alex Sheridan into the interview room which is remarkably similar to the waiting room, only with a laptop perched on top of a large table. A female officer joins us.

I go through the events of the evening from beginning to end. Somehow it's easier now I've already told Laura.

Then come the questions.

"Did you get a look at the car?" Alex asks.

"Not really." I try to picture the scene. "It was dark, no streetlights. He didn't have his lights on."

"You said 'he'? Did you see the driver?"

"No, I just assumed. I don't know."

"Don't suppose you got the registration number? Even a partial rego?"

I shake my head. I was useless.

"The make?"

"Sorry, cars aren't really my thing." With the exception of the Mini that Charlie bought for me. "The car was a four-wheel drive, deep grey or black."

Probably. I can't even get the colour right. It was dark. It happened so quickly. I have all the excuses.

The horror of Will lying on the grass outside his house comes back to me. *Will, please be alive.* The silence of the street, the only sound my footsteps and my panting as I ran across to him, my screams having faded into the distance.

And I wonder, will I have panic attacks about this too? Will this be the new nightmare that wakes me?

Alex Sheridan clears his throat. "Is there anyone you can think of who might have reason to go after you or William Sharma?"

"No."

"Did anyone follow you back to William's house, maybe someone from the Elysian Bar?"

"No, not that I know of."

Maybe I should've been more alert instead of getting my rocks off with Will. I did look around so it's doubtful anyone followed us, but who knows?

More questions. Do I think it could've been someone out for a joyride? Is it possible the driver didn't see Will?

I wait for a lull. "There's something you should probably know." I look at Laura and she nods.

"A year ago, I was involved in an attack. Not here. In Melbourne."

I tell him.

We met friends from the hospital for a late dinner at a new restaurant in the city run by some famous chef because Charlie liked to go to places that were 'in'. He had a few drinks to let off steam. Maybe things would've been different if he'd been sober, more alert, if he'd been faster. More to the point, if I'd been faster and acted sooner instead of waiting till it was too late.

A man came up and asked for our help because his girlfriend had collapsed so we followed him a short way. We had no idea he wanted to get out of view of the CCTV. Charlie, in particular, had no idea.

A multi-storey car park. *Didn't I always tell you they were dangerous?* That's what my mother said. Sometimes her words haunt me.

Fuck.

The guy is right in front of us. I see his face. I've seen it so many times, that night, on the police computer, in my dreams, my nightmares. That face flashes and pulses before me, going in and out of focus, like a movie projector gone wrong.

I take a deep breath and force myself to get a grip. White walls around me, dark-grey carpet beneath, Laura holding my hand, a police officer opposite. I'm safe.

Laura squeezes my shoulder. "It's okay, Kate. You don't have to keep going."

I turn to her. "Sorry?"

"The police can look up the details or I can brief them."

"Oh." I'm here and this is now. I clear my throat. "I've gone back to my maiden name, Kate Mamotte. In Melbourne I was Kate Best."

Or Katherine Best, as the courts and the media referred to me. Yep, only the newspapers and my mother use my full name. And now I'm back in my old town with my old name.

"I don't think there's any connection between the two events," I add. "I just wanted to get it out there."

My story doesn't seem to ring a bell with the officer, and I'm thankful. In Melbourne, everyone knew. Occasionally people came up to me on the street, other times they stared, or at least it felt that way. Or maybe it's been fading from people's consciousness since then. Other crimes and deaths must have taken prominence in the past year. Horrible shit continues to happen. It's the way of the world.

But this is my horrible.

Chapter Three

The only places I hate more than police stations are hospitals, yet here I am. I can't ignore Will after something like this has happened, especially after the way I treated him. And since I don't fancy visiting him at home, a trip to the hospital suddenly seems like a good idea.

He's reclined in bed, one leg in a cast, his arm in a sling, dark-green hospital-issue pyjama top buttoned up, his face and neck covered in bruises. Probably so is the rest of him. Shoulders slumped, he's staring at the phone in his hand.

I take a deep breath, knock on the door and step over the threshold. Will looks up, his face haggard, skin hanging from his swollen cheekbones as if he's aged overnight and maybe he has. I remember now, how much it hurts the day after a traumatic injury, and the pain you feel after the adrenaline and the body's natural protection responses have worn off.

"What are you doing here?" he asks.

"I won't stay long."

He doesn't tell me to piss off, which is as much as I can hope for, so I edge closer to the bed, holding a silver gift bag in front of me.

"I got you something. Buffalo Trace." I wait. "Bourbon."

"I know what it is."

The timing isn't right so I hold on to the bag for now.

"Never thought I'd see you again," he says.

"Well, that was the plan. *Before*, that is. Then things changed."

"Tell me about it. I made the news." He shows me his phone. "Police are searching for witnesses or dashcam footage from any cars in the vicinity of a hit-and-run in Dianella late last night. A man in his thirties. Me. You don't even rate a mention."

He places the phone face down on his lap, his movements stiff, and looks at me with an intensity that sends a bolt of guilt through my gut.

"I'm sorry," I mumble. "About your injuries, about everything."

"Really, *Asher*?"

I deserve this. "It's Kate. I figured the police must have told you my name. Our fling… getting together… it was only meant to be for one night."

I'm about to give another apology. I stop myself. I should let him talk. Or not talk.

My phone goes off loud and clear in the bag slung across my shoulder, letting me know there's a text message. It makes me jump.

Will gives me a dull look. "You might as well get it."

I pick up the phone.

Too busy for your mum?

I drop the phone back into my bag. I shouldn't have looked, except I'm nervous. No way can I deal with my mother right now. I'll set my phone to vibrate as soon as I'm out of here and ignore any calls in the meantime.

"What else about you is fake?" Will asks.

"The other stuff is true. I grew up in Perth, went to

Melbourne for uni and lived there for thirteen years, came back for a fresh start." I bite my lip, wondering if I should come out with the full truth. "I don't really live in East Perth. I didn't want you to know where I lived."

Silence.

"In Subiaco, if you want to know."

More silence. I shouldn't have come.

"I really am a writer. You can google Kate Mamotte, copywriter."

I had to get a new website with my new name after I got rid of the old one. It's a necessity for a freelancer. Of course, you can find anything on Google if you know where to look and you dig deep enough. I've got to hope people don't dig but I don't mind if Will does.

He won't find me on social media though, not since I deleted every account, personal and business, got rid of them all. No regrets. People were hounding me, journalists, the media, people I didn't want to talk to. Then there were others who were nasty, venomous, swearing, slurring, disgusting. So I pressed delete.

"How did you get the scars?" he asks.

My hand covers my abdomen, fingers spread apart, an instinctive movement. He's seen all of me, of course he has.

"You didn't say anything last night."

He shrugs. "Reckon I can ask now."

"I-I got attacked last year by a man with a blade. They're knife wounds." I put the bag on the floor, pull up my sleeves and show him the slash marks that have partly faded, unlike the gashes on my stomach, then pull my sleeves down again. "That's not a bullshit story. That's the truth."

Nothing from Will. *Please talk to me, give me something.*

"I don't like to talk about it," I say. "So I don't."

Will glances at me. "Did they get the guy?"

"No. He got away." I swallow. "And I got away with my life."

"Me too."

Charlie didn't, though. Still, I'm glad this isn't Will's funeral. Charlie's was hard enough to handle, the bits of it that I can remember, that is. I've blanked out so much. They held off the funeral till I was out of hospital, which meant his poor parents had to organise the whole thing, as if it wasn't hard enough for them already. Best friend Noah gave a beautiful speech, as did Charlie's father, Michael. His mum held herself together until Mike sat down afterwards and then she lost it, whereas I kept up a steady stream of tears throughout the ceremony. I felt for her, more than for anyone else, and for Mike.

Mum saw I needed help and came to stay with me for a couple of weeks. Laura did too, but then she had to go back home, and I worked out the rest of the world was carrying on as normal.

"Are you okay?" Will asks.

I place the gift bag on the bedside table. "I'll leave this here."

"Nice meeting you, Kate."

"You're such a lovely guy, Will."

"So people tell me. And that's really my name."

The need for some sort of explanation grips my gut, despite the fact I know there aren't always answers. "Do you have any idea why anyone would do something like this?"

"Nope, none at all. You?"

I shake my head. I remember the way the car was heading straight for him, how quick Will was in darting to the other side of the road, how the driver veered to make sure the car hit him.

I step back. "Bye, Will."

"Bye, Kate."

Have a good life, Will. I give him a wan smile as I leave.

One thing's for sure. Now I've got that out of my system, I don't need to hook-up with anyone again. Not for a while. I've got enough on my plate with setting myself up here and trying to pull in more work.

As I walk down the hospital corridor, there's a woman pacing at the other end, a crying toddler in her arms, the little boy's face red. His sobs are distraught, not tired or forced, and it grabs at my gut. I wonder if he's sick, but this isn't the children's hospital. Maybe they're visiting a sick relative. Though I don't know what's going on, it reminds me things could be a lot worse and that I shouldn't feel sorry for myself.

When the sliding doors open and the fresh air outside hits me, I scan the area as I stride to the car. There's nothing suspicious, yet something feels wrong. My whole life has felt wrong since the night Charlie and I were attacked.

I can't help thinking of the man who did that, because he's out there somewhere, probably still in Melbourne, only I don't know that for sure. I moved to Perth. He could have too. The police never got him. He could be anywhere and he might be out to finish what he started.

Maybe Will wasn't the intended target last night and there's someone who wants to get me instead.

Or maybe I should be more gracious because Will's the one who's in hospital and I'm not.

I park the Mini on the street outside the house because I'm too lazy to drive down the back laneway and reverse the car into the garage. Not lazy. Exhausted.

My phone vibrates with a text message before I'm even out of the car. Mum again.

I thought I might be seeing more of you now you're in Perth?

I sigh. She says this as though I've been ignoring her, whereas I've been trying to get her to come over but she'd rather complain than visit. I'll wait till I get inside, then call to set up a date. I'll keep the conversation simple because I can't tell her what happened with Will. She'd freak, and the last thing I need is to be blamed when I already feel bad enough.

The woman has a sixth sense, I swear. She knows exactly how to get to me and when I'm at my lowest point and that's exactly when she pounces. Still, I refuse to let her rile me. Mum is one of the reasons I came back to Perth, so I can try to rebuild the relationship and also to help take care of her. Not that she's old, but she needs help around the house and there's no one else around. Repair, replenish, revitalise, that's my new motto.

I get out and close the car door. I should think positive on a day like this, a magnificent sunny Perth winter's day, the sort of day visitors from England or Sweden might find hard to believe is the middle of winter. Maybe I should pretend to be from a cold climate, pretend to be someone who's not me.

The trees in Subiaco are wonderful, from ancient gnarled peppermints with straggly branches to vibrant poincianas that stretch out like giant umbrellas to massive white-barked gums with branches hanging across the middle of the road.

I should feel spoilt and make the most of this. It's nothing like the place where I grew up, a suburb way out of town, no trees, old houses, noisy neighbours. You could call it working class but that would assume most of the people were working. It's also nothing like the dilapidated share house I lived in while I was at uni in Melbourne or the tiny bedsit I moved into later. Mind you, I was so grateful for the scholarship that let me move across the other side of the country, and I loved that crappy bedsit and having my own space.

I should appreciate all the good things in my life, like Joel's house, a concrete bunker, an architectural masterpiece and a godsend all in one. I don't know where I'll be living a year from now but guaranteed it won't be as amazing as this, nowhere near it.

My phone vibrates in my bag as I reach the front gate. And just like that, it gets my back up. Surely it can't be Mum again. I pick up the phone. And stare. It's not Mum. No caller ID. A message. One word.

Bitch

A bolt of fear shoots through me. I look around as if someone might be watching. This can't be right. Because no one knows how much of a ruthless bitch I am.

Chapter Four

I do a little editing, not much work coming my way. I do a lot of cleaning, making sure the house is in a state of constant immaculateness. I've got the time for a lot of exercise as well, because too much exercise is never enough. I don't contact Will because that's not going to aid his healing or make him feel any better. I report the text message to the police, as per Laura's instructions, and try to put that behind me or I lie to myself that I'm not thinking about it.

I'm on my way to meet Laura now. Closing the front gate behind me, I scan my surroundings but nothing is odd and nothing is moving except the leaves on the trees. It's only a short walk to the train station. I'm lucky to live close to the railway line because Perth public transport is notoriously bad, even if it's a hell of a lot better than before I moved away.

A gust of wind whips along the main road, blowing a curl of hair across my cheek. I hold my hair in place as I cross the road. Walk. Don't stop.

"Kate! Kate!"

I hear my name and stop, my heart jolting me to attention. Where am I? I remember walking to the station but can't recall buying a ticket, getting on the train, getting off, all things I must have done. I've blanked out again. Crap. Major crap. I keep thinking those episodes are behind me and they keep happening. Now I'm in the city, buildings towering overhead, and a small crowd has gathered on the other side of the road, gazing up, arms raised, pointing.

Laura waves, motioning for me to join her. I take a deep breath and weave my way closer, greeting her with a kiss on the cheek, as if we haven't seen each other in months. I say hello to her husband, Theo. He said he'd try to make it, since Royal Perth Hospital is only a short walk away.

"Wow, I don't usually get to see you in work clothes," I say to Laura.

She's wearing a grey top and blazer with a black skirt, and she'd look quite lawyerly if it wasn't for the red boots and bag. She can't help but let a bit of personality sneak in.

"Good timing," she says. "Noah's team is next."

That's why I'm here – to keep her company and show Noah some support. Her brother is about to abseil down the AT Tower, along with a bunch of other people, all of them raising money for cancer research and of course Noah is determined his team will raise the most. Though he's not a doctor, he's joined a team of medics, friends of Theo's. Right now half a dozen people are dangling off the lower part of the tower, a few more at the top.

"That's them. Noah's on the right." Laura points to four dark figures at the top of the building, where they've set up scaffolding, for safety reasons probably.

"How can you tell?"

I don't wait for an answer. I squeeze her arm as Noah (or at least I think it's Noah) leans back at ninety degrees to the wall, the first of them to get going. Even from my safe position on the ground, the height freaks me out. No way would I do that. I don't like looking over the edge of buildings. Don't even like other people doing it.

Someone approaches. It's Ryan, my new neighbour. He seems to be popping up everywhere, in the laneway behind our houses, at the Elysian Bar a week ago and now here.

"Hi, Kate."

"I wasn't expecting to see you here," I say.

"Passing by. I had a meeting in the city. Did you enjoy the band the other night?"

"Oh, they were great."

"Did they play all the old rockabilly classics?"

"A few."

I have no clue about rockabilly. Luckily he spots Laura and Theo and leans across to say hello to them.

Laura smiles with pride. "My brother Noah's up there."

"Wow." Ryan looks up. "I've heard about this."

Meanwhile, I try not to stare at Ryan and fail. That's quite a nose he's got. I've never noticed it before, never seen him in profile, and maybe I shouldn't be looking anyway.

I stare at the building. Noah and his team have scaled the first leg of their abseil and are on the lower portion where we can see them more clearly.

"Um, is that Spider-Man?" Ryan asks.

"Yep," Laura says. "The team decided to dress up in superhero costumes to get into the spirit of things."

"Why not, eh?" Ryan turns to me. "How are you and Esmeralda doing?"

As well as housesitting, I'm looking after the world's most beautiful and most temperamental cat. Mum is coming around tomorrow to see the house and meet the cat. *That's* the part she's most excited about.

"Esmeralda is getting only the best of care," I say.

Laura stands on tiptoe as if that'll help her see better. "I think Noah's reached the bottom now. I'm glad he's safe."

Of course she is. She has two teenagers in the house, a legal career, a surgeon husband who's hardly ever home, and she cares about all the people in her life.

Ryan leans a little closer. "You said you're a copywriter?"

"That's right."

"I hope I don't seem like a stalker but I googled you."

Google sends a shiver up my spine. I hate Google, can't stand it, even though I use it every day, but I keep things light and smile. "I hardly think you're a stalker at all."

"Look, I've got a mate who runs an agency, web and design and that sort of thing."

This piques my interest. "Really, what's the firm called?"

"Hintons."

"I'll look them up, you know, stalk them a bit."

"Maybe we can talk another time," Ryan says.

"Sure." I nod, trying to look nonchalant rather than desperate. "I'd appreciate that."

He has no idea how much I'd love to get more business through the metaphorical door. Charlie always told me not to stress, that I didn't need to keep working all the time, that he'd take care of me. Instead it turns out that at age thirty-one I can barely make a living.

A group of men in superhero costumes make their way through the crowd, Noah at the front, his eyes on me when they should be on Laura.

"Laura's brother looks just like her," Ryan says.

"Really? I can kind of see what you mean."

"He seems very driven."

"Yeah, he is."

Noah's reputation must've preceded him. He works in finance and investments and a bunch of other stuff I don't understand. I guess when you've grown up the way he and

Laura have, you don't want to end up poor again. He and Charlie met back when they were both students doing different degrees, both of them hard-working and dedicated.

Spider-Man, Superman and Batman are grinning, on a high after their abseil and apparently unaware that they're grown men wearing their underpants on the outside, whereas Noah doesn't seem silly at all. He's dressed as Thor and looks like Chris Hemsworth only without the long hair and beard. Funny how he can be so good-looking but it doesn't make me feel anything. Maybe I've known him too long.

Then Noah hugs me and doesn't let go, always so effusive.

"Congratulations." I nudge him away. "That was a sensational abseil."

He hugs Laura, which warms my heart a little, while the other superheroes chat with Theo.

A woman I've never seen before comes up to me. "Hi, I'm Adrienne, a friend of Laura's."

"I'm Kate." I want to add that I'm not used to crowds and socialising.

"My husband is Batman."

"One of Noah's team?"

She laughs. "Men, honestly! Batman! Pete's a brilliant neurosurgeon but he's no superhero."

Standing there stunned, I get the rundown on how her kids and Laura's went to primary school together but her boys are at Scotch now, an expensive private school, and Adrienne is very busy ferrying them to and from after-school activities. Apparently it's nice to see a young person like myself moving into the area. How young does she think I am?

Luckily Batman comes along and I excuse myself. I'm exhausted already.

I turn to Noah. "Congratulations, by the way."

"Yeah," Ryan adds. "Fifty-five storeys. That's impressive."

Noah shrugs. "No big deal. It's not my first rodeo."

He's always doing daredevil things, one after the other and buying Harleys and sports cars, a bit like a mid-life crisis, only without being middle-aged. Charlie used to give him stick about it, the way men do. That was despite the fact Charlie would join him in heli-skiing and other assorted thrill-seeker activities, none of which were my cup of tea. I stuck to martial arts. Much safer.

"They made us watch a safety video up there," Noah says with an eye-roll. "They said we'd all feel terrified. *As if.*"

"From where I was standing, it looked pretty terrifying," I say.

"Oh, Kate." Noah smiles. "You don't have to worry about me. Today was a win-win situation all round. We raised a heap of money for a good cause and had fun doing it."

I look from Noah to Ryan. "You guys know each other?"

"Sure," Ryan says. "Everyone in Subi knows everyone else."

Noah has a house here because it's a good investment and he comes over regularly. But he lives in Melbourne.

He points to the top of the building. "You know my new office is up there? The refurb is nearly complete, Kate. You've got to come and see it soon."

I nod. "Sure."

"I'm changing things around, moving forward. I want to take my business to the next level, build up my clientele in Perth, so I'm making this my base. A permanent move. I can still fly to Melbourne once a month to keep things ticking over. Maybe more often if I need to."

My stomach sinks. Somehow even though I knew it was coming, it's not what I want to hear. I came here to get away. Can't he see that?

I straighten, suddenly stiff, then tell myself he has a right to live wherever he wants. Besides, I shouldn't get upset at someone in a Thor costume.

"I'll see you around, then," Ryan says as he leaves.

"I'm off too." I step away. "I'll say bye to Laura."

Noah takes my arm. "You've been through a lot, Kate."

I lower my gaze. *A lot* doesn't even begin to cover it.

"It's been a year," he says.

"I know."

"I'm not saying you should forget about the past. You can't. But you've got to start thinking about yourself. It's wonderful that you've come to Perth for a new beginning."

"Yep."

"And so have I. We can do this together, you know."

Which is not what I had in mind at all.

I say goodbye to everyone, then make it to the city station and get off the train in Subiaco without blanking out, a minor miracle. Sometimes you've got to take the small wins.

Chapter Five

So far, so good, no major dramas. Not that having my mum over should be an issue but it's better if I'm prepared.

Mum crinkles her nose as she pushes her empty plate back. "The cake's a bit dry."

"Is it? I was worried the orange syrup might've made it soggy."

"That's what it is! I couldn't put my finger on what wasn't quite right."

Mum looks around at the rammed concrete walls, their roughness a contrast to the immaculate polished concrete floor and perfect white ceiling. The furniture is verging on spartan, not even any window coverings in the living area, all part of the minimalist aesthetic. It's a lot to take in if you're not used to it.

Even for me. Laura gave me a rundown on the place and I checked out the online articles before I'd even spoken to Joel, the owner. I remember how nervous I was when he gave me a tour of the house, anxious he might change his mind. I still can't believe I've got this place for the next year.

I reach across for the empty plates and mugs.

Mum purses her lips. "I don't like to say it."

"Say what?"

"This house is terrible, so cold and empty. It's like a… like a prison or a concentration camp." She shakes her head. "The architect who designed this house must've been off his rocker."

"You know he lives next door?"

She waves it off. "If you don't like it here, you can come and stay with me, you know that, don't you?"

"Thanks, Mum."

"And I can introduce you to Renata. She makes the most amazing cakes. She's so clever. Very eloquent too. She used to be an English teacher."

"Great."

Renata is eloquent even though I'm the one who's a writer. Sometimes I'm not sure what's going on, with Mum, with me, with anything.

She tilts her head. "Your hair looks lovely like that."

"Thanks."

I'll take any compliment I can get from her. I used to keep my hair long and straight and lighter because Charlie liked it that way. No more. A few months ago, I cut my hair off to shoulder-length, dyed it back to my natural dark colour and left it to curl or wave or do whatever it's going to do. So liberating.

Mum stands. "Honestly, Katherine, your old house in Melbourne was much nicer than this."

It was the opposite of this with runners in the hallway, paintings on the walls, cushions on top of cushions, a soft furnishings overload, and ornaments on every shelf. Charlie took comfort in being surrounded by things. Me, not so much.

"Did you really have to sell it?" Mum asks.

"Yes, I really did."

Mum seems to think I'm rich. I used to think I was too. I tried to explain it to her and then gave up. It's the one thing Noah helped me with when I was trying to make sense of the mortgage and the bills and the loans. I guess he's not a finance guy for nothing and for that, I'll always be grateful.

I load the dirty dishes into the dishwasher. "Would you like to take some cake home? You'd be doing me a favour."

Mum wanders into the kitchen. "That'd be lovely, thanks."

I open the pantry to get a container and show her shelves so neat they'd probably make Marie Kondo weep. I wrap up half the cake for Mum.

"You've always been so organised and orderly," she says.

"Yep."

"Remember when you used to watch *Toy Story*? And you'd line up all your toys next to you, and they had to be in exactly the right order."

"They were mostly Jack's toys." Mr Potato Head was mine, though.

"He was happy to let you play with them."

Jack was always looking after me. When I was little, he showed me how to do things from drawing cartoon characters to making a doll's house. Later, we graduated to painting the lounge room and using a drill. He was a big brother and father-figure all rolled into one. I guess he had to be since it was only the three of us after Dad walked out when I was five. I can barely remember my father or maybe I don't want to.

Mum gets a faraway look in her eye. "Jack was such a good lad."

Till he wasn't. I don't want to ruin the moment.

"He got that from my side of the family," she adds.

"Sure."

Any negative traits come from my father's side of the family, the Mauritian side that I barely know. Nothing bad comes from Mum's Aussie side. Luckily, she doesn't go there, this time.

Esmeralda slinks into the kitchen, rubbing herself along Mum's legs and giving my mother her full attention with her amazing azure eyes. Of course, nothing less than a sleek Siamese cat would do for Joel. She's a stunner.

Mum bends over and pats her, murmuring pleasant words to her while Esmeralda lifts her head and purrs right back as if they're having a conversation.

Mum stands, so I try to take over but Esmeralda digs her claws into my hand and leaps away at a hundred miles an hour. She'll warm to me eventually, I'm sure. Meanwhile I rub my hand.

"It's only a scratch." Mum frowns. "Have you got a house key for me?"

I have no idea what she's talking about. "Pardon?"

"Well, you've always had a key to my place." She looks at me as if I'm an idiot. "I thought you'd give me a key to yours. I mean, what if you lose your key? You live on your own."

"There's a lockbox at the side of the house with a spare."

Joel apologised for the archaic measure, his words, not mine. He hadn't got around to setting up surveillance and security, and then he was called away for work.

"What if you forget the code?" Mum asks.

"I won't."

I used my usual code, Jack's birthday, the code I use for 'everyday' passwords.

"Fine," she says, though it clearly is not. She takes her bag and the cake and turns away.

"Mum."

Nothing.

I follow her down the hall.

"Mum."

Still nothing.

I sigh and pull the door open. It's always this way with her. Doesn't matter what I do, it's not good enough. I'll never be good enough.

As I'm walking Mum to the front gate, Ryan arrives, shopping bags in hand. He must've done a grocery shop.

"Hi there," he calls out.

Mum nudges me, asking in a low voice, "Is that him?"

"I'll introduce you." I wave at Ryan. He comes closer, depositing his bags on the footpath.

"This is my mother, Julia," I say. "And this is Ryan."

Mum's eyes widen. "So you're an architect? Katherine tells me you designed this house."

"Yeah, I'll be entering it in a couple of architecture competitions."

"That's so exciting," Mum says. "Where do you get your inspiration from?"

"Actually, this project was different from the others I've worked on. Joel wanted something that fit with his orderly lifestyle, so that led to a specific brief. As an architect, it was exciting to have the opportunity to work on something like this, but I was designing it for Joel. A dream come true." Ryan places a hand on his chest. "For me anyway."

"You're too modest. The house is like something from a magazine. It's beautiful."

"Not everyone thinks so," he says.

"Well, I do."

Does she? It makes my head spin.

Ryan turns to me. "It must be the same with your work. You work to a brief and sometimes you get a project where you can let loose."

I open my mouth to speak but Mum jumps in.

"Katherine? Let loose? You've got to be kidding. She thinks she's letting rip if she messes with the punctuation in her writing!"

Mum laughs as if this is hilarious. She doesn't seem to notice no one else is laughing.

"Your daughter is very talented." Ryan smiles. "I've checked out the writing samples on her website."

We chat a bit longer, then Ryan leaves.

Mum turns to me. "He doesn't know, does he?"

"No, why would he?"

"I can tell." She pauses. "Don't think you can catch a man like him."

Her comment leaves me gaping. Did I hear right?

"Oh, my Katherine," she says. "I was going to say… you're stronger than you know. You have to be to have lived through what you did, my precious darling."

"Please don't call me that."

It's never one thing with Mum. It's everything. We've been through this before. Charlie used to call me his precious, and I can't bear the name from anyone else.

I stand there while she gets in her car and drives off. Then I drag myself into the house, barely making it to the front door when the first spluttery sob comes out. I close the door behind me. I touch my face. Tears.

Mum is wrong. I wasn't 'strong' the night Charlie and I were attacked. I'm not strong.

I can't explain it to her. I couldn't even explain it to the psychologists, not the first one or the second one I tried. It's no wonder I stopped going when neither of them truly got it. I couldn't save the man I loved. Me, of all people, me with my focus on self-defence and years of training under my belt and an actual black belt while we're at it, and none of it helped. The second shrink nodded like she understood, asked me why I felt that way. Why the hell did she think?

Survivor guilt, she called it. Nope, that doesn't even come close. I don't want that label. Survivor failure, is that even a term? I should've been faster, quicker, smarter, stronger. I should've been everything I wasn't.

Chapter Six

A door is banging. My eyes spring open, my heart racing. I reach for the phone at my bedside. It's 2am.

Lying still, I listen. Sure enough, the door bangs again, the sound coming from inside the house. Then again.

I sling my legs over the bed and sit up, cold air biting my cheeks, my body still warm in Charlie's old Cookie Monster pyjamas. It's Charlie sending me a message because he's angry, maybe about Will, maybe about something else.

The door bangs, fainter this time.

I wrap my fluffy dressing gown around myself and slip my feet into a pair of Ugg boots, ugly but necessary. I stalk through the whole house, room by room, turning on lights, opening every closet door but even before I've made my way to the back of the house, I know I won't find anything. There are no drafts in this house built to precision standards with its sealed doors and double glazing, and there were no doors left ajar anyway.

My ears are still pricked as I slide onto a dining chair. It was Charlie banging that door, I know it, trying to punish me for getting together with Will, as if I haven't suffered and struggled enough already, as if I didn't try to protect him that night, as if I didn't get cut and stabbed too. I drop my head into my hands and rub my temples.

Don't fight the knife.

How many times have I heard those words, or a variation on it, during weapons training? A knife attack isn't like in the movies. An attacker won't come at you with one strike, wait for you to respond and then try again. It's not neat and clean. The guy will stab you over and over again. Like a sewing machine needle, in and out, cut, stick, slit, slice, slash, until you drop. Because he doesn't give a shit about your life. Chances are you won't see the knife coming and might not even know you've been stabbed till it's too late.

Run. If someone pulls a knife in public, always run if you can. Kick the guy away, make some distance, distract him, don't let him get close, know where the exits are and get the hell out.

Then there's the kicker, the proviso that always follows, because you can't run if you have to protect your loved ones.

I never thought that would be me.

Why? Why Charlie, of all people, a doctor, someone who helped people and saved lives? So pointless.

The lights go on next door in Ryan's yard. Maybe he can't sleep either. I know the feeling. No way am I going to be able to fall asleep with thoughts rocketing around in my head, about Will being hit by a car, Charlie who's both dead and taunting me, doors banging, knives slicing.

Maybe some fresh air will do me good. At the very least it should make me grateful to get back under the duvet. I open the sliding door and step onto the deck, the smell of mulch and eucalyptus engulfing me, cold air hitting me like a slap in the face. I tie my dressing gown more tightly.

There's a cough from next door. I jump.

"Is that you, Kate? It's me, Ryan. I thought you should know, so you don't get freaked."

Freaked? Me? Whatever could give him that idea?

"Hang on a sec," I say.

I step up onto a concrete planter box that sits in front of a feature section of dry stone that lines the fence, to find I have an amazing view of Ryan's yard. And of Ryan, who's standing on the other side, his hair tousled like a messed-up James Dean if the actor had got old enough for his hair to start turning grey. Also if he'd been Italian.

"Sorry if I scared you," Ryan says. "I take it you couldn't sleep either?"

"Nope. You must be freezing."

He's wearing blue checked pyjama pants with a grey hoodie thrown over the top, Birkenstocks on his feet, hardly sturdy cold weather gear. The term 'effortlessly handsome' comes to mind. I shouldn't think it. I shouldn't think anything.

"A bit," he says. "Ah, I know what'll warm us up. Wait right here."

Ryan steps inside, then comes out carrying a frosted bottle and two tumblers that he deposits on his outdoor table. He pours a generous amount into each glass, carries them over and hands me a glass.

I stare at it. "Will this help us sleep?"

"At this point, it's not going to hurt."

True. I sniff the glass. "Smells like…"

"Vodka, hopefully." Ryan knocks back a mouthful.

I take a sip. "I know. This tastes like caramel Drumsticks."

"It does a bit." He laughs, takes another gulp. "Maybe the marketing people at Absolut thought vanilla vodka sounded more sophisticated."

"Yeah, you know what marketing people are like." I give him a sneaky sideways glance and have another drink. The alcohol settles in my stomach. Soothing. I look across his backyard and to the night sky beyond. "It's pretty out here. Nearly a full moon."

"A gibbous moon."

"Sorry?"

"A three-quarter moon is called a gibbous moon."

Where on earth has this come from? I stare at him. So surreal to be looking over the fence drinking vodka with my neighbour, both of us in our pyjamas at two in the morning. Or three. Or whatever time it might be.

He shrugs. "Something I learnt back in science class. At high school, I went on a date with a girl who was seriously smart, not to mention very pretty, and I thought I'd impress her with my worldliness and knowledge. So I said something about kissing her under the gibbous moon."

I laugh. "Who said romance is dead?"

"It was pretty dead that night. She laughed at me too."

"So glad I'm not a teenager anymore."

"Me too."

"Was this in Perth?"

"Yep, Midland. I went to the local high school. My folks still live there."

A working-class area about as salubrious as the one I grew up in.

"I wouldn't have guessed," I say.

He raises his eyebrows. "And you?"

"I grew up in Kwinana." I smile. "It's where I learnt the ways of the world."

"I could say the same. A lot of rough kids. Sometimes it was hard not to get into fights. I let my Italian temper get the better of me a couple of times. After that, I learnt to talk my way out of things."

"It's a good skill to have. Better than fighting."

"My dad could see what was going on. He wanted to get me into boxing but that was never my thing."

"It's my thing."

"Really?"

I sip my vodka. "When I was at uni, I had a boyfriend who did boxing so I dabbled for a bit."

Nick was my first love, the first guy I had sex with, my first serious relationship. That was B.C. Before Charlie, who said he knew I was 'the one' from the first night we met, whereas it took me a little longer. We were at a party. We'd already been introduced and Charlie was on the other side of the pool from me, eyeing me up, motioning to me to ask if I wanted a drink. Then he grabbed a bottle of champagne from a table behind him, dived into the pool fully clothed, pulled himself onto the edge of the pool and popped the champagne while people cheered. The ultimate romantic.

"How did that work out for you?" Ryan asks.

Boxing, not Charlie, that's what we were talking about.

I clear my throat. "It didn't work out so well with that boyfriend, but boxing turned into kickboxing and that turned into Krav Maga. It's intense and a little bit crazy and very effective. I loved it right from the start."

Charlie thought kickboxing was too dangerous. I stopped sparring after he gave me the talk about concussions, then took up Krav but that wasn't any better in Charlie's view because of the never-ending bruises, the twisted ankle, the damaged shoulder, the fractured coccyx that I tried to hide from him, only to get in big trouble after he worked it out. Sometimes it felt like Charlie cared too much but, then, he was my best buddy looking out for me.

"You still training?" Ryan asks.

I shake my head.

"But you said you love it," he says.

"Oh, I got too busy with work and taking care of the house and other things. You know what it's like. Life gets in the way."

My voice cracks. I come out with it anyway. "I stopped when my husband got killed a year ago."

Ryan's eyes widen. "I'm sorry. He must've been young?"

"Yes, thirty-six."

A pause. "Shit, same age as me."

"It was a car crash." That's hardly a lie. It was the biggest car crash of my life, And Charlie's.

His eyes widen. "Were you in the car?"

"No, I wasn't."

A lie. I was there. I couldn't save him. And now I've started on this track, I can't stop myself. I create a story about a driver going through a red light, Charlie's car wrapped around a power pole, the other driver's remorse.

"I don't hold a grudge." I sip my vodka. "The other driver didn't mean for it to turn out that way."

So calm and controlled, I am such a good storyteller and such a good liar. I hold the biggest bloody grudge of all. I don't forgive *him*, the guy who killed Charlie, wherever he is. My heart rate rises. I want revenge, justice, someone to pay. The cops said it was a case of wrong place at the wrong time. I never believed them. There was more to it, even if I don't know what that was.

"It's okay if you're angry," Ryan says.

"What makes you think I'm angry?" I shrug, though my face has probably already given me away. "What about you? You know, in general, life, work, home, partner, girlfriend, take your pick."

"I used to be married," Ryan says. "We've been divorced for a few years now. Olivia's a good woman. She's moved on and I'm glad she's found someone."

God, he's so calm and reasonable, the opposite of me. Or maybe he's good at pretending too. After all, if his ex is such a great person, why aren't they still together?

I raise my eyebrows. "Things didn't work out between the two of you?"

"You could say that." He gives me a tight smile that doesn't reach his eyes. "Something I forgot to tell you. I talked to my mate, Dave Hinton, who runs the agency."

"Is he looking for a copywriter?"

"Actually, he said their usual copywriter has some large contracts and isn't doing smaller jobs anymore. And he's always on the lookout for new talent anyway. He suggested we catch up, the three of us."

"Absolutely. I'm sure I can squeeze that into my diary." Understatement of the century. "Thank you so much."

What an opportunity. The hard part about freelancing is always getting more clients, and that's exactly what an agency does, leaving people like me to sit back and do what I do best, write the copy. It might be the break I need.

Ryan shrugs. "No problem. Would you like another vodka?"

"Reckon I've had enough." I smile. "I need to sleep. You probably do too. Goodnight, Ryan."

I go to my room and wonder why I came up with the crap about Charlie in a car crash. Maybe I'd be better off writing it down instead, not that particular story, but something else. It's what the second psychologist suggested, that I put my feelings on paper and write letters to Charlie, especially since I'm a writer. So maybe I should write.

I close my eyes and I sleep. No dreams. Only nothingness.

Chapter Seven

It's not all right. It's never going to be all right.

I'm in my favourite Lululemon shorts, pacing the living room in its concrete magnificence, sweating before I've even started my workout. Ready. For what? I'm so wound up that if anyone looks at me or, God forbid, tries to come near me, I'll explode like a volcano spewing forth lava.

This isn't me. This isn't what I'm like. Shit, I want my old life back.

How I long for that good old boring, beautiful, everyday life. Making meals for the two of us to eat after Charlie got home from work. Snuggled up on the sofa, watching a movie or the Tour de France because Charlie liked the cycling and I liked the scenery. Coffee and croissants on the back patio while we played cards or did the word puzzles Charlie enjoyed so much. The nine-letter word was a favourite but he didn't like it when I got the word instead of him, like the time I got *inception* before we'd even got any of the other words it contains and Charlie told me I was spoiling our fun. I saw the word *point* was in there too, so I said, "That was the *point*" at the same time as he called out *point* and we laughed together.

Yes, we laughed and loved. He was my best buddy and he was so much more.

I remember once we had a bath together, though the claw-foot tub in the old house wasn't made for two. Charlie was waiting for me in the bath, then he took my hand to help me in and grinned as he started tickling me with his toes in strange places. All that skin on skin, it was hardly surprising we ended up in the bedroom before we'd even dried ourselves. I remember how I felt afterwards, sated and satiated with a hint of sexiness thrown in.

It wasn't always just the two of us. There was brunch with people from the hospital, with Noah, dinners out, the occasional housewarming or party.

I had a few friends of my own too, friends my age, not just Laura on the other side of the country. Until my friends pissed off or I pissed them off by being such a cow after Charlie died. Shit, I'm back to feeling like that volcano again.

Esmeralda slinks past, eyeing me suspiciously, though Siamese are known for being loving companions. Apparently. She looks so soft and warm, a creature of beauty. I crouch down and beckon her. She bares her teeth and screeches, perhaps not so beautiful after all. Then again, she can probably feel my bad vibes, the poor thing.

My phone buzzes on the dining table. It's my mum. More bad vibes.

Turns out I'm in luck. Mum's in a good mood, asking for my orange cake recipe, the cake that was too dry and also too moist. She even compliments me on it. I find the recipe online and send her the link. She sends back a love heart emoji. Conversation over.

I suck in a deep breath. What the hell am I doing? There's only one thing for it.

Time to get that cardio hit. I have to make this go away. I slide my phone and keys into my pocket.

I jog to the park in a new development on the other side of Subiaco. It's completely different here from Old Subi filled with federation houses featuring stained glass and bull-nosed verandahs and standard roses in the front gardens. Here, it's all contemporary houses with glass frontages, two and three storeys, taking up the entire block, and of course the biggest houses are the ones in the prime location overlooking the lake.

The hair on the back of my neck stands on end. Is that footsteps behind me?

I slow down and turn to check. No footsteps, but there's a black Merc crawling along at jogging pace. He pulls over. Shit. I was right. He's following me. A man gets out of the car. I look around, confident I can cut across the park and outrun him. Seconds later he's knocking on someone's front door. A woman opens the door, kisses him and pulls him inside.

Okay, I'm not being followed. That's good news. I'm paranoid. Not so good.

There's only one thing for it. At the park I sprint as fast as I can, legs pumping, to the next lamppost where I slow to a jog. I do the same again, sprint, jog, sprint, jog, the repetition soothing, the exertion burning my lungs. The burn is good. I keep going, for how long, I don't know. Time means nothing. Every now and then, I slow down long enough to catch my breath, then it's go, go, go.

I do the stair run, up and down, push-ups in between. I use the bench for step-ups and for triceps. This is all the equipment I need. No punching bag. Don't need my martial arts dojo.

For these moments, there is nothing else in the world, only my heart racing, muscles aching like I might break, lungs ready to collapse. Finally I feel alive, now when I can't breathe anymore.

I run. Past a little kid playing soccer with his dad, past a young couple lying on the grass, past a Labrador in the bushes. I follow the path around to the other side where it's quieter and find the perfect tree with a branch for pull-ups, so I get into position in a dead hang.

BANG. Shit, what was that? It sounded like a building falling down, a bomb, a small earthquake. I drop from the branch, then cower in a ball at the base of the tree.

Suddenly I'm in the car park, Charlie beside me, the two of us engulfed by darkness. I hear the soft squeal of tyres on the concrete in the distance. There's a figure in the darkness. A man is in front of us, telling us his girlfriend has collapsed, pointing to an old car in the corner with the boot up. She was putting something in the boot. He doesn't know what happened to her and he needs our help. Please can we assist him. I remember that word, *assist*, so carefully spoken.

"I'm a doctor," Charlie says.

Of course, he wants to help, but my gut tells me something's not right. I grab Charlie's arm.

He shakes me off. And I know exactly what's going through his head and how he's wondering why I'd stand in his way. He's annoyed because I should let him do his job; he's a doctor; he helps people and saves lives.

I don't want to be polite. I want to tell Charlie to shut up and pull him away and run. I want to do so many things and I don't. I am useless.

I blink, trying to get the guy's face out of my mind, but he's there. Here. Right in front of me, only now he's got the knife. Dark hair, olive skin, an ordinary face. Not mean, not snarling, no swastika on his forehead. And though he's stabbing Charlie, there's an unsettling calm about him, the cold composure of someone who's in control, like he's a regular guy going about his business. He could do this all day. He doesn't care that this is my life, Charlie's life, doesn't give a shit about what he's doing.

"Are you okay?"

A voice. A man standing in front of me. A dog barking.

That face, so calm. *It's him.*

Staying low, I ram my shoulder into his waist and take him down. An instant. Less than a second is all it takes and the guy's laid out on his back on the grass. Shit, it's lawn, not concrete, not a car park.

Breathing hard, I look down at the man. It's not him. What have I done?

"I'm so sorry," I mumble. The Labrador circles my feet, barking like crazy. "I thought you were… I didn't mean… "

I hold out a hand to help the man up. He takes it, gets up, then pushes my hand away.

"What the hell?" Scowling, he wipes grass from the back of his jeans. "Bloody lunatic. I should call the cops."

The poor man, the poor dog. I pity anyone who comes into contact with me.

"I'm so sorry."

He's already leaving, backing away from the lunatic before turning and storming off, his dog at his side. I don't blame him.

I fall into a heap at the base of the tree, my hands shaking as I reach for my phone to call Laura. It's hard for my brain to send the message to my fingers to swipe up and search for her in my contacts. She'll come and get me. *Please answer.*

This is Laura, who thinks I should join her at yoga instead of doing this crazy shit? How am I going to explain that I saw my attacker, that he's here… that it's all in my head.

My dearest buddy,

It's only been a year, not long enough for me to heal, and I don't want to. I'd rather hold you in my heart forever than let you go. Doesn't matter that it causes me pain, that grief is eating away at me on the inside, killing me bit by bit. That's the way it has to be. True love doesn't die.

You were the only one for me, and the longer we were together the more certain I became. There's that chemistry. Science and psychology have no chance of getting a handle on it. Researchers try to break down our reactions into synapses and biology and pheromones, but they're on the wrong track completely. They can't explain the miracle of the human mind and heart and how these things work. Some things you simply have to accept.

For me, there was life before I met you. And life after. They might as well be two different universes. You were named after a prince and that's what you are to me, my prince, the best thing that ever happened to me. I was nothing before we met and I don't want to be nothing again.

I'll write to you again, I promise, even though this is hard for me to do, more difficult than you might think. Even if I don't write to you often, you're in my heart. I carry a piece of you with me every day.

Love you always

xxx

Chapter Eight

Waves surge and crash on the shore, the foam on the shoreline swirling a dirty pale grey and white, compared to the deep grey of the rest of the ocean. The only thing that's darker is the sky, storm clouds looming low. Even the beach sand, usually pristine white, appears a pale shade of grey.

We've got the perfect viewing platform from the glass-enclosed outdoor deck at Sebastian's. Wind rattles the frames, cool air rising through cracks in the decking below while heat lamps hanging from the ceiling help counter the cold.

Ryan has set up a coffee meeting for me with his mate, David Hinton, whose agency does branding, web, digital and content, the full kit and caboodle as far as I'm concerned.

"Sorry I chose such a dire day to meet up," David says.

Crap, I should be paying attention. "No, not at all. The Indian Ocean is beautiful, any time of year."

Ryan smiles. "As long as you're not thinking of going for a dip."

"Not likely." I screw up my face. "There aren't even any surfers crazy enough to get out there today."

Conversation. Congenial. Making a connection. That's

what I've been doing by showing interest in David's business and talking about the clients I've worked with, the copy I've created, and the power of plain English.

It's been a week since the day Laura picked me up from the park, and my head has been all over the place. I haven't had my attacker's face come to me, as it did that day. Instead I have a vision of Will getting thrown by that car and then a vision of Charlie looking down on me, followed by a pang of guilt.

I force that stuff out of my head. I have to get through this meeting and make a good impression. I've got to get more work or my savings will run out. If I'm going to be honest, I've never had much work on. My own fault or maybe Charlie's because he didn't like me working too much, insisting my time was better spent in other ways because he couldn't be a successful paediatrician without my support.

No need to make it a bone of contention between us. That's what he used to say. He was right about a lot of things. The money he made crapped all over my earning capacity, after all, and he couldn't have anticipated the way things would turn out. No one could.

David takes his phone from the table. "We should get going before the heavens let rip."

"Sure." My stomach drops. He hasn't said anything about passing any work my way.

"It was great catching up," Ryan says, as he gets up and shakes David's hand.

"Lovely meeting you," I add. "Let me know if you'd like to see any more writing samples or anything."

"No, no, I've seen enough."

Great, what's that supposed to mean? I can guess. My website has examples of my work – everything from taglines and naming projects to web copy and reports – and I sent him a few additional pieces after he requested them over the phone. Not much more I can send him anyway.

We step outside and walk past a newsstand. A poster outside says *Is this the face of a murderer?* It features the face of an ordinary-looking, middle-aged bloke who killed a man in self-defence. A difficult subject but that's not me. I shouldn't let it get to me. The others don't take any note, and maybe I shouldn't either.

"Just smell that salt air." David smiles. "Don't you love working from home? I did the school run this morning and I can pick up the kids later on. Doesn't get much better than this."

"I forgot to ask how the kids are doing," Ryan says.

"They're great. You know what it's like. They grow up so fast."

Ryan nods.

The smile leaves David's face. "Sorry if I've said the wrong thing. And you? You seem to be doing okay?"

"Yeah, I'm doing pretty good, mate."

We say goodbye. David heads for his car and we get into the Mini. Looks like there might not be any new work coming my way after all.

I start the engine. "Thanks for the intro."

"Don't look so disappointed."

"I'm not." *I am.*

"Dave's a deep thinker. He might have something up his sleeve for you."

I drive off. "We'll see."

After a while, Ryan says, "Looks like it's about to start pissing it down."

"Sure does." In Perth, it's all about who you know. Might be like that everywhere, which makes me wonder about Ryan. "It must be hard starting off an architecture business. I mean, it's one thing to be able to design a house and another to be able to pull in the clients. And a house is a huge thing to trust someone with, especially if the architect is new and young. So how did you get started?"

"Yeah, I used to be young once."

I glance across. Ryan is grinning.

"You're not old," I say.

"Just jaded."

"Neither of the above."

"You're right. It's hard getting a leg up in this business. I started off in a commercial firm, doing detailing and construction documents, as you do when you're a grad. Then I got a job in a well-known firm that does residential."

"And how did you move into working for yourself?"

"Got lucky, I guess. My first private job was designing a house for my mother-in-law. Margaret lives in Cottesloe right on the beach so she's fairly well off. Some friends of hers liked the place so they got me to design a house for them. Those early jobs got me started."

I nod as I drive. "Connections."

"Absolutely."

"That's your *ex* mother-in-law?"

"Yeah, I'm still friends with her. Margaret doesn't feel like an ex."

"That's nice of you." A pause. I wait. "Sorry, I shouldn't be so nosy."

"No problem. Are you still in touch with *your* parents-in-law?"

"Yes, Charlie's mum is so wonderful. It was easier when I was back in Melbourne, though. I must give her a call."

I was always closer to her than to Charlie's dad. For months after Charlie died, they'd have me around for dinner. Jan loves to cook and I love to eat – or I used to – so we had something in common. She was always kind, much kinder than my own mum if I'm going to be honest.

Maybe all the talk about Charlie got to be too much for Jan

after a while, maybe that was why she started pulling away, and seeing less of me. The dinner invitations petered out and our get-togethers morphed into coffee catch-ups and phone calls.

We're close to home now, nearing a set of traffic lights. Green. Movement through the corner of my eye. A black car speeds through the intersection, its engine roaring.

I slam on the brakes and come to a grinding halt in the middle of the road. My heart jolts in my chest.

"Are you okay?" I ask Ryan.

"Yeah, are you?"

Though shaken, I nod and keep driving while we talk about the bloody idiot and how the traffic light in his direction must've been red for several seconds before he sped through. The rain is holding off, other than a couple of fat drops that fall onto the windscreen.

I let Ryan out of the car in the rear laneway before reversing into the garage. I'm an expert at reversing into parking spots, as a safety precaution, in case I need to get away quickly. A lot of good that did me.

Ryan's standing by the edge of the garage when I get out of the car.

"Are you okay?" I ask. "Do you need something?"

"Actually, I wanted to check that *you're* okay?"

"Fine."

"I thought the near-crash might've shaken you," he says. "You know, since your husband died in a car accident."

My stomach sinks. I stare at this man who's kind and considerate and who deserves better. I spend half my life pretending to myself but I don't want to lie to him.

"Look, that's not what really happened."

I give Ryan the full story from going out to dinner with friends and the guy in the car park with the knife to Charlie covered in blood and the guy running off. I don't skimp. I don't sugar-coat. There's no glamour or chivalry, only death. Ryan listens. He asks a few questions. He doesn't judge.

He reaches for my hand. "I'm so sorry for everything you've been through."

I nod. "Thanks."

"You said you'd done some martial arts and Krav. Surely your training must've saved your life."

He's right. I know this. And yet…

"It didn't save Charlie's." I blurt the words out.

"I'm glad you're alive and in one piece."

He doesn't say 'unscathed', the word people often choose. Maybe he does understand. Either way, I feel a little lighter.

"I'll show you something." I take my hand from his and slide my sleeves up to my elbows so he can see the scars.

"Bloody hell." He waits, stares. "You're a remarkable woman, Kate."

I remember knife training at Krav and how many times we were told that the number one rule of knife is that you *will* get cut. Blades are dangerous. My American instructor used to say he'd rather defend against a gun than a knife, that your chances were better. Now I'm living evidence.

I pull my sleeves down. "It was a big story in Melbourne at the time and I hated seeing my name in the news. Hated *being* the news. You know my mum calls me Katherine?"

"Yes, I noticed."

"When the case was in the media, they used my full married name, Katherine Best. I went back to my maiden name after that."

And chopped off my hair because that was the closest I could come to an identity change. I didn't want people to see me or to know. But Ryan isn't 'people'.

He nods.

"I know you'll google, and that's okay," I say. "I'd do the same."

I don't think he'll blab to the neighbourhood, though. He doesn't seem the type. I feel a little lighter.

"Take care, Kate."

Ryan leaves and as I get inside the house, the air crackles, followed by a thunderclap. In Perth, it doesn't drizzle so much like it does in Melbourne. Here, it's more like the rain clouds have an on switch and an off switch. One or the other, nothing in between. And right now, it's bucketing down.

Chapter Nine

A few days later David Hinton sends through a brief for a small piece of work, a badly written capability statement that needs revising. This is right up my alley and potentially a great start.

Laura drops by so I invite her in.

I usher her ahead of me. "Ooh, nice cardie."

"Just a little something I picked up in Melbourne," she says.

A running joke between us. I have the same red cardie with swallows on it, bought at a tiny goth shop in Fitzroy without knowing she had one the same.

We reach the back of the house where I've been sitting at the dining table with my laptop, notes scattered everywhere.

Laura points to the laptop. "It's a Saturday."

"Not for me. It's no skin off my nose and I like doing this stuff anyway."

"Then you'll need these." Laura pulls a small gold cardboard box from her bag. "I couldn't go to the John Walker shop without getting you something."

"You're the best!" I open the box and extend it to her.

"No thanks. I've got my own stash of choccies at home but, look, I won't stay long if you're working."

"You wouldn't be checking up on me, would you?"

She smiles. "I'm allowed."

"You sound like you're about six years old."

"I've learnt from the experts. Wasn't that long ago my kids were six. Or that's how it feels anyway."

"Yeah, six going on sixteen. Blake's having driving lessons, isn't he?"

"I know, it's a scary thought. He's seventeen, actually. That reminds me. If I get stuck for a lift for Mia after school, can I call you?"

"Of course."

Laura waits. "It's for her martial arts classes."

I clench my teeth, my natural reaction, then think about it. "No problem."

"Something else. You would've seen all that media about the middle-aged man and the home invasion in Canberra. I wanted to check it hadn't affected you too much."

The news was hard to miss, even for someone like me who doesn't read the news. A guy on meth broke into a house and was strangling a woman so her husband, who was ex-military, beat him to a pulp and got him in a sleeper hold that killed him. The police say it was excessive force and now the homeowner has been charged with murder. A tragedy all round.

"I'm fine, honestly," I say.

Laura purses her lips. "The Canberra cops are shockers. You can't trust the police. I'm glad you didn't have to go through that, not when you've been through so much already."

"It's strange, though. I felt almost relieved when I read about that case. Because it wasn't me. Is that mean of me?"

"Not at all."

We leave that dour subject behind and have a chat, it's

what friends do, though Laura doesn't take a seat. I haven't got over the novelty of living up the street and seeing her in person so often. She never pulls me too close or pushes me away when I become too much hard work.

My old friend Amy used to say "no judgement" and laugh, when judging was exactly what she was doing. At one point, she told me I should get used to being on my own instead of leaning on a man all the time. *All the time?* Because Charlie and I had been together whereas she was single. I didn't *lean* on him. We were married. I loved him.

She apologised afterwards, of course, and I apologised for my moods, for being short with her, for being a total nightmare. I wasn't an easy person to be friends with after Charlie died. Maybe Amy wasn't much better than the group of girls she hung with, the ones who used to talk about me behind my back.

I should get this shit out of my head. I shouldn't dwell.

My phone buzzes. Crap. "That's Noah. I'll call him back later."

"He cares about you," Laura says.

"I know."

"I'd better leave you to it."

"Sure." I swipe my phone up from the table. "I'll walk you to the door."

I can trust Laura with a secret, or multiple secrets, or just about anything. She's been through so much herself, which is one of the reasons she's so close to Noah. Their mother was abusive, fluctuating between mental health and addiction problems, and her dad left them with their psycho mother when Laura was a teen. A few years later, Laura moved out and took Noah with her to keep him safe. No wonder the two of them are close, despite the ten-year age difference and despite having lived on opposite sides of the country for such a long time.

The doorbell rings while we're walking down the front hall. I pull open the door. It's Noah. Funny how he and Laura look so alike with their blue eyes and brown hair but the same features that make Noah look manly – like he's the movie star who's going to fight off the forces of evil – make Laura appear thoughtful.

"I thought you might like to go out for a coffee," he says. The look on my face must give me away because he adds, "Only a coffee between friends, Kate, that's not much to ask."

Something in his pleading tone makes me feel guilty. "Maybe another day, thanks, Noah."

If I was going to have coffee with anyone, it's Laura. Uncomplicated, unromantic, unadulterated coffee. But right now I need to get in a couple of solid hours of writing so I can feel like I've done something. Writing used to be my big escape from the world and that's what I want now, an escape.

He steps forward. "No worries. We don't have to go anywhere. I can come in for a quick cuppa."

Something rubs me up the wrong way, his familiarity and forthrightness, and it only makes me want to stand my ground.

The fact is, I do still long for Noah as a friend. He's a link to my past in a way that no one else can be – because he was Charlie's best friend – and I don't want to lose the memories I have of him. I want to share them with someone who understands. Just not right now.

My phone vibrates in my hand. It's Mum. For once, she's my saviour. I take the call and ask her to hold.

"Sorry, guys," I say to them.

"Let's go get a coffee, bro, the two of us," Laura says.

"Bro?" Noah raises his eyebrows. "Since when do you call me bro?"

"If you keep going, I'll make you buy me cake as well." Laura takes his arm and they leave.

I close the front door and put on my happy voice. "Hey, Mum."

"Ooh, how are you, darling?"

Darling? She must be in a good mood.

"Great. I was working but I can take a break to chat."

I might as well with all these interruptions. As I wander back to the rear of the house, Mum gives me a rundown on the latest saga about her work and how they suspect someone is diddling the till. Mum is a different person at work, hardworking, patient in training new staff, happy to help out with anything that's needed. She's worked at the same bakery since I was a kid so I've seen her in action many times over the years. Always a smile on her face, a lilt in her voice, constantly asking about her regulars and how they're going. I used to wonder how she could be so different at home. I stopped wondering a long time ago.

"I've been doing some more baking," she says.

"You work at a bakery, don't forget."

"It's the raspberry chocolate cake I used to make years ago. I remember how Jack used to lick the bowl, even when he was fifteen or sixteen."

"Yeah, he was funny. But I was the one who made the choc raspberry cake."

"No, that was me."

Was it? "But, Mum, I remember that recipe came from my high school cooking classes."

I also remember being shouted at because the raspberries I'd bought from the supermarket were expensive and did I have to always be so careless about the cost of things.

"You made the cake once and it was all wrong." Mum raises her voice a notch. "So I tweaked the recipe, and the cake came out moist and delicious. Jack used to love the cakes I made. He had such a sweet tooth."

Until it wasn't sweets he craved but something else. I

remember how long it took to convince Mum that Jack had a drug problem and the way she took it out on me. Angry. Heartless. *I wish you were the one who'd run away*, that's what she said. I remember gasping, the breath leaving my body and the strange feeling that I must've got it wrong, which is exactly what she told me later, because there's no way she'd say something like that. Shit, this is more crap I shouldn't keep dwelling on.

"How are you doing all on your own in that concentration camp?" Mum laughs.

"I love it here." Which is true.

"Nicer than your mother's house, is it?"

I grit my teeth, not wanting to say something I'll regret.

"How are you really doing, Katherine?" she asks.

"O-okay. Still a bit anxious."

"Nothing's happened, has it?"

"No, not really. Sometimes I get a weird feeling like I'm being followed or like someone's there."

"But there's no one there?"

"No."

"Well, if that's the case, maybe the problem is you."

"Mum!"

"There's nothing for you to be scared about. If anyone should be scared it's the other guy. You know how to take care of yourself and you know exactly what I mean."

Do I? How can she even think that?

I see him in my mind's eye, the *other guy*, the one who attacked me and Charlie. That night fear gripped me, adrenaline coursing through my body, then my brain froze because this couldn't possibly be happening, followed by the knowledge that it was. Debilitating and electrifying. Life and death. Both of them resting on the flip of a coin, the slice of a blade.

Much later it hit me that this was nothing like training.

We were never trying to kill each other at training with our rubber knives and yellow plastic guns. No live blades. No psychopaths. These were two different universes and somehow I'd crossed to the other side. The only thing I'm sure of is that training saved my life.

Training.

For a couple of years, Charlie tried to talk me out of going to training because he needed me at home. But training was the one thing I wouldn't give up. He finally relented and said he'd *let* me continue with it. As if I was a child. Oh hell, I shouldn't think about the crap that went down, not when it's twisting me up inside, not when Charlie was such a wonderful husband.

If anyone should be scared it's the other guy.

Not true. I'm not Jason Bourne or Rambo. I'm not big or strong or savvy. I can't incapacitate attackers with a single blow. I'm not an action hero in a choreographed fight scene with stunt people and mats to land on. Life doesn't work that way.

Sometimes Mum sucks the life out of me. She always knows how to get me, such an amazing skill.

"I've gotta go. Bye, Mum."

I press the red button and stare at the phone in my hand.

The guy who attacked me and Charlie is still out there. I can't get it out of my head. Or my gut. I came to Perth to get away but what if this isn't far enough? How do I know he's not coming for me too?

Chapter Ten

I lie in bed, the duvet pulled up to keep me warm, wondering what it was that woke me. I hear someone calling my name, that voice I know so well.

A cool breeze sweeps across my face and tickles my nose. A gust, not a little breath of air. I wait. Will there be more? *I feel you. I know you're there.*

After a while I sling my legs over the edge of the bed and sit up. I'm wearing the Homer Simpson T-shirt that Charlie thought was so wacky, that was big on him and is enormous on me. Cold air bites into the exposed skin of my arms and legs.

My eyes have adjusted to the dark so I look around. No movement, nothing strange. Then the wind whips past me, blows my hair back. That wasn't my imagination. My imagination isn't a breeze.

"Charlie." I whisper his name.

He's here.

I stand. "Where are you?"

Nothing.

I wrap my dressing gown around myself and slide my feet

into my Ugg boots, wondering how he even knows where to find me since I've moved to the other side of the country.

Padding out of the room, I follow my heart, my gut, whatever you want to call it. I move slowly, willing him to come to me. I want to be his 'precious' again and to wallow in his presence, no matter the cost.

I stand in the doorway that leads to the living area at the rear, leaving the lights off so as not to scare him away. Moonlight streams in through the glazing.

I see everything. I see you, Charlie.

I see nothing.

Time passes, how much I don't know, and it doesn't matter because I've got all the time in the world. No way can I go to sleep after this anyway.

I can't feel him anymore. There's no breeze, no Charlie, no nothing. Disappointment settles in my chest.

Shoulders slumped, I shuffle to the dining table and drop down onto a dining chair. I can wait a bit longer. So I do. I wait for nothing.

Maybe the lights will go on in Ryan's yard again. They don't.

I think about watching some mindless television. I specialise in mindless, mostly because I can't watch dramas or the news or anything with conflict. It's too distressing. I've watched every home renovation and architecture show I can find, along with a heap of travel and cooking programmes until I couldn't face another *Bake Off*.

Charlie's not here so eventually I go back to bed, hoping for a sign that doesn't come. Sleep doesn't come for a long time either. When I awaken, it's a new day and I'm the same old frazzled mess.

I park the Mini in the garage off the rear laneway, scanning the area as I get out of the car. I remember watching *Cape Fear* with Jack when I was a kid and freaking out when Robert De Niro had hidden under the family car, only to creep out later to hold them all hostage. Jack teased me about it for months.

I unlock the back door and put the groceries away, telling myself it doesn't matter that I've had a bad night. I'm alive, living in an awesome architect-designed house in one of the most desirable parts of Perth. I have friends. I may have a new client. And I have a long life ahead of me.

Esmeralda slinks into the kitchen, looking up at me with those amazing blue eyes. I crouch down and beckon her, only for her to turn away, of course. The doorbell buzzes so I head down the hallway.

The front door is locked. Everything is locked, except for the back door which is left unsecured as a conscious decision on my part so I can step into my own backyard.

I open the front door to see a woman in her forties standing there, an expectant look on her face, about as far from threatening as you can get. She's holding an enormous bouquet in her arms. I glance behind her at the white van from Cottage Florist parked on the street. Flowers?

She holds out the bouquet. "I have a delivery for Kate Mamotte."

I place a hand on my chest. "For me?"

Noah is the only person I can think of who might send flowers and that makes me reluctant to take them. Still, I can't take it out on the poor delivery woman, especially since I don't know for sure they're from Noah.

She hands me the flowers.

"Thank you."

I close the door and wander towards the back of the house, admiring the flowers while trying not to. Magnificent white oriental lilies dominate the bouquet, complemented by red roses and sprays of small white flowers set against a background of glossy green leaves. I wish Noah hadn't done this.

Then, maybe they're from Ryan. There's a little burst of sunshine in my heart. But, no, he doesn't seem like the flower-sending type and why am I thinking of him anyway?

I place the flowers on the dining table and reach for the card tucked into the red ribbon wrapped around the bouquet, wondering if there's a vase in the house big enough to handle this or whether I should keep them at all.

The envelope is stuck down so I rip it open and take the card out. The message inside has been typed. Odd. I stare and wait. This isn't sinking in.

To my Precious
Love you always
Charlie xxx

Chapter Eleven

How long have I been standing here staring at the table? I have no idea. Staring but not seeing. I don't see the table or the flowers, though some distant part of my mind knows they're there.

I suck in a long slow breath. Oxygen. Brain. Try to get those cogs working. I've blanked out again. I tell myself that's okay. I'm at home, Joel's home, and I'm safe. Another deep breath. Breathing is good.

Panic. An urge overtakes me. I want to grab those flowers and throw them out the back door. Further. Into the laneway. Away.

Don't panic. Think instead. I am indeed going to grab those flowers but not like that. They're evidence. I stomp to the kitchen and take a pair of rubber gloves from beneath the sink. I rummage around in the drawer till I find what I'm looking for. I've seen them somewhere. Ziplock bags. Got 'em. And a garbage bag.

My hands are clammy, I struggle to get the gloves on before picking up the card by a corner like it's poisoned and sliding it into a ziplock bag. I shove the flowers into the garbage bag, the card in its ziplock bag following suit. I grip the top of the garbage bag so nothing can escape from it.

I get into the Mini and drive.

Same police station, same bland grey décor, different interview room.

The same police officer too, because I asked for him. Alex Sheridan is coming and he'll understand. Doesn't matter that he's young. He already knows my history, after all. Or does he? I struggle to think but, yes, I'm sure that when he interviewed me about Will, I told him about being attacked in Melbourne.

The officer at the front desk probably thought I was nuts, wanting to report a bouquet of flowers. I stare at the walls, wishing they'd turn the heating down. I'm sweating, my underarms damp, and I've already taken off my denim jacket. My neck rigid, I don't look at the garbage bag on the floor.

The door opens and Officer Sheridan appears, a smile on his face. Friendly. A wave of relief washes over me. Maybe this won't be so bad.

He shakes my hand. "Hi, Katherine."

"It's Kate, actually."

He takes a seat and places a laptop on the table and I go through everything with him.

Alex nods. "I can see you're distressed. It must be horrible for you to receive flowers that are supposedly from your dead husband. But I'm not sure this crosses into the area of criminal activity."

Wasn't he listening? Shit, I should have phoned Laura first – she'd know how to deal with this – but I didn't want to bother her while she was at work. My shoulders are scrunched so I roll them in circles, forcing myself to loosen them off. This is all wrong. You can't force yourself to relax.

Forcing and relaxing are at two different ends of the spectrum.

"Someone close to me sent those flowers," I say. "This is someone who knows me and Charlie, someone who knew Charlie called me his Precious."

"Then that should narrow down the number of people who could've sent you the flowers. Do you have any idea who that may be?"

My close friends? Laura, Noah, Amy. My family? Mum. My dad and brother are long gone. Have I mentioned the nickname in passing to other people? Had Charlie done the same, talked about his Precious to the staff he worked with, to patients, to friends?

I can't suspect everyone. I can't. That doesn't narrow it down at all.

"If I knew who sent the flowers, I wouldn't be here," I say. "I'd be on the phone blasting that person or maybe turning up on their front doorstep."

"Do you think that would be wise?"

I narrow my eyes. "I've got good reason to be scared and I'm sick of walking around in fear. The guy who attacked me and who killed Charlie is still out there."

The investigating officers in Melbourne said it was a random attack. They looked into Charlie's life – and mine – interviewing our friends, Charlie's colleagues, staff at the hospital, checking phone records, looking into every nook and cranny. They couldn't find anyone who had a reason to hurt Charlie, no disgruntled patients who wanted to make him pay for botched surgery, nothing like that. Far as I know, the police didn't even have any good leads or any suspects.

But it wasn't random. *Random* would have finished in Melbourne. *Random* wouldn't have followed me to Perth.

And the officer sitting opposite me should be taking this more seriously.

I change tack. "For a while now, I've had this strange feeling like I'm being followed. Maybe someone *is* following me. Maybe it's him."

"Who?"

"Look, I know the attack happened in Melbourne but for all I know, the guy who attacked us has come to Perth and tracked me down. There's a murderer out there. If he's killed once, he can do it again. Maybe he rammed poor Will with his car and sent me that *bitch* text message. Maybe he's the one who sent me those flowers. To show me who's boss."

"I'm sorry, Kate. You say the guy is still out there?"

"Yes."

He pushes his chair back. "Can you give me a moment?"

I thought I already had. "Yeah, sure."

Alex Sheridan leaves and I drop my head into my hands, my elbows resting on the table. Something about being here makes me feel like a criminal when I haven't done anything wrong.

The police officer pops his head into the doorway. "We're just checking out a couple of things. Please bear with us."

Us? Who is us?

"Sure."

I drum my fingers on the table, thinking they're not taking me seriously, so I take the phone from my bag and snap a photo of the card and bouquet to make sure I've got a record. The flowers are so beautiful-horrible I can't bear to look at them. Laura will believe me. I can show her the photos. She'll understand.

Alex strides in, an officer following close behind, an overweight man with greying hair and a forehead full of horizontal lines that tell me he's been around the traps. Looks like they're calling in the big guns.

"Kate, this is Sergeant John Cunningham."

"Hello," I say in a small voice.

"Nice to meet you," he says.

Alex takes a seat opposite while John pulls out a chair closer to me.

"Kate, I think there's been a bit of a misunderstanding here," John says.

Where? What misunderstanding?

He continues. "You've come to us because you received flowers and a note you perceive to be threatening."

I nod. "Yes, I've been sent flowers from my dead husband. I think that's enough to freak anyone out."

"Maybe someone is trying to freak you out, as you put it. But there's no overt threat in the card, no indication anyone wants to commit an act of physical harm against you."

I'm sick of being nice. "Honestly, I can't believe you said that. My husband and I were attacked by some guy with a knife. Charlie was killed. Multiple stab wounds. Horrific injuries. So much blood." Tears spring to my eyes. "You weren't there. You didn't see it."

Surrounded by a river of blood. On my hands and arms, my clothes, Charlie's white shirt, his throat, the concrete floor turning crimson. Sliding and slipping in blood. And it kept flowing. How could there be so much?

Charlie's face flashes before me, the way he looked at that moment, throat gurgling, the colour drained from his face, the life from his eyes. Cradling his head in my arms, talking to him, desperation and denial mixing in my gut. Shouting for help. Screaming. Whispering to Charlie.

John lowers his gaze. "We've accessed the files and seen the crime-scene photos. I'm sorry for your loss."

Sorry? They're trained to come out with these words and I'm tired of the platitudes.

"I was there." Getting to my feet, I pull my sleeves up, show them the slashes on my forearms. "I got out of it alive. Don't get me wrong, I'm grateful. But I ended up with *this* and my husband died and the other guy walked away."

"He'd been in prison before."

They know him? How can they know about the guy's prison record when they never caught him? I don't want the answer. They know…

I know too.

I've always known. My lips part but I can't speak.

"Your attacker didn't walk away that night." John pauses. "Kate, can you hear me?"

I drop back down into the chair.

"Can you remember what happened?" He pauses. "You and your husband were attacked by an assailant armed with a knife. Video footage shows the man approaching you and your husband, motioning for you to join him. At that point, the three of you retreat towards a corner that's out of shot of the CCTV, which is probably exactly what the attacker planned. Charlie tried to fight him. He had defensive knife wounds on his hands as well as other wounds that were fatal. You fought the attacker too. You killed him. Do you remember? He didn't walk away."

I killed him. It's true.

Chapter Twelve

My shoulders drop. He's right. He's wrong. Shit, these two cops weren't there and don't know what it was like.

"Melbourne Police put together what happened," the older officer says. "They had your statement and a statement from the middle-aged couple who heard you yelling 'stop' and calling for help."

Stop. Get back. The words we're drilled to yell out at training.

John continues. "There was substantial evidence at the scene, the knife with only one set of prints on it, the wounds you and Charlie sustained, the attacker's wounds, the positioning of the bodies."

Bodies. More than one.

"I was too late," I say.

John's lips go thin. "You did everything you could. You fought off an armed attacker. That's no small feat for anyone, let alone a woman your size."

I remember lying in a hospital bed afterwards, that night, the next day, I don't know when. Time had no meaning. There were people around me, Amy, Mum, Laura. And none of those people were Charlie. He was gone, my life torn to shreds, my heart ripped from my chest.

After a while, it was like my mind started attacking itself. I couldn't bear to constantly think about Charlie, the clawing pain too much for me, so I thought about something else. *Him.* And what I'd done.

That man had a family too, friends, people who loved him. Somewhere there was a mother who'd given birth to him, raised him, done the best she could. And now her son was dead. There was a father out there, most likely brothers and sisters too, cousins, relatives. He probably had a wife or partner. Shit, maybe he had kids. Oh God, what was I going to do if he had kids who'd had their father taken from them?

I killed him.

And maybe part of me died too.

Because I couldn't forgive myself, couldn't face the fact, couldn't grieve or breathe. The thoughts were a tape on a loop going round and round in my head like a video gone out of control, until I couldn't argue with the mess in my head anymore.

So I hid it from myself. I made up a different story, one my mind could cope with. Because I wasn't a murderer or a monster. I hadn't killed someone. Nope, that's not what happened.

John says, "You're lucky to have survived."

How many times have I heard this? No one says, *You're lucky to have lost your husband.* No one puts two and two together and realises they're the same thing.

I raise my eyebrows. "You reckon?"

Alex clears his throat. "I've read through the files. The man had already inflicted fatal damage to your husband, and you fought him off."

I didn't have a lot of choices that night. A knife doesn't let you choose. And if I had to do it again, I'd do whatever I had to do.

Yet none of that changes the fact that I killed.

And it's eating away at me.

"Kate," John says. "I hope you fully understand that the man who attacked you is dead. He can't hurt you anymore."

An image flashes in my head of a man with his arm around a woman in her sixties, a mother who'd lost a son. Another Scarparolo. He looked so much like my attacker that it made my stomach lurch, the same ridges in his brow, the same dark eyes.

"His brother's still alive, isn't he?" I say.

"Whose brother?"

It comes back to me. The inquest. I'd been sick at the thought of this, fearful of reliving that night all over again. Luckily the authorities had already gathered evidence and the coroner had had time to examine the evidence so it didn't take long for a decision before they confirmed I'd acted in self-defence against a larger, armed opponent.

"My attacker had a brother called Domenic," I say. "He threatened me at the inquest back in Melbourne. This was a definite threat. *You deserve to die for this, bitch,* that's what he said in front of a crowd of people, including lawyers, so stupid of him."

Alex raises his eyebrows. "You didn't mention this earlier when you told me about the text message?"

I shake my head. I have no clue how I could have pushed this so far back into the recesses of my mind. I am such a screwed-up mess.

"I'm sorry. It's only coming back to me now."

John straightens. "Thank you for telling us. We'll look into it. So this was in Melbourne?"

"Yes."

"Did the brother ever contact you again?"

"No, I don't think so. I can't remember. There was so much going on at the time that it's a bit fuzzy in my head."

They'll look into it. Like the Melbourne Police looked into it. They didn't come up with much.

Charlie didn't die for no reason. It wasn't a good reason – there's never a good reason for murder – but there was some reasoning behind it. Maybe Scarparolo had met Charlie somewhere and had some perceived grudge against him. Maybe the man was hired by someone. Maybe there's some other reason.

Whatever the case, I have to find the truth about Charlie's death.

Chapter Thirteen

First stop, the florist.

Google gives me the exact location of Cottage Florist. I drive to South Fremantle. I don't pass 'Go' and I don't wait for the police. They must think I'm a nutcase. Can't say I blame them.

A red light. I brake, take a deep breath, concentrate on driving. One thing at a time. I was in denial before. No more.

The main road is lined with Norfolk Island pines but the shopping centre car park has only a few scraggly trees. South Freo is filled with cute workers' cottages and has a vibrant strip filled with neighbourhood shops and cool cafés, whereas this shopping centre is a washed-out remnant from the seventies.

Against these bland surrounds, Cottage Florist is an oasis. Shelves are crammed with vases, stuffed toys, decorative plates and paraphernalia. I guess there's money to be made in the extras. But this is a florist, with flowers on a large oak table that dominates the centre of the room, flowers on the floor in front of the shelves and under the table, bunches in buckets, bouquets on display, flowers everywhere. Not surprisingly, it smells like an enchanted garden in here.

A man behind the counter who's working his magic with fern fronds and white roses calls out hello. I say hello back, feeling both conspicuous and overwhelmed so I figure I might as well buy some flowers, for Laura perhaps. Roses, orchids, irises, tulips, chrysanthemums, I don't know where to start.

Charlie never had a problem choosing the most beautiful flowers for me. Because I was beautiful, he said. He'd bring a single red rose to my bedsit when he visited and on the day I moved in with him, he filled the living room with lilies. Once, he had matching bouquets delivered for me and Amy for a girls' birthday lunch, which caused a lot of swooning and maybe even a little jealousy. A long time ago.

My phone pings so I dig it out of my bag to see a message from my mother. Her sixth sense seems to be working a treat. I can't deal with her now so I leave it.

"How are you going? Can I help you?"

I look up. The florist is the epitome of neatness in a blue floral shirt tucked into a pair of jeans with a crease line down the front.

"I'm looking for flowers for a friend," I say.

"Any occasion?"

"I guess friendship is an occasion."

We chat for a bit. He talks about the flowers and smiles a lot.

I pick up a bunch in vivid reds and oranges. "These are the ones."

He takes them to the counter and I pay for my purchase.

"Actually there's something else," I say. "Someone sent me flowers from here recently. It was kind of an *unwanted* admirer if you know what I mean."

"Oh."

"And anonymous."

He tilts his head. "Hmmm."

"Look, I think it might be an old boyfriend and if it's him,

I'd like to set him straight. So I was wondering if you could tell me who ordered the flowers."

"This is quite unusual. I'm really not sure."

"Could you take a look please?" He doesn't say anything, so I add, "I received the bouquet yesterday afternoon if that helps. I've got a picture."

I find the photo on my phone and show it to him.

He scoffs. "You put the flowers in a garbage bag?"

"I'm sorry. It wasn't the flowers. It was the boyfriend. He was a real piece of work."

The florist raises his eyebrows. "I remember that bouquet very well. If that was your boyfriend, then you must like them young."

"Sorry?"

"A teenager came in the day before yesterday. Not our usual clientele. He looked completely lost so I asked him if he wanted a hand, and he more or less grunted, then spent all of about three seconds making his selection. If you don't mind my saying so, he didn't seem like your type."

"What type is that?"

"Young. Smelled of cigarettes. Wore an Anthrax T-shirt. Looked like he couldn't get out of here quickly enough."

"How did he pay?"

"Cash. That's another reason he stuck out. We don't handle much cash since Covid hit. Nearly everyone uses a card, with the possible exception of our elderly customers."

I take the bouquet. "Thanks for your help."

Of course, the person couldn't go to their local florist or pay by card or order online or do anything to leave a trace. But paying a teenager fifty bucks to go inside and order a bunch of flowers is a different matter. So much more anonymous.

As I get into my car, I look for a young guy in an Anthrax T-shirt though I know he's not going to be there.

Chapter Fourteen

Laura is my lifeline, my phone-a-friend when I'm stuck, not that I want to be a millionaire and God knows I don't want to go on a television quiz show. I just want to get by.

She's so practical, her brown hair pulled back into a ponytail, as she makes us cappuccinos using the De'Longhi coffee machine Theo bought because her husband buys only the best.

Laura places two mugs on the marble benchtop and takes a seat beside me at the breakfast bar. She's already put the bouquet of gerberas in a vase at the other end of the counter. I'm glad I chose a large bunch or they'd be lost in a room this size.

I wait till she's got some caffeine inside her, then show her the photo of the flowers and give her the full story from the delivery van rocking up to the time I left the police station. I leave out the bit where I thought the flowers were from the attacker, the man I killed a year ago. Laura doesn't need to know about the crap going on in my head.

After I've finished, she shifts her gaze between me and the bouquet. "You didn't, did you?"

"Didn't what?"

"Come on, where did you get my flowers from? You went to the Cottage Florist place you just told me about, didn't you?"

I nod.

She sighs. "Did you think the police weren't taking you seriously? That they wouldn't investigate?"

I feel like she's looking right through me, that she knows the police think I'm a nutter. And maybe I am. But I'm sure as hell not going to admit it.

"You're the one who's told me the police aren't rocket scientists," I say. "I had to do something. I couldn't just sit here."

"Oh, Kate."

Laura slides off her stool and gives me a hug. For someone so slight, she gives one hell of a hug, securing her arms around me and holding me tight.

God, how I miss Charlie's hugs, his strong arms, the way he made me feel. It's the thing I miss most, pathetic though that may be. My throat tightens. I'd do anything for one of Charlie's hugs.

"I'm okay, Laura."

She sits back on her stool. "Obviously there was nothing to stop you making enquiries of your own. That's not it. Kate, I'm worried about you. Sometimes it's better to leave things alone."

There was a time when I'd have called Amy but Laura is older, more experienced, more likely to search for a deeper truth, more everything-that-I-need, even though I don't always like what she's got to say.

"Maybe I don't want to leave things alone," I tell her. "I left everything to the police before, and look where that got me."

"Okay." She purses her lips. "Look, the note was personal, I agree. And spiteful. This person *wants* to hurt you. It's what people like that thrive on. The best thing you can do is ignore them and get on with your life, especially since you've already done the responsible thing and gone to the police. Don't let this person get to you."

"It's a bit late for that."

"Oh, Kate, I know it's hard. And I'm glad you came over, rather than kept things bottled up."

The doorbell rings.

"Bugger, I forgot," Laura says. "Noah said he might drop by."

"That's okay. I'm good. I can handle this."

And if I say that enough times, I might believe it.

Laura leaves and seconds later I hear voices at the door, then the familiar sound of footsteps down the hall.

I stay seated. "Hey, Noah."

He greets me with a kiss on the cheek.

Laura remains standing and leans over the counter, silent, waiting.

Noah looks from his sister to me. "Is something up?"

"Yeah." I go through the story again. It's easier the second time around. Or maybe this is the third. I'm not sure.

Meanwhile Laura starts chopping up onions and peppers for dinner. Noah reaches for my hand to give it a squeeze.

I slide off the stool. "I should go."

"Me too," he says.

"But you just got here."

"I was dropping something off."

Or making excuses, more like it. Laura leaves the knife on the chopping board and walks us to the door.

Outside, Noah says, "I'll walk you home."

"But you drove here."

His car is parked a couple of houses up. Red and shiny, it's hard to miss. He's had a series of rental vehicles, switching and changing at will as if they were toys, until he decided to go electric and buy a Model S.

"It's not far and I can do with the exercise," he says. "Besides, you're the one who used to tell me how beautiful Perth winters are."

"Except when it's raining."

Which isn't happening now. Fluffy white clouds float in an azure sky as if we're in an Impressionist painting.

Back in the day, it used to be the three of us, me, him and Charlie. They liked their 'boy activities' – long bike rides together, elaborate ski trips, and Noah liked to go fishing out on the boat. I have no clue what he's done with the boat now.

I remember joining them on a ski trip in northern Italy, such a privileged life I led. One evening I suggested a day trip to Bolzano, and Noah said he'd rent a car and would take me there personally. Charlie made it clear that wasn't going to happen. Very clear. Not that I think Noah was seriously falling for me, then or now, but it'd be typical of him to want what he can't have.

"Earth to Kate." Noah waves his hand in front of my face as we walk. "Anyone there?"

"Oh yes, sorry." We've crossed the street and I barely noticed.

Then it hits me. Maybe it was him. Maybe Noah sent me the flowers, so I could go running to him for comfort. He knows about the nickname, knows a lot about me and Charlie. How could he do that?

And how can I even think that? But I do. Then I feel mean for thinking it. Noah wouldn't be that cruel.

"Is there anything I can do, Kate?" he asks. "You still miss Charlie. It's understandable."

I stop outside my gate. "It's not just that. Something keeps niggling at me, something I can't quite explain. Like I was living in a parallel universe with a different Charlie and there was something else going on."

"Is it because of the money? You have every right to wonder what he did with it all. When I looked at the numbers, they never added up."

"I don't know, Noah."

Charlie remortgaged the house and took big chunks of money out of our account, including several hundred thousand dollars before he died. I'd felt sick when I found out, this shock coming after his death, the biggest loss of all. It took a while for the magnitude of the numbers to sink in and it became clear I wasn't going to be left with much. It was hard not knowing what Charlie had done with the money and, worse, that the only explanations I came up with were dire.

I hold my hands out. "I can't go there right now."

"You must have wondered if he was seeing someone else."

"No."

Not my Charlie. My heart seizes up. I can't bear the thought. Charlie with another woman… It's not possible. He loved me. And if that horrible idea has entered my mind before, it's only because I was so distraught after his death.

"Did he ever say anything to you about a woman?" I ask.

Noah shakes his head. "At the end of the day, there were a lot of things Charlie didn't talk about. It's clear he was burning the candle at both ends. I think he had his secrets, if you will."

Secrets? From me? The look on my face must give me away, my shock, the pain.

Noah takes my hand. "I've reached out to you before, Kate. Anything you need, call me."

I open the gate and step away. "Bye, Noah."

I feel his eyes on me as I walk up the front path and unlock the door.

Inside, I head for the bedroom. The bed is perfectly made, the navy duvet smooth, two cushions neatly positioned by the leather headboard. Floor-to-ceiling windows look out onto a sheltered courtyard and a wall of ivy that brings the outside in.

I drop down onto the bed and stare at our wedding photo in the silver Vera Wang frame that Charlie chose. The picture sits in prize position on the low chest of Scandinavian drawers opposite the bed.

Of all the photos taken that day, this is the one that means the most to me, a selfie taken by Charlie, his outstretched arm disappearing out of shot. His other arm is slung around my neck, my hand covering his. Charlie joked that I was being possessive by hanging off his arm and I teased him back, saying he was being clingy first by putting his arm around me. The two of us are smiling, glowing with love, love coming out of our pores, radiating love.

Who is that man who looks so happy?

So many things I should have done differently. If only I'd been quicker. If only I'd dived in before Scarparolo pulled the knife on Charlie. If only I'd put my foot down earlier and said, no, we're not going to help this stranger who said his girlfriend had collapsed. Then we'd never have been backed into a corner facing a knife attack.

Why? Why had this man wanted to stab Charlie? Is it possible Charlie had some secrets I didn't know about?

"What was going on, Charlie?"

A memory flashes in my mind, makes me shudder. I was going crazy with grief. I'd see Charlie in the clothes in the wardrobe, in the paintings and furniture he'd chosen, everywhere in the house. I couldn't bear it, so I packed up his things and gave them to the Salvation Army. I kept a few items that gave me solace, like some of his T-shirts, his Peter Alexander pyjama pants with their novelty prints, the worn Carhartt windcheater I still wear and snuggle into.

There was one item that still sticks in my mind, not special but suspicious. I tossed it out anyway. And now it's gone.

It's killing me all over again. The Charlie I knew was a successful doctor, a pillar of society, a happily married man, one day to become a family man. The Charlie who proposed to me was a romantic, popping the question in Paris, getting down on bended knee at Girafe Restaurant with a view of the Eiffel Tower, sweeping me into his arms, everyone around us cheering.

Then there was this other Charlie who threw away hundreds of thousands of dollars and maybe got in trouble or had someone after him. Maybe he got involved in something dodgy and owed a lot of money and that's how he ended up dead. Who knows?

The problem is, I have to know and I don't want to know.

Chapter Fifteen

Hours pass, wonderful hours where I am normal again.

The back door is open, a gentle breeze wafting past the dining table, the crispness refreshing. I've got another small job from one of the other people at David Hinton's agency. The guy wants a quick turnaround and I am nothing if not quick, especially since there are no other jobs holding me back.

The client is a company that manufactures sheds for mining and industry, mostly up north, where the money is. The copy in one of their brochures is convoluted and full of advertising spiel, and they'd like it shaped into something more down to earth. This is right up my alley. Plain English. Crisp and clear. With manly overtones, given the client. I can be manly. I take on the persona. And I write.

When I'm writing, there is no time. Time disappears. Writing makes me free. Charlie never quite got it and maybe that's okay because he was off healing people and saving lives.

Years ago, I was upset after being turned down for a full-time senior copywriting position. Charlie pointed out there were probably people with more experience than me. When another job came up with the same firm, I called them to ask about it, only to find out Charlie had phoned them a few months earlier to say I couldn't take the first position because of a death in the family.

I was furious. Charlie was calm. He said a full-time position wouldn't have left me with enough time to take care of him and the house. It would have made me miserable. He did it because he loved me. Couldn't I see that? I let it go. The job was gone anyway.

The sound of kids in a neighbour's backyard laughing and playing floats in through the back door. Esmeralda mews and rubs herself along my legs, making me smile. I feel her through my jeans.

"Hey, sweetie." I lean over to pat her but she slinks away, her tail in the air, as if making a statement. Still, I like having her around.

Movement in the corner of my eye. I shudder. A cockroach scuttles across the polished concrete floor. Huge. The size of a small skateboard.

Horrible creature. Shit, shit, shit. How dare that thing scare the crap out of me? Someone's going to pay. *It's* going to pay. If I'm going to do one thing, I'm going to kill that sucker.

Its feelers keep twitching as I unlace my Converse sneaker and take it into my hand, sliding off the chair to get closer.

"Die!" I give it a big whack with my shoe. And miss.

He's moved.

I'm sweating in less than a second. I have to do this.

"Die, motherfucker!" I whack him again.

White guts spill out of the revolting creature. It twitches. I hit it again. "Die, die, die!"

So much concrete, the sound of my strikes and my voice echoing. I'm in the car park again and that man is in front of us, asking for our help. Friendly. Until he's not. His face is neutral, almost serene, the scariest thing of all because I know what Charlie doesn't. This man will do whatever he wants to do. He's not snarling or spitting. He doesn't have tatts crawling up his neck. He doesn't need them. He's not bulked up like he's training for the UFC. No, he's been training for this all his life.

Charlie's already been sucked in, so guileless when it comes to things like this. I don't see the knife, not at first, and Charlie doesn't see it at all. The rest, I see in slow motion. *Charlie, get away. Run. Don't be there.* My body is flooded with feelings of overwhelming love that mixes with the fear. And terror. I have to protect Charlie. I can't let this happen.

Whack, crash, crack.

"Die, motherfucker!"

I keep smashing, loud whacks resonating throughout the room, tears streaming down my cheeks.

"Motherfucker."

I yell at the mushed-up remains of the cockroach, the hard shell of its wings splintered into pieces, its soft white insides mixing with hard brown outsides. I scream. Die, it has to die.

A thump from the backyard doesn't quite register. Footsteps. Running. Suddenly there's a figure in the doorway, a man, panting.

"Stop!" I stand and yell.

He stops. I take a moment. It's Ryan from next door. *Calm down.* Everything's fine. I can't jump him like I did the man in the park.

He rests his hands on either side of the sliding door. "Kate, are you okay?"

I nod. I'm panting too.

His eyes dart around the room. "You sure? Is anyone here?"

"I'm fine."

I'm not fine. I'll never be fine again.

"Can I come in?"

"Sure."

His shoulders relax as he steps closer, still looking around as if to make sure it's safe. "Jesus, you scared me. I thought you were being attacked, like a home invasion or something."

I can't let him know he's right, that I was back in that car park with Andrew Scarparolo, the man who killed Charlie. I'm not there now. I let the Converse drop from my hand. It lands with a gentle thud.

"Was that you yelling 'die, motherfucker'?" Ryan asks in a soft voice.

I wish the concrete would split open and swallow me. I wish I could go back in time and kill the ugly insect in one fell swoop. I wish I was a different person.

"Um, yes," I say. "There was a cockroach."

Ryan points. "*That* was a cockroach?"

I nod.

"Come on, that's so OTT it's kinda funny." He must see the look on my face because he adds, "I'm sorry. You're crying."

I wipe the tears from my cheeks and force a smile. "It's not so funny for the cockroach."

"I guess not. Let me give you a hand."

"Sure," I say as if it's the most natural thing in the world for visitors to deal with cockroach smeared over the floor.

Ryan stares at the slimy detritus. "Normally I slide them onto a fly swat and get rid of them outside."

"Nup, not gonna work."

"Do you have a paper towel or something?"

I rush to the kitchen, my gait uneven because I'm only wearing one shoe, and grab a couple of paper towels.

Ryan wipes up the mess and deposits the remains in the kitchen bin while I sit down and lace up my shoe, calmly, like a rational person, not like a psycho cockroach-killer.

"Is it okay if I take a seat?" he asks.

I nod. "You don't have to be scared of me."

"That's good to know."

"Thanks. For cleaning up the mess, but mostly for taking such quick action and, you know, coming over."

Ryan sits down. "I had to jump the fence. Haven't done that sort of thing since I was a kid."

I remember the thud I'd heard earlier, not quite the practised pounce of a cat burglar.

"What were you doing jumping fences when you were a kid?"

He grins. "Not breaking into houses if that's what you're thinking. We used to steal grapes from a house down the street, that is, until the owner came out of his house one day and caught us. We made a run for it, went around the corner and scurried over a fence to hide. Came face to face with a German shepherd." Ryan laughs. "My mates and I learnt to run and leap pretty fast that day."

"That sounds even scarier than a cockroach."

He grins. "Depends on the size of the roach."

"Not sure I should trust a law-breaker like you."

"Hey, I was ten."

I picture a pint-sized Ryan running in fear and hold back a smile, then notice a soggy patch of brown covering the bottom of his pale-grey windcheater.

"What's that?" I ask.

"I was on the back deck having a coffee. I knocked it over when I heard you yelling."

I stand. "That'll stain. If you take it off, I'll soak it."

"Nah, don't worry about it."

"It's no trouble. And I'll make you a replacement coffee. It's the least I can do."

"Fair enough." He stands and whips the windcheater over his head. His T-shirt rides up as he does so, revealing a lean stomach, rather attractive if I was looking, which I'm not.

Leaning against the doorframe in the laundry room, he watches while I run some water in a bucket and soak his windcheater. Just as well Esmeralda's not here because this is her space and she doesn't like me coming in unless it's to feed or tend to her, though she might take to Ryan a bit better.

I turn off the tap. "I love that window."

A horizontal slot window with cupboards below and above looks out onto a mini-courtyard with creeper growing up the wall and a grevillea that's weighed down by a wattlebird sucking nectar from the flowers.

"Designed especially for Esmeralda," Ryan says.

"Really?"

"That's why her bed is on the cupboard, so she can look at the activity outside while feeling cosy in the enclosed space.

"You're very clever. She likes it here."

We move to the kitchen where Ryan takes a seat at the breakfast bar and I make plunger coffee that I pour into the white Villeroy and Boch NewWave mugs.

Ryan points at the mugs. "Very architectural."

"And expensive. I looked them up online and nearly had a heart attack at the price. Sugar? Milk?"

"Neither, thanks."

I add a splash of milk to mine and join him on the other side of the bench. "Can I ask you a question? If someone had been attacking me, what would you have done?"

"I'm not sure exactly. I would've called the police, obviously, but if something bad was going down it would've been too late by the time they got here."

He's nailed it. It's always too late by the time the police get there.

He takes a drink. "Turns out I didn't need to worry. The cockroach didn't stand a chance."

I laugh. This isn't so bad.

We converse. Like two normal people. We drink our coffee. After a while, I notice it's getting dark outside.

"Time to go." Ryan stands. "If it's okay, I might use the front door."

I get up and walk down the hallway. "Sure. I mean, you're welcome to jump the fence whenever you like but the front door's cool too.'

He smiles. "Phew."

Ryan is beside me as I pull open the door.

"Thanks for the coffee." And he's off.

Somehow it feels too soon.

I hardly ever yell. I got shouted at enough as a kid that I refuse to stoop to that level. After Dad left, Mum couldn't shout at him anymore, then Jack left too so there was only me to take the brunt. She's mellowed since then.

I've shouted *Die, motherfucker* at plenty of cockroaches, though.

And I whispered the words once. Once was all it took. And something died inside me.

Chapter Sixteen

"That's a common nickname," Mum says over the phone.

Instant regret. I should never have mentioned the flowers and card to her. Maybe I should've called Charlie's mum instead, a compassionate human being, only I wouldn't want to add to her pain with my problems.

"You're making a big deal out of nothing," Mum adds. "It's not as if someone sent you a letter bomb."

My heart rate rises. "Flowers from my dead husband are nothing? Come on, Mum."

"That's not what I meant. You've misunderstood what I'm saying."

The doorbell rings. Saved.

"Someone's at the door," I say.

"I can tell you're upset. You get like this so easily."

"I've gotta go. Bye."

My pulse continues rising as I storm down the hallway, so I take a moment to calm myself before pulling the front door open.

It's the police. Another jolt to my heart. Shit, I'm all over the place. And Ryan just happens to be walking up his front path at this very moment. He waves. I smile, pretending this is normal.

"Is it okay if we come in?" Constable Alex Sheridan asks.

"Sure."

"This is Constable Gabby Furlani."

I smile and she nods before I lead them to the living area at the rear of the house. They sit on the opposite side of the table from me, like it's a job interview or, worse, an interrogation. There's always an edge with cops or maybe it's me who has the problem.

"I thought this warranted a personal visit," Alex says.

Personal isn't good, not when the police are involved. Still, it's not as bad as the formal interviews I had with the police in Melbourne, the questions, the statements, not to mention the trauma that led to me being there.

I remember another cop in Melbourne asking me, off the record, what was going through my head that night during the attack, as if it had all been my fault. He didn't get it. There was no thought, no weighing up of options, no time to decide. There was only me trying to survive, trying to save Charlie, me failing.

Alex frowns. "Kate?"

"Go ahead."

"Firstly, the flowers. We followed through on your enquiry."

"Great."

"We paid a visit to Cottage Florist and talked to the owner, Julian Kelly, but you'd already been there, hadn't you?"

"Yes."

"The gentleman had already prepared a theory about how someone had paid a teenager to order the flowers for you."

"Okay."

Alex clears his throat. "It's extremely hard to get an accurate description of events from someone who's already made up his mind. There are certain protocols when we interview witnesses. We have procedures and defined ways we go about things." He sighs. "Sergeant Cunningham said we'd look into it and you should have left us to do our jobs instead of getting in the way of a police investigation."

He stares. For a young guy, he's got a determined glare. He's probably used to dealing with criminals and meth heads and people a lot scarier than me.

"I didn't do anything," I say.

"Your intentions may have been good but we can't have you leading people on when we're conducting an investigation. The sergeant went out of his way to attend to this personally," he says. "And your actions were highly inappropriate."

I made them look bad because I was quicker. Is that it? No doubt after attending to this *personally* the sergeant asked Alex to speak to me *personally*. Refusing to let him make me squirm, I sit ramrod straight in my chair.

"Remember, the flowers weren't a message from your husband's killer," Alex adds. "That man died in the car park in Melbourne a year ago. We're clear on that, aren't we?"

I nod. That's put me in my place then, the crazy woman who tried to tell the police a dead man was after her. A man she'd killed herself, no less. They don't come much crazier than that, and I don't need to be reminded. I want to disappear into a puddle on the polished concrete floor.

Alex says, "My colleagues undertook a thorough investigation of the man who attacked you. They were well aware of his associates, friends, family, an ex-girlfriend who was an English teacher. Which brings me to my next point about the attacker's brother, Domenic Scarparolo, the man who threatened you in Melbourne."

"That's right."

"We've spoken to him here in Perth."

"He's here?" My eyes widen. "He must've sent the flowers.

This is too much of a coincidence, even you've got to admit that."

"Slow down, Kate. So far we have no evidence to suggest he arranged for that bouquet to be sent to you. Anyone could have sent those flowers. For all we know, you might've done it yourself."

His words suck the air right out of me. How can he suggest such a thing? I blank out from time to time but I couldn't have done something like that, no way. Yet there's a niggling doubt… Maybe Mum's not the only one who thinks I'm making a big deal out of this. Maybe I created the whole thing. Maybe I'm a new level of unhinged.

No, I can't think that way.

Alex clears his throat. "I'm not saying it was you. In the course of our enquiries, we also questioned Domenic Scarparolo on his whereabouts on the night William Sharma was rammed by a vehicle."

Could he have done that? I hadn't even got that far. I stare at Alex. Wait for him to continue.

"He was working till midnight at a pub in Freo on the night in question. His manager has verified this, and after that, Domenic Scarparolo was at home with his wife."

"Yeah, and there's no way his wife would lie for him," I say sarcastically.

"There's not enough time for him to have made it to Dianella in time to drive his car into Will Sharma. Think about it, Kate. It also seems extremely unlikely he'd have known you'd be at that address at that time, given you'd only met the man that night. Scarparolo wouldn't have had time to follow you after he finished his shift."

Who knew I was going out that evening? I hadn't told anyone. I was hardly going to advertise that I was going out on the prowl.

It hits me like a battering ram. Ryan was there that night at the bar with a friend. He knew where I was, even if he didn't know what I had planned or where I was going next. Surely he wouldn't have followed me. He couldn't.

I drop my head into my hands. "Do you think Domenic Scarparolo followed me here to Perth?"

"It seems unlikely. He married recently, and his wife's from Perth."

I lift my head. "Which pub does he work at?"

"Don't approach this man. That would be irresponsible and extremely remiss of you."

And I am never 'remiss'. I am a lot of things – well-behaved, polite, sensible, logical, practical, controlled. I don't fly off the handle or seek revenge or shout and scream and swear. Except at cockroaches. I hate myself, my personality, my life.

And it's time to do something about it. I don't have to put myself in danger. I do need to talk to this guy. And if that means visiting every pub in Fremantle to find him, then that's what I'll do.

"Thanks," I say.

And I walk the two officers to the door because 'civilised' is another thing I am.

Chapter Seventeen

For someone who's so aware of their surroundings, I've done a stellar job of not noticing that the sky's so dark it looks like it's about to collapse.

The light in Perth can be harsh. Not now, though. The soft green lawn around the lake has a subdued glow, the water rippling without any sparkle, the air thick and heavy. Winter. It beats the hell out of strings of forty-degree days in summer.

I go to the park for my workouts, a different park each time and a different time of day. No routine for me because that'd make it too easy if anyone was watching. No headphones or earpods either. Always look confident; always look like I know where I'm going; don't be a target. God help anyone who tries to grab me and God help any cockroaches who get in my way.

My phone vibrates in the pocket of my shorts so I stop by the lake and pull out my phone. It's Mum. And it's not so bad. She's asking for a hand in the garden because the work that needs to be done is too much for her. I text her right back, telling her I'm happy to help.

I jog to the playground, slowing down as I get closer. I get that creepy feeling of being followed, the hair on the back of my neck standing on end, my senses alert even though there's no reason for it. I tell myself I'm full of shit for being overly cautious.

The only people left in the park are a group of three mums with their toddlers, and I'm pretty sure they're not about to attack me. A woman catches a little boy in a red puffer jacket at the bottom of a yellow slide and they giggle together. Two mums stand and chat, glancing from time to time at two girls as they climb up a brown plastic ladder to stop by a railing at the top of the play equipment and giggle. Huddled together, their little shoulders are scrunched as they chat. So cute, so innocent. A pang cuts through my chest. I shift my gaze to the mums. Could that be me one day?

I do some quick stretches, calf muscles, quadriceps, hip flexors. I've always wanted children of my own. Always. Charlie said he wanted kids too, and then never seemed so keen as time went on. He never said no. It was always *after*. After he got his residency, after we had a bit more money behind us, after he got his dream job at the next hospital.

When I gave him the news, he wasn't happy. I'll never know why. If I had a child, I'd have a piece of Charlie left. And now it's too late.

The woman at the bottom of the yellow slide stares at me while her little boy runs around nearby. Or maybe I'm staring at her. I'm such a klutz. I'm not stretching anymore and my eyes have filled with tears.

I wave and offer her a wan smile. She waves back. Does she know how lucky she is? Probably. Right now, she's the smartest person I know, her and her two friends, because nothing is more important than your kids.

A fat drop of rain lands on my cheek. Then another.

The mums swing into action, holding hands with their children as they run and giggle towards the road, while I stand there, unable to take my eyes off them. They get into their cars parked under the Moreton Bay fig trees that line the road. Children are loaded into SUVs, car doors slam, engines are geared up, tyres hum on the road, and they're gone. I'm still rooted to the spot, dripping with jealousy because I want what they've got, someone to care for, someone to love me.

Time to go. I jog along the path that winds through the vast green lawn, only to spot a car crawling along the road under the Moreton Bay figs. Might be nothing or it might be a problem. I'm not hanging around to find out which. I can double back or cut across the park.

Then I see it's not any car. It's a Tesla, Noah's new car.

He toots his horn and pulls over. I veer off the path over the grass and head for his car. He leans across the passenger's seat and pushes open the door. Yep, it's definitely Noah.

I rest my hand on the top of the open door. "I thought I was being followed. For crying out loud, Noah."

"For crying out loud, what? I live here, remember? Jump in."

I look down at the leather seats, new-car smell spilling from the interior. "I'm sweaty and kind of wet."

"I'm not precious about that stuff. Come on."

I hear the words he doesn't say. He's not precious the way Charlie was, so particular about all his belongings, making sure everything was perfect and nothing got scratched. I can't hold that against Noah when he's right. I get in, still panting, and pull my seat belt across.

He checks for non-existent traffic and pulls away. "What were you thinking, Kate? It's going to start pissing down any minute. The rain isn't like it is in Melbourne."

He says this like I don't know what Perth weather is like, when I grew up here.

A memory flashes in my mind, Charlie and me running to the car in the rain, him ripping off my wet cardigan after we got home and kissing me, holding me, making me hot chocolate. I miss him so much it hurts, but Noah is not Charlie.

On cue, the dam gates open above us, and rain pounds the roof of the car, pouring down the windscreen. As if the rain and Noah are conspiring against me. I drum my fingers against the leather seat.

"Were you on your way somewhere?" I raise my voice so he can hear me over the deluge.

"Home. I just had a meeting with some prospective clients."

"I thought your books were full."

He laughs. "You've gotta play the game. Treat 'em mean, keep 'em keen."

I'll never understand this side of running a business. Maybe that's why I'm so bad at it. Noah says he maintains a select client base, and now he's broadening that base to include medical contacts of Theo's. Doctors have money, after all.

Still it's hardly surprising that people come to Noah. Years ago he made a reputation for himself with some lucrative real estate deals, got named as a young gun in the industry and had his face on the cover of a couple of prominent business journals. Then he shifted into financial consulting and that's going equally well for him, maybe better. He says his nous and natural business instincts got him further than any MBA.

"Have you been busy with work?" he asks.

"Amaaazing." I draw the word out, thinking maybe two can play this game after all.

"Kate, don't try to kid a kidder."

"I didn't say 'amazingly well'." I shrug. "Maybe it's amazing how much business sucks at the moment."

Rain is still hammering down, the wipers pushing pools of water left and right, struggling against the deluge. Ahead of us the road is a river. Must be a blocked drain. Noah slows as he navigates through it.

"You can talk to me, Kate. You know that, don't you?"

"Sure."

"But I like your line about business being amazing." He shoots me a quick smile as he turns a corner. "I've got a lot on so I had to let a client go. It was no great loss, an annoying busybody, and I was more than happy to return her investments. Sounded like a case of a marriage on the rocks with a divorce around the corner if you ask me."

"Really?"

"And I've got another trip to Melbourne lined up but that's hardly news."

We pull up outside my house, or Joel's house, to be more accurate.

Switching the engine off, Noah turns to me. "You're a good writer, Kate. You just need more clients. Moving forward, that's what you need to focus on."

Moving forward. Noah is a master when it comes to clichés. It rubs me up the wrong way, maybe because I'm a writer so I'm always trying to avoid the overused phrases and sentiments.

"I think in some ways Charlie was holding you back," he says.

I press my lips together.

"He didn't want you to be too successful."

My fingers grip the door-handle. "That was only one side of Charlie."

"You came here to start over, so maybe you can write your own narrative." Noah glances at my hand. "It's been a while since you've worn your wedding ring."

I keep it in the sleek timber memory box that Charlie gave me years ago, along with a few birthday cards, selected photos, a Venetian mask, some other souvenirs, and old passports and documents including his death certificate.

I glare. "I loved him. I still do."

"I didn't mean that. I don't think Charlie appreciated you as much as he should have."

I push the door open.

"I miss him a lot too, Kate."

My arm is stretched out into the rain, water dripping down the glass onto the leather lining of the car-door interior. Noah said he wasn't precious so I'll see how *not* precious he is.

"Not like you do," he says. "I'm not comparing my grief with yours but I feel the loss and the pain too. It's one of the reasons I left Melbourne because, for me, in Melbourne Charlie was everywhere." He gives me a lingering look. "The other reason is… more obvious."

"Please don't, Noah."

He rests his hands on the sleek steering wheel. I don't want the glamorous life he represents, the cars, the overseas holidays, the real estate investments. I want a life, my life.

And maybe all I want now is a nice, relaxing bath to soothe my nerves.

"Charlie was a great guy," he says. "But he wasn't perfect. That's all I'm saying."

He wasn't perfect, but he was *mine*.

"Thanks for the lift." I get out of the car and trudge to the front door, letting the rain soak into my skin, my running clothes, my shoes. Noah doesn't drive off, not yet, or I'd hear the swish of tyres on the road. I feel his eyes on me, staring, admiring, wishing.

A shudder shoots up my spine. Something is wrong. My gaze is lowered, my eyes on the coir doormat trimmed in black with three black *fleurs-de-lys* spaced across the middle, an unusually ornate choice for someone like Joel.

The mat is crooked, pulled out from the door at a forty-five-degree angle. Nothing in the house – or outside it – is ever out of place. I glance around. Nothing else is odd so I stick the key in the door and wave. Noah finally takes off. I hate this feeling of being watched and followed. I'm not imagining this.

Someone has been here.

Hey Beautiful Buddy

You were always my best friend, my best everything, the best of me. Were. Past tense.

That's why I've got to do this for you. For once in my life, I know exactly what to do. I'll take my time and that's okay. No need to rush and I certainly can't expect everything to happen at once. It's not easy setting myself up in a new place or making enough money to get by or working out the details, but I've got a plan, and that's the main thing. A girl needs a plan, eh, honey? I'm not perfect, far from it. In the past, I've rushed in too soon and stumbled through life and made mistakes. This time, I'm determined to do things right and savour every moment because God knows there are so few moments in life that are sweet.

Everything's so much harder without you. Before, I had you pointing me in the right direction and helping me out. Now, I have to work it all out by myself.

I need to dig deep and not only find the truth, but fight for it. There are so many fakes around. Too many. I'm like Holden Caulfield. I can't stand all the phonies. I'll have to do a lot of searching and cut through a lot of crap to get to the truth, but don't worry, I'll get there. For you.

Love you always

Love you, love you, love you

Chapter Eighteen

Finally, the weekend. I've been waiting for this.

Fremantle becomes a tourist town when the sun is out, people swarming there from suburbs far and close, enjoying the cafés and al fresco dining and a pleasant walk. The perfect afternoon for a pub crawl.

Constable Alex Sheridan referred to the place where Domenic Scarparolo works as a pub, not a bar, so I've already decided to start with the bigger hotels, the Norfolk, the Sail and Anchor, the National and several places along High Street. That's a lot of pubs to get through.

I try the National first. Years ago, Mum told me this used to be a dump but that was before my time. It's a dump no more. Immaculate pointing on the red-brick exterior, intricate wrought-iron lacework and cast-iron verandah panels, concrete and plaster detailing over the arched windows. They didn't skimp on the renovation.

In contrast, the outdoor trestle tables and rough bench seats are rustic, not to mention extremely inviting. Vines growing from oversized pots add to the relaxed feel. No wonder all the tables outside are taken. Not many better places to be on a sunny afternoon than outside with friends having a beer. That used to be me and Charlie once. I remember a pub around the corner from our place in Fitzroy, the sun shining, water condensing on the outside of our pint glasses while we scoffed down hot chips and aioli. An ordinary memory, a wonderful one, a memory that makes me ache.

Focus. Luckily I don't want to sit outside. That's not what I'm here for. I wander inside, checking out the interior and looking for a familiar face behind the bar. *That* face.

I order a lemonade at the bar, choosing an older male bartender because I have a feeling a bloke will be more helpful. A nervous shiver shoots up my spine. I'm not made for this.

He laughs. "On the hard stuff, eh?"

I smile. "I'm a two-pot screamer, unfortunately."

"But this isn't even a beer!"

"Nah, I guess not. Hey, I'm looking for someone. A friend said he works here."

I give him the name. I try to sound casual. No, he's never heard of Domenic Scarparolo. He doesn't work here. The bartender has been here for over ten years and if anyone would know, he would.

"Thanks," I say.

I wander off with my lemonade past two old-timers who've probably been here since the year dot, past fresh-faced young people, past a couple with their two small kids. I leave my drink on a table around the corner, amble away and try not to feel like a sad loser with no mates.

Next pub. Look around. Order a drink. Ask the same question.

Another pub. Rinse. Repeat.

I've stopped counting how many hotels I've been to. Now it's the Red Lion, in a prime location on a corner. Though the aroma of freshly-poured beer and the low hum of chatter appeal to me, I've had enough and this will be my last pub for the day. Next time, I'll have to try some of the smaller bars.

My phone buzzes so I check my messages. Laura is asking if I want to pop around for a quick coffee. Hell, I can't have coffee with her today and can't possibly tell her what I'm up to. She'd freak. I take a deep breath and type.

Not today. Maybe tomorrow if you're free?

I slide my phone back into my bag and go inside. Magnificent stained glass, walls stripped back to bare brick, a long wooden bar with several sets of beer taps, green exit signs to my right, another set of doors to my left, people standing at the bar, people seated at tables, no familiar faces that I can see. No older male bartenders either, so I go up to the bar and try a barmaid with a tight black T-shirt tied at the waist.

"Hi there." I smile. "Can I get a lemon, lime and bitters please."

So much more exotic than a plain soft drink. She prepares my drink of choice and places it on the bar.

"I'm looking for a mate of mine," I say. "A friend said he—"

I freeze. His face flashes before me, *that* face, the one that's imprinted in my mind. I'm back in the car park. The world around me is dark. Tunnel vision. There's nothing else but me and him and the knife coming at me. I get cut, how many times I don't know. I have to stop this. I grab the man's knife-wielding arm with both my hands, putting all my weight on it, holding on for dear life. He's strong but he can't stab me while

I've got the arm. *Control the weapon.* I don't have control for long. He fights free. Slashes me. Heat. Blood. Fear. Terror.

"Hey." The woman bartender waves at me. "Are you okay? You look like you've seen a ghost."

I'm back. If only my voice would work. It's not *him*. It's his brother and this is the reason I came and I'd better get my act together quick smart because he's already got one over me. He knows who I am, no doubt about that, no uncertainty in his stare.

"I'm fine." The words come to me.

Deep breaths. I force myself to think. I'm in a public place. I'm safe. This is not the man who attacked me in the car park. This is his brother and I should be careful.

"I'll take care of this, Carly," Scarparolo says without taking his eyes off me.

The barmaid shrugs.

"What a surprise." He waits, then adds, "It's quieter outside."

A stocky guy in a black collared shirt strides across behind the bar and points to the beer fridges behind them, giving the barmaid instructions on something.

Domenic Scarparolo walks with his chest puffed out, his arms not touching his sides. I leave my drink at the bar, forced to follow behind because he's taking up so much space. Screw him.

We wander outside into the beer garden with its green planters, hanging baskets with ferns and tables surrounded by punters enjoying themselves. Everyone loves a beer garden. We stop by a limestone wall.

It's now or never. "What are you doing in Perth? Why did you come here?"

"What's it to you? It's a free country."

Great, now I'm dealing with a five-year-old, a potentially

scary one. I raise my hands and use them while I speak because it's safer to have your hands up.

"I liked it better when you were on the other side of the country," I say.

"Did you now? The cops came looking for me the other day." He folds his arms. "You *know* the cops came to see me."

I'm sinking. In over my head.

"I didn't send the police," I say. "I didn't know you were in Perth."

"Well, now you know. Seems you knew exactly where to find me. Don't play nice with me. You killed my brother."

That was the worst night of my life, the night I lost Charlie and my world changed. Yet somehow this is *his* loss? The breath leaves my body.

I gasp. "Your brother murdered my husband in cold blood."

"You killed him."

True, so true.

Andrew Scarparolo made a mistake, or maybe I did. Hard to tell when it happened so quickly. I had his arm, and we were both going to ground. Bad, bad, bad. So I sprawled, my legs back, my body on top of his. I knew if I ended up with him on top of me that'd be the worst possible position. Blood everywhere, Charlie behind me, fear coursing through me. Not fear. Terror.

I remember very well what happened after that – the moment before. Then there was after, and I've lived with that 'after' ever since. It's deep in my bones, the feeling that I must pay for this somehow, that this will always drag me down, that I'll never escape.

I get my shit together. "Your brother had a knife."

He mumbles something in agreement, I can't catch the words, then adds, "Andrew wasn't perfect and maybe he should've ended up in jail or something. I'm not saying he was a saint. But he didn't deserve to die. He shouldn't have ended up dead."

"Like my husband?"

He presses his lips together. "You don't give a shit about what you've done."

Fuck you, fuck this, fuck everything.

Laughter erupts from a nearby table, people having fun. The guy in the black shirt carries a platter across to a table in the far corner.

"He was my brother," Scarparolo says. "Andrew would never have laid a hand on a woman, let alone knifed one. I don't know what shit you made up for the police."

"Did I make this up?" I pull up my shirt and point at the scars, the puncture wounds and slashes, irregular and jagged, the mess on my torso.

A woman at a nearby table does a double take, then I drop my shirt. Mouth gaping, she turns to her friends.

From Scarparolo, nothing. No shock or surprise. No acknowledgement either.

He says, "The cops gave me some wild-ass story about someone getting rammed by a four-wheel drive. They looked my car over, like I had something to do with it. Asked me lots of questions. Talked to my boss." His eyes narrow. "I'm new on the job here. That fuckin' pissed me off."

I purse my lips. "Have you been following me?"

"Now there's an idea."

I'm on a roll. "Why did you do it? Why'd you send those flowers? What was in it for you?"

He leans closer. "What kind of fuck-up are you?"

My heart racing, I step away from him further along the wall, livid because his description is spot on. I have stuffed up in so many ways and my life is in shreds. This guy has a job and a wife, while I can barely make a living and that hardly rates a mention because I've lost the love of my life.

The stocky guy in the black shirt approaches. "Everything okay here?"

Scarparolo waits a moment, then nods, the silence between them comfortable.

I straighten. "No, it's not okay. He just called me a fuck-up."

Black Shirt gives me a look like I'm an annoying child, then turns to Scarparolo. "Carly needs a hand behind the bar when you're ready, Dom. No hurry."

Dom. So familiar.

Black Shirt turns and walks away.

Scarparolo grins. "Trying to get me in trouble with the boss, eh? You really are a bitch."

I stumble towards the exit, then look around to make sure it's safe. Scarparolo hasn't moved, an ugly grin still smeared across his face.

The next thing I know I'm halfway home, driving up the highway past blocks of art deco flats in leafy suburbs with no idea how I got here. Shit, I've blanked out again. I refuse to hit the panic stations. I maintain a reasonable speed, check my mirrors, do my best impersonation of a safe driver. I'm overcome with the horrible feeling I'm being followed, the hair on the back of my neck standing on end.

I drum my fingers on the steering wheel as I stop at the lights, my eyes on the rear-view mirror. Blanking out has caused me to freak out and I'm imagining things. Deep breaths. Everything is fine.

Everything is not fine. The manager at the Red Lion is mates with Domenic Scarparolo. That's probably how he got the job even though he's new in town.

And a mate would lie about what time Scarparolo's shift finished and whether he was working that night.

Chapter Nineteen

Another day, another workout.

It's been raining all day, the ground soaked, trees dripping with water, so I decided it was more sensible to work out on the back patio instead. That's me, sensible. It was go, go, go, sprawls, squats, push-ups with some other stuff thrown in for an efficient, killer cardio session. Sweating like crazy, lungs burning, legs like jelly, arms twitching, this is the life. Now that I'm done, the cold is sinking in, my skin clammy.

I sit cross-legged on the deck, my water bottle beside me, as I take a moment to appreciate my aching limbs and my lungs that have been pushed to capacity. Best of all, there's silence in my head. It's like a migraine lifting and floating away and leaving me alone, for a while anyway.

I hear the swish of Ryan's back door opening and closing. Voices sail over the fence from next door. No, only one voice. Ryan's.

"I'm sorry, Margaret, I know how hard it is for you."

He must be at the table that's by the fence only a few metres away from me. I'm not listening, not really. It's not my fault his voice is deep and crystal clear.

"I don't think she wants to see me anymore… No, it's not that. I think it's too painful for her. But we both know her husband's a good bloke. I get the feeling he understands how much we both lost… Oh yeah, you too, Margaret. Of course."

Should I clear my throat or make a loud noise so Ryan knows I'm here? He's probably so engrossed in his phone call that he hasn't wondered if anyone else is nearby. At least I assume it's a phone call.

"Maybe we can catch up for coffee and I'll tell you about it. It'll be easier that way… Nah, it's nothing terrible. It's good news actually… Sure… I'll come over tomorrow."

Listening in to him talking to his ex-mother-in-law makes me feel like I'm snooping or heading into stalker territory. I take a drink of water. Surely this call will be over soon. If I start moving, he'll hear my footsteps and the back door and he'll know I was out here, which is worse.

"I'd love to come over now, really I would," he says. "But I've got some final prep to do before a meeting tomorrow."

He makes lots of sounds from the other side of the fence, lots of yeahs and hmms and okays. A long silence follows. No hmms. He must be listening to what she's saying.

"Olivia is pregnant, Margaret. She's going to have another baby." A pang shoots through me even though I don't know this person. A long silence follows. Silence isn't good. This must be hard for Ryan. "Are you crying? Please tell me they're happy tears… Me? Yeah, I'm fine. I think she's moving on. No, she'll never get over it. I don't mean that…"

I'm in too deep and can't move away now that I'm a weird combination of embarrassed and engrossed. The sun has come out, raindrops glistening on the plants and leaves. Ryan's not going to head straight inside while it's so pretty out here.

"Sixteen weeks. Yeah, so still a long way to go. The morning sickness was pretty bad for the first trimester… Yeah, just like before… But she's come good now."

Is it bad to feel jealous of someone's nausea? It's wrong, so wrong. The pang inside me turns to pain. This used to be me. I used to be in a loving relationship. And now there's no Charlie. We should've had little Charlies. Or just one. One new life would've been enough for me. One little person to love and take care of.

I'm still stuck thinking about a baby that never was, whereas this baby is real, a new life coming into the world, and Ryan has to come to terms with it even though he's trying to sound happy for his ex. I hang my head. I shouldn't be listening. I should've gone inside sooner. So many things I should've done differently.

"I'd love to help, really I would, and I'm doing my best." Ryan's voice cracks. "It's hard for me too… Sure… Okay, then. Bye."

Ryan lets out a long groan. I freeze. None of this is my business.

"Why?" Another groan. "Fuck." Followed by footsteps and the swish of Ryan's back door.

I step inside as quietly as I can. I try not to think about what could have been. Instead I wonder how Ryan will be coping.

Charlie is falling. We're in the kitchen at our old place in Fitzroy. I'm leaning over the kitchen sink, the edge of the cupboard digging into my gut, as I hold on for dear life. Charlie's life. He's on the other side of the open window, dangling into a chasm so deep it has no bottom.

He's slipping from my grasp though I scream at him to hold on. There's no sound from Charlie. I can't see him anymore. *Where are you?*

Suddenly I'm out on a Melbourne street, the overcast sky

pressing down upon me. I try to phone for help but as I touch the screen, each button disappears. Then the screen becomes blobs of swirling liquid. Despair. Dread. I can't get the phone to work. A pedestrian smashes into me, knocks me back. Pain rips through my shoulder.

I sit up in bed, reeling, sweating. I'm always too late. Charlie has already fallen.

Just a dream. So why is my shoulder so sore? I give it a rub, grateful for the physical pain. I pick my phone up from the bedside table. Three o'clock. My heart sinks. I've still got hours to go.

I put my phone down and sling my legs over the edge of the bed.

"Charlie, are you there?"

I wait. Nothing. Charlie is gone, the room empty. He's never coming back. This isn't even my bedroom, not really.

I wander through the house, looking for something, I don't know what. My feet are cold on the polished concrete. Cold is good. I open the back door and step outside. Let me freeze. I need to feel. Not the feelings that swirl around inside me. I need to feel the night air. Cold, fresh, freezing. Outside, I look straight ahead without seeing. I don't know how long I stand there. My hands and feet are ice blocks, my nose frozen. I need to get colder. I rip off my pyjama top and let the cold night engulf me. I don't look down at my scars, an ugly reminder of a horrendous night. I never look at them. I'm shivering, my teeth chattering. I'm crazy.

No sound from next door, no lights going on. The only things that are going on are in my head.

I stomp into the house. I came out here to *feel* but I was wrong. I don't want to feel anymore.

Chapter Twenty

Coffee is good. Coffee is a lifesaver. Somehow I got through the rest of the night. I may have slept. I'm not sure. The only thing I am sure of is that I look like crap. Don't need a mirror to tell me that.

The ring of my phone makes me jump. Rachel Jones, a client and an old friend of Noah's. It must be after nine over there, a reasonable hour in Melbourne. Leaning back in my chair, I take a deep breath, pick up my phone from the dining table and put on my happy voice. Professional. Perky. If I pretend to be someone else, maybe I'll become that person.

"Rachel, how lovely to hear from you. You're up bright and early."

A pause.

"Hang on," Rachel says. "Noah mentioned you were going to Perth. You haven't moved already?"

"Yeah, I have."

"Oh no, I forgot. It must be seven in the morning for you. I'm so sorry."

I laugh. "No problem. I was just having a coffee."

Rachel apologises some more. Small talk, I can do this.

Every client is important and I always liked Rachel because she's down to earth, clever and caring. Caring, that's right.

"Thanks for the card you sent," I say.

"Oh, I'd forgotten about that," she says. "About the condolence card, I mean, not about Charlie. I'm sorry, Kate. Maybe I should've called you sooner."

"You're doing way too much apologising, Rachel." I keep my voice light. "I moved over here to be closer to friends and family. My mum's here, and Noah, and I'm good friends with his sister. It's not as if I'm on my own."

That's despite the fact I've done a pretty good job of alienating myself from any other friends I had. Not from my clients though, the few that I've got.

"How are you doing?" I ask. "How's business?"

"Things are going smashingly. I'm not quite in Noah's league but his style is different from mine. He's more of a risk-taker, whereas I'm pretty conservative. Even after all these years, I'm incredibly grateful to him. He was *cleaning up* his client list. That was the term he used, honestly, as if too many clients is a problem."

"That sounds like him."

"Some of the so-called cast-offs he sent my way have turned out to be quite lucrative. That's kind of why I'm calling."

A while back, I'd suggested some nice-to-have promotional materials, and now she's adding a few more even-nicer-to-haves, so there'll be a bit of work coming my way.

Excited after the phone call, I get my laptop and take another look at Rachel's website, feeling pleased with myself because the copy is holding up pretty well. She wants to update her Financial Services Guide too, a document that gives information on the financial services she offers, fees charged and how she deals with complaints. It's a legal requirement for all financial advisors in Australia and as I look at it again, I have a couple of ideas on how we can make it a tad more interesting.

I get to the end of the document where the small print at the bottom has her ABN, Australian Business number, and AFSL, Australian Financial Services Licence number. The last number looks so familiar. It starts off 669. I remember because it's nearly the number of the beast, only Rachel is as far from beastly as you can get.

And I'm feeling a lot less beastly now too.

Kneeling in front of Mum's new planters with a trowel in my hand and the sun on my back, I'm swelling with satisfaction. Doesn't matter that I'm not the world's best gardener.

The rear flywire door slams shut. It must be Mum, who's been scrubbing the shower recess. One thing I can say about her is that she's not lazy. She's always working on something or pottering around.

She hands me a glass of water.

"Thanks." I knock back a few mouthfuls. "I'm glad I can help in the garden."

"Me too." She drops down onto a white plastic chair. "But I thought you were going to do the painting first."

"What painting?"

"I told you about it last time we spoke."

"No, you didn't."

I rack my brain. I'm sure she didn't. I force myself to think positive. *Repair, replenish, revitalise*, my three R's, because I want to fix my relationship with my mother. It's not as though I've got a lot of family to choose from.

She leans back in the chair, looks around. "You're always forgetting things, Katherine."

"Sorry?"

"When it's something for me, that is. I'm sure you remember all the things you need to do for yourself and for your friends too. It's always like that for us mothers, always second best." She laughs, like this is a joke.

Did she tell me she wanted me to come over this weekend to do the painting? Maybe she did and I forgot. My head has been all over the place.

"It's the living room," she adds.

"Let's take a look then," I suggest.

Mum doesn't say anything. I untie my dirt-covered sneakers and leave them by the back door, then wave for Mum to join me. She does.

The lounge. I look around the room with its scuffed walls, the previously white paint turning pale grey, the room feeling dim even though the curtains are wide open with light streaming in.

And I feel bad for Mum because this is the room where she relaxes with a cup of tea during the day and where she sits alone on the sofa to watch TV in the evenings. It's not too much to ask that this one room is set up nicely for her.

"I reckon a new paint job would transform the place," I say.

Mum sighs. "It's too much for me. You'll see what it's like when you're my age."

"You're not old, Mum."

Her shoulders drop. "I don't have anyone to help me, you know. Your brother was so good when it came to the painting."

"I did my fair share of the painting too."

"Don't be silly. You've forgotten. I know Jack had his problems and he left us. I live with those memories every day. But he was such a lovely lad until those other boys led him astray."

I bite my lip. No one forced Jack to take drugs or leave. When he was sixteen, he confided in me that he wanted to run away – from home and from Mum, in particular – but that's too cruel for me to tell her. I never thought he'd do it and never realised that leaving meant he'd only get in touch when he needed money. The first time it happened I 'loaned' him some cash, only to find out he'd blown it on drugs. A mistake I made once, though since then I've paid some of his bills when he was skint. No, Mum doesn't need to know any of this.

She's right, though, about him being an awesome brother when we were growing up. After Dad left, Jack started taking on some of the more manly jobs around the house at the tender age of nine. He taught himself how to do the pruning and clear out the gutters and later to fix the broken towel rail. He was my star, my superhero.

I remember painting the bedrooms when he was fifteen and I was his twelve-year-old apprentice. Later, I took over, mostly because there was no one else to do it.

"Mum, I did a heap of painting for you. I remember telling my high-school friends about it and they couldn't believe I'd done that all on my own. Just before I moved to Melbourne. Remember?"

"Please don't run away like that ever again."

Hell, I wasn't the one who ran away. She's mixing me up with Jack again. I moved interstate because I got a scholarship. We're such a small family but there used to be more of us.

"Mum, do you ever wonder about Grandma and Grandpa, and if they need a hand? If they're even alive?"

"No, I do not." Her face reddens, white foam forming at the corners of her mouth. "Not after what they did to me. The things I've had to endure, the punishment. They used me, the two of them, so badly. No one knows what it was like or how much I went through."

I can't even remember what terrible crime Mum's parents committed against her but at least I remember them a little, whereas I have no memories of my dad's parents, only that we called them *Grand-mére* and *Grand-père*. Jack told me they had big smiles and French accents. Mum shouted at him that it was Creole and the language was a mutant, like them. I remember finding a pile of birthday and Christmas cards from them, hidden at the back of Mum's dresser drawer, and getting screamed at. Or was that a bad dream?

Mum puts her hands on her hips. "There's only so much a human being can take. I put up with it all for you and your brother until I couldn't bear it anymore."

"I'll clean up outside." I turn away and trudge out the back. So stupid of me to have brought the subject up. I put away the tools and sweep the paving where I've spilled potting mix and mulch.

Standing back, I force myself to think positive and admire my handiwork. I'm doing pretty well for a beginner gardener.

Back in Melbourne, Charlie always insisted he'd take care of everything outside the house, and that I should take care of the inside. The garden required heavy work, he said. Paving, landscaping, pruning trees, all things I wasn't up to. Apparently. So Charlie hired landscapers and gardeners and a handyman to do the maintenance because he was too busy at the hospital where people depended on him.

"Katherine honey, we've got a visitor," Mum calls out, her voice all sweetness. She's beaming, a woman I've never seen beside her. "This is Renata."

Renata smiles. "I've been dying to meet you."

She looks imposing beside my mother. Tall, broad shoulders, muscular arms. I don't know what I thought Renata would look like, but it wasn't like this. Honey-brown hair and a friendly face with a weight-lifter's body, such a strange mix. She's somewhere in her forties, much younger than Mum, which is fine, but there's no excuse for the cheap, old-lady perfume wafting off her.

Renata shifts her gaze between me and Mum. "I can't

believe the family resemblance. Julia, when I look at your daughter, it's as if your features were painted on a Mauritian face. The only difference between the two of you is the curly hair and skin colour."

"That, and about thirty years!" Mum adds.

"Julia, you look ageless." Renata tilts her head. "Have you lost weight?"

"Not me. If anything, I might've gained a kilo."

"No way," Renata says. "Those jeans look great on you, by the way. The dark denim is very slimming."

It's going to be a while before that smile comes off Mum's face.

"You've got such a way with words." Mum turns to me. "Renata has made one of her amazing cakes. Oh, and the other day she brought around some lasagne, the best I've ever had."

"My lasagne is pretty good too," I say.

It used to be Charlie's favourite. A few years ago I made a huge spread, including lasagne, for a dinner party for some of his doctor friends after he started a new job. It was nearly a disaster because I'd forgotten they were coming until Charlie reminded me. He saved the day. And made a sensational dessert, which topped off a wonderful night.

Mum snorts, covers her mouth. "Kate thinks she makes great lasagne!"

I shrug. "What?"

Still sniggering. "You're so funny, you have no idea."

She puts her hand on Renata's arm as if they're both on the same team, when it's me she's talking about. She's right about one thing. I have no idea.

A door slams and there are raised voices from next door. A child is complaining about something and a woman calls the kid a bloody idiot, then a male joins in and they're all screaming at each other.

Mum's shoulders drop. "Sounds like the neighbours are home. Let's go inside for a cuppa."

"Sorry, Mum, I've gotta go. Maybe next time we'll have a regular catch-up over coffee or shopping. Then I'll come back to do the painting another time."

"Fine," she says.

It's not. I grit my teeth.

"I'd love to get to know you better," Renata says, then waits till the neighbours have stopped shouting. "I've heard so much about you."

"Another time," I say.

I couldn't bear a bite of Renata's *amazing* cake, not that this is her fault. It's Mum, she has a way of getting to me. I get out of there as fast as I can.

Chapter Twenty-One

When Laura first told me Mia was taking up kickboxing, I was so proud.

She was younger then, not quite a teenager and easier to talk to. And I was a different person. I spent a lot of time at training and was more than happy to encourage her, especially since she seemed so interested. Laura told me later that she once heard Mia shouting at her brother that she was going to learn how to beat him up. Not quite the honourable motive I'd imagined, but it made Laura laugh.

Now Mia needs a lift to training. The dojo isn't far but Perth public transport is terrible and Laura doesn't want her coming home in the dark, which suits Mia just fine because apparently *anything* is better than taking the bus.

We get out of the car and Mia waves to a girl with the club T-shirt and a big bag slung across her shoulder.

"I told Mum she should get a Mini too," Mia says to me.

"Why?"

"Are you kidding? This is so much cooler than Mum's Honda."

I pause outside the door. Abrams Self-Defence Academy.

"I'll get a coffee," I say. "I'll be here when you get out."

Mia stops. Stares. She's got the same blue eyes as her mum, only on Laura they look thoughtful, whereas on Mia they're intense, verging on slightly psychotic because a teenage girl not getting what she wants can be a scary thing.

"Come on." She takes my hand and pulls me towards the door.

I make a small circular movement with my hand and twist out of her grasp.

Her eyes widen. "Hey, smooth move! You'll have to show me how to do that later."

"I'll see you when you're done."

"You don't want to come inside?" She gives me the harsh stare again. "It's not that big a deal, Kate."

The honesty of a fourteen-year-old girl throws me. I smile and turn away, leaving on my own. I get coffee. And I come back, drawn by that same honesty.

I'm outside the door, takeaway cup in hand. Maybe Mia's right and it's only a big deal in my mind.

God knows I used to love Krav. I already had to fight to get there because Charlie disapproved so much and then the whole aim of training was to fight. No wonder it was exhausting. And I loved it. It was part of me.

I tried to go back to Krav a few times last year but when I did, I was having flashbacks and getting stabbed all over again, even if it was only in my mind. I talked to my instructor, who could see the pain I was in, and he mentioned that a lot of people benefited from therapy. Such an American idea. Well, I tried that and it wasn't for me.

He also told me I'd done an amazing job that night and that I was awesome, but I couldn't bear it when the only thing I'd succeeded in was not dying. And I didn't want to be awesome. I wanted to be Kate Best happily married to Dr Charlie Best, yet now I'm Kate Mamotte again.

One thing he was right about. He said there were no winners after violence.

I promised myself I'd go back to Krav again as soon as I was ready, yet here I am struggling to walk through the doorway just to pick up Mia. There's a tightness in my chest, a sour feeling in my gut, my anxiety levels rising. I tell myself I can do this. It's like riding a bike. No, more like going for a swim in the ocean, where you've got to dive in all at once.

I pull the door open and scoot down the steps, the stale bacteria scent so familiar, only this time it doesn't bring on a panic attack. It doesn't bring on anything. I turn a corner into the dojo and slide down onto a bench, looking around at the padded mats, punching bags and boxing ring. Everything is slightly worn the way it always is at these places. Kind of comforting.

Mia spots me right away and waves wildly, her face lighting up. She's a good kid and I can tell she likes me watching her as she kicks the pads, then holds them for her partner. The instructor tells her she's done well, awesome, in fact. That word again. Mia smiles with pride.

It comes back to me. Training is fun. Violence is not. Violence has consequences.

Movies are full of tough guys who save the day and don't worry about the detritus they leave behind, the injuries, the trauma. In the movies, you can shoot a guy and walk away a hero, barely think about the event again, but that's not how it works.

Or the hero can take on five thugs, who come at him one at a time, as if that's what they'd do instead of jumping him from behind all of them at once. That same hero is then happy to leave these guys lying on the ground nursing their wounds. Well, I'm not a hero.

Violence changes people, the way it changed me, left me traumatised. The movies are wrong. Violence is wrong.

A guy in his forties approaches, shaved head, the club shirt, white judo pants, smiling. I should smile too.

"Are you Mia's friend?" he asks.

I nod. "I'm Kate."

"My name's Rob. Mia mentioned you trained in Krav and kickboxing."

Laura has primed her not to blab about the night of the attack, I'm sure, so this is Mia's idea of being tactful. I don't want to talk about myself so I ask Rob about his training, only for him to play down his experience. It's what people who are seriously good do, because they don't need to brag about it.

Which makes me think of my American instructor who trained with the best in Israel, spent years studying jiu-jitsu in Japan, kali in the Philippines and did a bunch of other stuff that falls under the category of 'weird shit'.

He also told us that if we were ever attacked and had to fight back, we should never say it was self-defence, because saying you hit someone in self-defence is admitting you assaulted them, which opens you up to a world of trouble, completely aside from what you've been through.

This fit in with everything Laura has said about how people may think they're in the right but they end up digging themselves into a hole with the police by talking too much. Her advice was always to talk to a lawyer first. So after Charlie and I were attacked, I didn't claim self-defence to the police. I said very little until I got a lawyer, and I was in hospital anyway with doctors telling the officers I wasn't up to being questioned. Otherwise, things could have turned out differently for me.

At the end of class, Mia runs up to me with a sweaty hug. As we're walking up the stairs, she says, "You did really good, Kate."

"So did you."

"You've gotta put yourself out there. Honestly, I was proud of you today."

"Well, I'm not the one who got sweaty."

I make light of it because that's what I always do. And it's okay. I can do this. What I can't do is go back to Krav yet.

Chapter Twenty-Two

I should be working. The copy changes Rachel asked for won't take me long and I shouldn't have to force myself but my concentration is shot.

A drink of water might do me good so I get up from the dining table. Though the cold water runs down my throat, it fails to refresh me. I look out through the window at the garden where it's drizzling, which of course makes me think of Melbourne.

I remember a dream, leaning over the sink at our old place in Fitzroy, Charlie falling. *Don't think about it. Don't go there.*

I'm still in the kitchen. Still standing. I feel strong hands land on my shoulders, a firm touch that makes me feel safe, yet I'm too scared to turn around. I close my eyes and melt. *Oh, Charlie.* He's behind me, his breath warm on my neck, as he peppers my skin with little kisses. This is where I belong. This is how it should be. Charlie nuzzles closer, murmuring my name, whispering that he loves me.

"I love you too," I say.

Turning around, I open my eyes. My heart is racing as I look around in the hope he might be hiding nearby. It'd be so like Charlie to play a trick on me or surprise me. The room is empty.

"Come back."

Is it wrong that I speak to him sometimes? I don't want to lose these moments with Charlie, even if they're not real. They're all I've got.

The front doorbell rings, sending a jolt up my spine. Great, that's all I need. I'm not going to answer it. Laura and Noah know they should text me first if they want to drop by, and I haven't ordered anything so it can't be a delivery. Besides, I don't want to think about the last delivery I received.

I lean against the sink. One breath in, one breath out, that's how you do it. A gentle breeze is wafting in through the back door. Soothing. I need to be soothed.

My phone buzzes on the dining table. Fine, I'll get it. Ryan: *Can you come to the door? Or is this a bad time?*

Well, it's a better time than it was five minutes ago. I text: *Be right there.*

I pull open the front door to find Ryan crouching down patting Esmeralda.

He looks up. "I found a little friend."

"Maybe she wants to come in," I say.

"I think she just wants to be patted."

He must be thinking of a different cat because that does not sound like my Esmeralda. I crouch down and can't believe it when she rubs up against my legs and lets me stroke her. She looks up at me with her glassy blue eyes, slinking away behind me eventually.

Ryan stands. "She wants to go inside. You were right."

I get to my feet too. "Maybe. But she likes you better than me."

"She's known me longer, and I've looked after her a couple of times when Joel was gone away. You know she comes by my place sometimes and follows me around?"

"Wow, you're privileged." I smile. "Sorry I didn't answer the door earlier."

"It's okay. I get it. Just as well I've got you in my phone."

"No probs. Would you like to come in?"

"Maybe another time," he says. "I wanted to let you know I saw a guy acting weird out here yesterday. Not sure it's anything to do with you but I thought it was worth a mention."

"What sort of guy?"

"A big guy, fortyish, dark hair, a bit of a bogan, out of place."

My stomach drops. Shit, no, it can't be. Scarparolo doesn't know where I live. I'm jumping to conclusions.

Ryan reaches for my arm, his touch warm through my merino jumper. "Are you okay?"

I force a smile. "Yeah, sure. So what happened?"

"Nothing much. He was parked a few houses up on the other side of the street. I saw the car when I went to buy bread in the morning. Didn't think anything of it. But the car was still there when I came back and that's when I noticed someone in the front seat. He wasn't doing anything, just sitting there, so I went up to him."

"Really?"

Ryan spreads his arms. "Well, I tried to. I thought it couldn't hurt to say hello and ask. But the guy drove off before I could talk to him."

"What kind of car did he have?"

"Drove a Jeep Cherokee, probably around ten years old, black, a couple of dings in the door. Not the sort of car someone around here would drive."

My stomach clenches. That fits the description of the car that rammed into Will Sharma. Surely the police must've looked into this.

It's got to be Scarparolo. Shit, he thinks nothing of ramming his car into a human being and he knows where I live. How does he know? The police wouldn't have told him. Maybe I'm wrong and it's not him. God, I hope I'm wrong.

"Don't suppose you got the rego?" I ask.

"I couldn't. He didn't have a rear number plate." Ryan holds my gaze. "Do you know him?"

"No, but thanks for keeping an eye out."

"Call me if you need anything."

"Sure, I'll walk you to the gate."

Though it's stopped drizzling, the air looks thick and grey. I check out the street, even though I know Scarparolo – or whoever was in that car – is long gone. There are always cars parked on the road because off-street parking is at a premium here, the street lined with trees, houses packed close together, gardens manicured. A magnificent, gnarled peppermint tree sits on the front verge, the branches sparse because of the age of the tree but trees are one thing they don't get rid of here.

A woman with cropped silver hair walks past, her tiny dog barking more loudly than its size would suggest.

"Morning," she says.

We return her greeting while she heads up the street. People. A neighbourhood. These are good things. There's no Scarparolo.

Ryan smiles as he opens the gate. "I know you can handle yourself. I've seen what you do to cockroaches."

I laugh. He's caught me off guard. I have the sudden urge to kiss him, an urge so stupid that I don't know what's got into me. Thinking about Charlie must have muddled my brain and God knows my hormones are all over the place.

"Thanks for coming by," I say. "I appreciate it."

As I walk up the front path, I tell myself I shouldn't think about Scarparolo. I don't even know it was him, and I don't need to feel scared all the time. But I do.

Chapter Twenty-Three

No rain or drizzle today. No clouds either to mar the magical blue sky. The perfect Saturday.

As I look up, the sky seems even bluer against the grey-green leaves of the giant gum tree outside La Vida. Two kids skip around the tree while their mothers stand outside the café and chat, both of them decked out in their finest Lululemon activewear, complete with padded down jackets. They probably think this is cold but it's like fairyland compared to a Melbourne winter.

Feeling lucky, I cross the street to buy a Lotto ticket, my final stop. I've already got fresh bread in my backpack, my excuse for venturing to the shops.

A woman comes hurtling out of the newsagent and stops suddenly to avoid crashing into me.

"Hello, Kate." Surprise in her voice. "Remember me?"

She's beautifully groomed, probably a bit older than Laura, possibly a friend of hers.

"I'm Adrienne." She places a hand on her chest. "In case you can't recall. So, how are you settling into Subiaco?"

Suddenly, it clicks. She's the woman who gave me her life

history in five minutes flat when we met, the wife of one of Theo's doctor friends who abseiled off the AT Tower.

I put on a polite smile. "Pretty well. I grew up here, so it's not so strange."

"It took me a while to get used to it after leaving Sydney. But that was years ago, before the kids were born. The only problem with Perth is that it's so far from anything which means the long-haul flights are a killer. I've booked tickets for Europe, the non-stop flight to London return. Business class for the four of us costs a pretty packet but it's worth it. I couldn't bear to be cramped up in economy. I'm so glad those times are behind us."

I open my mouth to speak.

"It's easy for Pete. I do all the organising and book everything well in advance so the trip goes smoothly when we get there. Mind you, he's pretty busy as a neurosurgeon."

It strikes me that her husband might be a brain surgeon but this woman is not. Time to get out of here.

"Enjoy your trip," I say.

"Oh, it's still ages away." She places a hand on my arm. "Just quickly, I forgot to ask Laura last time I saw her. How's Noah?"

"Fine."

A pause. "I thought you two might be close?"

"We've known each other a long time, that's all."

"I'm a bit disappointed with him. I thought we had everything ready with our investments and then he withdrew our deposit and gave it back to us."

Shit, I'm never going to get away at this rate. "Oh."

"I know what I'm doing. I used to work in finance, you know, many years ago." She waits for a reaction. "I was ready to go ahead with the investment. Then he returned our funds without even consulting us first. Honestly, as if our money wasn't good enough for him."

"I don't know much about his business, sorry."

Then the penny drops. He mentioned a busybody woman who needed her money back. He suspected a rocky marriage with a possible divorce looming, not that a family trip to Europe flying business class sounds like a marriage on the rocks. More likely she's a client Noah didn't want, and he probably gave her a story to get her off his back. Can't say I blame him.

I shrug. "I don't really know the ins and outs of his life."

"Well, it all seemed a bit strange to me." She points to the café across the road. "There's a group of us who meet at La Vida on Wednesday mornings. You're welcome to join us. It'd be great to have some new blood in the group."

"Thanks, but I should get going."

I turn and leave, hoping the look on my face doesn't give me away. No way am I joining her.

No Lotto ticket for me, not today. I can get one tomorrow. I'm feeling lucky just for getting away, as I cross the road to the paved mall outside La Vida where I've locked up my bike.

Two teenage girls are ambling towards me, chatting as they walk. They're wearing pale jeans, oversized black hoodies and Blundstones, both of them having gone overboard on the dark eyeliner. Individuals. I love the way teenage girls do things together. It makes me smile.

My phone buzzes as I unlock my bike and toss the braided steel cable into the basket at the front. I reach for my phone at the bottom of my backpack under the loaf of bread that's still warm to touch.

ID withheld. Probably a scam, someone asking to click a link, collect a package, telling me there's a new notification.

I swipe. I touch. I tap. A photo appears on my screen.

Charlie.

No.

My lungs crushed, I can't breathe. I stumble back to the red-brick wall behind me.

The two teenage girls stop and ask if I'm okay.

Act normal. Pretend it's nothing.

I force myself to speak. "Yeah, fine. Thanks for asking."

They wander into the frozen yoghurt place on the corner. Jealousy eats away at me, despite my pain. I don't want my life. I want theirs. How I'd love to be young again, not my fifteen-year-old self because I was so unsure of myself, but to be in someone else's skin. I'd love to be in love and to be loved. Not like this.

My hand trembling, I can't bring myself to look at the photo again. Until I do. Then I can't stop staring. It's tattooed onto my retinas. I'm going to be seeing this for the rest of my life.

It's a photo of Charlie, his arms around another woman. And she's naked.

I've seen this photo hundreds of times, maybe thousands, every morning when I wake up, every night when I go to sleep and every time I walk into the bedroom. I have the same photo of Charlie and me on our wedding day, only this is Charlie with someone else. A selfie. One of his arms is outstretched so he can take the photo, the other is slung around the woman who's topless, her arms folded to cover her boobs. The photo captures an intimate moment, but that's a moment I had with Charlie too. Not a moment. A life. We had a life together.

Had. Past tense.

And Charlie was having an affair.

Chapter Twenty-Four

Like a lunatic, I cycle to Laura's. I don't bother to get my act together first. I don't give a shit about cars and traffic and road rules. A car honks. Screw them. They can give way to me for once.

I keep pedalling, past the Federation cottages, past the pristine gardens, past the shady verge trees and towering gum trees on the median strip, past a boy playing footy with his father on the oval, past parents pushing a pram on the footpath. Happiness everywhere I look. Screw them too.

When I get to Laura's house, I veer onto the footpath and through her front gate which one of the kids must've left open. I let my bike fall onto the grass, then race up her front steps and bang on the door.

Laura has led me into the study and closed the door. Her family is home. Somewhere. I'm slumped over the small sofa while she paces the room in front of the cast-iron fireplace, two cups of supposedly calming green tea growing cold on the coffee table.

"I'm so sorry, Kate," Laura says. "Did you have any idea?"

I shake my head.

Pacing again. "Jesus, neither did I. Charlie, of all people. Seeing someone else. That…" Bastard? Her mouth twists. "Do you have any idea who the woman is?"

"None at all."

Younger than me, mid to late twenties, fine features with a full mouth and straight brown hair as if she's stepped straight out of the salon. There's a youthful glow about her, a bit like the teenage girls I saw earlier, an almost childlike air of innocence. Innocent while sleeping with my husband. The irony sucks the life out of me.

I stare at the photo on my phone. Who is she? Who sent this to me? And why? To hurt me. To drag me down even further.

I look up. "Um, can you stop pacing please. It's making me dizzy."

"Sure." Laura drops down beside me. "Can I take another look?"

I hand her the phone. Thumb and forefinger on the screen, she expands the photo and examines it. The silence in the room and Laura's frown unnerve me.

I clear my throat. "You're not going to tell me it's fake, are you?"

"I wish I could." She frowns. "This is so tacky. The same photo, the same pose, except for the obvious difference. It's also very like Charlie to do the same thing over again. He never had much imagination, not like you."

"Yeah, well my imagination's going crazy at the moment."

My head is a car crash, images banging around in my mind. Charlie with this woman in his arms, Charlie in bed with her,

Charlie laughing with her, kissing her, holding her, doing all those things he did with me – with her. Hell, this isn't the truth I wanted or ever expected. The truth sucks. It hurts. I was happier before.

"I can't believe how stupid I was," I say. "I thought he was career-focused, long hours, double shifts. I guess he wasn't spending as much time at the hospital as I thought he was."

"You're not stupid, Kate," Laura says.

My life has been shattered and shat upon all over again. Charlie's gone, my previous life in Melbourne a remote memory, and maybe I've been kidding myself the whole time.

A sudden chill takes over the room. I turn to the window where Laura has pulled back the plantation shutters to let the sun through, only now it's bucketing down, the downpour arriving sooner than I thought. That's the thing about the rain in Perth. It's relentless. Doesn't give you a break. The weather will fool you, breathtakingly beautiful one minute, miserable the next.

"Talk about double standards." I slump forward, my forearms resting on my knees. "He'd get pissed off at me for glancing at another man. He was jealous of Noah, despite the fact they were best friends. Didn't like me spending any time alone with him."

"Yeah, Noah has mentioned it."

Maybe I should have told her too. After all, there are hundreds of other things I've told her about Charlie and me and everything else.

"I need to know." I scrunch my hands into fists. "Who was she? Where did they meet? Did he love her?"

For all I know, this woman may have had something to do with Charlie's death. Maybe she had a husband who hired a thug to beat Charlie up. Maybe Charlie dumped her and she was a jilted lover who wanted to make him sorry. Maybe there's some other scenario. And sure, maybe my mind and imagination are working overtime, but I don't think so. All I know is that this changes everything.

"I want the truth about Charlie," I say. "Good, bad or ugly, I need to know or I'll spend the rest of my life wondering."

Even though it sucks.

Laura's frown deepens.

"What?" I ask.

"Did the Melbourne Police say anything to you about Charlie having an affair?"

I shake my head.

"They do a victimology study as part of their investigations. They would have looked into every facet of Charlie's life to try to find links between him and the attacker. They searched the house and interviewed you and all of Charlie's friends and colleagues to build a picture of his life. You know that. You were there."

"So how come they didn't find out about this?" I whisper the words, barely daring to believe.

A spark lights up in my heart. If the police couldn't find anything about an affair, then maybe I've got this all wrong and it's some sort of hoax. The light goes out. I'm not wrong. That picture reeks of sex and intimacy and betrayal.

"The police aren't always thorough or smart," Laura says, not for the first time. "They checked his phone, didn't they?"

"Y-yeah."

"If he was having an affair, there would've been phone calls, messages, photos. All these things leave a trail."

An image flashes before me, a mobile phone in my hand. "Maybe he deleted them."

"Police Forensics would've been onto it. No, he had a second phone. I've seen it happen before."

My heart sinks even further. James, one of Charlie's colleagues, came to see me to return some things they'd found in Charlie's locker at the hospital. I remember James's reluctance to hand the bag over and the pain in his voice when he told me he was sorry about Charlie. I wondered why he'd bother to give me Charlie's belongings when there was nothing there of any value.

Then I found the phone.

It was pretty easy to work out why Charlie had a second phone. For secret calls. James knew too, no doubt.

As soon as he left, I stormed through the house to the back patio and stamped on the phone with my Dr Martens. Smash. Stomp. Crush. I threw the broken pieces in the bin. Gone. No second phone and no need to give it another thought. Until now.

"I've gotta tell you, Kate," Laura says. "I'm pissed at Charlie for what he's done. He was always so charming and personable but there was an undercurrent, as if he wanted to keep you in your place. There are things you've told me…"

I hold a hand out. "Let's leave it for now."

She bites her lip. Nods. Laura has made similar hints before and I've always cut her off. More than ever, since Charlie died, I haven't been able to bear a bad word said about him. Now I wonder where the truth lies.

Laura sighs. "If anyone would know about Charlie seeing someone, it'd be Noah. But I don't think he knows. He'd have told you, me, the police, everyone about it."

That's right. He's in Melbourne for business, coming back tonight, and I couldn't bear to talk to him about this today anyway. I've had enough angst for one day. Tomorrow it is.

Chapter Twenty-Five

Tomorrow happens sooner than I think.

I awaken with a jolt. Though my eyes are pressed shut, I am as awake as I've ever been, thoughts rocketing around in my brain, memories, discoveries, disturbances. My skin crawling, I scratch at my pyjamas as I sit up in bed and reach for my phone to see it's 3.05am.

Except these aren't pyjamas. I've gone to sleep in one of Charlie's old T-shirts. How can I have done that? The fabric is sandpaper on my skin, scratching and scraping. I swear there's a rash forming. I stand, rip the T-shirt off, throw it to the floor and stomp on it.

"Arsehole."

The words are a whisper, no venom in them, no relief.

I grab some fleecy pyjamas from the drawer. Mine of course. I don't need anything from Charlie. I get back into bed and roll onto my side, my stomach, my back. Nothing is comfortable. I punch the pillow to soften it up, then slam my head onto it and pull the covers up around my neck.

Pressing my eyes shut, I try to force the horrid thoughts from my mind. *Think of something soothing. Think of emptiness.*

Think of blue skies and a gentle breeze over the ocean. Waves crash in my head, the breeze becoming a storm, my body tossed in a cyclone.

I know exactly what to do. I turn on the lights and slide into my Ugg boots because whatever else is going on, my feet should be warm. It doesn't take me long to rifle through my drawers and find what I'm after: Charlie's Carhartt windcheater, his Cookie Monster PJ pants, the oversized T-shirts that used to give me comfort.

There's more. I find the Tasmanian Blackwood memory box Charlie gave me and dig out the birthday cards, photos and souvenirs I don't want anymore. They're trash, memories no more. I catch a glimpse of the signature Tiffany Blue box that contains my wedding ring, and freeze. Glitzy, expensive, Charlie's choice. It can stay there, along with the other documents of my past and Charlie's, the wedding certificate, the death certificate. Everything dead.

I storm through the house, turning the lights on as I go, slamming cupboards in the kitchen till I find a green garbage bag. Back in the bedroom, I pick up the remnants of my life with Charlie from the floor and shove them inside the bag. Everything. Finished. Over.

There's more storming through the house, then I switch on the outside lights, the garden coming to life like it's ready for a civilised gathering of people standing around with cocktail glasses. I stomp through the backyard to the bin shelter because, heaven forbid, Joel couldn't have something as unsightly as a rubbish or recycling bin in sight, and I dump the bag in there. The cold cuts into my skin, reminding me I'm alive. Also reminding me of the importance of good footwear.

Back inside the house, I think about making myself a calming camomile. Screw that, I'm calm. No I'm not. Screw the camomile too. I grab a bottle of vodka from the freezer, my emergency bottle, because this is an emergency. I find a glass and tip in a generous amount. It burns the back of my throat. I should've bought some of the vanilla stuff that Ryan has. Not to worry. This'll do the trick. My gut is churning by the time I've finished the first glass and poured a second shot, also generous. I finish it, of course, and now the same waves that were crashing in my head are creating havoc in my stomach.

The crashing turns to rolling as I make it into bed and pull the covers tight around me. I can throw up or go to sleep. Either would be fine by me. I'm fine. I've never been finer. I close my eyes. I picture another night, a gibbous moon, sipping vanilla vodka, chatting over the fence, Ryan's soothing presence, the way it seemed perfectly normal, the sort of thing that happens in any suburban backyard. Soothing. Like waves lapping on the shore. I drift off.

Chapter Twenty-Six

A coffee shop. A nice neutral meeting place. I can't cry here and won't let myself create a scene.

So much damn sunshine. I can't stand the stuff. Why can't it be drizzly and miserable like Melbourne? The footpath still glistens with puddles from a downpour last night, a reminder of how quickly things can turn.

Noah arrives at the same time as me. I'm on foot while he slides out of his red Model S. He's found a parking spot right outside the café, of course, because things always work that way for him. He opens the back door, reaches inside and saunters over to the tables on the pavement where I've stopped.

"I got you something from Melbourne."

I recognise the box right away, pale pink with large purple lettering and a cellophane window that gives me a peek of the world's best cupcakes. In my humble opinion.

My eyes widen. "I can't believe you did this."

"I made sure to get some red velvet."

From my favourite cupcakery in Melbourne. My heart softens a little.

"I had to take these as hand luggage," he says. "Some idiot

nearly threw his case on top of them in the overhead racks so I set him straight. Then I nearly left the box on a counter when I had a coffee at the airport. Talk about a close call."

"Thank you so much." Taking the box from him, I lean over and kiss him on the cheek. Maybe it's the Hemsworth resemblance that does it, the hunky good looks, but sometimes I wonder if he's acting.

Noah smiles and points to a table. "Outside, perchance?"

"Sure."

We sit down in that damn sunshine that was annoying me five minutes earlier. I'm all over the place. A waitress clearing the next table asks if we're ready to order. I was ready before we got here. She takes our order, a cappuccino for me and a long black for Noah.

He grins. "I'm really glad you called. I thought about dropping the cupcakes off last night but it was after eleven when I got back and I didn't want to disturb you."

"Yeah, I was in bed by then." No need to mention I wasn't asleep.

"I thought you might've wanted cupcakes for breakfast."

"Hey, I only did that once. Or maybe it was twice. I only ever eat healthy breakfasts nowadays."

He nods. "Sure you do."

The teasing tone in his voice reminds me that we go way back, me and him and Charlie. Also, if it wasn't for Noah, I'd never have met Laura and my life would be so much the poorer. I should be grateful.

I ask about his flight and how things went in Melbourne. Business is always good according to Noah. No surprises there. He's always monetising and strategising and building and growing.

Our coffees arrive. I take the phone from my bag, open up the photo and slide it across the table. He brings the cup to his lips, then stops and puts it down.

"What the hell, Kate?"

"What the hell indeed," I mutter.

"Do you want to tell me what's going on?"

"I got a text yesterday from an unknown number. No message, just that photo attached."

Noah's brow furrows. "You seem pretty cool about this."

"No, this is my brave exterior."

I don't tell him I spent half of yesterday crying my heart out to Laura. I can tell him later or maybe Laura will.

He covers my hand with his. "I'm here for you, Kate. It's okay if you cry. Perfectly understandable, in fact."

It wouldn't be the first time. My crying was non-stop when Charlie first died. I pull my hand back, cupping my cappuccino in both hands, not that I need to warm them on a day like this.

"This must be a huge shock to you, Kate." Noah clears his throat. "I'm sorry Charlie was such an arsehole."

Was he? I didn't think he was, at the time. There were his moods, the days he'd sigh and slam doors and give one-word answers. There were plenty of times he'd shout at me but that was always because I'd done something wrong. I knew the drill. I'd walk around on eggshells and take extra care with everything, and he'd get over it within a few days. It only ever happened because he was under such pressure at work.

"He was your whole life," Noah says. "You thought you'd found your soulmate."

I don't believe in soulmates or the idea of one perfect person you're destined to be with. But I believe in love, or I did.

"We loved each other and built a life together."

Noah nods. "It's like your dreams are being shattered all over again, if you will. First when he died, and now when you're finding this out."

I've barely had time to process the affair, yet Noah has nailed it in seconds. Surely not… He couldn't have…

"Was it you?" I grab the phone. "Did you send this to me?"

"Me?" Eyebrows raised, shock in his eyes. "I guarantee if I'd known about *this*, I'd have told you."

I believe him, because Charlie's affair would've given Noah an opportunity. With me. I swallow.

"Maybe it was the same person who sent you that *bitch* text," Noah says. "I'm sorry to bring that up. You're as far from a bitch as you can get. You're a wonderful person, Kate."

I'd pushed that to the back of my mind. I can't forget these things, not if I'm going to put together the pieces, which is what I should be doing now. The uncertainty feels like insects crawling across my skin.

Noah holds my gaze. "You always wanted kids, didn't you?"

"Why are you bringing that up now?"

"And Charlie kept putting it off. Didn't he?"

I open my mouth to speak. I ponder. I wonder why the hell I'm pondering anything. Why should I stick up for Charlie?

"Yeah," I say.

"You'll be an amazing mother one day, Kate. I feel it in my bones."

I press my eyes closed for a moment. "Please don't tell me I'm still young."

"That's not what I was going to say. Just let me know what you need, Kate. A shoulder to cry on? I'm here. Need some company? I'm your man. No strings attached. I can do coffee, beer, bar-hopping, dinner, takeaway, whatever. Or if you need space…" He takes a deep breath. "I can do that too."

What do I need? I need to go back to Melbourne, a short trip to catch up with a few people, ask some questions and find out what the hell Charlie was doing. Maybe all I need right now is a normal conversation. I have so much trouble just doing 'normal' nowadays.

"I had dinner with Michael and Jan when I was in Melbourne," Noah says.

Charlie's parents. Do they know about Charlie's affair? I doubt it.

So selfish of me even to be asking myself that question. If anyone's in more pain than me, it's them. They lost a piece of their hearts when Charlie died and they're never going to get over it, though they have to find a way to live with it.

Meanwhile I haven't been in touch with them nearly as much as I should. And though I've got an excuse, a wave of regret washes over me.

"They must've loved seeing you," I say.

"Yeah, they're good people. I used to spend a lot of time at Charlie's place when I was a teenager and his parents were always very generous. They were an anchor in my life, them and Laura, of course." He grins. "They spoilt Charlie rotten. Me too, for that matter."

"You're not the only one who got welcomed into the family."

I remember the first time I met them and the way his mum gripped me in a bear hug that went on a little too long. A couple of years later, Jan told me that she'd known from the way Charlie talked about me that I was 'the one'. And I believed it one hundred per cent.

Happy-sad memories with Charlie's folks. I should focus more on the happy and less on the sad. His parents deserve all the good thoughts and wishes I can send their way.

"When we were younger, Charlie used to really push the envelope when it came to his folks," Noah says.

"What do you mean?"

"Occasionally, he'd tell me how his parents thought I was hanging around too much. Once he said they only had me around because they felt sorry for me."

My mouth falls open. "No. Jan and Mike would never have said that. They didn't think that way."

Noah keeps his eyes on me. "I didn't say *they'd* said it."

But Charlie had. This must've wounded Noah, who only had his big sister, whose folks had practically abandoned him, who didn't have the parental love that Charlie did. The worst thing is I can almost hear the words coming from his mouth.

"I didn't believe him for a minute," Noah says. "With someone like Charlie, you can only show strength or he'll walk all over you. I'd done it tougher than him and it had hardened me so I could hang in there."

Perhaps Noah is made of sterner stuff than me. No matter what I went through it never seemed to toughen me up, or I don't think it did. I'm suffocating in this conversation so I try to lighten up.

"Did Jan cook one of her amazing dinners for you?" I ask.

"Nope, haven't had one of those for a while."

Which makes me feel better because it's been a long time since I've had a dinner invitation too.

"We went to Sears," Noah says. "My shout."

A classy restaurant, for sure, located at the casino, which is the sort of glamour Noah likes. The more expensive, the better.

"There's something else," he says. "Michael doesn't say much. You know that. At one point, he said…" Noah's voice cracks. "He said I was like a second son to them."

"Oh, Noah."

Funny how he can be hardened and sensitive all at once. He doesn't cry though, whereas tears prick at the back of my eyes for the parental love he's getting from these people who aren't his parents. Before Charlie and I got married, Jan used to tell me I was like the daughter she never had, and my heart would swell each time, so I have some idea how Noah must feel.

"I might catch up with them myself," I say. "In person. It'll be good to see them again."

"You're going to Melbourne?"

"Sure, I can see some friends too while I'm there."

He shrugs. "Great idea."

As soon as I get home, I'll book that airfare. I'll have to find someone to look after Esmeralda and let Joel know what's going on. He can't possibly mind if I tell him I'm leaving for a family emergency. That's not lying. Charlie was my family.

And talking about Charlie's folks has reminded me I have my own mother to take care of. Because life still goes on.

Chapter Twenty-Seven

Return ticket to Melbourne booked. The tickets for an immediate departure were twice the price so I'm leaving in several days' time. Gone are the times I could indulge myself with large expenses.

I lean over my laptop on the dining table. This would've been a lot easier if I hadn't got rid of Charlie's second phone but at the time I couldn't bear to have that thing near me. So now I'm searching the dregs of social media to see if the other woman is lurking in the background of a photo on one of Charlie's accounts or those of his friends. I scroll through pages and pages, examining every face, wondering where she might be, reading every comment, trying to read between the lines.

My neck is stiff, pain creeping into the back of my head. I try to loosen up the muscles, then give up.

I'm investigating, I guess, though it's not in the same league as hands-on research. I remember being invited to the firing range at the police academy by one of the guys at training who taught there. I was slow to put on the hearing protection and had my eardrums blasted. I learnt real quick how loud gunfire is. I also learnt how much fun it is shooting a gun. I loved it. Felt like I was in an episode of *Hawaii Five-0*.

Charlie hated it, told me never to go there again.

I loved gun defence at training too, even if I'm not convinced it'd work. The principles seem fairly straightforward: clear the body, control the weapon, counter-attack. Then there's the unsaid principle – try not to get shot – all of which is easier said than done. Even with our yellow plastic guns there'd be an adrenaline rush, a lot of fear and fumbling, and that was without any actual danger. My American instructor said they used to do the same drills in LA with real guns and blanks. He said this like it was a good thing.

There's nothing online so I lean back in my chair with a thump. I'm the world's worst detective. Charlie was right when he said I shouldn't worry my pretty head about so many things, that not everyone is cut out to make the big decisions, that I wasn't as clever as him. In fact, most of the time I was downright useless.

Did he really use that word? Did I really take it?

Pain spreads from the back of my neck, engulfing my head, pressing down on all sides. I can't get the picture of the two of them out of my head. It used to be my attacker's face I would see, then it was Will being thrown into the air by that car, now it's that fucking photo.

"How can you do this to me, Charlie?" I yell. "You were my husband, my lover, my best friend. *Were*."

I get to my feet. "Screw you, Charlie."

For seeing someone else, for always being so superior, for holding the high ground, for taking all my happy memories and casting a shadow over each and every one.

I wait. Nothing. He's not here.

I pull up in the driveway and kill the engine. I know exactly where I am, parked in the driveway in the Mini outside the house where I grew up, Mum's house.

But I can't remember how I got here.

Shit, I've blanked out a fifty-minute trip. Nearly an hour of my life. I remember having breakfast, getting in the car and the speed bumps in the rear lane, then merging with traffic on the freeway. After that, nothing.

This is downright dangerous. I've got to be more careful. It's always this way after a particularly bad night. I woke up at 2am and read my Kindle. My Kindle is a lifesaver. Then I fell asleep a couple of hours later. More dreams, more nightmares, more memories coming back to me.

I make a vow to myself. From now on, if I've had a bad night I won't get in the car. I'm okay now, though, wide awake and fully conscious.

Before I've even opened the car door, I hear shouting from next door. When I was growing up, we had a beautiful neighbour, Sally, whose adult son died of brain cancer many years ago. She never got over it. Didn't matter how many grandchildren came along. I couldn't stand it when Mum spoke to her about Jack as if she understood and it was the same thing. My brother may have absconded but he's still breathing.

The house has changed hands a couple of times since then and Mum has told me about her new neighbours, who aren't quite as beautiful as Sally. Cigarette in hand, an overweight woman in leggings and a too-tight windcheater is shouting at a bloke with a long grey ponytail, something about the lawn needing to be mowed. What lawn? Looks like weeds to me.

I get out of the Mini.

"What are you staring at?" the woman yells.

"Good morning," I yell right back.

"G'day, love," the bloke says with a laugh.

Then he shouts at the woman about the lawn and how he's not the bloody hired help.

Seconds later, I'm at the front door of Mum's house, my key in the door. She's so proud of owning her own home, of what she's achieved, and rightly so. It is indeed an achievement. She grew up poor, which was completely her parents' fault according to her, and she always wanted to do better than they did.

I stamp my feet on the mat and call out, making a lot of noise so Mum knows I'm here, though not as much as the neighbours, before stepping inside.

"Come in," Mum calls out from the back of the house, which is not that far from the front.

She's wrist-deep in detergent suds at the sink. The kitchen is old but clean and well-kept, built in the days before dishwashers were common.

"Are the neighbours at it again?" she asks.

"Sure are. How are you doing?"

"Great, now that you're here." She pulls the plug and dries her hands. "It's so lovely to see you. What a surprise."

"I texted you yesterday to say I was coming."

"No, you didn't." She rolls her eyes. "You only think you did."

Who knows? Maybe I didn't. My mind has been all over the place lately.

"I brought chocolate biscuits," I say.

"Oh, good, because there's no cake in the house."

I don't mind that there's none of Renata's *amazing* cake. I open the packet of Tim Tams and the packaging rips, a biscuit landing on the counter.

"You've always been so clumsy," Mum says.

Something Charlie used to say too. We make small talk and

after we're seated at the table, I explain about the photo and show it to her.

She puts on her glasses and stares. "Are you sure it's real?"

"Yeah, I am."

"They can doctor photos and make it look very realistic. There's a programme called Photoshop that people use."

As if I've never heard of this. "The image is real, Mum. Just look at it."

Their heads, arms and bodies are too intertwined, the lighting and tones the same on both their faces, no tool marks, shadows or reflections, no digital manipulation going on there.

"It's a photo," Mum says. "So what?"

The breath leaves my body. Why does she always do this to me?

"She's got no top on and, as if that's not bad enough, it's a replica of my wedding photo, Mum. It's Charlie with another woman. He was having an affair."

She pulls her head back like a turtle. "Do you think so?"

"Yes, I'm certain. That's why the picture was sent to me."

"Who would send you something like this?"

"I have no clue."

She asks the same question several different ways, as if this is the most important thing about it.

Eventually she says, "I'm so sorry, Katherine. I don't know how he could do that to you. There's no excuse. And that woman is obviously a bitch."

Finally. Was I fishing for her to say something like that?

Mum adds, "You'll get used to being on your own and then you'll find someone else, I know you will."

I smile wanly. "Don't try to marry me off just yet."

"It'll be easier for you than it was for me. I devoted my life to you and your brother. You two were always my number one priority and I never wanted another man to interfere with that.

I was a single mother trying to bring in an income while looking after two small children."

She keeps on going in this vein. Once she's started, it's hard for her to stop. This is a hell of a lot better than when we were teenagers and it wouldn't take much for her to get worked up into a shouting and swearing frenzy. Then we'd tiptoe around, always on edge, never sure when she'd blow up again. Jack used to say he couldn't stand it any longer and that it was no wonder Dad left. Mum's mellowed since then, a little.

A horrible memory hits me. We'd made Father's Day cards at school and one of the kids told me I shouldn't have bothered when I didn't have a dad. I was trying to fit in. I failed. I was in tears when I told Mum about it after school but she was in one of her moods and told me I was forcing tears to get sympathy, that I should be ashamed when she was the one who'd been wronged. Cruel words to a little kid.

Now she starts telling me about the latest exciting thing that's happened at the bakery and how they suspect one of the juniors is diddling the till. I feel like I've heard this story before.

I interrupt. "Mum, I've just found out my husband was having an affair."

"I didn't think you'd want to dwell on it. There are other things we can talk about. I thought you came over for a pleasant visit."

Yep, that's me. Pleasant, clearly out-gunned and thoroughly exhausted. I let my mind wander while Mum talks. I think about buying groceries for dinner, split peas to make a big pot of dahl, and a few other things.

Mum finishes her story while sipping her tea.

I scull mine, then stand. "I should get going. I've got to stop at the shops on the way home."

"I need to stock up and do a few errands too. You don't know what it's like when you work full-time."

She's not full-time. I don't point that out to her because I don't think she was referring to herself but to my dismal work status. Still, I can be the bigger person.

The bigger person makes a hasty exit. I check my messages when I get in the car. There it is. A record of my chat with Mum yesterday where I said I'd pop over, complete with a thumbs up icon in return from Mum.

Chapter Twenty-Eight

Later, much later, I reach home.

After my earlier debacle, I drove safely, concentrating every step of the way. I leave the car on the street outside because I'm too lazy to park it in the garage off the laneway. Mum has that effect on me sometimes.

As I walk through the front gate, I think how funny it is that this concrete architect-designed bunker feels more like home than the house where I grew up. The sky is clouding over, the weather forecast for heavy rain and squally winds, yet that won't be a problem for me when I'm cloistered inside. And that's exactly where I plan to be tonight.

The front door pivots open, closing seamlessly behind me. I head down the hall towards the kitchen, stopping at the threshold of the rear living area. Esmeralda slinks towards me, blue eyes blinking against her dark face as she mews. Like everything else in the house, she is perfect. She brushes against my legs, an unusual show of affection for her, so I crouch down to stroke her.

"What've you been doing, Esmeralda?" I ask. "I hope you've been a good girl. Have you missed me?"

She slinks off, her tail high in the air, poophole on display. She turns as if to check whether I'm watching. I laugh. That's me told, then.

As I stand, something seems different. I sniff the air. Perfume? That's not possible. Nothing is amiss in the kitchen, the benchtop's clear, no prints on the stainless-steel fridge. I'm a neat freak. It's how I got the housesitting gig.

I check the back door. Locked. Noise from outside makes my ears prick, some sort of rustling sounds from next door. I unlock the door and peer outside to see the branches of Ryan's lemon tree shaking, a pair of giant gardening shears held high. He must be doing the pruning.

Inside, I head for my bedroom, then freeze in the doorway. The cushions on the bed are slightly askew, sitting at uneven angles. And the duvet cover that I stretched across so tightly is wrinkled on one side, as if someone has lain down.

My heart rate rising, I force myself to think straight.

It could've been me. As much as I hate to admit that's the case, it's a possibility. I could've blanked out. I might've been in a hurry or angry or sloppy or done any number of things that were out of character. And then blocked it from my memory. Wouldn't be the first time.

Esmeralda mooches into the room and mews loudly, looking up at me. She's telling me something. She knows. I reach down to pat her, only allowed one swift stroke before she skulks away.

As I straighten, I see it. Or rather I don't see it.

My wedding photo is gone.

My breaths come hard and fast now as I stalk across the room and stare at the top of the low chest of Scandinavian drawers, as if… As if what? I don't even know. My heart lurches. Someone has been here.

"Noooooo."

I yell and shake my head, though there's no one to hear

me. I yank open the drawers into which I've laid out my clothes, all carefully folded and neatly aligned. I'm about to close my underwear drawer when I see a flash of silver underneath the perfect piles of knickers and socks and bras.

It can't be. I reach for the photo frame that's face down at the bottom of the drawer, taking care because it feels somehow more fragile than before. As I turn it over I see the glass has been smashed, a spider web of cracks emanating from a central point as if someone has taken to it with a weapon or broken it over their knee. My wedding photo, shattered, like my life.

I spot something else at the back of the drawer, a small hammer, not mine, not something I've seen before. I dig it out, hold it in my hand and try to picture what has happened.

It wasn't me. I didn't do this. Surely I'm not that nuts. So why is my chest gripped with terror?

The hammer is evidence, something I could show to the police so they can send it off for testing, except now it's covered in my fingerprints. I've seen enough crime shows to know that. I have the photo frame in one hand, the hammer in the other, hoping like hell I haven't stood in this same position before.

I place the photo frame on the bed and stare at the cracks in Charlie's face. And mine. The hammer slips from my fingers, landing on the rug with a thud. I need help. I call Laura and get put through to voicemail. I can't get it out of my head that someone has been here. This wasn't me. It can't have been. Panic rushes through my veins. Next I try Noah. Same deal. Anxiety simmers in my gut. All I know is I want to show this to someone who'll understand why this is all wrong, someone who knows me and how neat I am.

I text Ryan. Two seconds later a message comes through.

Be right there.

The hammer. I grab it from the floor and run through the house into the backyard to the bin shelter by the shed because it wouldn't do to have the bins in view. So unsightly. I lean into the wheelie bin, lift out a rubbish bag, drop the hammer and dump the bag on top.

I can't hear Ryan in his backyard. He must be on his way over. I run back inside and head for the front door, panting.

Chapter Twenty-Nine

Ryan stands in my bedroom, looks at the photo frame on my bed, the glass smashed. "Are you sure?"

I'm not sure. "Yes."

His jeans have dirt smeared on the knees, his long-sleeved T-shirt stained with sweat, a pair of old Nikes on his feet. Gardening clothes. His hair is mussed up, a lock hanging over his forehead like he's Elvis. I don't know how Ryan does it but there's something about the greying temples that only makes him look more youthful.

"I was out this morning, and then home all afternoon," he says. "I didn't hear anything or notice anyone lurking."

I lean against the chest of drawers. "I realise how ludicrous this whole thing sounds."

"Not necessarily. I haven't forgotten there was a guy hanging around last week."

Scarparolo. Or at least I think it was him. Did he do this? I should've thought of him right away, yet somehow I can't quite picture it. It seems so restrained. There are a lot of things I can imagine him doing – ransacking the house, threatening me, fighting me, getting even – all things that take gross physical strength. Then, I haven't had any experience with stalkers. Don't they start small and escalate their attacks? Shit, this has 'stalker' written all over it.

"Kate." Ryan rakes his hair back into place. "Why would someone come in here and smash your wedding photo?"

My heart sinks. "You don't believe me."

"It's not that. I can see how upset you are. I don't think you're worked up about nothing."

I look into his eyes but I can't tell whether he thinks someone has broken in or that I'm an attention-seeking nutcase who smashed the photo herself.

"If you're this worried, you should report this to the police," he says.

There it is, the doubt, the *if*.

I shrug. "They won't do anything."

"I'm not saying there's anything the police can do, but at least they'll have a record in case something else happens. This is strike two. First the strange guy, now this."

"Actually there was something else." I might as well tell him. "A couple of weeks ago, I received a bunch of flowers. The card said they were from Charlie, from my dead husband."

I stop there. I don't tell Ryan about the *bitch* text message, Will Sharma getting rammed by a car or the photo of Charlie sent to me anonymously. A lot of things I don't tell him, or he's going to think my life is a train wreck.

"That's horrible, Kate," Ryan says. "Look, it's all the more reason to go to the station. I'll take you."

I remember the police officer saying I could have sent the flowers myself and I've got a pretty good idea how this will go down at the station. I don't need Ryan at my side to find out what a loser I am.

"Thanks, but I can ask Laura to come with me," I say.

He nods. "Sure."

I glance at my phone. "That's her now. Hang on and I'll text her back."

I send a quick message that everything's fine and I might pop around later. I sound normal. I don't sound like a crazy woman who thinks someone broke into her house with the express purpose of smashing her wedding photo. I'll message Noah later too, so he doesn't worry about calling me back.

"Is anything else missing?" Ryan asks. "Your laptop, valuables, that sort of thing?"

I've barely looked. "I don't think so."

"Any sign of forced entry?"

"I haven't checked."

"I'll take a look around if you like?"

"That'd be great, thanks."

Ryan pulls out a phone from his jeans. "Okay, I'll take a couple of photos and send them to you."

"Of the mussed-up bed? Doesn't look like much."

"No, but I get it." He snaps some photos of the bed and picture frame with its smashed glass.

"Thank you." Relief washes over me. Maybe he believes me after all. "My friends used to make fun of me for being a neat freak."

"I'm fairly fastidious myself, though not quite as anal as Joel."

"Oh, I'm anal!" I nod. "I don't even think that's an insult."

Ryan laughs. I don't smile. A memory comes back to me, Charlie coming home one evening after doing a double shift, or at least that's what he told me he'd been doing. He got pissed because I'd left a dirty plate and cutlery in the sink. I'd made burritos and told him there was a plate for him in the fridge. Another vision. Charlie storming out, because he couldn't live in these conditions and eat when the kitchen was filled with crap. And how could I do that to him after he'd been working hard and helping people at the hospital?

For so long, I haven't let myself think about these moments, his faults and flaws, all the times he freaked out at me over nothing. I had no clue what he was doing behind my back.

"Are you okay?" Ryan asks.

"Sure."

"I'll take a look through the rest of the house, if you like."

"Thanks. Can I follow you?"

House. Follow. Check. Forget about Charlie.

The rest of the house is perfect. The worst thing that's happened is a layer of dust on the furniture in Joel's bedroom and the other rooms that I don't use. I'll make sure the whole house is pristine by the time I hand it back to Joel, of course, but that's months away.

I wish it wasn't immaculate. I wish for a broken window, muddy footsteps in the house, other signs of a break-in, evidence, confirmation, proof. Someone has been in here and smashed my wedding photo – I know it – only they didn't enter or exit through the deadlocked doors. There must be some explanation. I think about the hammer I've hidden in the bin and turn on my heels.

I crash into Ryan's chest, bouncing right off it as he steps back, his arms outstretched, his hands on my shoulders.

"I'm so sorry," I say.

"No, I should be more careful. You're on edge after what's happened. It's perfectly understandable."

"I'll be okay."

"Look, if you don't want to be on your own, you can come to my place. I'm making chicken curry for dinner. Might not be the most exciting offer you'll get but I'm a pretty reasonable cook."

"You're kidding."

He raises his eyebrows. "My offer's not that bad, is it?"

I smile. "No, that's an amazing coincidence. I was going to make a big pot of dahl."

"Ah, the perfect accompaniment."

Actually, I'm thinking Ryan is the perfect accompaniment, with or without chicken curry. The thought shouldn't have come to mind. How can I think that? How can I not?

I walk him to the door, then lock the back door before taking a shower. It's a basic security measure because I wouldn't be able to hear anything if someone broke in while I was showering. Yep, a lot of good my security measures are doing me.

When I reach the bedroom, my phone pings, still on the bed where I left it. It's Noah messaging me about the missed call, so I send him a quick text.

One thing at a time. Tomorrow I'll go to the police station. And talk to Laura. I leave for Melbourne in a couple of days. When I get there, I'll catch up with James who handed me Charlie's second phone, with Charlie's folks of course, maybe Amy, the only friend worth seeing.

I stare at the fractured picture frame, the photo that used to mean so much to me. In the en suite, I remove the glass, putting the broken pieces in the bin that's hidden in the cupboard. I'm careful. I'm not someone who smashes things. Taking the photo and frame with me, I step towards the Scandinavian chest of drawers, the magnificent grain of the birch unmarred by any decoration.

I open a drawer and shove the photo face down under a pile of T-shirts. I don't need to look at it.

Chapter Thirty

I've wondered what Ryan's house looked like inside, and now I know. The glimpses I had from over the back fence don't do it justice.

A good meal, good company and the fifties music playing in the background have calmed me down. I lean back in a dining chair.

"Your place is the polar opposite of Joel's," I say. "It doesn't look like the same person designed both."

It's a lot more modest, for one thing. Ryan's not afraid of a bit of colour, though you'd never guess if all you'd seen was Joel's house. The walls in the dining area where we're seated are a deep emerald green, the ceiling too, which might feel oppressive if not for the wall of glass doors leading onto the patio that add a feeling of lightness even at night. He's switched the colours around in the kitchen with deep-green cabinets, white benchtops and white walls, so the rooms are like pieces of a puzzle that fit together effortlessly.

Ryan shrugs. "Designing Joel's place was a dream. It's not hard to create beautiful spaces with immaculate finishes when money's not an issue." He laughs. "I didn't have Joel's budget."

"Honestly, you can't tell. Your place is awesome."

As much as I love my concrete bunker, I love this too. I can imagine myself having breakfast on the patio, sitting at the table with my laptop, giving Mum a tour. The place is comfortable all right.

"I did a lot of the work myself." Ryan stands and pats a section of exposed brick. "This used to be two rooms till I got to it with a sledgehammer and opened the space up. Made a hell of a mess but I knew exactly what it'd look like when I was done."

So he's not afraid of hard work. I picture him covered in dust, strong and muscular, slinging the sledgehammer. Maybe I'm picturing too much.

Ryan has already offered to drive me to the airport. He also said he'll look after Esmeralda when I'm in Melbourne, that he's done it once before, straight after Joel moved in. So he's not afraid of doing favours for friends either. I talked to Joel, who suggested Ryan, and gave me the name of a fancy cat-boarding place, just in case.

"What's this music?" I ask.

"Right now? This is Eddie Cochran. That night at the Elysian Bar, you said you love rockabilly. Surely you'd recognise the classics?"

"Um, some of them."

Ryan smiles. "And your cardigan is very rockabilly with the tattoo-art swallows."

"Is it?" I bought it because I liked it and didn't think much deeper than that. "I have a confession to make. I wasn't really at the bar because of my love of rockabilly."

His eyes widen in mock surprise. "You don't say."

"You knew?"

"I'm teasing."

And I like it.

"Okay then." I pretend to be slighted as I reach across for

the dirty plates. "Enough about me. What's your dream for this place, you know, if money wasn't an issue?"

He takes a moment to look around. "My dream isn't about the house. It's about the people in it."

What people? I take the dirty dishes into the kitchen where Ryan is soaking the pan he used for the curry. This reminds me of home, but not any of the homes I've had, certainly not my life growing up with Mum and not my life with Charlie. He didn't cook, except when we had friends around, didn't clean up, and didn't let up if the place wasn't perfect.

It strikes me that this is what life should be like, preparing meals together, pottering in the kitchen, chatting as we work. Is that what Ryan meant?

Outside there's a flash of sheet lightning and a distant rumble of thunder followed by a sudden downpour. Despite the darkness, I stare at the rain mindlessly through the kitchen window, the steady patter on the tin roof comforting.

"At Joel's, it's so quiet when it's raining because of all that concrete." I turn to Ryan. "Unless the doors or windows are open, of course."

"Of course." He smiles. "I like the sound of the rain."

"Me too."

We move to the living room in one of the original Federation rooms at the front and Ryan downs another beer while I sip mineral water. The room is filled with period features, ornate cornices, a picture rail and wrought-iron fireplace with Art Nouveau tiles set into the surround.

The home renovation and architecture shows I've watched put me in good stead for our discussion about houses before we move on to other subjects. Ryan likes old movies, classics, Hitchcock movies, anything with Humphrey Bogart and especially *Casablanca*. I mention Audrey Hepburn and he says she was wonderful in *Roman Holiday*. I'm in awe.

He's obviously very close to his family, a mum and dad (one of each), his sister and a much-adored niece and nephew.

"I take it your dad's not on the scene?" he asks.

I shake my head. "He left when we were little. Mum said he went back to Mauritius but I'm not so sure. The only thing I'm sure of is that he never got in touch again."

Every time I ask Mum about Dad, she goes off her rocker at me. Meanwhile I barely know what it's like to be Mauritian. If it wasn't for my skin colour, I could forget completely.

"I can't imagine it," Ryan says. "Having a beautiful daughter and not seeing her grow up, that's... something."

I'm not beautiful.

"I didn't know otherwise at the time, and I had my brother, Jack." I talk about how we used to play and argue and talk, before the drugs kicked in. "I think he has an addictive personality. When he got into skateboarding, he lived and breathed it. Didn't want to do anything else. When he got a new computer game, it was impossible to get him off it. Maybe drugs were a problem waiting to happen. I don't know."

"Is he still in Perth?"

"Last I heard he was in Sydney but he's drifted in and out. It's been a couple of years since we've seen or heard from him."

Addiction is an illness. It's in the Diagnostic Statistical Manual, or so one of Charlie's doctor friends told me, not that it's changed my opinion. Jack had everything going for him. No one forced him to do drugs or leave or become so selfish. Still, I long to hear from him, if only to know he's okay. He's always losing phones and changing numbers, hard to get hold of.

I change the subject. I think of nicer times and tell Ryan a little about living in Melbourne, not too much, because I don't know what's true and what's not anymore.

"What's your dream, Kate?" he asks.

"Sorry?"

"It's the same question you asked me earlier."

And it takes me by surprise. Dreams are for people like Ryan who can create amazing spaces such as Joel's bespoke bunker and this house that's moody and bright and comfortable.

My dreams were simpler: a life with Charlie, raising a family, taking the kids to school and the park, the child that will never happen, all things that are in the past tense.

"I try not to dream too much," I say. "If I can just get by, for me, that's an achievement."

He looks into my eyes. "Sorry, I shouldn't be so inquisitive."

"Not at all." I stand. "I should probably go."

I don't want to go.

My insides start to melt. If he gives me one small sign, I'll stay and I won't regret it. I want to feel close to someone. Not just anyone. Ryan. Maybe this will be a one-night stand and maybe it won't. Right now, I don't care. I'll take whatever I can get.

He stands too, so polite. "I hope you enjoyed the meal."

"I enjoyed everything about tonight."

"I'm glad you texted me earlier."

We are both so glad and polite and full of enjoyment. And I am none of those things, my heart rate rising, my head filled with lustful thoughts, blood rushing through my body, and we haven't even done anything yet. We might not for that matter.

"Let me walk you to the door." Ryan follows me down the passage, the hallway way too short for my liking, the stroll over before I know it. Lightning flashes on the other side of the stained glass inset in the front door, the wind howling outside.

Ryan edges closer. "If there's anything you need, call me, you know, like you did today." I look into his eyes, unwilling to leave or move, hoping for something. "You can call or text or give me a shout-out over the fence."

He reaches for my hand, his touch reassuring, the small sign I've been waiting for. He waits. *Don't wait.* He caresses my cheek, then slides his hand along my jaw.

"Or I can whisper it to you now." I stand on tiptoe, closing the space between us, my voice low. "I'd like to stay."

Ryan takes his time, brushes his lips against mine in a kiss that's barely there. Over before I know it. He's close, so close, looking into my eyes as if ready to give me an out. I don't want an out. I snake my arms around his neck and he pulls me tighter, kisses me in a way that leaves me in no doubt.

Yes.

I'm a teenager out on my first date. I'm heady with expectation, with a sense of the unknown, with a desperate need to be fulfilled. I'm ready for his naked body against mine. I want to feel. And to forget.

Eventually Ryan breaks the kiss. "Are you sure?"

"I'm sure."

I take his hand and pull him away from the front door, but I don't know which door is the right one. Ryan pulls me into the bedroom and switches on a lamp sitting on a dresser, bathing the room in a soft glow. I see only the bed. I don't take in the details. This isn't an architectural tour. The only tour I want is of Ryan's body.

He presses himself up against me, throws us into another intoxicating kiss, his hands on my waist, my ribs, my breasts. Sensation courses through my body. My hands on his chest, I fumble with the buttons on his shirt. There is only now, the moment before, and then there will be after. I slide the front of his shirt apart. I kiss his chest and slide the shirt from his shoulders.

That's when I see it, a large framed photo on the dresser, more photos, lots of family snaps. A baby, a toddler, a little girl with wavy blonde hair. My eyes glued to the largest photo, I step closer to the dresser, pick up the photo and stare.

"You have a little girl." I turn to Ryan who doesn't say anything, then look back down at the picture in my hands that fills me with sudden, unforeseen joy, the kind of joy I haven't felt in a long time. I see fun and family and love. I see afternoons at the park and baths and bedtime stories. I see Ryan chasing after a little girl. I hear her calling "Daddy, Daddy." I hear her giggling when he tickles her. Yet he's never said anything.

"She's gorgeous," I say. "I didn't know you had a daughter."

A pause.

"Chloe was a beautiful kid."

Was.

I place the photo back on the dresser with shaking hands, then cover my mouth as I take in the other photos, a grainy black-and-white of Ryan holding a newborn, a baby crawling on carpet, a toddler playing with pegs, a little girl sitting cross-legged on a pink bed, surrounded by soft toys. A celebration. Joy and sadness.

Tears in my eyes, I take a moment to compose myself as I think of Ryan, his heart broken in the worst way possible because there's no getting over what he's been through. I think of Charlie's parents and their pain. I think of this little girl who should be alive, and my heart breaks all over again.

"I'm so sorry." I take Ryan's hands into mine. I wait.

"She was four when she died. A car accident." He pauses. "That was four years ago."

"Four years," I whisper.

Some things you never get over. Maybe he needs to forget too. For a while. For one night.

Ryan cups my chin in his hands and presses another kiss to my lips, first gentle, then probing. He peppers my neck with little kisses. I hook my fingers over the hem of my T-shirt, pull it over my head and toss it to the floor. He skims his hands over the scars on my stomach, then higher. He slides the straps of my bra over my shoulders. I step towards the bed, motioning for him to come closer, then kiss his neck, his shoulders, that magnificent chest. My hands slip to the waist of his jeans, unbuttoning, unzipping, undoing the pain of the past. I can hope. I can try.

I don't believe in fate or destiny or afterlife. I believe in now, in the bare-chested man in front of me, in the desire thrumming through my body and the feelings that have led us here.

We make love that's slow and languorous, dripping with desire, bodies moving like liquid. He knows exactly what I like, where to touch me, each stroke familiar yet a surprise at the same time. It's as if we've always known each other, yet this does nothing to diminish the excitement of a first time. I'm swimming in a warm spring, bathed in warmth and beauty, water lapping around my body, engulfing me, my most intimate parts.

It's only later, much later, that I realise the lights stayed on. No more hiding.

Chapter Thirty-One

I cross the road and walk down to Laura's. After last night's storm – the one I barely noticed – the street is littered with branches and twigs, the smell of eucalyptus rising from the soaked earth. Dirty water has pooled around a blocked drain. I step around a branch that's blocking the footpath.

A breeze blows across the back of my neck, sending a shudder up my spine. It's Charlie following me, I could swear. I look around but there's no one there, of course.

Ten minutes later, I'm sitting on the polished concrete steps at the side of Laura's place while she hangs the washing. Her enormous back deck is behind me, the pool and greenery that surround it just around the corner. The sun has come out. The puddles have dried but the garden bed on the other side of the washing line is still damp, last night's downpour bringing out the smell of the mulch.

Where to start? I went to the police station on my own this morning and thought it lucky the same young police officer was there. We're on first-name terms, after all, and he knows me so I didn't have to repeat my whole life history. I told Officer Alex Sheridan about the break-in and how someone smashed my wedding photo. I showed him the photos Ryan took, well aware that displaced pillows don't make for an emergency. I was calm and articulate, unlike yesterday when I found the smashed photo and 'calm' went out the window. I told him how Scarparolo had been hanging around. At least I think it was Scarparolo. Ryan saw him. He's a witness. That has to count for something.

And now I regret it. I should've known how this would go down. I did know, and didn't want to face it.

I tell Laura the story. She's listening while she hangs out the clothes.

We're interrupted, Theo's voice coming from the top of the stairs.

"Hey, Kate," he says, then shifts his gaze to Laura. "I'm off, honey. Be back by two. I told Blake I'd take him to footy."

Theo keeps a low profile when I'm around or things get too intense for him. Meanwhile Blake is holed up in his room and Mia is out with friends. I guess that's life with teenagers.

"See ya, hon," Laura says. "Love you."

"Love you too." He blows her a kiss.

"Bye, Theo," I call out as he leaves, feeling privileged to glimpse this little slice of their life.

"You say you went to visit your mum that morning," Laura says while she picks pegs from the basket. "How were you feeling after seeing her? Agitated? Relieved? Happy?"

She's playing psychologist, only she's better than the two shrinks I used to see.

I shrug. "I wasn't so good earlier that morning. I blanked out for a bit."

Laura glances in my direction. "For how long?"

"The drive to Mum's."

"The whole trip?"

I nod.

Laura bites her lip. "And you told the police?"

"I didn't tell them I blanked out."

I didn't need to. They already thought I'd lost the plot.

She leaves the half-full washing basket and sits by me on the step. Close. Our knees touching. Close is good.

"Kate, you need to slow down and take a deep breath. You're still grieving and you've only just found out your husband was having an affair. You've been under a lot of stress and you blanked out in the morning, then found the smashed photo later in the day."

She lets this hang. She thinks I smashed the photo and blanked it out in some sort of self-preservation mechanism. There's another explanation. There has to be. Can't she be wrong this one time? To save my sanity. For my peace of mind, or whatever mind I've got left.

At least the way Laura puts it, I don't feel completely crazy, just a bit lost. Or a lot.

I drop my head into my hands. "Okay, I get it."

Laura wraps her arms around me. I rest my head on her shoulder, wondering how it ever got to this, then pull away.

"It's okay," I say. "Really. Look, no tears."

Because I'm too freaked out to cry. I don't know if it was better thinking someone else smashed the photo or believing I did it myself.

"I wish you'd told me right away," Laura says. "Yesterday, not today. If only I'd got to my phone sooner. You shouldn't have been alone at a time like that."

"I wasn't alone. I had Ryan with me."

Laura's eyes widen. "Ryan?"

"I like him a lot, Laura. This feels… different."

"I hope you're taking care of yourself. I mean, Ryan's a lovely guy and all, a great guy. But isn't it too soon?"

"Probably."

Laura does that thing where she doesn't speak. She waits. I made a mistake, once, and had sex with the wrong person but she doesn't need to know about that. Besides, this isn't a mistake. It's everything that's right in the world.

I clasp my hands together. "Life is short. Charlie's death taught me that in a way I hadn't known before. It's the old cliché. You can be here one minute, gone the next, no second chances. So I should make the most of every moment and live my life to the full. At the very least, I should get my shit together."

"One thing at a time," she says.

"I also know life is for living. And maybe I need a little more love in my world."

"What about…?" She holds out her hand. "No, don't worry."

She's thinking of Noah and how this will make him feel. He's her brother and she doesn't want to see him hurt. I don't have an answer for that. I don't tell her this might help him move on, though that's exactly what I hope will happen.

Laura throws her arms around me again, only this time when we break the hug, there are tears in her eyes – for Noah, no doubt.

She gets to her feet. "I've got to finish hanging that washing."

Laura is a good friend, the best. It's understandable if she feels a bit conflicted over Noah's interest in me. I feel conflicted about a lot of things myself.

At least Ryan doesn't think I'm a nutter. Unfortunately he doesn't know me very well.

My darling

I sense you at the strangest times. I feel you. I know you're there even if I can't see you.

You come to me in my dreams. Sometimes they're nightmares. That can't be helped. At other times the dreams are so normal, the two of us chatting on the sofa or walking down the street or having a drink at a bar. During these dreams, I'm content and loved and laughing, filled with the joy of the ordinary, relishing every moment.

Those dreams are the worst, much worse than the nightmares, because the dreams are beautiful and then I wake up and you're dead and I'm shattered all over again. It's not the dreams that are dire. It's real life.

Sometimes I think I should've appreciated you more when you were alive and then I realise I did as much as I could during the short time we had together. And yet, until it was ripped away from me, I didn't understand how much I had. And how little.

I'm constantly contradicting myself. And second-guessing. I lurch from one problem to another without the time to work out what's going on. I have strange visions, so many things I don't want to believe, so much crap in my life. Sometimes I think nothing is sinking in and other times it feels like I've got the knowledge of the world hanging around my neck.

I don't know what's real and what's not anymore but I can't let that weigh me down. And I don't know what to do. I don't know what to feel anymore. And I wish none of this had ever happened.

Sometimes I'm not even sure how much longer I can keep loving you. We'll have to see.

Chapter Thirty-Two

I spend the evening with Ryan. Cook, eat, make love, not such a bad combination. Pretty bloody good, in fact. The next day Ryan goes to work, doesn't seem to have to force himself, unlike me.

Tomorrow, I'm off to Melbourne. I'm scared of what I might find and of facing the truth but I'm doing it anyway. Right now, the supermarket.

I find a drive-through parking spot under a light. Perfect. Saves me having to reverse in. I glance around as I get out of the car, but no one is hanging around the car park.

The smaller places inside the shopping arcade have closed – the bakery, the butcher, the sushi place – whereas Farmer Joe's is open till ten. I walk through the turnstile into the fruit and vegetable section. My self-defence instructors used to say you should look around for a weapon. What would I use? A bunch of bananas? A pineapple perhaps? At least I know where the exits are. I always know.

My mission is specific. I must purchase John Walker chocolate liquorice, locally made and as good as the best from Belgium, to take to Charlie's parents in Melbourne because Mike has a thing about liquorice and Jan has a serious sweet tooth. Cadbury Roses simply aren't going to cut it. I pop a couple of packets of chocolate liquorice into my basket. I've already bought them a bottle of Little Things gin, made at a distillery around the corner. Australian botanical gin, whatever that is, I'm sure they'll like it.

Movement in the corner of my eye. I do a double-take. It's Scarparolo, practically right next to me. Shit, I've let my guard down.

I step back. "What are you doing here?"

He grins. "You know the old saying, what goes around comes around."

I don't know anything. My heart has jumped to my throat, perspiration beading on my brow. No fast movements. No need to argue with him. I want to walk away but I'm frozen to the spot. *Unfreeze, damn it.*

"My brother was minding his own business, just like you, and look what happened to him." Scarparolo keeps smiling. Why won't he stop smiling? "You didn't think about his life or what this would do to my mother. Did you now?"

His mother? I've thought about her more than he knows, about the pain of losing a son, the pain I caused to others. It still tortures me that I killed a man.

"You'd better watch your back." He edges the front of his jacket aside, revealing a black handle sticking out of his jeans. A knife, a threat. Fuck.

I ram the shopping basket into his chest. He stumbles back, laughs. I turn and run. A shop assistant is walking across the front of the shop. I slow down but can't stop myself from slamming into her, knocking her to the side. She grabs her arm, hunches over, hurt.

"So sorry." I glance up. Scarparolo is headed my way. He's holding a shopping basket, mine, I think. I hurl a stack of cans at the end of the aisle across the floor between me and him. Shocked, the shop assistant steps back.

I leave Scarparolo with the liquorice. I leave the shop assistant with the hurt arm. And I run.

Behind me, Scarparolo's voice. "Hey, miss, you forgot your chocolate."

I keep running.

I'm on the leather sofa in Ryan's lounge room, leaning forward, Ryan's arm draped around me. I stare at the abstract patterns on the rug, strange shapes and colours melding into each other and disappearing by the time the rug reaches the floorboards.

Scarparolo knows where I live, where I shop, where to find me and exactly how to scare me. I shouldn't let him get to me. I should get my act together.

"You should go to the police," Ryan says.

They won't believe me. Sometimes I think *I* wouldn't believe me.

We go through it together. The shop assistant didn't see the knife, only a frightened woman, me, making a run for it. I pushed her, then ran off, so she probably thinks I'm a nutter. She's not much of a witness, not for what I'd need.

"Maybe I'll report it after I get back from Melbourne," I say. Only a small lie. "It's not as if Scarparolo can hurt me while I'm on the other side of the country."

"You can stay here tonight, of course. I'll drive you to the airport tomorrow. I won't let you out of my sight until then."

I'll stay safe. That's important. And when I get back, maybe my life will be closer to normal.

"There's something I don't get," Ryan says. "A year is a long time to wait if this Scarparolo wants revenge. The guy's an arsehole, that much is clear, but why wait a year?"

"I don't know. Maybe because that's how long it took for me to turn up in Perth."

And I let him know I was here, such a stupid thing to do.

Ryan pulls me close. "At least I don't need to worry about you while you're in Melbourne."

I like that he's worried about me. He cares. I throw my arms around him for a hug, then take a deep breath and lean back into the sofa. I care about him too. It's selfish of me to think only of myself when he's been through a huge loss himself.

Something strikes me as I look around. "You don't have any photos of Chloe in here?" None in here or the hallway or the kitchen dining area or any of the 'public' parts of the house.

He shrugs. "Guess I don't want to inflict that on everyone who walks in."

"I'm sorry it's hard for you but the photos are beautiful. Was Chloe as cute as she looked?"

"Cuter." Ryan smiles, his expression softening. "And very chatty. I tell you, once she started talking, she didn't stop."

"Really?"

"We'd get a non-stop commentary on everything she was doing and everything she saw, then she'd repeat things we'd said to her verbatim. It was kinda scary."

"And fun?"

"Loads of fun. I remember when she had an accident with toilet training. Olivia walked into Chloe's bedroom while she was rubbing the floor with her clean white dress, saying *Naughty Flossie, Flossie shouldn't have done that and now Chloe's cleaning up your mess*. Floss was the cat."

"So Chloe had weed on the floor?"

Ryan chortles. "And thought she could deflect the blame onto Floss."

"Clever girl."

"She was smart, all right. She got that from her mum."

"Her dad's not so bad either." I pause, wondering if I should ask. "Did you and Olivia break up *after* Chloe passed away?"

"Yeah, it was after. I changed. My hair turned grey practically overnight for one thing but, really, that was the least of my problems. Olivia changed too. She's always been a hard person and then she became even more rigid, no tolerance, not even for me." He shakes his head. "Oh hell, I'm not explaining that very well. I don't blame Olivia. It's just the way things were. She's a good person. It's not like there were any third parties involved or anything."

Third parties. I stiffen.

"Is something wrong?" he asks.

"I'm sorry for everything you've been through." No one should have to go through the sort of loss Ryan has experienced. My heart bleeds for him and maybe also for myself.

"You can talk to me," he says.

I pull my phone out of the bag at my feet and show Ryan the photo of Charlie with the other woman.

Ryan looks at the picture, screws up his face, turns to me. "Far out, Kate. I don't know what to say."

I tell him the real reason for my trip to Melbourne. I tell him everything. Or nearly everything. My heart clenches when I think of Charlie with another woman. I start sobbing, which is inevitable. Ryan holds me close, which is wonderful. I think about the magnitude of his loss and pull myself together.

"I want to find out what was going on," I say. "We were together for ten years. I thought I knew him, and I was wrong. If I can find out the truth, maybe I can put all this to rest."

Ryan presses his lips together. "He didn't deserve you."

The words are strange to me. They float on the surface, not quite soaking through my skin. It's not what I'm used to.

Sympathy, sure, I've had loads of that. Platitudes, I get plenty of those. But I've also had years of Charlie niggling at me and putting me down, years of believing he was right.

"I'm not perfect," I say. "I'm screwed up."

"Perfect is overrated."

I wring my hands. "I failed. In the worst way possible. That's what really gets to me. I couldn't protect the man I loved."

"The guy had a knife. I read the reports online. Kate, you were amazing."

"Not amazing enough."

Other people don't get it. I stopped talking about it, stopped speaking about what matters. I only talk about everyday things, work, books, TV shows, mutual friends, the new person down the street, the acquaintance I bumped into. But I don't talk, not properly. Maybe it's time I started.

"I've done years of martial arts and self-defence stuff. You haven't seen me smashing the pads at training, sparring with guys who are bigger than me, throwing them to the ground, putting on chokes. I loved that stuff. It made me feel like a million dollars."

"You must be pretty good, Kate. I don't doubt it. But look at the size of you. And the other guy had a knife. There's only so much you can do."

It used to shit me, the way men are so much stronger than women. Still does.

I try to explain. "You're right. Logically, I know that. But in my gut, I believe I should've been able to do something. What kind of martial artist am I? Me, of all people, I should've done better and stopped Charlie from dying."

Problem is, I think these things at once – that there was nothing more I could do and that I should've been able to save Charlie. No wonder my head is such a mess.

Tears spill down my cheeks. "I had choices. At every turn,

there was a different choice or decision I could have made. And I chose mediocre, and ended up with a world of excuses. The other guy was too big, too fast, too determined, too whatever. What good are those excuses? I still feel the guilt every day. I didn't save Charlie. Didn't even come close. Was that really the best I could do?"

Ryan brushes the tears from my cheeks. "You're really hard on yourself."

"I know."

"It's good you're getting this out of your system. I'm glad you're talking to me. Sometimes you need to nut things down to their simplest level. Charlie was no match for the knife. I'm sorry. But you survived, and I'm glad you did."

I killed a man, and it doesn't make any difference that it was self-defence. It was still a person's life.

Also there's one small thing Ryan's missing, one thing that haunts me, that no one knows. I let it rattle around in my head. I don't let it out.

Ryan takes my hands into his. "You came out alive."

"And Charlie didn't. That's my point."

Ryan pulls me close and I rest my head against his chest, sobbing gently.

After a while he says, "You can wipe your tears on my shirt. I don't mind."

Sure enough, his shirt is soggy. I loosen up a little as I sit up and run my fingers through my hair and try to make my curls settle down.

"Sometimes I can't get it out of my head," I say. "I should've done more. I saved myself but not Charlie. I couldn't help him."

"There's something you're forgetting." Ryan presses a kiss to my hair. "Charlie couldn't protect you either."

I stare at Ryan's rug and the patterns start to make sense.

Chapter Thirty-Three

Ryan drove me to the airport this morning, as he promised. He's true to his word and that's exactly what I need right now, someone I can depend on.

I dropped my bag at my Flinders Lane hotel, then had a light lunch which was either early or late, depending on which time zone you look at. I texted Charlie's folks to confirm I was coming for dinner. Laura had asked me to message her after I landed so I did that and sent Ryan a selfie of me with a cappuccino, entitled *Melbourne coffee*. They know how to do coffee here.

It's so familiar catching a tram to Fitzroy, the place that used to be home. I don't go anywhere near our old house. I don't need to do that to myself, so I stay on Brunswick Street, the main drag, which is exactly as I remember it. Hardly surprising since I haven't been away for long. And it feels altogether different, like a foreign city.

I push open the door and walk into Bonomi's. I've never been here before, probably because Charlie said the place was too middle-aged for us, which meant it wasn't hip enough for him. There's lots of dark wood, leather booths, crystal chandeliers, flocked peacock-pattern wallpaper, red velvet curtains hanging at the back where there's probably a way out to the rear lane. I'd put it partway between a classy brothel and a gentlemen's drinking club. I quite like it, actually.

James waves at me to join him. He was Charlie's senior at the hospital but he's one of those men who looks ageless. He has a serious cycling habit that keeps him fit, a few lines on his face, a fantastic head of hair with only a few greys. Boyish good looks, some would say.

He gets up to greet me. I go for an air kiss, while he presses his lips to my cheek and takes my hands into his with rather too much enthusiasm, not to mention too much aftershave.

"So good to see you, Kate," he says.

"Hi." I'd forgotten how earnest he is. It's all coming back to me.

"What can I get you? A martini? A gin and tonic?" He motions behind him to a table with a cocktail glass on it. "I've got us a booth."

"Maybe a lemon, lime and bitters."

"Come on, you can do better than that."

He has a charming grin, I'll grant him that, but I stick to my guns when we order.

Drink in hand, I slide into the booth, ready for the requisite small talk. "How's Emily?"

"We broke up ten months ago."

My mouth falls open. "Really?"

"Things hadn't been good between us for a while." Matter-of-fact.

"But, that last night when we had dinner…"

Charlie and I'd had dinner with them the night we were attacked, the night everything changed.

"We were hanging in there by a thread," James says. "Broke up not long afterwards."

"Sorry, I didn't know."

He smiles, squeezes my hand. "That's understandable. You had a lot going on at the time, Kate."

I draw my hand back, unsure if I'm reading too much into this. I was the one who got in touch with him, not the other way around, so it's not as if he's stalking me. Still, he'd made a big deal of it over text, insisting he'd like to meet up for a meal, while I'd played it down, suggesting coffee. Coffee turned into a drink, his choice of venue, and here we are.

"How are the twins?" It's been a while so I can't remember their names.

He laughs. "They're at that stage where they just want to hang out with their friends. They know everything and of course I know nothing." He rolls his eyes. "Why would they want to be seen with the likes of me?"

I smile. "Yep, teenagers. Gotta love 'em."

"I do. I love them with all my heart. They're with their mother." His gaze lingers. "So I'm free all weekend."

"And how's work?"

He leans closer. "Let's talk about you, Kate, and how you've been doing. You've been through so much and I'd like to know more."

I give him a rundown, keeping things neutral. Meanwhile he goes overboard with the intense looks and if I had any doubts about his intentions, I have none now. I sit up straight, willing the hair on the back of my neck to settle down.

He sips his martini. "I might even be able to cook for you on the weekend. How does that sound?"

"Thanks, but I'm not here for long."

He smiles. "I'd like to return the favour, that's all."

"What favour?"

"You and Charlie had us over for dinner, along with two other couples from the hospital, and we never reciprocated. You cooked a fabulous meal, as I remember."

"Oh that, don't worry about it."

The dinner that nearly didn't happen because I'd got the night wrong. Or had I? A conversation with Charlie comes back to me. I reminded him my girls' weekend at a Yarra Valley retreat was coming up and all of a sudden he said his doctor friends were coming for dinner on that same Saturday. He insisted he'd told me a few nights earlier and that I must've forgotten, when I was certain he'd never set a date.

It hits me that Charlie was the one who'd got it wrong, not me. On purpose. He didn't want me going out with the girls because he didn't like any attention being diverted away from him. And he convinced me that *I* was wrong. My stomach sinks.

James frowns. "Are you okay? You look worried."

Not worried. Angry. I wish Charlie was here so I could hit him.

"No, all good." I snap out of it.

James smiles. "We could go to a restaurant if you prefer."

"Thank you but I'm busy all weekend." And for the rest of my life, the words I don't say. "I wanted to ask you about Charlie. You worked together and you knew him well."

James leans back. "Shoot."

"I know everyone at the hospital loved Charlie."

The smile leaves James's face.

"I got the impression he was very popular," I say. "With the staff, the patients, with everyone."

"Go on."

Another truth is starting to sink in. I've been had. Again. I took everything Charlie said at face value, believed every word he said. No, I can't have been that gullible.

"His patients adored him." Now I'm trying to convince myself.

"Great bedside manner, I'll give him that."

"You say that like it's a bad thing?"

"As doctors, we spend limited time with our patients and generally they're grateful for the care we provide, so it's relatively easy to get them onside. It's different with colleagues. When you work with people day in, day out, people get to know you better."

"Are you saying people didn't like Charlie when they got to know him better?"

"Not at all."

But that's not what his face is telling me.

"Charlie was good at his job," I say.

"Yeah, he was."

"He told me about some of his cases. There was a toddler, too young to speak so he couldn't say what was wrong. The poor thing couldn't move his legs, but his reflexes were fine and there were no fractures. Then the mother came back to the hospital the next day and said the boy could barely move his arms. Charlie ran more tests, talked to other specialists but no one could work out what was wrong till Charlie came up with the diagnosis. Guillain-Barré Syndrome, an autoimmune thing that causes paralysis."

"I know what it is."

"Sorry, of course you do."

James's eyes hood over. "Charlie didn't make the diagnosis. The neurologist did. And the mother was very grateful."

"Are you sure?"

He laughs as if that's a stupid question. "Yes."

"And Charlie took credit for it?"

"It wouldn't be the first time."

James is so certain and, as much as I hate to believe this of Charlie, part of me knows it's true. That's the worst part. Yet another item to add to my list of things-I-didn't-want-to-know-about-Charlie.

Time to cut to the chase. "There's something else. Did you know Charlie was having an affair?"

"No," he says, his voice even.

"You don't seem surprised."

"Hmm, I often got the feeling he might've been looking out for something better."

I press my lips tight. Better than me? Is that what he's saying?

"That's come out all wrong." James gives my hand a quick squeeze. "If you ask me, Charlie didn't know how good he had it with you."

"Thanks."

"You're a very attractive woman, Kate."

I pull out my phone and show him the photo. "Does she look familiar?"

"I've never seen her before." James sips his drink. "I gave you that box of Charlie's things. You must've found the phone in there and worked it out. Is that where you found the photo?"

"No, someone sent the picture to me."

"But surely you've known for a while?"

I shake my head. I don't explain my feelings or why I threw that phone away.

"I gather it's time for you to start moving on," James says. "I can be a friend, perhaps more than a friend."

"That's not why I came here."

He shrugs. "Still, it might be pleasant, to say the least."

Not what I had in mind at all. I slide along the seat and get up. "I should go."

James stands between me and the door. "You don't have to leave so soon."

Encroaching on my personal space. It gets my goat up. Yet I don't want to be the one to step back. Just because he's a man doesn't mean it's okay for him to stand in my way.

"I'm free for the rest of the evening," he adds. "We can think of this as more of a fling, if you like."

"I do not like."

His mouth falls open.

I step across, knocking his shoulder as I pass. And I leave.

Chapter Thirty-Four

My knuckles hover over the front door of Charlie's parents' place. I'm early. I should have texted to say I was on my way but my head was a bit of a mess after meeting up with James.

I stopped at my hotel to pick up the gifts I'd bought, then came straight here. Jan and Mike were always lovely company. I'm sure they still are.

I knock on the door. Voices sail across from the back of the house. Charlie's folks live on a tree-lined street in Glen Iris, a leafy suburb that's so much nicer than where I grew up it's not funny. Charlie used to put the place down and say it was full of old people, which I don't think is true. He thought he was too cool for suburbia.

Charlie's mum pulls the door open. She looks exactly the same, except for the open mouth and stunned expression.

"Hi, Jan." I put my bags down and throw my arms around her.

She hugs me back. Just. Then calls out, "Mike, Kate's here! She's early."

"That's okay, isn't it?" I ask. "I thought it'd give us more time to catch up."

I also thought I was family. I'm not so sure now.

"Of course." She takes both my hands into hers, then turns to call out again. "Did you hear me, Mike?"

"Yes, love." His voice comes from the distance.

"It's wonderful to see you."

"I've missed you both."

Seeing her reminds me how much. When Charlie was alive and life was normal, I kept in touch with his mum more than he did. Text messages, phone calls, coffee catch-ups. She liked to drop by with leftovers for Charlie and I'd tease her about cooking for her six-foot-tall baby. Other times, I'd come by their place after I'd done some baking to show my appreciation.

I got on well with Mike too but it wasn't like my bond with Jan. The bond we used to have. Somehow we both got lost in our grief after that.

She gives me another hug. Maybe she's feeling the same way.

"Can I come in?" I ask.

"Oh, of course. I don't know what I was thinking."

Jan shuffles back like an old woman, though she's far from that. As far as I know, she still plays tennis and goes for walks.

I pick up the gift bags and close the door behind me, turning to see Jan has stopped in the middle of the hall, staring at a black-and-white photo from our wedding, framed and blown up to practically life-sized. Not *that* photo, a different one thankfully. The happiness in our faces pains me. The fact that Charlie is gone kills me. No matter what he's done, he didn't deserve death. And his folks didn't deserve to lose their only child. My throat tightens.

Jan tilts her head to stare at the picture. "I look at this photo every day."

I used to look at our wedding photo every day too. Hell, I

can't stand here. If I do, I'll burst into tears or scream or fall apart.

I pull myself together. "Do we have time for a cup of tea before we head off to dinner?"

"Sure." She takes my hand, then shouts again. "We're ready for a cuppa, Mike. Better put the kettle on."

He calls out. I don't catch what he says.

We amble down the hall. Jan still has my hand as we wander past the other framed family photos, bald baby Charlie wrapped in a blue blanket, blond toddler Charlie with his proud parents. I'd forgotten how blond he was as a small child. Then there's the three of them in ski gear on holiday, Charlie's graduation, extended family at a gathering, a lifetime of memories, each one simultaneously painful and beautiful.

When we get to the back of the house, I break away from Jan.

"Hey, Mike," I yell, though I can't see him yet.

The open-plan living area has a modest footprint but feels large thanks to the wall of windows that flood the room with light, though 'flood' might be an exaggeration on an overcast afternoon like this. Kitchen, dining and lounge, every area is immaculate, which is nothing less than I'd expect from Charlie's neat-freak parents. It's where he got it from.

But I spy imperfection in the corner of the lounge, colourful items that look out of place.

"What's all the commotion?" Mike calls out. "Kate, it's you."

Movement in the corner of my eye by the glass sliding doors at the back, I hear Mike's voice but don't focus on him, my gaze riveted to the colours in the corner. A playmat with zoo animals printed on the cover. A blue plastic crate filled with toys, a teddy sitting in front of it, a baby rocker pushed to the back.

How can this be?

I look from Mike to Jan.

Jan sighs. "I told you to put that stuff away."

Mike spreads his arms. "I was going to. Got carried away outside with the new shelves I'm making."

Silence.

I see. I hear. It's not quite sinking in.

"We're sorry," Jan says. "We were going to tell you."

No, they weren't.

I put the pieces together. Jan stalling me at the door, calling out to Mike I was here. She wasn't asking him to put the kettle on. She wanted the baby things out of the living room. Baby things. In the living room.

Jan and Mike only had one child. And now they're grandparents. Charlie's child.

Chapter Thirty-Five

The tears on my cheeks have dried, tears of shock and dread. Jan is perched on the sofa beside me, Mike leaning forward on another chair.

Jan places her hand on my knee. "You caught us unawares. We should've been better prepared. You should never have found out like this. I'm sorry, Kate."

"It's okay," I say.

It's not. Nothing is ever going to be okay again. I came to their house with gifts that now sit unopened by the entry to the living room. Presents from Perth. I was armed with a photo of the other woman, wondering how to tactfully ask them if they had any idea Charlie was having an affair, wondering if they'd recognise her. They knew. They'd always known. I'm the one who didn't know a thing. Useless, just like Charlie told me I was.

"You've got a grandchild," I say.

"He's a beautiful healthy boy," Jan says. "That's what everyone wants, a healthy baby."

It's what I'd wanted too, before I miscarried. Oh God, this

is too much. The child I'd never been able to have with Charlie…

Someone else has had that child.

I should scream and shout. I should be hysterical but there's nothing left of me, no dreams left intact, no emotions that haven't been crushed.

"This is Charlie's child." Jan keeps her voice low. "You've got to understand. This is our flesh and blood, our grandchild, and we love him."

She's right. Their son is dead and they've suffered immense grief. They don't have other children and won't be getting any other grandkids. Of course they love the little boy. He's a baby. Innocent. All babies deserve the best.

"I'm happy for you," I say, even if it's only one per cent true. "But I'm still in shock."

"You're a kind and generous soul," Mike says.

I shake my head. I'm desperate and that's quite a different thing.

"We weren't expecting any of this," Mike says. "At first, we thought it was some kind of cruel trick or joke."

Pain grinds inside my gut. "You knew Charlie was having an affair."

"No, Kate. We knew no such thing. That came as a shock to us too, you know. That's partly why we didn't believe it at first. It's not the way we raised him or the example we set. Jan and I have been married for over forty years and neither of us has ever strayed."

No, but they mollycoddled Charlie, made excuses when he did something wrong. Not their Charlie, he could never do anything wrong.

I've heard the stories about when he hit another boy at school and it wasn't his fault. The other kid started it. Then there were the speeding fines Jan and Mike paid for when Charlie was a medical student, because he couldn't afford it.

And when Charlie was going to lose his licence because he'd lost too many demerit points, Jan said she was the one who'd been driving. Nothing was ever Charlie's fault.

"So, when did you find out?" I ask.

"It was five months after Charlie passed away. We got a phone call out of the blue. Couldn't believe it. We'd never even heard the name Sophia till she called."

"Sophia…" I try to think if Charlie ever mentioned her name and come up blank.

It explains a lot. That was about the time when Jan and Mike started to get distant. Jan got in touch less often, stopped inviting me over, said she'd rather get out of the house and meet me somewhere else. It didn't seem strange to me at the time. Grief causes people to do weird things.

Mike clears his throat. "She was thirty-nine weeks gone, a huge belly, ready to drop. She'd waited till the end of her pregnancy to tell us. We didn't dare believe her at first. We had no clue about any of this and she came out of nowhere."

"It must've been hell for you." I can't help my sarcasm and jealousy.

Mike ignores my bitter tone. "Kate, for us, this child was nothing short of a miracle. It was beyond our dreams. The grandchild we thought we'd never have. Maybe because I'm a man you think I don't feel this so strongly but I do. Blokes want to be grandparents too."

Silence. Despite what Charlie has done, I can't take away their joy at being grandparents. I'm not that heartless.

Jan clears her throat. "I'd always hoped you and Charlie would have children. We both did. Charlie said he was keen but that you wanted to wait because you were younger than him."

My chest tightens. Why would he have said that?

"That's not true," I say.

"It's okay, Kate. We respected your decision."

"No, you don't get it. I wanted kids and Charlie kept putting it off, first one thing, then another. *Him*, not me. I didn't want to force him."

I ball my hands into fists. If they make an excuse for Charlie now or tell me I've got it wrong, I'll lash out.

They don't.

No, I didn't force Charlie. I got pregnant by accident instead. *You should've stayed on the pill*, he'd said. Furious. *It would've been safer*. I didn't want to stay on the pill. I wanted to be ready whenever Charlie said it was time to have a baby.

A pregnancy. A tiny foetus. Then I miscarried after the attack. Despite this, I was 'lucky' because the knife wounds weren't deep enough or in the right place to hurt the foetus. The knife didn't get any arteries either. Lucky. The miscarriage happened a couple of days later. Emotional trauma.

I didn't tell Jan and Mike about the pregnancy or that I lost the baby, not after the reaction I got from my mother. So I'm not going to tell them now. They don't need any more loss in their lives.

"Why didn't you say something?" I ask in a small voice.

Mike shakes his head. "I knew we should've told her."

Jan glares at him. "Yes, and you wanted *me* to do it." She turns to me. "A couple of times I tried but I knew it'd break your heart. And then you started talking about moving back to Perth and I thought…"

I can work out what they thought.

After a while, Jan adds, "It was wrong of Charlie to have had an affair. I'm sorry."

Yet somehow I doubt Charlie would've been sorry. He'd have been the cliché husband, making excuses, saying the affair meant nothing, promising it would never happen again. How the hell would he have explained a baby?

Jan fiddles with her fingers. "Naturally we asked for a DNA test, to be sure. But truth be told, we knew as soon as we saw him. He's the spitting image of Charlie when he was a baby. There was no mistaking it."

My throat that's already tight threatens to close up completely but I force myself to speak. "D-do you have any photos of the baby?"

Jan reaches for her phone on the coffee table, scrolls through and keeps hold of the phone as she shows me some pictures.

She can't stop smiling. "This is when he was newborn and that's the world's proudest grandfather."

In the photo, Mike is beyond beaming. I nod.

"This is him at three months."

I stare at the picture. There's something about the baby's smile, the blue eyes and blond hair, the expression that is so like Charlie. Jan picks out other photos. The baby laughing, playing with broccoli on a tray in his high chair, sitting in a kiddie swing, cuddling a teddy, sleeping.

If only I wasn't so riveted to every picture. Instead I can't stop staring, though I know lives have been lost and other lives have been changed and life as I know it will never be the same again.

"What's his name?" I squeak out the question.

"We call him CJ. Charles James."

She named him after Charlie, of course she did.

Suddenly this all becomes so much more real. It's not a nameless newborn. This is a small human with needs and wants and a personality and people who love him.

Why did I come to Melbourne? Or to this house?

To find out more about my husband and now I'm finding out more than I wanted to know. Charlie had a life I didn't know about, and maybe it's connected to the night he was killed and maybe it's not. But I came here to find out more and I'm bloody well going to do it.

"I'd like to meet her," I say.

"Who?" Jan asks.

"Sophia."

Jan's mouth falls open as she turns to Mike. He spreads his arms, doesn't say anything.

"Look at me, I'm not angry." I lie. I'm a seething, molten mess of emotion, my insides ready to erupt and engulf everything around me. So calm on the outside, I add, "I'm not going to stab her in the back or do anything silly. I'm upset, yes. I've been crying, yes. Surely that's only to be expected. You've had months to get used to this whereas I've only had five minutes."

Jan straightens. "Leave it with me and I'll get back to you later. We'll see."

"It can't wait, Jan. I'm only here for the weekend."

"If she'll talk to you, you can always do it over the phone."

"Some things are better done face to face. It'll feel more real if I can see her." I hold my hands out. "Just her, not CJ. That'd be too much for me. Please, let's do it while I'm here."

"She's right, Jan," Mike says.

Silence.

After a while, she says, "Okay."

"Why don't you go and call her now," Mike adds.

"Sure." Jan stays put for another minute, then leaves the room, phone in hand.

Mike and I have the world's most uncomfortable conversation while I strain to listen in to what Jan's saying, the words a faint drone in the distance. Instead the two of us talk football, a safe subject despite the fact Charlie was the footy fan, not me.

Jan comes back and sits beside me. She pushes a piece of paper across the coffee table. "She'll see you tomorrow."

I point to the paper. "What's that?"

"The details, the name of the café where you can meet."

"Can I get her phone number?"

Jan shakes her head. "You can reach her through me if you need to."

Not very trusting and maybe I don't blame her.

"Do you have a photo of Sophia on your phone?" I'm not even sure why I ask, maybe because Jan has been so careful to edit the pictures she showed me.

Jan's fingers turn white as she grips the phone in her hands. She looks across at her husband.

"Might as well," he says.

After a bit of fumbling, she shows me a photo of a woman on the outdoor suite in their backyard, a baby on her knee. CJ is giggling, a happy baby.

But that's not the woman in the photo I was sent. The woman Charlie had his arms around had brown hair, whereas the woman on the screen of the phone is blonde. This is a different woman.

Chapter Thirty-Six

I'm early, checking out my surroundings and wishing the woman hadn't chosen Segovia. I love this café. Or I used to. Not so much now.

The place is archetypal Melbourne. It runs off a lane that's filled with people despite the constant drizzle but, then, that's Melbourne too. Small tables, cramped wicker chairs, lots of wood in the interior, framed photos lining the walls. The coffee is excellent, the food even better, but I'll stick to a cappuccino today.

I grabbed an inside table, my back to the wall so I can see who's coming. Somehow I can't shake those primal survival instincts.

She said two o'clock. Five more minutes. What if she doesn't turn up? I drum my fingers on the table.

Through the window, I see a woman under the awning, scanning the tables. Yesterday I was in too much shock to get a proper look at the photo. Blonde, that part was imprinted on my mind. Attractive, I remember, the rest a blur.

The woman lingers in the doorway, taking off her coat to reveal a tight sweater and slim legs clad in skinny jeans, so tiny there's an adolescent look about her. Fresh, as if her whole life is ahead of her.

As soon as her eyes land on me, she freezes, then smiles. She must've seen my picture in the paper after Charlie died. Maybe the sunglasses I wore at the time didn't cover up as much as I thought. I lift a hand to wave but can't bring myself to smile as she comes towards me.

"Hello, Kate," she says when she reaches the table. "Is it okay if I call you that?"

"Only my mother calls me Katherine." I motion to the chair on the other side of the table, grateful she doesn't want to shake my hand. "Take a seat, Sophia. I've already ordered, as you can see. You might want to do the same."

So civilised, that's me.

She turns to a waiter clearing plates from the next table and asks for a decaf soy chai latte. There she is, slim, delicate, fine features, a little younger than me, mid-twenties perhaps. The woman who stole Charlie, who slept with my husband, who gave him a child. The woman who still has a piece of Charlie in her life and a beautiful baby to bring up because, despite everything, that baby deserves to be loved. Jealousy burns inside me.

"Thanks for coming," I say.

"I've heard a lot about you."

"And I know nothing about you. Funny, that." She remains frozen in her seat, so I add, "I'm not trying to give you a hard time. Just saying."

She tilts her head. "Sorry we had to meet this way. It's true, Charlie hardly mentioned me to anyone. I was his little secret."

"It's a bit harder to keep things a secret when there's a baby involved."

She nods. If I didn't know better, I'd think that was a guilty expression. I need to draw her out.

I shrug. "I know what Charlie was like. Attentive. Saying all the right things. Making you feel special. He was like a drug that made you want more." I sip my coffee, peering over the top of the cup like an understanding girlfriend. "Things must've been different after you found out you were pregnant."

"You got that right. Charlie was furious. He blamed me." She sighs. "It took him a little while to get used to the idea but I was like, no, this can't be a secret forever. It's not how I wanted things to be. He came around pretty quickly in the end." She presses her lips together. "There's something you should know. Charlie loved you. I have no doubt about that."

Is she trying to make me feel better? She can't be a good person. Someone who's kind and thoughtful wouldn't carry on an affair with a married man, would they?

Her decaf soy chai latte concoction arrives and she thanks the waiter.

I hold her gaze. "I had no idea Charlie was seeing you."

Because I thought he was seeing someone else, a brunette. I cover my mouth to stifle a giggle. I shouldn't laugh when this is too tragic to be funny.

"Are you okay?" she asks.

I take another sip of coffee, my lifesaver. "Charlie was always working long hours, so I didn't pick up on anything."

"He was pretty good at keeping the two things separate," she says. "I felt like I never had enough time with Charlie, like he was always being pulled away from me, so I took whatever time I could get with him. It was a bone of contention between us, that's what Charlie called it."

Of course he did.

She sips her coffee or chai or whatever the hell that is. "Sorry, I didn't intend for any of this to happen and I certainly didn't get pregnant on purpose, I want you to know that."

But you're the one who's got his baby. My heart clenches. I didn't get pregnant on purpose either and I'd do anything to be able to go through that pregnancy, to have a child, our child.

Yes, even after all this, I'd kill to have Charlie's child. I'd give up my soul and my self-respect to be the one who was having an illicit affair, to be the one doing wrong, so I could be the one with the baby.

My throat tight, I swallow. "Go on."

"It was after Charlie got over the shock of the pregnancy that I realised he was never going to leave you. Like, never. That was when it really sank in. I mean, if he wouldn't leave for the baby, he wouldn't leave for anyone or anything."

Her voice drips with jealousy, as if she doesn't understand she has the most important part of Charlie that's left.

"How far along were you when Charlie died?" I ask.

"Sixteen weeks."

And I was only six weeks pregnant at the time. Charlie, how could you do that? And what the hell were you planning on doing about it?

Sophia prattles on. "I was already showing. People at work were giving me strange looks and a couple of my friends were even asking, hey, are you pregnant? I was the first in my group to get to that stage of, like, starting a family and stuff. And it was pretty obvious we couldn't keep it a secret forever." She stops, her brow crinkling. "Hey, are you okay?"

I roll my shoulders. "Yeah, I'm fine."

"I'm sorry. Charlie wanted to do the right thing by the baby. He was working out how. He'd already got a nice apartment for me and the baby. That helped big-time. Don't know what I'd have done, otherwise."

Her words aren't quite sinking in. "He bought you an apartment?"

"Yeah, well not outright obviously because that would've been too much money." Sophia stares at me, perhaps taking in my shocked expression. "It wasn't for me. It was for the baby. Charlie wanted his son to have a roof over his head."

Leaning back in my chair with a thump, I bite my lip and

look around the room. I see everything and nothing. A cosy café. Walls, closing in on me. Sounds, stuck in my head. Chatter from nearby tables. I'm surrounded.

I should've known. How can I have been so stupid? I knew Charlie had made large withdrawals from the bank. Huge, in fact. He'd also made sure there was no money trail or none that I could find.

The apartment is in her name. I don't even need to ask. Meanwhile young, pretty Sophia is happy to tell me everything. So naïve.

His son…

"Where's CJ now?" I ask.

"With my mum."

My heads spins out of control. I don't know why I'm here or what I wanted to get out of this. Where did they meet? Was it love at first sight? When did he see you? Where did you go together? How long was this going on for? All questions I don't want answered. I even wonder if she was at the funeral and whether that really matters.

Resting my elbows on the table, I rub my temples and force myself to focus.

"I'm sorry," she says. "I've said too much."

If she says sorry one more time I might toss her decaf soy chai crap bullshit latte across the room. I'm fooling myself again. I don't have it in me.

"Did the police ever get in touch with you after Charlie was killed?" I ask. "You know, when they were investigating his death."

"No."

So the police never found out about the affair. They didn't do their job properly. They're not rocket scientists, as Laura tells me.

"And you didn't think to contact the police yourself?" I ask.

"No, what for?"

I swallow back the pain, the resentment, my pride. "You saw a side to Charlie that I didn't. Do you have any idea why someone would have wanted to hurt him?"

"No."

"Do you know anything about Andrew Scarparolo, the man who killed Charlie?"

Her brow furrows. "Only what I've read."

"You hadn't come across him somewhere before? Even in passing?"

She shakes her head.

"Had Charlie ever done anything to make someone mad?" I ask. "Did he mention problems at work or someone who might hold a grudge?"

"No."

"There's something I want to show you." I scroll several years back through my phone and show her the picture that used to be my favourite in the whole world, our wedding photo, Charlie with his arms around me, the two of us young and in love.

Her mouth falls open. "Oh my God, I've got the same photo, only it's me and Charlie."

She's reaching for her bag at the foot of her chair. I hold my hand out. She stops and straightens.

"That's not what I wanted to show you."

I find the recent photo of Charlie with the topless woman, the brunette, the one who's not Sophia, and hold my phone out. I give her time so it can sink in, her eyes widening, brow furrowing, her expression changing from composed to confounded.

She presses a hand to her chest. "Who is she?"

"Charlie's girlfriend, I presume."

"When? Charlie? No, that must be from a long time ago."

"I checked the metadata." I stand, retrieving my coat and

bag. "That photo was taken twelve months before Charlie died."

Her face clouds over like a thunderstorm, pale skin turning grey. I don't need to ask her if she was seeing Charlie then. Her expression says it all.

Am I a bitch? I don't care.

I slide my arms into my coat and get the hell out of there. Drizzle has turned to rain. My coat is showerproof. My hair is wet in seconds. I push through the crowd, trudging along the main road, not sure where the hell I'm headed. I'm not used to being a bitch and maybe I do care just a little.

Too many people here, even in the rain. They're crazy, all of them. A laneway. I turn and stalk along the bluestone paving. Graffiti covers the walls. Rain mixes with the tears on my cheeks. Nothing much here, other than a green wheelie bin ahead.

"Motherfucker," I mutter.

I kick the bin over. A powerful push kick. Rubbish bags and refuse spill out onto the ground. Not my problem. Breathing hard, I stagger to a stop.

A wiry guy with long grey hair tied back in a ponytail is sheltering in a doorway. Cigarette in hand, he stares, then draws back on his cigarette and blows out the smoke.

He can stare all he wants. He doesn't know me.

If I can do one thing, I can punch and kick hard. I can do a lot of nasty shit. I can choke and throw and take a man down and spit and grab his balls and twist them. I can fight. And kill.

Chapter Thirty-Seven

One more person I need to catch up with in Melbourne.

I've been back to my room, showered, blow-dried my hair, repaired the damage. I also grabbed something to eat before meeting Amy for a drink. She couldn't stretch to dinner, not when she might be stuck with me for a lengthy period. That'd be too much of a commitment. So, after years of friendship and one year of not-really friendship, we're having a drink.

As soon as I see her walk into the bar, my heart fills with warmth. Her cheeks are rosy from the cold outside, her hair a magnificent mess of amber curls as always. She's wearing about fifty layers, as she's wont to do in winter, ripping off her scarf and shrugging out of her coat as she walks. A wool skirt hugs her ample hips, an oversized jumper covers her huge boobs. She always thought she was fat. To me, she looks perfect.

I stand. "Oh, Amy."

She hangs her coat and scarf on a hook behind my chair while I hold my arms out, wondering if this will be like old times or like more recent times. To hug or not to hug. I hope she's not asking herself that question.

"What the hell?" She throws her arms around me.

We fall into a hug that's warm and reassuring and reminds me of the friendship we used to have. Amy is soft yet firm, holding me tight, her cold cheeks warming up from resting against mine.

The memories come rolling back. Eleven years ago, my first holiday with friends, a girls' long weekend in Sydney. It was when I got to know Amy properly. We were having so much fun we stayed an extra couple of days, sunning ourselves at Bondi and shopping during the day, hitting the bars at night, giggling on the way back to our room.

Years later, there was a distinct lack of giggling after a painful break-up. Amy had taken her long-term boyfriend's odd behaviour as a sign they were on the verge of an engagement, whereas he was on the verge of breaking up with her. Which he did. It took her a long time to recover from that. I helped her find a new place to stay, dragged her out of the house to go out, invited her around for meals, nurtured her till we got the old Amy back.

It's her again, the old Amy.

"Let's get the ball rolling," she says. "What would you like to drink?"

"Oh, maybe a mineral water."

"Mineral water?" She gives me a look like I've spat on the grave of a loved one. "Nothing less than a margarita will do. Be right back."

I'm not so good with alcohol anymore but I'm very good with Amy so I let her buy the first round. She comes back grinning and sets two salt-rimmed margarita glasses on the table. I take a sip. It tastes good. Too good.

"How are you doing, Kate?" she asks. "How's Perth?"

"I'm settling in pretty well." Perth's not the problem. It's everything else. "You look sensational, as always."

She gives me a shy smile. "No, I don't."

"Well, beauty is in the eye of the beholder and I'm the one doing the beholding." I smile right back at her. "How's your mum doing, Amy? I don't even know how her treatment is going."

Amy has spent a lot of time looking after her mum, or last I heard that's what she was doing. Guilt swamps me. One of the reasons I moved back to Perth was so I could help my mum out and she's relatively healthy, not like Amy's mother. Breast cancer, surgery, chemotherapy, they're all life-changing things that she's been through with her mum. I visited Michelle a couple of times after she came home from hospital, once before Charlie died and once after. I must've started off being a friend to Amy and to Michelle. But cancer treatment is a process. It takes time. Months.

"I'm sorry I wasn't there to help you through it," I say.

"That's okay." Amy shrugs. "It's not like you didn't have anything else on your mind."

She tells me about the chemo and the radiotherapy, and how her mother is on the road to good health.

"Mum would love to hear from you," she says.

"Of course."

I make a mental note to call her. It's a small thing that might make a big difference.

"I'm seeing someone," she says.

"That's fantastic!" I reach for her hand. "You're glowing."

She can't help but smile as she tells me about her new fellow, an accountant-turned-graphic-designer who's changing his life around and wants her to be part of it. It's been a long time between boyfriends and I know how keenly she's felt the absence.

"And the girls? How are they doing?" I ask.

She gives me the rundown on Mel and Steph, the girls we used to hang with. I wasn't part of the group in the same way as Amy. They were her friends and I always felt like a hanger-on.

Or was that the way Charlie used to make me feel? He liked Amy, my fat and frumpy friend, he called her. Not to her face, of course, and I never let on but it occurs to me that he liked her because she admired him and agreed with everything he said, practically putting him on a pedestal. Unlike Mel and Steph who once teased him when they were tipsy, something Charlie never forgot. No, he didn't like them at all.

"Can you tell me something?" I ask.

"Sure."

"Is it true that Mel and Steph were only friends with me because of you?"

Amy scrunches her face up. "What? No. Where on earth did you get that idea?"

From Charlie. He said they used to talk about me behind my back, that someone had told him, a reliable source. I surmised it was probably Amy but maybe it was Charlie all along.

My mum used to say the same thing back when I was in high school, or a version of it, different versions depending on the occasion. *She doesn't really like you. She's only friends with you because you help her with her homework. They only invited you to that party because they felt sorry for you. He's going to leave you soon, mark my words. A doctor will never stay in a serious relationship with you.* But he did.

First my mum, then Charlie. Shit, were they both that mean and manipulative, and I didn't notice?

I change the subject. "I found out something about Charlie. He was having an affair."

Amy's eyes widen. "What? No. Charlie? You're kidding."

Then later, "What a bastard. I'm so sorry, Kate. I had no idea he was such a prick."

I love Amy's over-the-top reactions, her certainty. She asks all the right questions. She listens. She knocks back her margarita and orders a second from a passing waiter. I hand over my credit card, refusing to let her pay.

"Look," she says. "As much as I liked Charlie, I sometimes got a strange feeling from him, not like he wanted to get it on with me, but more like he was toying with me."

True. He flirted with her just enough to make her feel special and get her on side. It didn't concern me at the time because I knew there was nothing in it. Now I think that's exactly why I should have taken more notice.

I tell her about CJ, the baby. Shocked at first, Amy gives me a hug. She holds on tight, doesn't want to let go. When she returns to her seat, her face is wet with tears.

The waiter slides Amy's margarita onto the table, gives us a strange look and leaves. Two drunken females, that must be what he thinks, except I'm not drunk. I've barely touched my cocktail.

"There's something I never told you," I say. "I should have. I'm sorry."

"What? What else can there possibly be?"

She knocks back a mouthful of drink, tosses her head back, curls flying, dramatic and down to earth all at once. I've got the old Amy back and I adore her.

"When Charlie and I were attacked, I was pregnant," I say. "A few days later, I-I miscarried. I lost the baby."

Another hug, heartfelt reactions from Amy, more tears – from her, not me. Somehow I've run dry.

"Oh, Kate, I'm so sorry for everything you've been through."

Acknowledgement is exactly what I need. The sympathy is nice too, even if I may have headed too far into pity territory. We talk. I explain. I tell her about my sorrow in a controlled manner. Yep, that's me, controlled.

"I wish you'd told me," Amy says.

"Me too. Honestly, I wish I had. Don't know why I didn't." But I do. My mother's face flashes before my eyes, her horrible words ringing in my ears. "I was beyond talking after Charlie died. My life was shit. Things are better now."

Amy nods. "Better than shit. Wow, that's some improvement."

She makes me smile.

"Miscarriages are more common than you think," she says.

"Have you…?"

"No, not me. I was thinking of some of the women at my work. One of them was forty-two at the time and didn't think she'd get another chance. She didn't, in fact."

"That's tough."

"Whereas you're still young."

My breath catches in my throat. *Don't say it.*

"You've got your whole life ahead of you," she adds. "You'll get snapped up by some fabulous guy, I'm sure of it."

"Thanks."

Stop there, Amy.

She doesn't. "You can have another baby."

And just like that she cancels out every pleasant word she's said tonight. I can never have that baby, that remaining piece of Charlie, our baby. That baby is gone.

It hits me like a punch in the face, and I've had a few of those at training so I know what it feels like. This is why Amy and I aren't friends anymore. Suddenly I can't wait to get out of here and back where I belong.

Chapter Thirty-Eight

I've never been so glad to be home because maybe this is home, after all.

Ryan picked me up from the airport. I'd already told him about CJ over the phone. Sometimes I have to remind myself that the phone isn't only for texting. It's for talking too. And then I talked some more in the car. Talk, talk, talk.

This man is a star. Ryan has already cleared and wiped the table, pushed the chairs back in, put the leftover Mexican takeaway in the fridge and the plates in the dishwasher because he knows I'm not going to relax while the place is messy. He's so at home here with me and also Esmeralda. Meanwhile I put my feet up on the sofa. Shoes off, of course.

He brings me a Curly Wurly, which I savour because you're never too old for a Curly Wurly. He lets me eat and I let him talk about what he's been doing over the last few days – a bit of work and a considerable amount of time pining over me, if he's to be believed.

"I was surprised that first night when you asked to stay over," he says.

So was I. "I hope it wasn't too much of a shock for you."

"Remember when I saw you at the Elysian? I was with a mate and you were meeting someone."

I swallow. "Sure."

"I can't tell you how disappointed I was that you didn't come with us for dinner."

How differently that night could have turned out if I'd joined Ryan. I wouldn't have met Will and he wouldn't have ended up in hospital.

"That's sweet," I say.

"So how did your evening go with Noah?"

"What evening?"

"I saw him outside the pub that night and figured you were meeting him."

"N-no, not him."

Noah was there? Shit, maybe he followed me and rammed poor Will with his car, out of jealousy perhaps. Is that possible?

No, now I'm getting ridiculous. First, I'd suspected Ryan, and now Noah. He'd never do something like that, but he *is* the sort who might send me an anonymous photo of Charlie with another woman, even though he denied it. That'd be more his style.

Esmeralda joins us, settling on my lap, a welcome distraction.

"Thanks for taking care of her." I pat her soft fur and she purrs. "She's clearly not traumatised by my absence."

Ryan slides his arm around me. "She's a survivor."

"And not spoilt in the slightest."

Esmeralda rubs her face against mine, bringing a smile to my face.

"I think she's trying to come between us," I say.

"It won't work."

"You sound very confident."

"Always."

Esmeralda looks at Ryan, then at me, as if deciding what to do, then leaps onto the rug. I should've got Ryan a small gift for looking after her but I've been so consumed by my own problems that I forgot. It's never too late to be more caring, because I do care.

"Is it okay if I ask more about Chloe?"

Ryan smiles. "Man, she was so much fun. She was hilarious, curious, inquisitive, always asking lots of questions. She looked just like her mum, you know."

"Do you have more pictures?"

"I have a whole album at home."

"Any on your phone?"

"Of course."

We sit side by side looking at the photos that are beautiful and sad and many things all at once. His ex-wife is in some of the photos. Olivia's a very attractive woman, not that I should be surprised.

Ryan stares at his phone. "It's amazing how much she resembles her mum."

"She does." I examine the photo. "But I think there's a hint of Italian in there too, despite the blonde hair. There's something about her expression that reminds me of you."

She doesn't have his nose, which is a good thing for a little girl, but her dark almond-shaped eyes have come straight from Ryan.

"Thanks," he says. "It's nice to hear that."

"So, was Chloe a girly-girl?"

"She was a real mix. She knew how to twirl her hair and look cute when she wanted to get her way. And she loved singing and dancing. Once when Christina Aguilera was on the TV, Chloe copied all the sexy moves." Ryan's eyes widen. "It was a bit of a worry. She was only four but I could see her at fourteen, putting on the moves, with boys chasing after her."

And now he'll never get to see her at fourteen. Or twenty-four. More of those tears in my eyes.

"She was also into climbing," he says.

"Really?"

"Onto the furniture, mostly. One time when she'd got up early in the morning, we put *Bluey* on for her so we could get some extra sleep. Then we heard her crying out so we jumped out of bed. She'd pushed the sofa and the coffee table up against the TV cabinet. I don't know how she did it. It must've taken considerable muscle power from a little kid. And she'd climbed up onto the TV cabinet and couldn't get back down again so she was panicking."

"What a hoot."

Nerves simmer in my stomach because I haven't even touched on the most difficult question of all.

"I know this is difficult for you. Can I ask what happened with Chloe?"

Ryan breathes in through his teeth. "There was a car crash. Margaret was driving."

"You mean Olivia's mother? Chloe's gran?"

I'm bowled over by a wave of guilt, by not being able to imagine what that must've been like, and by imagining the horror all too well.

Ryan nods. "Margaret had taken her to see her sister who lives in Gidgegannup. It's not far but that's a country road. Margaret went through a stop sign, drove right through, didn't see it. A four-wheel-drive slammed into her, and the car rolled. It was quick. Catastrophic injuries. Paramedics said Chloe died immediately."

"God, I'm so sorry." I cover my mouth. "And Margaret?"

"Serious injuries, hospital, rehab, like you'd expect. It's not been quick for Margaret, though. She's tortured by it. Sometimes I think she's dying a slow death."

"But you still see her, your mother-in-law?"

He nods. "I might be all she's got. Olivia refuses to talk to her, so the poor woman has lost a daughter and a grandchild."

"I'm so sorry." Repeating myself but I can't help it.

"People are shocked I'm still in touch with Margaret but she didn't wake up one morning and think, today I'm going to act recklessly and crash the car and kill my beautiful grandchild." His voice cracks. "The bizarre thing is that she drives like an old lady, lets other cars through in the traffic, never goes over the limit. Not that she drives anymore. But when she did."

I raise my eyebrows. "You've forgiven her?"

"Not at first."

So much compassion in one man. "That's incredibly kind of you."

"Not really. Margaret's a good person who made one terrible mistake. I couldn't walk around with all that hatred in my heart."

Is that what I'm doing? I haven't even forgiven myself yet, not properly. I'm human and I've erred and maybe that's okay.

He adds, "Despite everything that's happened I can't bear for Olivia to walk around with it either. I know how much better she'd feel if she forgave her mum and let her back into her life."

"Do you still see Olivia?"

"Nope. I see her husband from time to time. He lost both his parents when he was younger and he really gets it."

"You see your ex's new husband?"

"Yeah, we go back a long time. He can't stand seeing Olivia that way either. He wants her to forgive and move on, especially since they're having a baby."

"That's wonderful, um, for them." I bite my lip. "Must be hard for you."

"Yeah, it is."

Nothing I say is going to fix this. I pull Ryan into my arms and hold him close. He hugs me right back.

Other people have tragedy in their lives. I'm not the only one. And Ryan's loss is immense.

Chapter Thirty-Nine

Another week has passed and I don't know what I've done with myself. I've spent as much time as I can with Ryan, had a couple of coffee catch-ups with Laura, been to the park for my workouts, and drafted some copy for David Hinton and another guy from his agency. Though I've got a foot in the door, I'm still trying to prove myself with them. And I've been distracted, I must admit.

The good thing about working for myself is that I'm not confined to a nine-to-five. This morning I got up early and got stuck into some editing, so now I can go for a walk in the middle of the day while everyone else is working. Because it's sunny and I feel like it. Sadly, also because I don't have nearly enough work to keep me occupied.

I lace up my much-loved purple Converse. Back door deadlocked, check. Bag slung over my shoulder, check. I close the front door behind me, in awe of the beauty of a fine Perth winter's day. Sun filters through the trees, the leaves backlit against a pristine blue sky. No dark clouds, not even any fluffy white ones. I'd missed out on this living in Melbourne.

Mum texts me about painting the lounge room for her. I text her back, letting her know I'll get onto it soon.

A gentle mewing comes from Esmeralda as she slinks around my legs and looks up at me with her stunning blue eyes.

I crouch down. "Are you lonely?"

She rubs her face and neck along my legs, then rests her front paws on my knees. I run my hands along her smooth fur and keep stroking her. The amazing thing is, she lets me. She feels warm.

"Have you been lying in the sun? Can't say I blame you." I pick her up and keep stroking. She nuzzles into my neck, such a turnaround. I never want to leave this house or this beautiful cat who's finally come to like me. I like her too. And Ryan. Well, Ryan probably comes before those other things.

I wander down the front path with Esmeralda in my arms, feeling slightly guilty at the sight of my car out on the street. I was too lazy to bring it in last night, or too preoccupied with Ryan, one or the other.

A vehicle catches my eye. I know that car from Ryan's description. Subiaco is full of huge SUVs driven by women who can't park them and men who drive them to the holiday house down south where it's freeway all the way, never taking those things off the road. But this four-wheel-drive doesn't look the part. It's unwashed and old with a couple of dings in the door and side panel. I can't make out the figure through the tinted windows, can't even be sure it's male, yet I'm certain that's Domenic Scarparolo sitting in the driver's seat.

Ryan's at work, not at home. I could scream for help. Or call someone. I should probably take a photo of the car, then go inside and phone the police, but Scarparolo will be gone by then and the cops will think I'm overreacting. After all, I'm the nutter who thought my husband's attacker was still out there when I knew he was dead, the crazy woman who freaked when she found a smashed wedding photo, who probably broke it herself.

Above all, I should be sensible. Blood rushes through my veins. Screw sensible. I'm sick of this shit. What good has it done me to be smart, aware, careful? It didn't stop Charlie having an affair, one, two, how many I don't know. Didn't stop him from dying in that car park.

My breaths come short and sharp, my mind buzzing, filled with white noise, like someone has turned the volume up in my head. A survival response. I've been through this before. Then the sound recedes.

Suddenly I'm in the car park. Andrew Scarparolo – I know his name now – has told us his girlfriend has collapsed. He's not frantic or breathy or worried like a man with a sick partner. He is none of those things, but Charlie's in doctor-mode and doesn't notice.

Pointing towards the car with an open boot, Scarparolo stands back to let Charlie go first between the cars. He steps ahead, of course, because he's Charlie. The hair on the back of my neck is standing on end.

"Hang on, Charlie," I say.

He holds a hand out as if to silence me. As much as I hate to admit it, this is typical Charlie. Superior. He always knows better. He takes my arm and drags me with him. Dismissing me. *Not now, Charlie.* Something is off here, even if I don't know what. He lets go of me, then steps to the back of the car and sees there's no one slumped in the open boot, no girlfriend lying on the floor.

He looks around. "What? Where?"

The attacker barges through, and heads straight for Charlie. I'm too slow. I can't believe this is happening. Charlie's hands are by his sides, hip height. *Raise your hands, get them up there.* I want him to do that one thing. *Please, Charlie, please.*

Tunnel vision. The guy is standing between me and my

husband. My eyes are riveted to the frayed edges of the neckline of the T-shirt under the guy's windcheater and the hair on the back of his neck, then on Charlie's expression. Annoyed. He doesn't even know trouble when he sees it.

Charlie doesn't see the knife.

I don't see it.

I see Charlie slump over, his hands clenching his stomach. He's been punched in the stomach, that's what I think. Then the guy's arm moves like a sewing machine needle, in and out, stab, slash, slice. Blood runs through Charlie's fingers. He's trying to grab the knife, blood dripping from his gut, his internal organs.

My heart jolts. I can't run. I can't leave the man I love here. He's everything to me and I would die on the inside if I left now.

I try to get Scarparolo's back. I'm fast but he flings his hand backwards and slashes my arm. The first cut. I try to block the next strike. Too slow. He slides the knife into my stomach. A shallow or deep wound, I don't know. Hot, it feels hot. I stagger back. Fear grips me. Adrenaline surges through my veins. Debilitating.

He jabs Charlie with the knife again, so quick, so easy. I try to grab him from the rear again but all he has to do is fling his knife-hand back. I've got my arms up, thank Christ. More cuts to my arms, both of them bleeding.

Charlie is hunched over, swaying, blood everywhere. Scarparolo grabs Charlie's hair and yanks his head up like he's a sheep at an abattoir. He slashes his throat. A river of red. The horror.

Desperation gurgles inside me because it's too late. I've failed. All I can do is try to get away. I turn to run. Scarparolo reaches for me, shoves me and I hit the concrete. I roll onto my back. He's coming at me but I can kick while I'm on the ground. *Smash*, the first kick lands. *Crack*, I got his knee. *Kick*,

kick, kick, each one for Charlie. He might be gone but he's still my reason.

Scarparolo doesn't care about the pain. The time it takes me to get up is the time it takes him to get between me and the way out.

He's not breathing hard. He's contemplating, calm, composed. There's no evil grin, no nasty glint in his eye, no sweat beading on his upper lip. This is not fury or desperation or revenge.

This is just business. And that's the scariest thing of all.

Esmeralda screeches and leaps out of my arms. Circling behind me, she makes her escape. Thank Christ for Esmeralda.

A flashback. Over. She's brought me back to the moment. I'm not in that car park. I'm at the front of my house. And I'm not putting up with this shit.

My chest heaving, I storm through the front gate because one way or another I'm going to have it out with Domenic Scarparolo. I'm reaching for the phone and keys in my bag. To take a photo, run my key along the side of his four-wheel-drive or start my car, I don't know.

It's him. He looks at me and waves. The prick.

The engine revs as his car starts up. Movement ahead. He's taking off. I get the car rego, repeat it in my head, since he's got a rear number plate now. My fingers won't work properly as I try to take a photo. The phone clatters onto the asphalt. Halfway across the road, I scramble for my phone, unlock the Mini and dive into the driver's seat. I say the rego number out loud as I take off, imprinting it in my mind.

I drive. I follow. I'm sick of doing the right thing. The world isn't doing me any favours so I should stop being so prissy and get my hands dirty instead.

For once in my life, I wish my car wasn't so conspicuous, a red Mini with a white roof. Not much I can do about that now. The traffic is heavier on the main road. I keep a couple of cars between us, unsure whether it makes any difference if he sees me or not.

I keep driving. We're on the freeway, the endless freeway, everyone heading in one direction along a treeless tarmac lined with concrete barriers and mesh fencing.

Eventually Scarparolo takes the off-ramp. So do I. The lights go red and I have to stop. Bugger. Maybe I've lost him. I repeat the rego out loud and in my head, my mantra, the numbers and letters I don't want to forget. As soon as the lights turn green, I take off like the clappers.

He's up ahead, turning a corner. I make a mental note of the street names. A people-mover shoots out of a driveway, then slows down like he hasn't just cut in front of me. Useless bloody Perth drivers. He speeds up, slows down, driving down the middle of the road so I can't overtake. I can't see past the car and have no idea if I've lost Scarparolo. Finally he takes a right and gets out of my way.

The street ahead of me is empty. In the distance, a four-wheel drive sits parked in a driveway. No, not parked. It's edging into a garage, or at least I think that's what's happening.

A group of kids is kicking a footy around on a stretch of treeless verge. The ball bounces onto the road, then off at another angle. I slow down. A boy rushes towards the road, then stops himself. I come to a halt and wave so he knows it's safe to step onto the road to get the ball. I wait until he's back on the verge before taking off, my eyes on the driveway Scarparolo went into. I pull up outside the house. Number twenty-one. At least I think it was his car and I think it was him and I think it was this driveway.

Biting my lip, I stare at the house. I should leave. Even if

I've got the right place, it won't do any good to talk to Scarparolo.

I open the car door and get out because I don't give a shit what's sensible and what will work. I'm dealing with a stalker and I've been giving him way too much attention, which is exactly what he wants. He sent me flowers – I'm sure that was him – and I freaked. He broke into my house and smashed my wedding photo. I went to the police and he got more attention.

I'm done.

Breathing fast, I knock on the front door before I change my mind. I've read so much about personal safety and security and stalkers that I'm practically an expert and know exactly what to do. I'm going to talk to him one final time and make myself very clear. Then I'm going to cut off all communication and refuse to give him any response. He wants attention and thrives on my fear. No more.

A woman pulls open the door. Her long bleached hair is pulled back into a ponytail that exposes her dark roots. A scrubbing brush and a couple of rags in one hand, she looks like she's been caught in the middle of something. She's wearing tracksuit pants with a cropped windcheater that exposes her substantial midriff. Strange to have your stomach bare while you're cleaning.

"Is your husband home?" I ask.

She pushes the gum in her mouth to one side. "Who said I'm married?"

"I'd like to speak to Domenic."

"And who are you, that you think you're so special?"

"Why don't you just get him?"

"It's okay, babe." A man's voice in the distance. "I got it."

I step backwards off the porch onto the front path while I wait, checking out the street but the only other people I've seen so far are the kids playing footy.

Domenic Scarparolo swaggers through the open doorway

and comes so close I'm forced to take another step back. His wife joins him, standing by his side.

"I don't know what you think you're playing at." I raise my hands, using them to talk. "But I've had enough."

He grins. "Darlin', I'm not playing."

"Listen carefully. Stay away from me. Don't come to my house. Don't wait out on my street. I don't want to see you at my local supermarket or suburb. Stay away."

Nothing moves, no breath of air, no sounds of life from the surrounding street. A magpie's call breaks the silence, the pretty song failing to soothe.

He folds his arms. "Actually, I've been wanting to talk to you for a while."

I stare at him. He's not agitated, not much of anything. I've said what I had to say, and now I'm not so sure. Whatever's going on, maybe we should get this out of the way.

"Do you know what it's like to lose a child?" he says.

My heart sinks. *I do.* I was pregnant and lost my baby. This is too close to the bone. How can he know? He can't. He's playing with me.

"My mother committed suicide thanks to you." His voice is matter of fact like he's telling me he had eggs for lunch.

"What?"

"She died of heartbreak. Andrew was always her favourite, ever since we were little kids. It was always *Andrew this* and *Andrew that,* and the rest of us kids got left to fend for ourselves. But she was still our mother, *my* mother. When she lost him, it sucked the life out of her. She should never have outlived her son. It's not natural. Then she topped herself." He jabs a finger in the air. "And that's all down to you."

I shake my head. "She didn't die because of me. I didn't kill anyone."

But I have. I have killed.

He sneers. "Lying bitch. You are so full of shit."

Bitch. Did he send me that text message? I step back and he takes a step forward, like an evil shadow.

He keeps up the finger-pointing. "You don't know who you're dealing with. You think you're so smart. My brother was a psycho." Smiles. "Me, not so much."

I walk backwards, unwilling to take my eyes off him till it's safe, my hands held out.

"See, I believe in family," he says. "Blood is thicker than water and all that shit. Family first. And you fucked with my family."

I won't go near his family. Don't want anything to do with them. He doesn't need to worry about that. This is the last time I'll go near him.

"Stay away from me, that's all I want." Those will be my final words to him. I turn away.

And get hit in the back of the head. Pain mixes with shock. Something clatters onto the path. I stagger forward, then turn back to look. There's a scrubbing brush on the path – that's what hit me in the head – and a dirty rag on my shoulder. I pull it off with two fingers and let it drop to the ground.

Scarparolo's wife laughs, takes aim and throws the plastic bottle of Jif at me. I lift my arm to cover my face. It's the laugh that gets to me. A switch flicks inside. No more.

I crouch to pick up the plastic Jif bottle, throw it back at her, then the scrubbing brush, while she cowers, a nervous giggle escaping her lips. Scarparolo shifts across to stand in front of her, his arms outstretched as if protecting his wife.

"Stay away from me and my family," he yells, louder than before.

Gladly.

I turn away. There's movement on the footpath. An old woman has come out of nowhere. Either that or I wasn't looking. She stops.

"It's okay," I say to her.

She glares at me.

"Goodbye, darlin'," Scarparolo shouts. "And good riddance."

That's exactly what I'd like, never to see this guy again, good riddance, this person out of my hair and my life.

I get in the car and start the engine. The white-haired woman is shuffling up her front path. I pity her, living next to these two. Scarparolo has barely moved, his arm around his wife, standing his ground like a proud husband.

I drive away.

Chapter Forty

Painting is the perfect occupation for me right now. Though it's been years since I've done this, it's all coming back to me. Mum has already done most of the prep by patching up a couple of chips in the wall before I arrived. Then we pushed the furniture into the middle of the room and covered everything with drop sheets. I've already painted the ceiling so I'm halfway there already.

I mix the wall paint with a wooden stirrer to blend in the shiny film glimmering on top, then tip a good amount into a plastic bucket to use for the cutting in. I climb up the ladder and start at the top, painting the cornices first, then cutting in around the doorframes and skirting boards. I'm lucky the enamel paint on the frames and skirtings is in good condition so that's one less thing to do. I've used a heap of blue tape to make sure I don't go over the edges.

Jack used to say the cutting in was the most boring bit, even more boring than the prep. Not surprising I should think of him when I'm in the house where we grew up. I don't find it boring, though, far from it. It's soothing, or it might be if my right shoulder didn't ache from the repetition. One thing's for sure, I'm going to appreciate a nice warm bath after this, a long soak till I turn into a prune.

My phone buzzes. Laura has texted to wish me luck with the painting and with my mum. *Only one of those things is hard work*, I text back with a smiley face. There's also a long message from Amy, apologising because she realised how harsh it sounded when she said I could have another baby. She must've talked to someone who explained it to her. I don't reply. But I must call or text her mother to see how her recovery is going after radiotherapy.

Mum stands in the doorway. "Are you ready for lunch?"

I straighten to stretch my back. "I'm all right, thanks, Mum. I've already eaten."

I get back to work, enjoying the repetition, the smooth movements, even taking perverse pleasure in the ache in my shoulder. It feels good to be doing something manual and to be helping.

The roller is next, my favourite part of the job. I tip white paint into the tray and dip the roller into it, making sure it's thick with paint. Then I roll it along the walls.

You roll it, Kate. That's why they call it a roller. My brother's voice is in my head, followed by his laugh. It's good to have my head filled with talk about the roller, instead of the other crap it's usually filled with. I start to see the dull walls transformed. First coat, done.

Mum comes back, placing a tray with a plate of muffins and mugs of tea on the table. Her eyes are wide. "Oh, Kate, I don't know what I'd do without you. This looks so much better than before. I can't wait to see it finished."

"Won't be long now," I say.

She hands me a mug. "I've made tea."

I wrap my hands around the mug and take a sip. Normally I'm a coffee person but this hits the spot, soothing and refreshing.

I sit cross-legged on the drop sheet. Mum hands me a muffin and I dig right in.

"Renata made them," she says.

"Delicious," I say, though if she'd told me that sooner, I might not have had one.

"She said to me, *Julia Mamotte, you deserve them*." Mum peers into the lounge room. "Renata's a great friend but I can't ask her to help with things like this. It's too big a job, the painting, that is."

"No need." I sip my tea. "That's why I'm here."

"I'm lucky to have such a wonderful daughter."

Her blue eyes light up and I think, it's true, we do look alike except for the colouring. We chat for a bit. We drink our tea. We act like a normal mother and daughter, which makes me think I'm finally making inroads with her.

The second coat of paint rolls on faster than the first. Maybe that's my imagination or perhaps my good mood, not that it matters. I'm in the zone.

Still, the other things in my life don't leave me, not completely. I haven't seen Mum since finding out about CJ, though we've spoken on the phone. Sophia has Charlie's baby, the baby I should have had. The thought makes me nauseous, or maybe that's the *delicious* muffin.

I've already started cleaning up when Mum comes back into the room. "This is amazing." She can't stop smiling. "I can't believe what a difference the second coat has made."

"I can."

"You should've called me. I'll help with the cleaning up."

Mum gets to work, carefully peeling back the blue tape at one end of the room while I start at the other. She's my mum. I should tell her. A baby is a public thing. There's no hiding it.

It's easier to talk while I'm cleaning up. Then I don't have to look at her. I remember Laura telling me this was a technique she used with her kids. None of this face-to-face stuff because they're more likely to open up if they don't have to look her in the eye.

Mum follows me into the laundry room where I rinse out the roller and brushes while I give her the full story.

"I knew it as soon as you showed me that photo," she says.

"Did you?"

"I had a feeling. You've always had such rotten luck. Why should this be any different?"

Deep breaths. I concentrate on running water over the roller. It comes back to me, how much paint has soaked in, the way it takes ages till the water runs clear. I hear Mum's voice behind me and try not to tune in.

She places a hand on my shoulder. I stop. This is too much. She puts her arm around me.

"Oh, my poor Katherine." She passes across a towel for my hands, draws me into a hug and holds me. How long since we've had a proper hug like this?

Eventually she breaks the embrace. "You must be devastated. I had no idea. I can't believe Charlie would do that to you." Her lower lip quivers. "So Jan and Mike are grandparents?"

And she's not. I stiffen. *Work. Keep busy. Keep moving.* I place the roller and brushes on some newspaper so they don't drip and take them outside. Mum follows. The noisy neighbours are at it in their backyard, music playing, adults shouting, a few swear words thrown in, kids squealing, barbecue smells filling the air.

At the edge of the garden, my back to Mum, I flick the roller to get the water off, once, twice, many times.

"The news about the baby has hit me hard," I say. "Especially since I was pregnant when we were attacked and then lost the baby." Mum looks blank, so I add, "You must remember. It was just after that night."

"Darling, are you sure?"

"Of course I'm sure."

"I think you're confused."

No, I'm devastated. There's a big difference.

Something else I remember. That night, when I was fending off the knife, I was fighting for Charlie even though I'd seen the blood. Even though I thought he was dead, my love for Charlie was driving me. My reason for living. I felt guilty later because I should've been fighting for my baby. Too late, always too late.

I feel Mum's hand on my shoulder from behind.

"It's understandable that you're muddled after everything you've been through," she says in a low voice. "But I think you're mixing this up with something else. After your father left, *I* was the one who miscarried. I only found out I was pregnant after he'd gone and then I was all alone. As if that wasn't bad enough, then I lost the baby."

I was a kid then, five years old, but it's never left me. Mum made it clear to me and Jack, the pain she was in, the loss she felt.

"I hid it from you at the time. To protect you."

No, she didn't.

"I talked to you about it when you were older."

She did.

"The stories are too similar. You've got it mixed up in your head."

I turn to her, the roller still in my hand. "Mum, I was pregnant. I miscarried. That baby is gone. I can never have that baby again."

She presses her lips together. "They were my exact words at the time. *I can never have that baby again.* You see, this is why you're confused. Trust me, you weren't pregnant when you and Charlie were attacked and you didn't miscarry. You've been through a lot, such terrible loss and grief, but not that particular loss. You're in great pain, Katherine, and you're confusing that pain with my experiences and the things I've told you in the past."

The racket from next door makes it hard to think. Mum's not lying to me. She's my mother. Surely she wouldn't crush my feelings at a time like this. She's not that conceited.

My heart crumples, a strange sound escaping my lips.

She places her hand on my shoulder. "Deep breaths, darling. You've let this get to you but you'll get through it."

At the time, I didn't tell anyone else about the miscarriage. Maybe this is why. Maybe I've got it all wrong.

A memory lingers. I was still in the hospital after the attack when I had a blobby bloody discharge, and I knew what had happened even before I called for the nurse. Mum was there later. I can picture myself curled on the hospital bed. I'm looking down at myself right now.

It's a memory. It's real. It has to be.

Or maybe I've created this stupid, sad, tragic fantasy after finding out about Sophie and CJ, and it's all in my mind. I need help. I need to get this stuff out of my head.

Surely I can't be this deluded. Or perhaps I can.

I'm suddenly tired, fatigue sinking into my bones, settling in my gut, nausea setting in. Before, all I wanted was a warm bath. Now I feel an overwhelming need to lie down. To escape. But I can't do that and show Mum yet another sign of weakness.

My darling

That's what you were once.

Sometimes I can't feel you anymore. And it scares me. Despite everything, I can't bear the thought of being without you.

I used to feel you all the time: when I woke up, when I went for a walk, when I lay on the bed, in the sunshine, in the shadows. In the summer, you were a cool breeze brushing past. In the winter, a burst of warmth. Not always, though. It's cold in Perth and plenty of times you made it colder.

Where have you gone? I've been through so much loss and change and hardship that I cling to the things I know. My safety blankets.

Fortunately or unfortunately – I don't know which – I still love you and always will. Therein lies the tragedy. And now that you're gone, no one new can enter your life and love you. Maybe I'm all you've got too.

You weren't a saint. No one knows that better than me or feels it more than I do. So many things I'd like to forget or block out. You've caused me unbearable pain. You ripped my heart out when you died and you keep ripping out little pieces, big pieces, rubbing sandpaper into the wounds.

I can't bear the pain you caused when you were alive and I can't bear it now you're gone. How can you do this to me? Why can't you leave me in peace? Yes, I scream out those words and want you back in my next breath. Which is what I do. I force myself to take a deep breath.

Whatever you did, whatever happened before that night, you didn't deserve to die the way you did. No one deserves that.

Sometimes I think I can't go on, but I do. One foot in front of the other, as they say. Not that I think of ending it. I only have one life and I'm not giving it up, not when I know how precious life is and how fleeting.

Besides, I can't get justice if I'm dead. I'm searching for the truth and for what's right because those things will set me free. I'm getting closer too, so close. I've come this far. There's no backing out now. I have to be strong.

Love you always

Chapter Forty-One

Though I was tired when I got home, I didn't let that stand in my way. I wanted to phone Michelle, Amy's mum, before I forgot. She sounded like a mother, concerned and kind, and made me feel better, which was exactly the effect I was trying to have on her. That, along with a warm bath, hit the spot. Both were exactly what I needed.

I'm walking out of the bathroom when I hear it, a baby crying, the plaintiff cry of a newborn, its tiny lungs filling with air. I stop, startled. It sounds so close, almost as if it's in the house but that's not possible.

Is it one of the neighbours? I pad to the rear of the house, unlock the back door and check outside but the crying disappears, then gets louder when I go back inside. Perhaps it's someone walking down the street. My phone pings. I ignore it. Instead I stride through the house, determined to check out the front but the doorbell rings before I get there. I imagine someone standing outside with a little baby, someone who needs my help.

I pull open the front door. It's Noah. I jump. Nearly have a heart attack.

"Kate, are you okay?" he asks.

A hand on my chest, I try to shake off my shock. The infant's cry sounded so clear but there's no baby. It's in my head, my imagination going crazy. If I didn't know better, I'd say Charlie was finding some way to taunt me from the grave.

"I'm so sorry," Noah says. "I texted you to say I was coming up your front path."

"Oh, I didn't check my phone."

"I'll try to be more careful next time." He motions to the paper bag in his hands. "Anyway your Uber Eats order has arrived."

The idea of an intimate dinner, just me and Noah, doesn't feel right, not when I've done such a good job of avoiding being alone with him.

I'm going round to Ryan's later. He's at a family dinner and he invited me, but I didn't feel comfortable with the whole meeting-the-family thing. He understood. He always does.

Meanwhile Noah is likely to tell me I'm overreacting to a simple suggestion to eat together, especially when he's already turned up with a takeaway. Maybe he's right. This doesn't have to be a big deal.

"You look like you need some cheering up," Noah says.

"Is it that obvious?"

"And I have Thai food."

"You know, that sounds better than the ham and cheese toastie I was going to make." I hold the door open for him. "I need to get an early night but a girl's gotta eat."

His face drops, only for a second, and I sense he doesn't like it when I set the boundaries, then he smiles and steps through the door.

In the dining room, we chat while I get plates and utensils from the kitchen. The spicy smell of green curry and Pad Thai fills the air as Noah opens up the containers, and any doubts I had disappear.

He's also brought along a bottle of champagne and though he's often generous, I've never been less in the mood for bubbles and celebration. Or losing my senses, for that matter.

My eyes on the bottle, I set the table. "I won't have any, thanks, but I'll get you a champagne glass if you like. Or I can get you a beer from the fridge."

He gives me that same face-dropping look for a moment. "A beer would be beaut."

I come back with the drinks, sit down and clink glasses with him. We eat. We chat. We act normal. Noah is excited about his office renovation and the bespoke furniture but doesn't want to say too much because it'll spoil the surprise. He invites me to come and see it. Soon.

Now that Noah's here, the truth is bubbling beneath the surface, the things I've found out about Charlie, things I should tell Noah because if anyone will understand, it's him. He and Charlie had been through thick and thin together over the years. Besides, I'm turning over a new leaf. No more secrets.

So I tell him. I go through the whole story about Sophia and CJ and once I start, I can't stop. I feel as if I'm hovering above the table looking down at the two of us. Distanced. Watching someone else's life, not mine.

Things look different from above. I see Noah's readiness to console me and, most of all, the lack of surprise. I drop down to earth with a thud.

"You knew, didn't you? You're the one who sent me the photo of Charlie with another woman."

Lips tight, he lowers his gaze. "I didn't know how to tell you. You loved Charlie so much I thought you wouldn't believe me and that it'd break your heart."

"When I first got the photo, I asked if you'd sent it."

A pause. "I'm sorry."

"And you knew about the baby? You knew all along."

"No, Laura told me about the baby but that was only the other day."

I raise my eyebrows. "You didn't know before?"

He shakes his head.

I wait, like a television detective who sits quietly while the person they're interviewing speaks to fill the silence.

He rubs his temple. "Not so long ago, I hired a private detective to look into Charlie's life. He's the one who gave me the photo but he must be a pretty crap detective because he didn't find out anything about a baby."

Or the other *other* woman. The woman in the photo is a brunette and Sophia has blonde hair. And there might've been more for all I know. A crap detective indeed.

"A few things make sense now," Noah says. "It was very unusual for Jan not to invite me over for home-cooked meals, and now I can see the reason for that. Not that I minded shouting them dinner, not after the number of times they'd fed me when I was a student."

"They had baby things in the house."

Pain rips through my chest. I see it before my face, toys in the corner of Jan's living room, photos of their grandchild, Sophia sitting opposite me at Segovia.

"Kate, I'm sorry. You deserve better than this. You deserved better than Charlie." He pauses. "I always thought so."

I didn't think so at the time, whereas now it seems obvious that Charlie and I were probably over anyway. Could we have survived an affair? Or affairs? Maybe. Some people do. But there's no way our relationship could have survived him having a child with someone else. That's the end, right there. Marriage over. God, I'm so sick of Charlie and the weight in my gut. How can he continue to do this to me?

My phone buzzes behind me. Glad for the distraction, I get up and pick up my phone from the kitchen counter. It's Ryan, sending a photo of the tiramisu his mum made for dessert, saying she'll be sending me a large piece. It throws me. I don't know how to reply so I send back a smiley face.

"That's Ryan, isn't it?" Noah is standing behind me, so close I can feel his breath on my neck.

I drop the phone face down on the counter and spin around, stepping to one side to give myself space. "Does it matter?"

"Come on, Kate. You know exactly what I'm talking about. I can see what's going on. I'd whisk you off to Paris if I could. Or Rome. Or New Zealand. The snow's good there right now. I'd do all that and more if I thought for a minute you'd say yes."

I push past him to the table. "I should clear up."
And you should go.

Noah is silent, sorting the empty containers into a pile and putting lids on the ones that still have food in them, while I whisk the plates and cutlery into the kitchen. He puts the leftovers in the fridge, the giant paper takeaway bag still in one hand.

He hands it to me. "I wanted you to find this when you were fishing out the containers."

I peer inside. At the bottom of the bag lie a bunch of unused serviettes and a burgundy velvet box that makes my heart thud in the worst way possible. "I can't take this."

He stares at me, waits, then slides his hand into the bag and opens the velvet box. An antique bracelet lies inside, a magnificent setting, Etruscan style, red stones and pearls set in burnished gold. It's exactly my taste.

I shake my head slowly. "I can't."

I know this and I've been denying it. I'm so good at blocking out the stuff that's too hard to deal with. For months, I've been trying to make sure I don't lead him on, careful to keep him at a distance, but things weren't always this way.

"Kate, you mean everything to me," he says.

"Noah, please don't."

"No, I've got to say this. I've admired you from afar for years but I would never have approached you while you were married. Never. I had too much respect for you. I never crossed that line. You can vouch for that."

Though it's not a question, I nod. Still, I often felt he had an interest in me. Charlie noticed too.

"I waited a year to give you some time to grieve," he says. "Maybe I left it too long. I moved to Perth to be closer to you, so we can both start afresh and build a new life together."

"You don't need to say any of this." My face hot, my voice breaks.

"But I do. We've shared so much together, the two of us, tender moments. I know you better than anyone else. No one else understands you the way I do. No one else can compete. You know it too, Kate."

Tender moments, no, please don't go there.

But he does. "I've been waiting for the right moment, then I realised that moment is never going to come."

I step back. "Noah, I can't do this. I can't be with you in that way. You were a dear friend to Charlie and you're my friend and that's where it has to stay."

"We were so good together."

No, don't bring that up.

"In fact, I'd say we were extremely compatible. You know exactly what I mean. You weren't faking. What we had was real and alive and intense. It's what's kept me going all this time."

My skin burns, flames engulfing me, the mistakes of my past.

One night.

Charlie had been dead six months, only six months, and I wasn't coping. I remember the tension, frustration, something building up inside me, feeling like I was going to explode. I didn't know what I was doing, not exactly, or why my body was doing that to me, only that I had to get things out of my system. It was too easy. Noah was there, ready, willing. And so was I.

I also remember feeling like a freak. What kind of grief was this? What kind of person was I?

"It was only sex, Noah." I blurt the words out.

"No, it was much more than that, and you know it. We made love. You called out my name."

Images flash before me, like previews from a steamy movie. Noah kissing me, his tongue in my mouth. The way I ripped my shirt off and pulled his hands onto my breasts. Electricity surging through my body as he pulled my nipples into his mouth. That moment of no going back. The desperate need. Primal. Impulsive.

Memories I don't want to have. Afterwards I worked out I should've searched for someone further from home, a man I didn't know and would never have to see again. Like I did with my second one-night stand. And then with Will, after I came to Perth. I'd learnt my lesson by then.

Hell, I never wanted to hurt Noah. I wanted to get the hurt out of my body and that's quite a different thing.

"You have to understand," I say. "It may have been a wonderful evening but it can never happen again. It's not what I want."

"Kate, you have no idea the things I've done for you." His voice trails off.

He's still holding the velvet box with the bracelet. I tip the box closed, grab both his wrists and lead him towards the door. He doesn't resist.

I pull open the front door. "You're my friend and you have to go."

Noah's shoulders are slumped, his face washed out but

there's still a glimmer in his eyes. "That's where you're wrong. Friends is the one thing we can't be, Kate."

He presses a gentle kiss to my lips, a kiss I don't want. Now he's crossed a line. If it was anyone else, I'd shove him hard right through that door.

"Please leave."

I close the door behind him and lean back against it, wiping the back of my hand across my mouth. My knees weak, I wonder how much lower I can sink. I don't want to remember that night. I want to forget.

Chapter Forty-Two

Somehow Ryan makes everything all right.

Later that evening, he texts me that he's on his way home from his parents' place, then messages as he's coming down the rear laneway.

Tonight has been too much for me. Unable to wait, I lock up the house and run out the back as he's reversing into his garage. After Noah left, I put on some comfort clothing so I must look like an apparition in my fluffy dressing gown and Ugg boots.

As soon as Ryan gets out of the car, I launch myself at him and don't let go.

"Wow, that's some welcome," he says. "Are you okay?"

"Yeah, I'll tell you about it later."

He's still holding me. I want him to hold me forever. Eventually I stop acting like a crazy woman and loosen my grip on him.

"Let's get you inside." He takes my hand. "Hang on, first things first."

He reaches for a container on the front seat, then leads the way through his back garden, which looks pretty at night illuminated by bollard lights. The light's on inside too, warm and welcoming.

"Can I get you anything?" he asks as soon as we're inside.

I shake my head. "No. Yes. A glass of water."

In the kitchen, he puts the container in the fridge, then pours a glass and hands it to me. "That wasn't meant to be a trick question."

I smile between sips of water. I love that he can make me smile. I love being around him. I need him.

Ryan stares into my eyes. "You look exhausted. Has something happened?"

"Yes. No."

He gives me a moment. "Well, that's a big improvement from your previous answer of *no, yes.*"

I don't want to talk about what's happened with Noah. I couldn't bear it if Ryan thought that was how we started, when our first night together meant so much more to me than the things that came before.

"You're so patient." I lean against the kitchen bench. "Whereas I'm such hard work."

"You're struggling," he says. *Understatement.* Then he adds, "But the fun parts of your personality keep filtering through."

"Fun?"

"Like the way you kill cockroaches and drink vanilla vodka at three in the morning."

"No, the vanilla vodka was you." I smile wearily. "I hope it's okay if we go to bed."

He leads me to the bedroom and slides the dressing gown from my shoulders, then wraps his arms around me, rubbing my back.

"Who said fleecy pyjamas with polar bears weren't sexy?" he whispers in my ear.

I rest my head on his chest. "I'm not feeling terribly amorous tonight. I hope you don't mind."

He presses a kiss into my hair. "I know just the thing. Why don't you get into bed?"

Ryan comes back five minutes later with two mugs of steaming hot cocoa. I wrap my hands around the mug he passes to me, while he settles on top of the duvet beside me.

"My sister was disappointed you didn't come along tonight," he says.

I am too. Big mistake. I sip my hot chocolate.

"Maybe next time," I say.

"She's even nosier than my mother. Both of them are dying to meet you."

"Sounds like you've got a lovely family."

"I do. Except for the nosiness. And the screaming children."

"Screaming?"

He shrugs. "Not really. Alice and Luke are only four and six, so it was a late night for them. They got a bit overexcited."

"I hope you weren't the naughty uncle who got the kids revved up before bedtime."

"No, we threw the ball outside for a bit when I first got there, then I toned it down after that. I was the responsible uncle who read them stories."

I picture Ryan with two little kids snuggling up beside him and listening intently while he puts expression in his voice as he reads out loud.

His eyes are on the photos of Chloe on the dresser, the silence between us telling me he's lost in his own thoughts. He had a life and a beautiful daughter and a wife before I knew him. It helps put things in perspective and evens out my mood, not that grief is a competition.

We sip our hot cocoa. I enjoy the warmth of Ryan's body beside mine.

"I didn't mean to tease you," I say. "I'm sure you're a fabulous uncle."

"I try."

"And I'm sure you were a wonderful father."

"I tried to be a good husband too. It wasn't enough. Sometimes you can be the best that you can possibly be, and it makes no difference."

"You make a difference to me, an enormous one." I place my empty mug on the bedside table and reach across to wrap my arms around his strong chest. "Can you get into bed and hold me?"

"I can hold you forever."

He presses a kiss to my forehead, then lets me go long enough to take off his clothes, pull on his pyjama pants, and get into bed. I feel his bare chest against my back as he spoons himself around me, one arm under the pillow beneath my head, the other draped over my waist.

My eyes are closed, my mind still spinning, my thoughts out of control. After a while, the sound of Ryan's rhythmic breathing tells me he's asleep. It's where I'll be soon too, I hope.

The next morning we tumble out of bed. I'm still in my fleecy nightwear while Ryan rips off his PJ pants and rummages around in the chest of drawers in the corner.

I wrap my dressing gown around me. "You should always walk around like that."

I'm not kidding. That is one sensational butt.

He pulls on underwear and a pair of jeans. "Are you joking? It's cold out here. Not that you'd know, wrapped up in layers like that."

"I can share my body warmth."

I pull my dressing gown undone and draw Ryan into a hug, wrapping the sides of the gown around him.

"This thing ain't big enough for the two of us," he says. "Besides, I'm noticing some inequity here. You're dressed for an Arctic winter while I'm not allowed to put a shirt on."

"You're allowed." I turn away and look over my shoulder. "It's not encouraged, that's all."

He laughs.

Ryan insists I sit at the table while he makes breakfast. Apparently he makes the world's best scrambled eggs but he's run out of eggs and doesn't know how that could have happened.

"I've got sourdough for toast or I can run down to the bakery for croissants," he says. "Or there's always my mum's tiramisu for breakfast." When my eyes widen, he laughs and adds, "Tiramisu it is."

Oh yeah. I nod.

Ryan makes enough toast for both of us. And coffee of course. You can't live without coffee. I eat a small slice of toast to pretend to be healthy, then have dessert for breakfast. You only live once.

"Oh my God," I say between mouthfuls. "This is the best tiramisu I've ever had."

"Not as good as my scrambled eggs." Ryan scoffs.

I give him a smug look. "Well, I wouldn't know."

He asks about the night before, which is just that, a night that now seems like it happened a hundred years ago, so I give him the quick version, explaining I was very clear with Noah that I didn't share his feelings.

Things Ryan doesn't do: he doesn't go all macho and ask if he needs to talk to Noah, or ask if I've done anything to lead him on, or question my feelings for him. This man is too magnificent for words.

Charlie would've been furious if he thought for one moment I'd shown the slightest interest in another man. Or even if I hadn't. I remember when one of his doctor friends sidled up against me at a party, I had to 'accidentally' spill my beer on the guy to get him away. According to Charlie, I must've done something to encourage him and then I caused a spectacle. Charlie gave me the silent treatment for days after that, all the while maintaining he was tired and I should stop being immature. But, then, it doesn't matter what Charlie did, except for the fact I'm grateful that Ryan is Ryan.

A thought pops into my head. "Esmeralda will be starving."

"She'll survive."

"Not for much longer." I stand. "You know how fussy she is, and she's only started to like me. Don't want to get into her bad books."

Ryan gets up too. "Far be it from me to stand in your way."

I reach across for the plates but he covers my hand.

"I'll do that," he says.

The magnificence continues.

Grinning, I tie my dressing gown a little tighter. "I'll go out the back way."

"Sure. I'll walk you through the garage."

We walk through the backyard and he opens the garage door for me. I give him a goodbye kiss.

"Gosh." Smiling, his eyes dart from side to side. "Anyone could see."

I smile right back at him. "Better get back to my place before the crowd starts taking photos."

As I press the code to open the rear gate, I hear the even sound of Ryan's garage door being lowered. The house keys are still in my dressing gown pocket so I unlock the back door, calling out to Esmeralda who will no doubt slink out of some corner at any moment. Inside, I head for the laundry room where I tip a good amount of cat food into her bowl, which I've washed of course because Madam needs a fresh bowl. She has standards and I don't blame her. I top up her water too.

Comfortable though my fleecy PJs may be, I get dressed so I can maintain some semblance of decency. Jeans, Converse, a long-sleeved T-shirt, windcheater, my winter uniform.

I get a drink of water, then start tidying the kitchen, which is pretty clean to start with, yet I can't help myself. The house demands immaculateness. My arms laden with bottles and a few plastics, I head to the recycling bin at the rear of the yard. The bottles clatter as I dump them.

Esmeralda is lying near the bins in the shade. That's unlike her on a sunny day like this. One thing I know. Esmeralda likes the sun. Two things I know. Esmeralda is not stupid.

She's so still, lying on her side, her back to me. Her head is resting on the paving, a pool of vomit by her mouth. She's sick. Did she eat something bad?

I crouch down, my fingers hovering over her soft fur, too scared to touch her.

"Esmeralda," I whisper.

It takes all my strength to stroke her but she doesn't move, can't move, won't ever move again. My heart lurches. Esmeralda, who disliked me for so long, how can this have happened?

She's lying on something powdery like dried paint on the far side from where I'm crouched. I move across to get a better look, my eyes glued to her stomach. It's not paint. That's blood. Esmeralda's belly has been slit open.

I stand and scream. This time it's my stomach that lurches, bubbling with bile. I turn and step away and throw up. Vomit bounces off the concrete onto my Converse as I hunch over, my arms wrapped around my gut, wondering who and why someone would have done this to you, poor Esmeralda, who lived a quiet life, and thinking maybe tiramisu for breakfast wasn't so wise after all.

Chapter Forty-Three

"I know who did this, Alex," I say to the young policeman. "This is down to Domenic Scarparolo."

How can this be happening and how can I be on first-name terms with the police when I've only been in town a couple of months?

"I'm sorry you're so upset," he says.

Of course I'm fucking upset. I fold my arms, turn away and stomp across to the other side of the yard to stare at the concrete paving and the pristine garden bed that's as immaculate as everything else at this house.

Ryan was awesome, of course. I try to calm myself by concentrating on how he's taken care of me. He heard me scream, raced outside and jumped the fence. I guess he's getting a bit of practice at that now. He held and consoled me, then took over and did what needed to be done. He took photos of Esmeralda in situ, then got some gloves and placed her in a box lined with a blanket so I wouldn't have to look at her anymore.

Meanwhile I sat on a garden chair unable to talk or help. This is me, the woman who was assaulted by an armed attacker, who fought him off and killed him, who watched her husband die, then instructed the passers-by to call for an ambulance and the police. That *was* me. Now I'm a mess because my cat has been killed and she's not even my cat.

Luckily I have Ryan. He also called the cops, who are here now. They speak in soft but firm tones to Ryan, probably thinking, *it's only a cat*. No, it's Esmeralda who toyed with me and grew to like me, Esmeralda who had her own personality and idiosyncrasies. Yep, plenty of those, and now they're all gone.

I take a deep breath to join Ryan, who takes my arm.

Officer Alex Sheridan clears his throat. "Can you tell me if there's anything that makes you suspect Domenic Scarparolo of doing this?"

I raise my eyebrows. "Other than the obvious?"

He tightens his lips. "We'll investigate. We also need to know if you saw anything suspicious, if you sighted his car in the vicinity, or if he's been in contact with you."

"Nothing like that. He didn't leave a calling card."

He ignores the desperation in my voice and asks a few other inane questions while the other officer takes notes.

"So the house was locked when you came home?" he asks.

"Yes, always."

Noah comes to mind. He was here last night and that didn't go well but, no, he would never have hurt a defenceless animal. For one thing, he doesn't like getting his hands dirty and he'd never have done this, regardless.

"Can we take a look in the shed?" Officer Sheridan asks.

"Sure."

"Is that locked too?"

I stop in front of the shed door. "Everything is locked."

My hands unsteady, I fumble for a moment, then punch in the code. I use the same code for the gates and the lock box at the front. Pushing open the door, I switch on the light and let the two officers go ahead. Alex pulls up the blinds, letting in more light.

The shed is more like a showroom, the polished concrete floor practically glowing. Two carbon fibre bikes hang side by side on the wall. A wall-mounted tool rack has a glass surround, presumably so the tools don't get dusty. Labelled plastic crates are stacked in a corner. Perhaps Joel ran out of room on the shelves, where a stainless steel watering can sits by gardening implements and clean gloves, other items in equi-sized boxes, all labelled, of course.

Ryan and I stay by the doorway. Alex opens a cupboard where a rake, shovel and other unsightly implements stay hidden behind closed doors. He crouches down and pulls out a black-and-yellow cardboard box.

"Do you have rats?" he asks.

"No," I say.

Ryan clears his throat. "Actually, there was a bit of a rat plague in the neighbourhood about a year ago. I used to hear them in my backyard at night, till I set out some baits. Wouldn't surprise me if there'd been rats here too."

As if they'd dare. I doubt Joel would have put up with them for long.

"Didn't think you'd have that sort of thing in Subiaco," Alex says. How very dry of him. He stands, the box of rat poison still in his hand, and flips open the cardboard top. "It's been opened. Someone has used this. There was white powder on the cat's whiskers."

"Was there?"

Ryan turns to me. "Yeah, there was."

Surely I would've noticed. Then, maybe it was the shock that did that to me.

"Poison is one thing," I say. "But why cut her open like that? It was horrible." Like someone wanted to make sure she was dead or leave a message for me. That's how it feels, personal. Maybe they even took some sick pleasure in the act. "It's Scarparolo. It has to be."

"Does anyone else have the code to get into the shed?" Alex asks. "Or a key?"

Ryan had a house key while I was away and he was looking after Esmeralda but he's given that back to me. No way would he do something like this. Shit, first Noah, now Ryan, how can I even consider them capable of such terrible things?

"Not that I know of," I say. "Joel, the owner, let me choose my own code when I moved in and I presume he has an overriding one so he can remove my access after I leave."

"And where's Joel?"

"London. He wouldn't poison his own cat. He adored her."

Alex glances around. "There's no sign of breaking and entering, and the shed was secured. You're the only one with a code, the only person who can get in and out of there."

I could never have given Esmeralda rat poison and I sure as hell could never have slit her open. I have problems, plenty of them. I'm stressed, yes. Maybe slightly unstable. I'm not sick, not like that.

The officer stares at me, his gaze intense now.

My eyes widen. "You can't be serious?"

From Alex Sheridan, nothing. Ryan slides his arm around my shoulder and pulls me close.

Is that what they think? That I killed a man in self-defence so killing a cat would be no big deal. My stomach that has nothing left in it but bile starts to boil. I don't care what they think. I just want them out of here.

Chapter Forty-Four

The next day I feel dirty from dealing with the police and lost because there's no Esmeralda, no small creature to feed. I even miss the way she used to ignore me. I spoke to Joel yesterday to let him know she'd been killed, a difficult phone call but one I had to make.

Tossing my phone onto the bed, I decide a bath might be soothing, then my phone pings. It's Amy. I stare at the phone in my hand, realising now that she was practically the only friend Charlie allowed me to have. And I wasn't lonely when I had Amy.

I swipe up to check her message. She's returned from the specialist with her mum and the doctors don't need to see her again for another twelve months. That's great news. Also, her mum appreciated my phone call and said I absolutely have to see her next time I'm in Melbourne. Apparently her mum even said she'd take up Krav Maga and find me if I didn't! I text Amy back about the three of us catching up next time I'm in town.

There's no point holding a grudge. (I don't text that part.) Amy and I can be friends, maybe not best friends, but we can still be something. It's not right that we're ghosting each other or doing whatever we were doing.

I run the bath and then come back to the bedroom. A new text. Amy tells me her mum would love that and so would she. But we'd better not let her mum get started on the margaritas. It seems we're having an actual conversation. And I like it.

After a bit more chat, I take a photo of the bubble bath I've prepared and shoot across the image, saying I'm busy for the next half hour. Amy sends a smiley emoji and the words, *So jealous*.

Warm water engulfs me as I sink into the bath. Leaning back, I close my eyes. I remember how Amy was in awe of Charlie, his medical knowledge, his knowledge in general, and how she'd listen attentively to his every word.

I remember Melbourne, another time, another life, when Charlie and I had a bath together, followed by sex that fell into the category of mind-blowing. His tongue on my nipples taunting me, his fingers gently caressing, tension building, his erection sliding into me. Oh God, the memories.

My eyes spring open. I remember something else. It comes back to me, the moment I walked back into the bathroom after running a bath for myself, and Charlie was soaking in the water acting as if nothing was unusual.

"What are you doing?" I giggled, thinking he was teasing me. "That's *my* bath."

But Charlie wasn't laughing. He insisted he'd run the bath for himself.

"You must be imagining it if you think you did." That's what he said. "Maybe you heard me do it and got the idea in your head."

And I thought maybe I had.

It's not that he was cheeky and took over my bath. That wasn't the problem. It was that he told me I was mistaken. Me. When he knew damn well he was lying.

It makes me wonder how many of my memories are tainted and how much I've got wrong.

———

Days pass. As they do.

This morning I forced myself to write copy for a capability statement for a small engineering business, another job I got through David Hinton's agency. I also have to edit a blog for a company that does electrical engineering, only I'm dreading it because I don't understand the article or what the company does, so I do the mature thing. I procrastinate.

Rachel Jones, Noah's financial planner friend, has emailed me to let me know how happy she is with her web updates. I always like to read through the copy after the sites have gone live to make sure there are no small mistakes. People sometimes add in random capital letters or headings don't get formatted properly, that sort of thing. I read through the copy on her website. Looks good.

I spot a sentence where I'm not sure of the phrasing. I stare and wonder what I wrote for Noah's website, so I navigate there and scroll through. A number at the bottom of the screen leaps out at me. The AFSL number that every financial planner must have.

I've seen that number before – 669, nearly the number of the beast.

My fingers clench the mouse. I stop. I must be wrong. I go back to Rachel's website. I check and double-check. It's the same number. I drum my fingers on the table. Something is wrong, very wrong.

I can't phone Rachel and ask her why this number is the same as Noah's. No, but I can make a follow-up business call to ask how the print job for her brochures turned out. I pick up the phone before I change my mind. She's chatty, which makes my job much easier.

"I didn't mention this before," Rachel says. "I've got news, rather large news. You'd have seen how big I was if you were here. I'm twenty-four weeks pregnant."

A pang of jealousy shoots through me. Pregnant, I remember what that was like, the excitement, the fluttering in my stomach, the overwhelming fatigue, only you're supposed to have a baby at the end of it. Not twenty-four weeks. I never got that far. But I was definitely pregnant despite what my mother tried to tell me.

I shouldn't be jealous. I should be happy for Rachel. And I am.

"Congratulations, that's wonderful news."

I ask about morning sickness and pregnancy and how she'll balance running a small business with having a baby. Rachel assures me she's got this under control and gives me the rundown on how her mother is coming over from Singapore to stay with them indefinitely. And Rachel already works from home so the office is set up.

"Enough about me," she says. "I'm sure you didn't call just to listen to me rabbiting on."

"Not at all. It's great to get your news. I called to check you were happy with the print quality of your financial services guide."

"It turned out really well," she says. "I went to the printer you recommended, and the guides look very professional."

"That's great. There's something else I wanted to check too. I had a minor panic because I thought there was something I didn't proof properly. Can you check if that's the right AFSL number at the bottom?"

"Hang on, I'll take a look."

I wait.

Rachel comes back. "Yeah, that's the right number."

"And each business has their own AFSL number, don't they?"

"Yes, that's the whole point. They're unique. It's a highly regulated industry."

"Okay, great. I'm glad you're happy with the guides."

I congratulate her again before hanging up.

Noah has been using another financial adviser's licence. I'm certain it's not the other way around and that Rachel hasn't appropriated his licence. She's so unpretentious and had no qualms about taking Noah's leftovers, as she put it, and has built up her business slowly. Noah is the opposite, a risk-taker, living life on the edge. And for as long as I've known him, he's been first class all the way.

I wonder why he'd use Rachel's AFSL number and what good that would do him.

Chapter Forty-Five

No more police stations for me. Nope, this time it's the Central Law Courts in the city.

Yet again, Laura is my lifesaver. It hadn't occurred to me to get a violence restraining order against Domenic Scarparolo till she suggested it, and there's no one I'd rather have by my side while I'm doing it.

I've filled in an application form naming the respondent, Scarparolo, because you need to know the legal terminology to get a VRO. I'm up on the acronyms now too. I've outlined the events and threats in a separate document. Laura was a great help with that and helped me describe the incidents, including stalking and threats, culminating in the suspected killing of Joel's cat. I mention the flowers and the text message, citing that as further evidence of intimidation, though I don't have evidence this was down to him. Now I'm making an affirmation before the clerk that this is all true.

"I sincerely declare and affirm that this is my name and my signature, and the content of this, my affidavit, are true and correct," I say.

Now that's done, I want nothing more than to get out of

there quickly. Luckily, this is a lot easier than getting in, which involved security worthy of a presidential visit.

We step out of the eighties beige building, at least I think it's eighties, and into the sunshine outside. The warmth seeps into me. A couple of men in suits walk past. Cars drive slowly over the paved road in front of us.

"I'm glad that's done," I say.

Laura waits beside me. "That's Step One out of the way. I can come back with you this afternoon."

She explained this to me yesterday evening. The application and affidavit have been lodged, but I still need to go before the magistrate who'll ask to hear a bit more about why I want a VRO. It usually happens pretty quickly and Laura assures me the magistrate will issue an interim VRO against Scarparolo. It's interim until it's made final, which is what I need.

Laura takes my arm. "We might as well head straight for the train. There's nothing you need from the city, is there?"

"You're such a calming influence on me," I say, as we walk. It was worth waiting a few days till she had a day off work and could come with me. "Something about the sunshine makes me feel right about all of this."

She smiles. "Lucky it's not raining then. Or snowing."

"Yeah, not a lot of snow around."

I point ahead as we walk home from the train station. "That looks like..."

"I think it does," Laura says.

Up the street outside my house, a couple of police officers are getting into their vehicle. I recognise one of them, Alex Sheridan, so I wave wildly, figuring he might have uncovered evidence against Scarparolo or that there may be some other recent developments. He and his mate, an older guy, stop by their car while Laura and I speed up.

"Hi there, Alex," I say. "How can I help you? Is something up?"

He nods. "A couple of things I was wondering about. Kate, you never mentioned anything to us about an incident at Farmer Joe's in Subiaco."

"No, perhaps I should have. There's been a lot happening." I take a moment to think. "Why bring this up now? I mean, how do you even know about it?"

"Can you tell me what happened?"

"Sure, I was in the chocolate aisle at the supermarket and wasn't paying attention to much else, when all of a sudden Scarparolo was there right next to me. He threatened me, told me I'd better watch my back. He must've followed me there. It's the only way he could've known where I was."

"Domenic Scarparolo says it's a coincidence he was at your local supermarket, that he was in the area and decided to purchase some sweets for his wife." Alex pauses and I'm thinking I don't like pauses. "You pushed the shop assistant, nearly knocking her over, then purposely hurled a display of canned goods across the aisle."

I shake my head, wondering how I became a hurler. "That's not what happened, not exactly."

"The shop assistant who was present has confirmed these events."

So they've interviewed her?

"Scarparolo threatened me," I say. "He had a knife in the waistband of his jeans, I bet he didn't show that to the shop assistant."

The officer continues. "There was no mention of a weapon or threatening behaviour. Apparently, afterwards the shop assistant was shaken, so Scarparolo called for help and then attempted to restack the cans."

I purse my lips. "Because he's trying to make out like he's the innocent party. That was after he scared the crap out of me, don't forget."

Laura reaches for my arm.

Maybe this is why I didn't report the incident, because I had a feeling something like this would happen. I'm having another feeling now, of my life reeling out of control, of forces much greater than myself bearing down on me, of getting into a bigger mess than before.

"There's something else you didn't mention to us, Kate Mamotte," the officer says.

I hate the way he uses my full name. "Yes."

"I'm talking about your visit to Domenic Scarparolo's house."

Laura turns to me. "You don't need to say anything. I can take it from here."

I don't want her to take it from here. I want this man to understand.

I grit my teeth. "Did Scarparolo tell you how I found out where he lived? He was stalking me, parked in his car outside my house. It wasn't just one thing. It was lots of things. I was sick of it, so I followed him."

"Kate, please." Laura raises her voice.

I can't stop. "He already knew where I lived. He'd been there before. My neighbour saw him, or someone who fit his description. It was him, I tell you."

"Domenic Scarparolo says that you came to his house and assaulted his wife," the cop says.

Laura's fingers dig into my arm. "Kate, this is getting serious."

"Thank you, Laura," I say. "But I want to clear this up. I did not assault that man's wife."

Alex looks down at a piece of paper in his hand, then back

up again. "He alleges that you threw several items at her, a cleaning product and a scrubbing brush."

I press my lips together. I should have kept my mouth shut and even as I think this, I know I'm not going to be able to.

"Actually," I say, "she threw those things at me."

"There was a witness, an elderly neighbour, who saw you throw the scrubbing brush and saw it land on the lady in question. Then Scarparolo asked you to stay away from him and his family."

"No, she's got it the wrong way around. I told *him* to stay away from me."

But of course the old lady didn't hear that. She only heard what *he'd* said.

"It's lucky he doesn't want to press charges," the officer says.

Over a scrubbing brush? I grit my teeth. Laura was right. It would've been better if I'd left this to her.

"You might find this amusing," he says.

I shake my head. "That's where you're wrong."

"But an assault on a pregnant woman is a serious matter."

"Pardon?"

Pregnant? How can everyone around me be pregnant? I remember the cropped top and thick waist and wondering why she was showing off her belly in that unflattering outfit. Shit, this is worse than I thought.

"In fact, that's why Domenic Scarparolo was at the supermarket the evening he bumped into you," the officer says. "His wife has been having cravings."

Great, this is all I need.

Alex continues. "He pointed out he was concerned for his safety and that of his wife and their unborn child. You're an accomplished martial artist, Kate."

My stomach boils.

"In his words, his brother died at your hands and he didn't want to end up the same way."

Andrew Scarparolo had a knife. He'd already killed my husband. I'm back to where I started in that car park, fighting for my life. I'm stuck. It's *Groundhog Day* gone wrong. I'll never get away.

I'm bleeding, terrified, and that knife keeps coming at me. He's already killed Charlie and I'm trying to defend myself. I've yelled *Stop* and *Get back*, the words that have been drilled into me at Krav, but this is a hundred miles away from training. I can kick and punch and throw and incapacitate but not against a knife. Training doesn't stop me getting cut, my arms, my stomach, my ribs, my sides. I'd run if I could. My attacker stays between me and the exit.

He slashes. We struggle. My two hands are wrapped around his wrist. No control. Not good for me and he's strong. I yank his arm down, yank and yank. Suddenly his hand is on the ground, the knife still in his fingers. I stomp on his fist, a miracle. Another stomp. I feel the knife beneath my shoe, then slide it away across the concrete.

He's not done, though. He dives in to take me to the ground. It's like a jump cut in a movie, one moment I'm on my feet, the next I'm on the ground. I land on top. My lucky break, thank Christ, thank my lucky stars, thank Saint Vincent, thank fuck. I have hope. If one of us is going to die, I don't want it to be me. I want life, today, tomorrow, next year, always.

I never planned for anyone to die.

My stomach that was boiling erupts inside me, bile rising to the back of my throat. I cover my mouth. I'm not going to throw up, not here.

Laura's hand slides up under my arm so she's practically holding me up.

"Hang on right there," she says. "I think you might show Kate a little more respect after everything she's been through.

Her husband died at the hands of this man's brother. Meanwhile he's been harassing and stalking her, hanging around on her street so she doesn't even feel safe in her own house. We've come from the Law Courts where we've applied for a VRO against him."

Something part-way between a grimace and a look of resignation crosses Alex's face. He hands me some papers.

"What's this?" I ask.

Another bloody pause, so long I can't stand it.

"Domenic Scarparolo got in first," he says. "He's taken out a restraining order against you, Kate."

My mouth falls open. Laura is left without words too. This can't be happening. I'm going crazy. I didn't threaten Scarparolo. I haven't done anything wrong.

And clearly none of that makes any difference.

Chapter Forty-Six

Laura implores me to keep my appointment with the magistrate that afternoon. I don't. She explains I can file an objection to the restraining order against me. Maybe I should, perhaps next week. I have twenty-one days to do this and right now I have very little energy. As long as Scarparolo stays away from me, I don't care. Except I do. I have both emotions at once. I need a break, so I'll forget about Scarparolo for a bit and tackle the easier things first.

I've scoured Noah's website and financial services guide looking for answers, even though I know the content inside out. I could ask Noah or raise the subject with Laura. One thing I don't do. I don't call ASIC, the Australian Securities and Investments Commission. I don't dob.

Instead I drop by La Vida on a Wednesday morning. Never thought I'd be having coffee with Laura's friend, Adrienne, but I recall her saying Noah returned the money from her investments after she'd asked him lots of financial questions. And I'd like to talk to her. She's pretty good at talking, as I recall.

I order a cappuccino from the takeaway window. Adrienne

is sitting at an outside table with three friends, all of them rugged up in puffer jackets and scarves though it's sunny and twenty degrees, hardly a freezing winter's day. They wouldn't last a day in July in Melbourne. Then again, maybe I'm being mean. I used to find Perth winters cold when I was growing up here too.

Adrienne waves as I approach.

"Hi there," I say.

"Kate, lovely to see you." She motions for me to come closer. "Pull up a chair. I'll introduce you to the girls."

She does the introductions as I take a seat. The three women say "hi," then huddle closer together and keep talking.

"Have I interrupted something?" I ask in a quiet voice.

Adrienne shrugs. "One of the girls' husbands has left her and two teenaged kids to shack up with a thirty-year-old."

"Oh, which of your friends is it?"

"It's not one of *these* friends. It's someone else. The poor woman's shattered. I'm not surprised, though. Her husband came onto me one night, the rotter."

I picture Adrienne with a man sidling up to her, then decide it's better if I don't.

"I chose my husband much more carefully," she says. "And if he tried anything, I'd take him for everything he's worth." She motions to her friend across the table. "Nat's husband is a doctor too, an ophthalmologist. They charge through the nose." She laughs. "That's an eye doctor, charging through the nose. Pretty funny."

I smile, thinking I'm back to where I started, talking to doctors' wives. "It's not very funny about that woman's husband doing the dirty on her, though."

"No, it's not," she says. "How's that friend of yours doing?"

"What friend?"

She nudges me. "You know, Noah. I imagine he'd be quite a catch. He's very successful."

By that, I guess she means rich. She's presuming a lot, and it rubs me up the wrong way, when I should be grateful because she's raised the very subject I wanted to talk to her about.

She places a hand on her chest. "I don't mean he'd be a catch for *me*. I'm taken."

I raise my eyebrows. "But you were looking, all the same."

"I thought we had a certain rapport, that's all. The man has a certain *je ne sais quoi* about him. He's the full package, you know, the looks plus the business smarts. And don't try to tell me you hadn't noticed."

"You once said something about Noah returning your investments to you?"

Her shoulders sag. "Yes, that was rather a disappointment."

"Any idea what happened?"

"At first I thought it might be personal. There was certainly an attraction between us, but I'm married. Not available."

Noah? Attracted to Adrienne? Somehow I doubt that.

I keep my expression even. "But you think he's got the business smarts?"

"Most definitely. I asked lots of questions, and I mean *lots*. I was on the lookout because if it seems too good to be true, it usually is, whereas the investments he recommended had healthy returns, not ridiculous ones. Also, I've had dealings with other financial planners before and the only thing they're interested in is making money for themselves. One planner tried to pressure us into selling a property to invest with him instead. I can tell you that didn't go down very well with me."

"And Noah wasn't like that?"

"Not at all. I had a couple of in-depth discussions about his investment philosophy. I asked if I could get in touch with some of his clients. A few of the other doctors have invested with him but they're all new investors and I wanted to talk to some longer-term clients."

"Did you?"

"It didn't get that far unfortunately." She shrugs. "I'm not used to being slighted. Maybe I shouldn't take it so personally."

"I'm sure it wasn't personal."

No way was Noah attracted to this woman, but that wouldn't be enough reason for him to turn down her and her husband as investors. Business is business. And he came to Perth to build up a portfolio of investors from medical backgrounds because they've got money to invest. My guess is that Adrienne was a pain in the neck.

I sip my coffee. "I should get going."

"Come and join us any time," Adrienne says. "Or at least any Wednesday!"

"Thanks."

I stand, suddenly overcome by a wave of tiredness, my legs weak. I blink to keep my eyes open. Adrienne's friends who'd been ignoring me tell me I should stay. Strange.

"Lovely meeting you." I lie. I'm good at lying.

And I'm out of there. I toss my coffee cup in the bin and walk home, dragging my feet every step of the way.

A few minutes later, I step through the front door and head straight for my room. *Sleep. Rest. Right now.* It's not only the mental exhaustion, the heavy head and the limbs that feel like they're about to fall off. I'm so tired I feel sick. My entire body is staging a revolt and telling me to take it easy.

I can't remember when I last felt this tired. Except I can.

I drop down onto the bed. And I'm out.

Chapter Forty-Seven

Laura's crouched in front of a garden bed, a giant weed in her hands, squinting as she looks up at me. "Are you nuts? Gardening sucks. I'll have a sore back after this and so will you, probably."

"I don't mind," I say. "I can help you do the weeding and then we can have a cup of tea."

She gives me a what-the-hell look. "Sure. There are plenty of weeds to go around. Gloves are over there."

I pull on the gloves that have been tossed onto the middle of the front path. "These must be Theo's. They're big but they'll do the trick."

"You're welcome to come to yoga with me tomorrow, if you like. It's great after gardening."

"Maybe another time."

I ask about the kids. Chat. Small talk. Then she mentions Noah. Finally.

"How's he settling in to Perth?" I ask, though that's not the question I want answered.

"Pretty good. Not everything has turned out the way he

hoped. With you, that is." Laura straightens, rubs her lower back and gives me a sideways glance.

"He talked to you, did he?"

"I worked it out, Kate. It wasn't that hard." She gets back to the garden. "I told him before he got here that he'd end up disappointed if you were the main reason he was moving to Perth."

"You never said anything to me."

"None of my business, not really. Noah came over for business too. I knew that part would work out for him."

My lucky chance. "Business seems to be good."

"Sure."

"So, why is it that you and Theo have never invested with Noah?"

"Theo's the reason. Property is the only investment he's ever been interested in. Bricks and mortar, solid and reliable. We've got superannuation, of course, but that's different."

Great, another dead end when it comes to Noah and his business. It's not Theo's investment strategy I'm chasing.

Laura is incensed about Scarparolo getting a restraining order, but not particularly surprised, not after her experience with past injustices. The part that surprises her is that he was smart enough to get one.

"I don't know what I'd do without you." I bite my lip. "You don't believe I could've killed Esmeralda, do you?"

"What? No."

No, I'm not a killer. Except I am.

Laura stands, hands on her hips. "Sometimes it's as if Charlie's still here. I think you know what I mean."

Charlie is often here, in the wind, hovering, lurking, watching. I feel him. But she doesn't know that. No one does. Shit, maybe I am crazy.

"I'm going to be straight with you," she says. "First off, I really wish you'd get professional help. I know a great psychologist, a friend of a friend, who could help you out."

I don't say anything.

She continues. "Secondly, Charlie wasn't good for you. I don't even think he was a good man. A decent person wouldn't have done the things he did."

I stand too, stretching out my legs. "I was in shock when I found out." I'm still in shock.

"I'm not talking about the affair and the other woman. I'm talking about the other things that happened during your relationship, the way he used to put you down and made you think you were responsible for things that weren't your fault. It sucked the confidence right out of you."

"I don't think so."

My voice is weak, my protest pointless. Charlie wasn't the selfless, loving husband he made out to be. He had me fooled for a long time. Not so much anymore.

Laura reaches for a plastic pot with a small groundcover, the tags from the nursery still on it.

I clear my throat. "You never said anything before."

"You never let me."

"That's not…" *True*. Oh yes, it is.

She passes me the seedling. "Reckon you can handle planting this? The watering can is just behind you, along with the trowel."

"Sure," I say because this has got to be more exciting than weeding.

She gets back onto her knees to tackle the weeds. "While Charlie was alive, it was hard to talk to you about him. I put the pieces together from things you told me, information from Noah, and from the times I saw Charlie. He always acted like a loving husband in front of me. *Acted*, being the operative word."

"But I did talk to you about Charlie. How could I not?"

"Yes, but you were quite selective. And protective. And I understand. He was your husband, but it was different from when you talked about your mother. You confided in me when it came to her."

"What's she got to do with it?" I ask. "I mean, she's a bit of a cow, but she's still my mum."

"Exactly. You love her despite the way she acts towards you. Because we're wired to love our parents. I was the same. I craved love from my mother. I get it."

If my upbringing was screwy, Laura's was worse. It's one of the reasons she and Noah are so close. They have that bond.

I point to the hole I've dug. "Is this about the right size?"

"That's plenty big enough. Your mum was constantly manipulating you, so you didn't know where you stood. She had no empathy, certainly not for you. It always had to be about *her*. She had to be the centre of attention and if she wasn't, then you had to watch out. You used to say she was mean. I think she was worse than that."

Laura's said this to me before. And I've pushed it to the back of my mind.

"But you held back when it came to Charlie," she adds.

Because I chose Charlie whereas I have no control over my mother. Because I loved him. Because Charlie was the only thing I had going for me and if I'd got that wrong, I'd be a complete loser.

On my knees, I drop the plant into the hole and scrape the dirt in around it, pressing the soil down to compact it.

"I didn't mean to… I just…" Hell, I can't even complete a sentence anymore. I tip water from the watering can into the hole and wait for the soil to soak it up.

"I couldn't talk to you about Charlie before," Laura says. "And then, after he died, there was no way I could say anything vaguely negative about him."

It's been blow after blow with the things I've found out

about him. Like I've had the crap beaten out of me. I'm a boxer with bruised ribs and two black eyes, staggering rather than standing, then one more strike knocks me down. The referee is counting and I get up. Each time I stand up, I find out something else about Charlie and get knocked right back down again.

I look at Laura. "He was an arsehole, wasn't he?"

She nods.

And I was blinded by my grief. Until I wasn't. I drop down onto my haunches.

"You don't have to do my planting for me," she says. "Or the weeding."

"I'll be all right. Just give me a sec."

She does.

After a while, she gets up and extends her arm. "Hey, I'll give you a hand up."

I take it, brushing off my backside as I stand.

"Kate, you must've heard about coercive control? That was Charlie through and through. He didn't like you working and wanted you to be dependent on him. He separated you from your friends, slowly, over time, so it didn't seem suspicious. I think I was okay because I'm Noah's sister and I live on the other side of the country, but your Melbourne friends started dropping off. I'm sure he peppered you with stories about some betrayal or something they said behind your back. It's what your mother used to do."

I stand up, staring at the garden bed like an idiot, because that's what I am. How can Laura know all this? Is she a mind-reader, a soothsayer, a psychologist? How can I not have seen what was right in front of me?

"He didn't want you doing Krav and martial arts either, did he?" she says.

"No, he didn't."

"Too many men around, too many other people for you to

talk to, too much opportunity for you to build your self-confidence." She raises her eyebrows. "You must've really put your foot down about that one."

"Yeah, I did."

That was one fight with Charlie I was determined to win. *After everything I've done for you!* That's what he said when I refused to give up training. I could endure the huge argument, that only lasted a few days, but the months after that were hard, months of walking on eggshells with Charlie blowing up at the smallest thing. Still, I knew I could hang in there and outlast him. Hell, I'd stuck it out with my mum long enough. I'd had the practice.

From my upbringing, I got resilience, determination, the survival mindset, which is probably why I was drawn to martial arts, and also why I got through the knife attack. Because I believed I could survive and I didn't give up.

"Charlie was just like your mum," Laura says. "They're made of the same stuff, those two, both of them controlling and manipulative."

I can't look at Laura. I want to scream and argue. I want her to be wrong.

"You married your mother," she says.

Shit, maybe she's right. Maybe when Charlie spotted me across the room – or the pool to be more precise – he wasn't seeing the real me. He was seeing my vulnerability. He could smell it.

I was set up for this by my mother through my upbringing. First Mum, then Charlie, they made me feel I wasn't good enough. They both got under my skin and took advantage of me, moulding me into something I wasn't.

I can't speak so I nod. Laura rips off her gardening gloves and draws me close. I hug her right back.

Chapter Forty-Eight

My eyes spring open. Awoken by a breeze. There it is again, a gentle wind blowing at the back of my ear and across my cheek, coming from behind.

I turn over in bed. There's nothing. Of course there isn't. I try to think pleasant thoughts. Ryan. Lucky. Love. I don't know if it's love but it's certainly something wonderful. He cooked me dinner tonight because, hey, I'm just next door and it's no more trouble to cook for two than for one. So practical. And caring. Also, his mother had made more of her tiramisu, especially for me, and he wanted to make sure I could enjoy it. Tiramisu, a good memory. I didn't throw it up this time.

He wanted me to stay but I told him I needed time on my own. No complaints from Ryan, only reassurances, because I know where he is if I need him. That's what a caring partner should be like. Not like Charlie. Crap, I need to think pleasant thoughts, not Charlie thoughts.

A gust of wind brushes the back of my head, messes up my hair. And my mind.

It's him.

My heart racing, I sit up in bed. I tell myself there are no ghosts. They don't exist. My husband is not here. He's dead. This is my mind playing tricks on me, mean tricks, like the sort he used to play. But I can't be sure.

"Charlie." I shout his name. "I'll tell you once and once only. You can't do this to me. I won't let you."

I sling my legs over the edge of the bed. I'm invisible. No one can see me because I'm the only one here. My fingers hover over the switch for the bedside light but, no, that's not the light I need. Besides, it's not so dark that I can't make my way through the room. I need to do this. I creep around, checking the corners of the room, inside the closet, the en suite. I pull open the curtains and peer into the courtyard lit by a couple of small bollard lights.

Doesn't matter that I can't see him. I feel him. I turn back to face the bed.

"I loved you," I say. "Part of me will always love you, but now I hate you for the things you did. Because you were never a good person. You're a selfish dick, Charlie."

There, I said it, and I'm not done yet.

"You're dead. Do you get that? Dead. And I'm alive. I'm still young, Charlie, and I have a new man in my life, a good man, who's nothing like you. And there's something else too, but I'm damned if I'll talk to you about that before I talk to Ryan. I have to live my life my way and you have to go away. You don't belong here."

I listen for a sign. Nothing.

"Get out and stay out."

I stomp to the chest of drawers and take out the wedding photo, still in its frame, the glass long gone. I raise it high, fling it to the floor, then stomp on it.

"It's okay."

Charlie's voice. Shit.

No bloody way am I staying in here on my own. My hands shaking, I grab my phone and type a message to Ryan, hoping like hell that his insomnia has got the better of him tonight.

Are you awake?

The dancing dots appear right away, thank Christ.

No, I'm asleep.

Then:

Are you okay?

Followed by:

I'll be right over.

A minute later, I hear shuffling noises at the front door, then Ryan calls my name. I open the door, pull him inside out of the cold and throw my arms around him. He smells of sleep and the outside dew, warm and cold at the same time, and he is everything I want right now.

"Are you okay?" he asks. "Did something happen?"

"Just a bad dream." Taking his hand, I lead him to the bedroom and slide under the covers. "Can you stay with me tonight?"

"Of course."

In bed, we hold each other in a long, reassuring embrace. I roll onto my side facing away from him, and he spoons himself against me. He doesn't feel ignored, or at least I hope he doesn't, yet I feel guilty for turning my back to him.

"I know this sounds dumb," I say. "But I want to be able to see if anyone's coming."

"Makes as much sense as anything." He presses a kiss to the back of my neck. "Goodnight, Kate."

"Night."

I squeeze my eyes shut. *Sleep. Go to sleep. Sleep now.* I don't. Ryan's breathing becomes more rhythmic and I'm pleased he can finally get some rest.

Sometimes I think it's a miracle he can sleep at all with the grief he must be carrying at losing Chloe, though maybe she won't be his only child. Despite his anguish, he's managed to forgive his mother-in-law for driving the car that killed her. That's a lot of pain and a lot of compassion and a lot of man.

Me? I'm not so forgiving.

Charlie was a mammoth arsehole and maybe that can make it easier for me to reframe the way I look at this. I have choices and a life ahead of me. I don't have to be gripped by fear. I'm still coming to terms with the whole Charlie thing, but maybe now I can hold onto my grief more lightly and learn to breathe again.

I can't feel him anymore, thank goodness. I hope that for once in his life he was listening and that he's finally gone. I can't speak out loud or I'll wake Ryan, so I say the words to myself. In my head, I'm shouting.

Screw you, Charlie.

And I fall asleep.

Chapter Forty-Nine

Another couple of weeks have passed and I do what I should've done a while ago. I go to the chemist. Sounds simple enough. I ride my bike there, walk into the pharmacy and look around for what I need but can't find it.

"Excuse me," I say to a middle-aged woman on her knees stacking tubes of toothpaste. "Where are the pregnancy tests?"

She gets up, making a joke about her creaking knees, and shows me a couple of different types of tests. A few minutes later, I'm back on my bike on my way home.

Ryan's car is parked on the street, which means he's home. It sends a tingle of excitement through me, in the best way possible. I don't wait. I take my bike around the rear of the house and go in through the back, then head straight for the bathroom.

It's not the first time I've done this. I remember what it was like in Melbourne over a year ago when I suspected I might be pregnant. I waved the pregnancy kit in front of Charlie after he got back from work, a smile on my face but not on his.

"What's that?" he'd said, even though he was a doctor and knew damn well what it was.

His face fell, for a moment, a single second that told me he wasn't as pleased as I was, nowhere near it. And though that second spoke volumes, I ignored it, told myself it was only the shock.

A couple of days later, I said how hard it was to believe that a tiny little foetus could make me so hugely, phenomenally, unbelievably tired. And he cut me right down, saying I'd know about tiredness if I'd had to work double shifts like him.

Another time, I remember his head falling into his hands while he mumbled something about it being too soon. More than that, I remember the fear in his eyes as I pulled his fingers from his face and asked him what was bothering him. It was too soon to tell people, that's what he said, before asking me if this was what I really wanted. As if there could've been any doubt.

These are memories, not fabrications, no matter what Mum tried to tell me. Why would she even come out with such selfish bullshit? For the attention? And what was Charlie doing with a pregnant wife and pregnant girlfriend? He must've been stressed out of his mind at the mess he'd got himself into.

Get out of my head, Charlie. I won't have him ruin this moment. This is my life, my way, and this time it's going to be different.

Leaning over the bathroom basin, I take the plastic stick from the packaging and read the instructions. I follow the directions and wee on the stick, then place it on the cupboard beside me. I wait. I'm not good at waiting. I breathe. I'm not particularly good at breathing either. Yes, I am. I can do this. I can do anything.

I'm still sitting on the loo as I reach across for the plastic stick. Two pink lines. They're not faint. They're leaping out at me. Like my heart is jumping out of my chest.

Yep, my body is working that double shift.

I know exactly when it happened. My first night with Ryan

we'd been lost in lust and we hadn't bothered with a condom, hadn't even given it a second thought until it was too late.

Sloppy. How wonderfully sloppy. Sloppy has never felt so good. I'm a grown woman and I'm ready for this.

No point waiting around. I pop the stick into the pocket of my windcheater, make sure I've got my phone and keys, and I head straight for Ryan's. He opens the front door, leans against it and sighs.

"Sorry to disturb you," I say. "I know you're working."

I'm not sorry, not one little bit.

He takes my hand. "Not at all. Your timing is perfect. I need a break but I was doing that thing when I tell myself I'll finish one more detail first."

I follow him to the back of the house, thinking I'm gonna give him a little detail that'll blow him away.

He wanders into the kitchen while I lean over the other side of the counter.

"Coffee?" he asks, switching the kettle on.

"Could I have a cup of tea?"

"Sure. I hope a mug is okay."

Is coffee bad for pregnant women? Not in moderation. I hope he doesn't offer me any soft cheeses. What else is on the list of stuff pregnant women shouldn't eat?

One thing I know. From now on, I'm getting my act together. Fast. Right now. This very minute. No more taking shit from the people around me, well, from my mother anyway because she's the main culprit. No more over-exercising when I should be taking better care of myself. I've also got to be sensible and make sure I can earn a living. If I can't make enough money working for myself, I can always get communications work in an office. I have skills and expertise. I can do this.

Two things I know. I'm going to be a wonderful mother. I was made for this. It's in my biology and in my heart.

"Are you okay?" Ryan asks.

A picture speaks a thousand words. I pull the white stick from my pocket, place it on the kitchen counter and give Ryan a long look. His gaze drops. He does a double take, his eyes widening.

"What…?"

I nod. "I'm pregnant."

The mug slips from his hand, smashing onto the tiles. Hot tea splashes in all directions, landing on the leg of his jeans. Shit, he's taking this worse than I thought. I wait for that 'single second' that happened with Charlie, wondering how Ryan feels and what's going on inside him.

Please don't let this be like Charlie all over again.

I'm holding my breath, then that second is over or maybe it never happened. Suddenly Ryan's not in the kitchen anymore. He's here, his arms around my waist as he sweeps me off the ground, spinning me around. I hear laughter. Ryan's laughter, and mine.

He lets me down slowly, but keeps one arm around me, his other hand resting on my stomach.

"I'm so happy, Kate, for me, for you, for all of us." He stops and stares. "I mean, you're happy about this, aren't you?"

"I want this baby more than I've ever wanted anything in my life."

He lets out a long sigh. "Thank Christ for that. We can do this, me and you."

As much as I adore Ryan, I don't know if we'll stay together. There are no guarantees in life. But I know that if he wants me, I'll be there and I'll try my best. He'll be a fantastic father. This baby will have two parents, which is one more than I had. And Ryan's a better person than either of my parents were.

It's a start and it's everything.

Chapter Fifty

Laura has to sign some papers, something to do with her superannuation, which Noah is managing. He suggested I come with her because I haven't seen his new offices yet.

He's already shown us the reception area, fitted out according to his specifications so it captures the feel of a 1930s gentleman's boudoir, even though there's no actual receptionist. He has a PA but she works from home in Melbourne.

He ushers us ahead of him. "The boardroom, ladies."

"For all your board meetings?" I say, then wish I could take back my sarcasm. "I mean, your clients must be impressed by all of this."

"One must make a good impression." Smirking, he has put on his posh voice, but he's still half serious.

Noah stands by the window, so we join him. The view is clearly the big drawcard, and Laura and I can't help but be pulled towards it. The river sparkles even in the fading light, the sun about to go down over Kings Park, a wall of green to our right. Traffic has banked up on the Narrows Bridge, making me glad I don't have to commute. We're in the middle of the central business district and yet we're cloistered from the city outside. This is a different world.

"That's some view," Laura says.

Noah smiles. "Sure is."

"It doesn't get boring," she adds. "Do you want to show Kate your office?"

Turns out his office is just as impressive as the boardroom, no surprises there. His desk faces a large window with the same view, making me wonder how he can ever get any work done with such a huge distraction right in front of him. Speaking of distractions, the antique-finish Chesterfields on the other side of the room look inviting.

"I'll show you something else."

Noah pushes open a door to reveal a bathroom that's straight out of a New York art deco apartment, complete with porcelain tiles on the floor and marble on the walls, a chandelier hanging from the ceiling. He's turned the light on, of course, so we can admire it in all its glory.

"Wow," I say. "An executive washroom? I thought they only had them in the movies."

"I can have everything I want." He turns to me. "Or nearly everything."

He makes it feel so personal. I wish he wouldn't.

"Hope you don't mind, Noah," Laura says. "But I need to get a move on and get dinner started."

"Sure."

Laura reads through the papers on Noah's desk while he and I admire the view some more. I'm trying to think of how to bring up the subject of why he's using Rachel's financial licence number or maybe I've got this wrong and it's the other way around. Either way, I can't get it out of my head.

"I'll leave this here."

I turn around as Laura places the pen on top of the pile of papers.

"Sorry, but I can't hang around," she adds.

"Okay." I step towards her.

"Surely you don't have to go too, Kate," Noah says. "There's something I wanted to show you. I mean, you don't have to get home to cook for the family."

Laura leaves, insisting she can find her own way to the lift.

I turn to Noah. "Did you want to talk to me about something?"

"Much better if I show you."

He reaches for a swipe card under the pile of papers on the desk, then motions for me to follow him, but he's taking his time and I can't help but walk one step ahead of him. Eventually we reach the lift. He presses the button to summon it.

I raise my eyebrows. "We're going up?"

"To the top of the world."

"Is the view different from up there?"

"Something like that."

We get out on the top floor, then I follow Noah to another door, where he swipes for entry to a stairwell. I'd thought we were as high as we could go. Apparently not.

Noah pushes open a fire door with a '*No unauthorised entry*' sign, holding it open for me. There's a lot of concrete here at 'the top of the world', a concrete floor and waist-height rendered balcony, a shelter that probably houses some utilities, a couple of warning signs and not much else. Glamorous, this is not. Unlike the rest of the building, this place isn't meant for public consumption.

I wander ahead. "Are you sure we're allowed up here?"

He shrugs, pockets the swipe card. "I paid a guy to turn a blind eye."

I decide to take a look around, then get going. It's not often I get a guided tour of Perth's tallest building. Well, never. Though the view is much the same as from Noah's office, there's a feeling of freedom from being out in the open and the evening couldn't be more perfect with hardly a breath of air. Very unusual for such a windy city.

For once, Noah doesn't talk too much. We stand and breathe and enjoy the surroundings. I should do this more often, take the time to appreciate what I've got. Sometimes all we have is this moment and maybe the one that follows, and you never know when that can be taken from you. A dour thought, perhaps, yet somehow liberating.

"So why'd you bring me up here?" I ask. "Was it for the view?"

He gives me a sideways glance. "For me the view is great when I'm looking at you."

A corny line that I don't want to hear. I ignore him, leaning over the balcony to look down at the sheer drop. Fifty-five storeys. Vertigo hits me, my stomach lurching, or maybe this is a result of my pregnancy. Either way, it's not good and I stretch out my arms to give myself some distance. I tell myself there's nothing to worry about. It's a concrete balcony, as solid as they come, and tall enough to protect me.

"You've been up here before, haven't you?" I turn to Noah. "When you did that abseiling thing for charity."

"Yeah, but that was on the other side, where the building is stepped down. Then we abseiled down in three sections. The longest section was just over twenty storeys, so it was no problem."

I manage a wry smile. "No problem at all."

"There's something else."

He motions for me to follow. On the other side of the utilities shelter, he's set up a picnic, complete with a hamper, an ice bucket with champagne and another bottle, a tartan picnic rug and cushions for us to sit on.

I stiffen. "Please don't, Noah."

"You don't have to drink the champagne. I got mineral water for you."

"It's not that."

"Then don't have it. Sit down and make yourself comfortable. All I'm asking for is a little of your time. It's not too much to ask."

If it was anyone else, I'd tell them where to get off. But this is Noah. Besides, he doesn't look like he's going to jump me or take me into his arms.

Still, I thought I'd been clear with him before. Or did I imagine that?

I settle onto one of the cushions. Cross-legged, my back is straight and I must look about as comfortable as I feel, which is not at all. Meanwhile, Noah pours me a Perrier and hands it across. I have a sip and place the glass on the ground. His brow furrows as if deep in thought. Unease brews in my stomach. He can do his thinking in his own time. I'm about to get up when he reaches into his jacket pocket for his phone and taps it a couple of times.

He hands it to me. "This is what I wanted to show you."

I look at the Qantas booking on the screen. "You're going to Paris?"

"Two tickets, Kate. First class."

I swallow.

"For me and you," he adds, as if I couldn't work it out.

I'm not going anywhere and I'm certainly not going to be swayed by first class. I shouldn't have given him a chance, not after the mistakes I've made before. A memory flashes before me, of the two of us in bed together, only it's not erotic. It's terrifying. Maybe I was wrong about Noah. Maybe we can't be friends. Maybe we can't be anything.

"I'm not going to Paris with you, Noah."

"This would mean everything to me."

I drop the phone onto the rug. "You've got this all—"

He grabs my wrist, holds it tight. "Hear me out. Just this once, then it'll all be over."

The escape from a wrist grab is easy, but that's not my first instinct, not with Noah. I lower my gaze to his hand and he lets go and says sorry. He doesn't sound sorry, though.

He opens the picnic basket and lays the items out, one by one. He's thought of everything, a selection of cheeses and smoked meats, crusty baguette, cloth napkins, a platter for the cheeses, side plates and mother-of-pearl knives. Problem is, this is everything I don't want.

"Kate, you've been through so much," he says. "Life has been unfair to you, when you deserved so much better. It's time to take life by the horns, to follow your dreams, to make new dreams and memories. We can get an apartment in the fifth arrondissement, or anywhere that you like, and start the day with croissants and coffee. We can go to galleries and for walks along the Seine and after we've finished playing at being tourists, we can find our own cafés and bars to go to. You can still work if you want to. And if you don't want to, that's fine by me too. I'm happy to share everything I've got with you, because I want to share my life with you. We've known each other for so long and been through so much that I truly believe you can grow to love me. And if you don't, well, I have enough love for both of us."

My heart sinks a little deeper with each word from his mouth. I don't know if they're words of love or desperation. I feel guilty at my own part in this because I've led him on, though that was never my plan.

"This stops here," I say.

Noah holds my gaze. I can't make out the look in his face. It's not one I've seen before.

"Don't you get it, Kate?"

There's a hint of anger in his voice, enough to make the hair on the back of my neck stand on end.

"Careful, Noah. We might not be friends anymore if you keep going like this."

His face drops. "That's the sad part of it all. It's not just this. It's everything. It was all for you."

"That's not true."

And I'm not going to take crap from him. Noah is a lot of things – forceful and ambitious and successful – but he has never been selfless. He's been building his own empire, for himself, which was perfectly reasonable until he started dragging me into it.

"I'm not going to Paris on my own." He raises his arms to the sky. "I'm going out in a blaze of glory."

"You're not talking sense." I brush my hands on my jeans, ready to stand. "I wanted to ask you something but now I think it's better if I go."

"What, Kate? Ask away. This might be your last chance."

It might too, because at this rate, it's looking like I might never want to talk to him again. "One question, then I'm out of here. This is going to seem strange, but I was wondering why you're using Rachel Jones's financial licence number?"

He laughs. It's a nervous laugh if I've heard one, making me edgy in return. This is the Noah I know, yet there's another person hiding in there. I'm missing something.

"What's so funny?" I keep my voice even.

His laughter dies down, the grin on his face unnerving. "You told Rachel. You, of all people."

"Told her what?"

"About the AFSL number, of course."

"I didn't *tell* her anything."

I called her up and asked her about it, which is quite a different thing. I didn't even mention Noah's name.

"She worked it out."

"Worked what out?"

He gives me a lingering look. "You're such a beautiful

person, Kate, inside and out. You don't have a mean bone in your body."

"Actually, I do."

And I'm getting pissed off with this ridiculous game of cat and mouse.

"Problem is, you hit the nail on the head," he says.

What nail? What the hell is he talking about?

He continues. "A direct hit. You couldn't have been more concise and now that the wheels are in motion, there's nothing I can do. Absolutely nothing. The repercussions of this are much bigger than you can know."

"Noah, you're rambling."

"It's okay." Compassion in his voice. "I know you didn't intend this. I was angry at first. Not so much now. What's the point? You weren't to know."

My lips tighten, I stare at him.

He takes a deep breath. "Years ago, I asked Rachel if I could use her financial licence number. You can't practise as a financial advisor without one. So I asked. And she refused. I used it anyway. Quietly. No one else knew. Until now."

"I don't get it. Why wouldn't you simply apply for your own number?"

"You never got it, beautiful Kate. I didn't finish uni."

"Look, I know you didn't finish your MBA. Charlie told me about it. He said you didn't want your clients to know, so you made out like you'd finished it because you were embarrassed, or maybe you didn't want people to think less of you."

He tosses his head back. "Screw the MBA. I didn't get close to it. Didn't finish my degree. I knew the subject matter inside-out, better than the lecturers, but they were full of the theory and knew nothing about how to succeed in finance. In the end, I failed too many subjects. When you fail the second time around, you don't get another chance. They kicked me out."

"But you went to uni. Before I met you. You and Charlie were there at the same time."

"I went to campus to the library."

But he didn't go to university.

Shit, these are some lies he's been telling. I've read about people like that who pretend to go to university so their parents don't know they've failed, people who lose their jobs and then supposedly go to 'work' so their partners and friends don't know. People who lead a double life. Like Charlie did. Maybe he and Noah had more in common than I thought, except Charlie actually had a medical degree and a job. He had a lot of things in his life, too many, in fact.

My stomach clenches. I didn't know Charlie and I don't know Noah. I don't know anything.

Sudden movement. A flash of mother-of-pearl. Noah reaches for a knife. My vision narrows, my breaths coming fast. Fight or flight. I've been here before.

"What?" he says.

I'm on my feet already. Panting. My hands out, I step back. I have to protect my baby. An overwhelming drive to stay safe for my child rips through my entire body and being.

He drops the knife. "Oh, Kate, you've got this all wrong. I'd never hurt you."

Relief. Christ, he's not attacking me. Of course he's not. I'm having a panic attack. Still, I need some air. I lurch towards the balcony, dragging my feet each step of the way.

"Kate?"

I hear a voice behind me.

Chapter Fifty-One

I'm in the car park. I've been here before, too many times. Engulfed in darkness, my vision has narrowed. Tunnel vision. I turn to Charlie lying on the ground. I crawl across the concrete on my knees and one hand, my other arm clutching the slashes in my stomach. Blood drips to the concrete, large splotches, rivulets streaming down my arm.

I don't look at where I've been and the other body. I can't.

There's only Charlie. I can't reach him. My knees scrape along the ground, the sound echoes, a definite echo, background noises. Far away, everything is so far away.

Somehow I make it there, my knees sliding in a pool of blood, Charlie's blood, its metallic smell filling the air. I'm choking, unable to breathe. *Charlie, breathe. Please. You have to breathe.* The gash in his neck has gushed red, blood smeared on his face, his shirt, through his hair. I lift his head carefully, afraid it might come off or that I'll cause him more pain. Even as his head is heavy in my hands, I know how stupid this thought is because I can't hurt him anymore. No one can. I cradle his head in my lap. I'm muttering to myself, running my fingers through his hair, trying to neaten it. He never liked messy hair.

Charlie doesn't die in my arms. He's already gone by the time I get to him. I don't watch the light leave his eyes or tell him to hang on. I whisper, "I love you" instead, because I don't want to disturb him by raising my voice.

My heart clenches, getting tighter with each passing moment till it feels like my chest will collapse. Time passes. I can't say how much, five seconds or five minutes. No time or an eternity, it's all the same to me. Because my world has been shattered and nothing will ever be the same, so how can it matter how long I stay here? Finality and fear pool in the pit of my stomach like cement.

The echoing gets louder. Footsteps, voices, a gasp. I look up to see a middle-aged man slide his arm around a woman, probably his wife, who's covering her mouth in horror. It strikes me how ordinary they look, how normal, in their jeans and warm jackets. I see what lies between me and them. My husband is covered in blood while I caress his hair and another man is sprawled on the concrete, not moving.

"Ambulance," I say, as if there's anything paramedics will be able to do. "And police."

"Kate."

I hear my name. How can those people know my name?

"Kate."

Breathing hard, I'm leaning against something, my arms resting on a hard surface. Suddenly, my eyes are open. I'm at the top of the AT Tower with Noah. Was that a panic attack? No, a flashback. Same difference.

"Are you okay?" Noah asks.

He has his hand on the middle of my back. It's to console me, nothing more, I'm sure.

"I'm…" I'm what? I'm with Noah, who never finished university and who's acting weird. Noah who doesn't have a financial licence number and why should I even care about that? "I'm upset, that's all."

"We can still go to Paris. It's not too late."

"No." I swing my arm around to fling his hand off my back, then stop myself and turn to face him.

"If you don't come with me, I'm done for." Pleading with me now.

I shake my head, confused. Didn't he hear me?

His face turns white. "Rachel has reported me to the authorities."

Noah is all over the place today, speaking in riddles and expecting me to know what he's talking about. I'm not getting anywhere by asking him questions. I keep my mouth shut. I let him dig a hole.

His shoulders slump. "She's such a do-gooder she even called to tell me so. Can you believe it? I've done so much for her, helped her with business, gave her clients on a plate, and this is how she repays me. She knows exactly what happens from here. The authorities will investigate."

So what if he used her financial licence number? Maybe it's against the law, but it's not murder or rape or some heinous crime. He'll get over it.

I stare at Noah. His face is like iridescent fabric, glowing pale grey one minute and glimmering another colour the next, changing with every movement and minute. Somehow the sheen seems to be wearing off, the colours getting softer so that maybe I'll be able to see through him soon.

"I know their procedures and protocols," he says. "They're very quiet as they investigate. Thorough too. At no point do they let on who they're investigating. They gather all the evidence first, get everything lined up and then they swoop. I'll be ruined, Kate. They'll go ahead with this and there'll be nothing left. The houses, the car, the money, it'll all be gone. I'll end up in jail."

So dramatic. He's annoying the hell out of me now. My husband got murdered in a car park. That was a tragedy. Using someone else's licence number is no major disaster. He can pay the fine or pay a lawyer or work something out.

A memory comes to me. The first time I heard about AFSL numbers was through Charlie. I was in the kitchen of our old house, tipping a can of tomatoes into the pan for pasta sauce, while Charlie leaned over the counter, grinning.

"It's an Australian Financial Services Licence number, that's what it is," he said.

I frowned because I didn't know what he was going on about or why he'd brought this up.

"It'll all become clear soon enough," he said. "And you'll be very surprised when you find out exactly what. You'll see."

But I didn't see anything because a week later Charlie was dead.

Though I'm still not sure what Charlie was going on about, it hits me that he was onto something. That's why he looked so excited that evening.

I stare at Noah. "Charlie knew."

Noah's face turns white.

"Didn't he?" I raise my voice.

"Charlie was always so superior. He was going to turn me in, for the fun of it."

I poke Noah in the shoulder like a tough guy in a lame movie. He doesn't say anything, so I give him a sharp shunt in the chest that knocks him back half a step. Now I've got his attention.

I glare. "So what?"

"It wasn't the financial services number. It was where the number would lead. I'm ruined, Kate. I took a lot of money from people. I started off with real accounts and small profits. Then I saw how I could make more money and do it better. So I took more funds from clients. And these people let me. They kept on giving me their money to invest. I gave them good profits, not so huge that they looked suspicious but good enough to keep them happy. Everyone's happy when the profits are coming in. And as long as I could keep bringing in more clients and more money, I could keep distributing those profits. I was killing it, Kate. I was good at this."

So these were fake accounts. Is that what he's saying? He's talking about some sort of Ponzi scheme. Did people even do that nowadays? Was it still possible? I think back to one particular news story several years ago. Yeah, seems it's extremely possible.

Meanwhile, Noah was living it up, first-class travel, five-star hotels, only the best for Noah Bentley.

My blood is boiling, and I've barely even started.

"Charlie knew." I say it again.

Noah nods. "He worked it out."

Charlie knew and Charlie's dead. That wasn't a random attack.

"I did it for you, Kate."

It wasn't for me. Everything Noah did was for himself.

"Charlie found out," I say. "Just before he and I were attacked."

Noah spreads his arms. "I didn't mean for it to happen that way. This got blown into something big and ugly that wasn't my doing. You've got to believe me. None of this turned out the way I intended. Andrew Scarparolo was only meant to rough Charlie up so he'd keep his mouth shut. He wasn't supposed to kill him. I didn't know Scarparolo would have a knife or that he was a psycho. It was *his* fault. All of this. He was sick. A killer. On some sort of power trip."

Charlie dead. His attacker dead. At my hands. How many lives affected by the aftermath? And all for what?

My heart clenches, my chest caving, so I can't get enough breath.

This was all down to Noah. The knife. Scarparolo. Charlie's death. The worst night of my life.

Noah.

"Charlie died," I say.

"Charlie was a dick. He didn't deserve you."

"He was your friend."

"I told you. I didn't mean for it to happen that way." Noah looks up into the evening sky as if the answer is there, then back at me, though I am not the answer. "Then I saw that things might work out for the better now you were free. I had to give you time, a year, after everything you'd been through, and I was at your side the whole time. I was there for you."

I can hit Noah and run. I have to get out of here, keep my baby safe.

But then I'll never get the full story and this may be my only chance. And I have to know the truth.

Think, Kate. I can't think. My head is jammed. I can't move. What to do?

My mouth dry, I swallow. "The flowers from Charlie, breaking into my house, smashing the wedding photo. That was you."

"No." His eyes widen. "I don't know what was going on but I supported you. You remember, don't you?"

"I met a guy at a bar and went back to his place. Someone rammed their car into him. He ended up in hospital."

Noah blinks rapidly. "I don't know what you mean."

I don't trust the blinking. "That was you, wasn't it?"

"I'm sorry. I couldn't bear to think of you hooking up with some random prick. It should've been me with you, not him. I saw red, couldn't help myself. And I went too far."

I'm struggling to put the pieces together. I remember feeling like I was being followed that night but surely that couldn't have been Noah. "It wasn't your Tesla."

"I had a hire car before the Tesla." He shrugs. "A four-wheel drive. It didn't even make a dent. We can put that part behind us. It was a mistake. I admit it."

A mistake? Charlie's death, was that a mistake too? It takes my breath away.

I have to get out. I have to think.

"You killed Esmeralda."

"I didn't touch your cat. I love animals. I couldn't do that."

He sounds so convincing. And Esmeralda is so dead.

"You're lying," I say. "You lie about everything. You're a fake."

"My love for you has never been fake." The softness in his voice throws me. "I've loved you for years."

Love? This isn't love.

He throws himself against me, pain jarring my lower back as he presses me against the balustrade. His body is hard. He's a man. Much stronger than me. He's grabbed my wrists, his grip tight, pressing my arms against the balcony so the edge cuts into my arms. My hands are useless to me. I'm stuck. Shit, I should never have let myself get in this position.

His lips parting, he leans closer, presses a kiss to my cheek. He lingers, his breath warm, then he nuzzles against my neck, as if we're lovers.

"Stop, Noah."

He tries to kiss me but I turn my head. I lean back, my upper body tilting over the balcony. Fifty-five storeys lie below. The tallest building in Perth, the street bustling below, the brick balustrade cutting into me. I can't lean back further. I can't topple over. I can't. Fear pulses through me.

"Oh, come on, Kate. We've done much more than kiss before."

I send in a headbutt, not a good one, but a distraction, enough for an opening.

He loosens his grip on my wrists. I grab his head with both

hands and press my thumbs into his eyes. I'm breathing hard. I let go.

Noah staggers back, his hands covering his face. "No, Kate, no."

I try to make a run for it but Noah swipes at me. I veer away, my eyes on the door, the exit. I have to make it.

Noah stays where he is and swings his legs up onto the balustrade. Stands on it. He's teetering on the balustrade, swaying, the sun setting in the background. Shit, he's going to jump.

No, this can't be happening. I'm rooted to the spot.

There's been so much death already, all of it senseless, and I can't let him die too. Charlie's death haunts me. Maybe it always will. I held his dead body in my arms. I killed a man that night, another death that haunts me. Maybe there was no way around it, but he was still a human being and I took a life. Death isn't the answer.

I'm selfish too. The truth has come out this evening. Maybe there's more truth, a greater truth, or maybe there's nothing else. I only know I can't let Noah die.

"My eyes. What've you done, Kate?"

"Don't look down," I say. "Look at me, Noah."

I give him time. He turns his head and squints at me, then stares with an empty gaze.

I step forward, no sudden movements. "Maybe we can talk now."

"Don't come any closer."

I take another step. "Come down, Noah."

"We could've escaped together. Paris. But you didn't want me."

I can't say yes to Paris now, and he wouldn't believe me anyway.

"I love you, Kate."

His face falls, sadness glimmering in his eyes. He turns,

holds his arms out like Christ the Redeemer, closes his eyes and lets himself fall forwards.

Nooooo!

I leap forward, swiping thin air, then I grab an ankle as he's on the way down.

I've got him, I think. His body slams into the side of the building, a horrible thud.

"Noah!" I scream his name.

No response. Was he knocked out? No way will I be able to hold onto a dead weight.

I'm leaning over the balcony, breathing hard. *Don't look down.* The balustrade digs into my ribs. My body slides forward with his weight. Pain in my gut. No, not my stomach, not my baby.

I can't do this.

I have to do this.

His arms move. He's conscious.

"I've got you."

Only just. His life is in my hands. I don't want the responsibility and I can't let go, no matter what. I can't watch another human being die. There are people below. What if he lands on someone? He'll kill them too.

This is Noah. He might be a crook but he deserves to live, to speak for himself, to tell the truth.

My right hand is gripping his ankle. The other hand slips. I reach for the leg of his jeans. I've only got the hem. It's not enough. If I can pull with my left, it might ease the pressure enough so I can get a better grip with my right. I try. It doesn't work.

Noah lurches lower. One of my feet lifts from the ground.

I'm overbalanced, hanging over the edge. I can't breathe. Can't think or find a way out.

"Let go, Kate."

I hear a voice but I don't know if it's Noah's voice.

Desperation drips inside me. He can't die. Not another death.

There's so much more I need to find out about how Noah could possibly have paid some thug to put an end to Charlie.

Besides, Noah knew I'd be there that night. Didn't he care that I'd have to watch my husband get beaten up, or worse? Didn't he care that my husband was murdered and I killed a man that night? Because I sure as hell care. Noah didn't learn his lesson then. He can't have, not when he followed me and rammed his car into an innocent man, and I can't forget that either.

His life is hanging by a thread and so is mine. He kicks. A death wish. No, not that. I try to hold on. I grip. I squeeze.

He slips from my fingers.

Chapter Fifty-Two

"You're not going to overdo it, are you?" Ryan takes my hand as we wander down the gentle incline to the lake, not a big lake but it's our lake. Well, ours and everyone else's.

"We're not exactly running, are we?" I smile so he knows I'm taking his comment the right way.

I'm tempering my exercise and developing a gentler routine with focus on strength and conditioning, and I'm even looking into throwing some yoga into the mix. No more killer cardio for me because it's not good for pregnant women to get their body temperature up too high, and I'm going to do everything right.

"From now on you can call me Ms Moderation," I add.

There's a freshness to the air that you only get early in the morning, that certain crispness, rolled up with the promise of a new day. Two black swans flap in the lake, the sound reverberating through the air, water rippling around them. The path meanders around the lake and we meander with it.

Ryan slows as we near the playground, then stops. It's early so there's only one family here. The mum has a toddler seated on the bench beside her, as they share a croissant and she passes a sipper cup to the little fella. Dad is watching a slightly older child on the climbing frame, giving her instructions on where to put her hands and feet. Meanwhile Ryan has gone quiet.

"Are you thinking of Chloe?" I ask. "You said she was good at climbing."

He stares ahead. "She wouldn't have needed any help on that thing. She was a natural, like a little monkey."

"Are you okay?"

"Yeah, I'm fine." He turns to me. "That'll be us one day."

"I hope so."

"I know so."

I'm glad he's not as melancholy as I thought.

"You're allowed to be sad sometimes," I say.

He smiles. "I'm happy too."

We set off around the lake, taking our time, enjoying the calmness of our surroundings, and the ordinariness. It's so good to feel normal or something close to it. And right now, close enough is good enough.

It's less calm on the other side of the lake where a group of cockatoos have settled in the gums and other trees packed together on a small island in the lake. The squawking and clattering is an assault on the ears, in the best way possible.

Ryan starts to say something.

"What?" I say.

He laughs and takes my hand as we make our way along the grass away from the lake. Funny how when I was jogging, this gentle incline seemed like a mountain worthy of the Giro d'Italia but now that we're taking our time, it's a walk in the park. Literally.

"Don't suppose you've heard from Laura?" Ryan asks.

"No."

"She'll come around."

Theo said the same thing. He should know, I hope, since

he's married to her. So far, Laura has flat out refused to believe Noah orchestrated Charlie's death. And I understand, or I try to, because it's a horrendous thing to believe of your own brother. Laura's response to the accusations of fraud are another matter, however. Theo said she didn't argue when the authorities told her Noah had orchestrated a massive fraud, and that they were fast gathering evidence against him.

Theo also confessed he never quite trusted Noah with their family investments so he made excuses instead, investing in real estate because it was rock solid. A lot more solid than Noah's financial scheme, as it turns out. Theo also asked me exactly what Noah had said on the rooftop, so I went through it with him. Laura might not be speaking to me but Theo is. It's something.

I'd rather come out with the truth. As far as I'm concerned, there'll be no more secrets, no more keeping things to myself and I'll tell Ryan everything. I can't lumber him with it all at once though, poor guy. Feeling a stab of guilt, I suck in a big breath. Soon.

"One more thing." I tell him about the Elysian Bar and how Will ended up in hospital after Noah rammed into him with his rental car. I'm pretty sure I haven't mentioned this to him before and, judging by the look on Ryan's face, I'm right.

"We're talking about the same night I saw you there?" Incredulity in his voice.

"Yes."

"I can't believe it." He shakes his head. "And Will was the Indian guy at the pub? Have I got that right?"

"Yeah, how did you know?"

"I saw him looking at you. And I wanted you to look at me."

"Oh, Ryan. I don't know what to say. I'm glad you weren't the one who ended up in hospital. You never liked Noah, did you? Maybe you were right."

"Doesn't matter who was right. What matters is that you're safe and sound."

"It doesn't all fit. Some of it does, but there are too many missing pieces." Before we cross the road, I stop to look for traffic even though there are no cars out on the road. "Lots of weird stuff happened, and I don't think it was all down to Noah. I mean, look at Esmeralda. He said he didn't kill her."

We amble across the road.

"He might've been lying. He was pretty good at that."

"True, but it doesn't seem like his style. Neither does sending me flowers from Charlie or smashing our wedding photo. Those things were meant to freak me out."

"And maybe send you running into Noah's arms," Ryan suggests.

"Maybe."

"The police are investigating. You heard what they said. They've got a lot of evidence to get through to build a complete picture. Let them do their jobs."

"I will." I stop at the next street, a busier one, where mums in four-wheel-drives are taking their kids to school. "I wish Noah hadn't jumped. Anything but that."

I'm trying to keep a grip and hold it together, for myself, for Ryan and for the baby.

Ryan takes my hand. "I'm sorry you had to go through that, Kate."

"I wish he was still here, in custody, in jail, on bail, whatever. What he got wasn't justice. It was death. They're not the same."

"No one said it was fair." After a while, he adds, "Maybe you'll have to learn to let it go."

Maybe I will.

Chapter Fifty-Three

Mum's eyebrows go up the middle. "I wanted to check you were okay. And since you wouldn't come to me, I had to come to you."

I drum my fingers on the kitchen counter. "Well, I'm as okay as I can be, under the circumstances."

She comes around to my side of the kitchen bench and covers my hand with hers to keep my fingers still. "That's exactly what I mean. I've been so worried about you. I thought this might be the last straw."

I shrug. "Sometimes I wonder how many last straws there can be."

"I thought you might…" She bites her lip. "You know, try to finish it all."

"Me?"

Despite everything it hasn't occurred to me to 'finish it all' as she has put it. I don't for a minute think that things can get any worse, and I have every reason to live. I'm carrying a life inside me and I have a wonderful man living next door.

The kettle boils so I take my hand back and pour hot water into the coffee plunger.

Mum gives me a pathetic look. "You didn't inherit my strength, unfortunately."

So Mum is strong and I am, what? Weak? She presses my buttons. I know she's doing it, yet somehow I can't make it stop. Was I weak when I killed a man in self-defence? Andrew Scarparolo's name will be forever etched in my mind. Was I weak when I faced Noah?

"I'm not contemplating suicide," I say, though right now I may be contemplating murder.

"You don't know what it's like being a mother, the pain that goes with it, how hard it is." She lowers her gaze. "But you'll find out one day."

That day might be coming sooner than she thinks. She's my mum and I want to tell her I'm pregnant. I bite back my words because I also want this to be a joyous moment.

I pour the coffee into pristine white mugs and get the milk from the fridge. Mum sighs. Moans, actually, her shoulders slumping.

"Are you okay?" I pour a dollop of milk into each mug and put the carton back in the fridge.

"You have no idea what it's been like for me." Her voice is a croak. "I've been having migraines every day, worrying about you, but I still have to dust myself off and go to work to earn a living. A mother's pain is the deepest pain of all. It's been agony for me, watching you withering away like this."

I didn't think I was withering. "Mum—"

"It's okay for you. You've got friends, people looking after you, and you're getting so much attention. I know what you're like. You've always loved the spotlight. But I'm the one with the headaches. No one is thinking about me or worrying about me. I'm on my own, like always." She sighs. "It's okay. I'm used to it."

My blood pressure rises. "What about Renata?"

At the mention of her name, Mum's eyes light up and she forgets about her headaches.

"She's the one person I can rely on. The only one, really. She says *I'll keep checking up on you, Julia, I won't let you down.* I'm too ashamed to let anyone else know it was my daughter up on that roof with that man, Noah Bentley, my daughter who got herself into a dangerous position. Again. What will people think? The shame." She scoffs, tosses her head back. "It's not natural, the number of times you've been in such serious trouble. This doesn't happen to normal people. It's as if there's some sort of curse on you. You attract all these terrible misfortunes."

Ashamed. Not normal. Cursed.

Is that how she feels about me? It sucks the air from my lungs, even though I shouldn't be surprised. I always wanted a mother, someone who believed in me and loved me unconditionally, but somehow it always comes back to *her*.

"It's always been like this," she says.

She's not done yet. She's never done.

I nod. "Yeah, it has."

"You have no idea what I've been through, the hopes and dreams I had for you. All shattered. I've worked so hard all my life, did everything for you. I gave up my own dreams so you can follow yours."

There's one thing I can give her that Renata can't. A grandchild. It's petty of me, I know, yet I can't help myself.

"Actually, I have some rather amazing news," I say. "I'm pregnant."

Mum's mouth falls open. She looks down at my stomach, then back up again, speechless for once.

"I'm serious, Mum."

"Oh my God, how? What? Who's the father?"

"Ryan, from next door."

Silence. It's probably a lot for her to take in.

Then, "You didn't tell me."

"We haven't been seeing each other for long."

"My baby is having a baby." Her voice cracks.

She raises her arms in a giant hallelujah, then throws them around me and pulls me close. Mum's not big on hugging so this tells me how excited she is. When she lets go, tears are glimmering in her eyes. In mine too. I'm shaking.

"I'm going to be a grandmother. Finally!"

There's a little too much emphasis on the 'finally' but I let it go. "Yep, we're both really happy about it."

"So Ryan is fully on board with this?"

"Yes."

"He's not going to leave you to be a single mother?"

I frown.

Mum's lips spread to a smile I can't quite trust, then she splutters and laughs, slapping her hands on her thighs as she doubles over.

"What's so funny?" I ask.

She catches her breath and places a hand on her chest. "Oh, nothing."

Whatever it is, she'll get over it and I probably don't want to know so I don't ask. I take a sip of my coffee.

"It's just," she says. "It's just you can't even take care of yourself. How are you going to take care of a baby?"

Every muscle in my body stiffens.

I am five years old and she's telling me she doesn't deserve such a naughty child. I'm ten and I've broken a glass, and she scolds me because I'm useless, no good at anything and I should get out of the kitchen before I break anything else. I'm fifteen and she's telling me it's no wonder my friends feel sorry for me. I'm twenty-five and she's predicting Charlie will leave me, of course he will.

No, I am better than this.

I press a hand to my temple. "You know what? I've got a migraine too."

Her eyes narrow. "Pardon? Are you trying to get rid of me?"

I don't have your strength, remember? I need to rest. I can't take care of myself. I also can't let her get away with this. No more Mr Nice Guy. I am Ruthless Bitch.

"Actually," I say, "until you start showing me some basic human respect, don't bother."

"Don't bother what?"

"Don't speak to me like I'm some no-hoper. I'm a good person and I'm going to be a good mother."

She takes a step back. "So that's it, is it? What about showing some respect for me, your mother? I can't say anything without you getting mad at me for no reason. And now I may never see my grandchild because of it."

What?

I shake my head. "It's better if you leave."

"Don't tell me what to do." She stalks to the dining chair and grabs her bag. "One day you'll know what it's like, and then it'll be too late."

The tears streaming down her cheeks are real. She leaves.

There's a hole in my heart. And also a sense of relief.

My dearest Andrew

I think about you every day, every waking minute. We were together such a short time but it meant everything to me, just like I know it meant everything to you.

I confess I'm tired of hearing your brother Domenic's name. That stupid woman has mentioned him many times, too often for my liking. He's not half the man you were, Andrew. He's done nothing to avenge your death, though he has followed that Kate around, scared her, put her on edge. It's something, at least. Now it's up to me to write a better ending for this story.

That bitch, Kate, can't see me, can't see what's right in front of her eyes, though I've been here the whole time. I could've done this more quickly, got it over and done with, but where would be the fun in that? It started in Melbourne but I couldn't bear to stay there without you, and I chose Perth for a reason. Because Kate's mother was here. I chose to ingratiate myself. I knew I could find a way and I did.

In fact, it's worked out better than I could possibly have planned. That silly bitch, Kate, went snooping and searching, trying to find out about her husband's life. Her mother told me all about it. Serves Kate right. She thought she was too good for the likes of me. Her and her precious doctor husband.

That was why you killed him, wasn't it? Because you've always hated doctors, lawyers, the lot of them, those so-called professionals. Because they think they're so smart and have such a superiority complex, the arrogant pricks. Well, you showed him, even if it was the last thing you did.

I've taken my time, cultivated a fine relationship with the bitch's mother and played with Kate every step of the way. In some ways, this is my life's work, the greatest novel ever written. I used to dream of writing a modern To Kill a Mockingbird, of taking the literary world by storm and leaving a legacy for future generations. God knows I was wasted as an English teacher, and then those bastards wouldn't let me teach anymore, said I wasn't stable, not fit to be around students. All because of one stint in a mental hospital.

Instead I've done something better than compose a novel. I'm a great writer. With my actions since you died, I've crafted a multilayered story of lasting love and revenge that's building to a magnificent denouement.

But first, the climax.

That bitch is going to pay. Her suffering has to equal yours. And mine. For I have lost so much. You didn't visit me when I was in hospital. I could see it was too much for you to bear, my love. I also used to see the look in your eyes when we were together. You were waiting for the right time to propose, I'm sure, but then you were taken from me too soon and it was too late. We should have been together forever.

I'll love you always.

Now it's time.

<h1 style="text-align:center">Chapter Fifty-Four</h1>

My knuckles hover over the door. I've only been here once before, on the night when I was getting my rocks off with Will Sharma. And I probably wasn't paying much attention to his front door but I know where he lives.

I turn to wave at Ryan, waiting in the car. He waves back. Of course he does, because he's a good man.

I've told the police everything that happened when Noah jumped off the building and everything he told me, and the cops might be satisfied but I'm not. Will ended up in hospital and he deserves an explanation – from me, not only from the authorities – because I still feel partly responsible.

Sucking in a breath, I rap on the door. Eventually there's a strange thunk, thunk and the door is pulled open. Will stands in the doorway. He's on crutches. He opens his mouth to speak, then looks at me like he can't believe I'm here.

I get in first. "I'll be quick. I won't take up much of your time."

He nods. "Actually, it's okay, Kate. Do you want to come in?"

Such a nice guy.

"Out here is fine," I say. "I could've done this over the phone, only I didn't have your number. Have the police been here?"

"Yeah, they have. Look, I'm sorry about the guy who jumped. That must've been terrible."

Will just got even nicer.

"Thanks," I say. "So you know he was the one who rammed into you with his car?"

He nods.

I raise my eyebrows. "And *you're* sorry?"

"Don't get me wrong. I was pissed when I first found out, but I've had time for the news to settle now. The guy must've been obsessed to have been pursuing you, to have used his car as a battering ram, to have jumped off a tall building. Normal people don't do things like that."

There's more I could tell him about Noah's business activities or how he hired someone to rough Charlie up and how the guy took it too far. If we were mates, I could tell Will, but I don't think he wants me as a friend. And I don't need the sympathy. Much better to stick to the point.

I hold Will's gaze. "I wanted to say I'm sorry for giving you a fake name that night, for getting you involved in something outside your control, and for being the reason you ended getting hit by a car and badly injured."

"I think you already apologised when I was in hospital."

"Did I?"

"Besides." He points at his broken leg. "This isn't your fault. It was that guy, Noah's fault."

I open my mouth to argue and find I can't. Those things are down to Noah, not me, with the possible exception of the fake name. Still, I felt compelled to face Will one last time, probably because I'm a better person than Noah, though at the moment I don't think I'm a better person than Will.

"Thanks, Will."

I hear clattering from inside the house, followed by a female voice. "Is everything okay, hon?"

"Sure," he yells. "Won't be long."

I smile and wave and turn away. He's someone's honey and I'm pleased for him. And my very own honey is waiting in his car.

Ryan has texted to say Margaret, his mother-in-law, is next door at his place and that she'd love to meet me. His second message comes later:

I told her. Hope that's okay.

I don't mind, not after everything he's told me about her, even though it's still early days and we're not telling the whole world about the pregnancy. But I understand. Margaret's a significant part of his world.

We've already told Ryan's folks and his sister that I'm pregnant. We did the big Italian dinner with the family thing, with tiramisu, of course. They made such a big deal of our news that it did feel a bit like telling the whole world, only in a good way. His mum started fussing as soon as I walked in the door and the fuss levels went up after we made the announcement. Ryan's dad didn't say much. It's probably hard for the poor guy to get a word in edgewise. But he did say it was wonderful to have a new member of the family and since I'm carrying a grandchild, that's even better. His sister thanked me for taking care of Ryan and bringing so much happiness into his life, only I think it's the other way around.

At least Ryan has taken care of telling Margaret about the pregnancy on his own. I close the front door and stride down the path to see him with a middle-aged woman in his yard. That must be her.

"Hi," I call out.

By the time I'm out of my gate, the two of them are on the footpath outside our houses.

Margaret looks more demure than I expected, more Cottesloe-by-the-beach, with a sleek dyed bob, diamonds glinting in her ears, manicured hands and white pants, though thankfully they're not linen.

She becomes less demure as her eyes fill with tears and she throws her arms around me, babbling about how she's so pleased for us and how she's been dying to meet me and then she's so thrilled all over again. She says my name over and over again like she doesn't want to forget it and grips me tightly.

Ryan places a gentle hand on her shoulder. "It's okay, Margaret."

She pulls back. "It's just that I'm so happy for you."

"Yeah, we got that," he says.

She takes his hand into both of hers. "And I'd like to be part of this baby's life."

"Sure you can."

"I know your baby already has grandparents but you know the saying about how it takes a village. Maybe I can be like a surrogate granny. Or a great aunt. Or at the very least, something like a wise woman from the village. I won't interfere, I promise. But I'd like to be there for the two of you and for the baby. And I'm available for babysitting duties whenever you need me." She stops as tears spill down her cheeks.

Ryan pulls her in for a hug. "It's okay, Margaret."

"I shouldn't think so much about what's been." She steps back, wipes away the tears, her gaze lowered. "I miss her so much."

Chloe. Of course.

"So do I," Ryan says. He waits, then adds, "I'm excited to be a dad again."

She nods. "You'll be a wonderful father."

"And you'll be a wonderful step-granny."

"Hey." I spread my arms. "We'll definitely take you up on the babysitting."

She smiles. "Wonderful."

"See, everything's great," Ryan says. "Is that your Uber?"

"It is." She kisses Ryan on the cheek, then me, and gets into the waiting car, turning to wave as the SUV takes off.

"You're right. Margaret will be a wonderful step-granny." I say this with great assurance even though this is the only time I've met her.

Ryan slings his arm around me like he's relaxed but I can see his jaw is tight, his gaze distant.

"Do you want to talk?" I ask.

"I've spent way too much time talking lately. Some quiet would be nice."

He's been agonising over the last few days, trying to come to terms with something, despite his excitement about the baby. Since Chloe died, he's wanted his ex-wife to forgive Margaret for the car crash, because he knows how good forgiveness feels and because he wanted to reunite a mother with her daughter. But now that Olivia is pregnant again, Ryan has had to accept that she'll probably never forgive Margaret. If expecting another child hasn't changed Olivia, nothing will. So he has to leave that behind him.

Though I'm sad for Ryan, I'm glad our child will have good people in their life: Ryan's folks, his sister, Margaret, Laura maybe if she starts speaking to me. When it comes to my mother, I'm not so sure, and it pains me. Pain after pain after pain. I wonder how much of what she told me about the rest of my family is true and how much is spite on her part. It can't be the case that every member of the family has committed unforgivable wrongs against her, that they're all evil, that no one understands her. Meanwhile I don't know my grandparents or even my own father.

"I can go back to my place if you need some quiet," I say.

"That's not what I meant at all." He takes my hand into his. "Hey, are you okay? Are you thinking about your mum?"

"Something like that. I'm thinking about my dad." I bite my lip, wondering if I should come out with it. "I don't know if he's still in Perth. Mum said he went back to Mauritius but I don't know why he'd go back there when he'd grown up in Australia or why he's never been in touch."

"Maybe he has."

"Sorry?"

Ryan raises his eyebrows. "Do you really think your mother would've told you if he'd called? When you were kids, he might've tried to get in touch but she could've blocked him?"

Now he's mentioned it, that sounds exactly like what Mum would do. I grit my teeth.

"Well, I've been an adult a long time and he hasn't tried to contact me," I say.

"Don't forget, you moved to Melbourne and your brother ran off. It might've been hard to find you."

Another thought hits me. "Dad's parents were around when we were little too, *Grand-mére* and *Grand-père*. Jack remembers them but all I recall was two old people watching me when I came out of kindy a long time ago. I don't know if that was them or if it was my imagination."

Then there's Jack. I'd take him back into my life in a heartbeat if he cleaned up his life. Maybe one day.

"What about your mum's folks?" Ryan asks.

"They're still alive as far as I know. And I have a feeling they're not as horrible as Mum said they were. I'm not even sure where to start."

"Start somewhere." Ryan presses a kiss to my cheek. "Your

dad might be hanging out to be a grandparent for all you know. And if he's not, then that's his loss. He might not be as nauseating as my mum, who's going to be the happiest, effusive, most over-the-top grandma around."

Start somewhere. Good advice.

Chapter Fifty-Five

"You can come if you want."

It's Laura's name flashing on the screen of my phone when I pick up, and that's Laura's voice at the other end.

"Hi, Laura," I say.

We have the world's shortest telephone conversations. It's exactly what I need. Such a relief. I want to be there for Laura at the funeral even if she's barely speaking to me. In a strange way, I also want to say goodbye to Noah, if only to put that chapter of my life behind me. It may be the closest I can get to closure.

Yet another funeral, yet another life gone to waste.

That's how it feels, even if Noah did this to himself. He's also brought enormous grief to his family, to his sister who loved him, and to his niece and nephew who adored him. For what? For money, for a lifestyle filled with first-class air travel and fancy cars, for the illusion of success.

A private service. Laura didn't know what to do, only that

she couldn't face a crowd and she certainly felt a celebration of her brother's life wouldn't be right, given the allegations against him and the evidence that's being gathered.

Only a handful of people are present, all of us sitting at the front of the crematorium looking through a wall of glass onto a small courtyard with giant tree ferns.

I don't hear the funeral celebrant's words. I find it hard to focus. She says something about a photo montage but I can't look up at the screens at the front. I can't bear to look at Noah's childhood photos with Laura, pictures of his teenage years, or to think that Charlie might be in some of the photos. They were best friends, after all. I stare into my lap instead and at my hands twisted together.

What am I even doing here? This is all wrong. Noah was a murderer. He wasn't a good person. He lied to everyone, stole their money, ripped off their life savings and, worse, got his best friend killed. If Noah were here, he'd be telling more lies, trying to talk his way out of it and causing more pain. All he did was create pain for the people who loved him. In many ways, it's easier that he's gone. Yet somehow the finality and the waste and the shame of it all hasn't sunk in.

Shit, my head is a mess. If that's true, why did I try to save him? Why did I hang over the edge of a fifty-five-storey building, endangering the life within me? What the hell was I thinking?

I try to concentrate on taking deep breaths, one in, one out. I take Ryan's hand into mine and squeeze it. This is the life that matters, the life that's here. *Lives*, I correct myself, three of us.

I have my act together by the time Laura gets up to the podium to make a speech that's as beautiful as she is. She speaks in a neutral tone, no platitudes, as she goes through Noah's life from the beginning, their life together and their 'dysfunctional' family. Laura is so polite. Her parents were both useless, so she had to be a mother to Noah and help take care of him. She talks about his friends, happy years at uni, studying and hanging around. Lots of hanging around, as it turns out. She talks about the man who was a generous uncle to her kids but, other than that, it's as if Noah's life stopped in his early twenties. She doesn't mention a university degree or his business accomplishments or the fortune he supposedly accumulated or the way he used other people's money to pursue a lifestyle worthy of the rich and famous. She can't talk about that without lying, and Laura is not a liar.

The celebrant closes the event and suddenly it's over. The world's shortest funeral and also the world's longest. Laura and Theo get up and walk down the aisle and out of the room, their kids behind them.

Relief washes over me. It's finished. I check my phone before we get up, not that I get a lot of messages. There's one from Mum. I'll read it later. If it's full of self-pity and accusations, I won't reply, but I live with a glimmer of hope that the promise of a grandchild might make her change her ways.

Outside, Laura and her family have moved away from the covered area with the hearse to stand in the sun in front of a bed of rose bushes. Theo gives me a hug, makes me feel good, or better at least. The kids are rather fabulous too. Blake shakes my hand and tells me they all appreciate me coming. Mia leaps into my arms, clinging like a koala that's dug its claws in, and I mean that in the nicest way possible.

Next, it's Laura. She takes my hands into hers, holding me at arm's length. She's holding me, that's the main thing. I open my mouth to speak but she gives a curt shake of the head, then she pulls me close, drawing me into the warmth of her embrace.

She's right. We don't need to speak.

Chapter Fifty-Six

After a couple of days, I get a message from Mum.

Sorry I've been so mean to you.

Only all of my life. I might not have been able to see it before but I can sure as hell see it now, clear as daylight, clear as the phone in my hand. I lean back in my chair with a thump.

"Something up?" Ryan asks from across the table. The sun has come out so we're making the most of the fine weather on his back patio, which may one day be my back patio, and most certainly would be if Ryan had his way. Meanwhile I said we should take baby steps for our baby.

"Honestly, my mother never ceases to amaze me." I hold my phone out so he can read the messages she has sent. "I don't know if this is good or bad."

He frowns. I scroll down.

I'd like to talk things through with you over a cup of tea, just the two of us.

I hadn't replied to that message so she sent another.

After that I'd like to get to know your lovely young man a bit better. But first we need to talk. Mum x.

"She's got that bit right." Ryan grins. "Of course I'm lovely!"

"So what do you think?"

That wipes the smile from his face. "I don't like the things you've told me about her or the way she's treated you. She hasn't earned your trust or respect, not yet."

I bite my lip. What Ryan says is true, and yet it doesn't matter. The pull is too strong. This is my mum we're talking about.

He must see the look on my face because he says, "Do you want me to come with you?"

For a mother-daughter tête-à-tête? I shake my head.

"Be careful," he says. "I don't want you to get hurt."

I pipe up with great confidence. "Everyone deserves a second chance."

"Just because she's your mother doesn't give her the right to treat you badly. That's all I'm saying."

I nod, my face lighting up as I type a message.

Okay, I'll come.

It's party-central at the house next to Mum's, cars clogging up the street and covering the neighbour's front verge.

There's a bunch of kids on skateboards who've taken over the road and aren't in any hurry to get out of the way of my car. I don't mind. I worry that other drivers might not take it as slowly as I do. A few teens sitting on the kerb are sharing a cigarette, or maybe a joint. I don't look too closely. None of them seem to be taking any notice of the younger kids running around, dodging the beer cans on the front lawn.

The noise is coming through loud and clear as I pull into Mum's driveway, despite the fact I have Foo Fighters blaring through the car stereo. Sounds like the adults are out the back, their sound system pumping out *doof doof* music, which means they all have to shout to be heard, creating even more noise. I've never been a fan of that stuff. It's the sort of music I suspect only sounds good after a lot of drugs, and that's not my scene.

I wave as I clamber out of the Mini. "Hi."

A couple of the younger kids say "hi" back. The dope-smoking teens are too preoccupied to acknowledge me.

I stop myself from stepping into a puddle of vomit. In Mum's driveway, not theirs. *Nice.* The teenagers laugh. If this was down to one of them, I hope they've got that out of their system. I grab the hose and spray the vomit into the garden bed so Mum doesn't have to deal with it, my actions eliciting a second round of laughing from the teens that gets my goat up. I turn the hose in their direction as I drag it away, 'accidentally' spraying them.

"Hey!" they yell.

I give them my sweetest smile.

Brats, I think.

"Sorry," I say.

I knock on Mum's door, then let myself in with the key, yelling out "Hey, Mum" so she knows it's me. I make sure the door is locked behind me. Habit.

"Come in. I'm here." Mum's voice sounds faint against the backdrop of techno that's reverberating through the walls.

"I'm glad you called." I'm still yelling, unsure if she'll be able to hear me and hoping she doesn't tell me off for shouting. I lower my voice as I near the dining room and kitchen. "I brought some Tim Tams to have with afternoon tea. They're your fave—"

I stop. The biscuits slip from my fingers. My bag slides from my shoulder to the floor, as I raise my hands and take it all in, in one terrible glance.

A gun is pointing right at me, an actual gun. It feels surreal, like I've walked onto a movie set. It's Mum's friend, Renata, only this is no friend. My heart rate skyrockets.

Mum is tied to a chair. A gag in her mouth cuts through her cheeks, terror in her eyes. That can't have been her talking earlier. Must've been a recording. She rocks back and forth in the chair, soft grunts the only sound she can make. The phone in her lap clutters to the floor.

Dread seeps into my bones. Any thoughts this might not be real evaporate. I've walked into a trap.

I could run. I flinch.

"You won't make it," Renata says. "I can't miss from here."

She's right. Shit, I'd run if I had a chance. No point at such close range. All she has to do is pull the trigger. Bullets will cut through the cheap doors and plasterboard walls. I can't leap and tackle her to the ground. I'd be dreaming if I thought for one moment that would work.

I swallow but my mouth's dry, the lump in my throat getting bigger. No one will hear anything, certainly not the neighbours. No one will call the police and it'd be too late if they did anyway.

Mum continues to rock back and forth on the chair, struggling against the restraints and making whimpering noises. Without taking her eyes off me, Renata whacks Mum across the middle of her face with her forearm, the gun in her other hand still pointing in my direction. Mum stops, her head hanging forward, blood dripping from her nose.

"It's about time you shut up," Renata says. She circles right, as she motions for me to move. "Over there, bitch."

Oh hell, it was her all along.

I take a few small steps. This isn't some heat-of-the-moment idea that came to her. She's supposed to be Mum's friend but clearly she's not.

She must've messaged me earlier using Mum's phone. Renata's shown patience and perseverance and planning skills.

She's practised this over and over in her head. She's not some random psycho and she certainly didn't get this far by being dumb. I can't underestimate her.

Can I reason with her? With a gun? Shit, I have to do something.

"Renata," I say.

"You still think my name's Renata!"

She laughs, like she's got one over me, and she has. Any words I had leave my head. My mind is empty. Bolts of fear shoot from one side of my brain to the other. My head's going to explode. I can't breathe. I don't move, don't touch my stomach. And though I try not to give anything away, I'm certain my mother has blabbed to her so-called best friend that I'm pregnant.

"Move it!"

She wants me to stand next to Mum. I move it, just like she tells me. She lets out a long, slow, satisfied breath.

"This is justice," she says.

What is? I want to ask, but my tongue is swollen in my throat. I don't want Mum to die, and I don't want to die, no way. Above all, I want my baby to live. The tiny life inside can't make it without me. Bub needs me. Ryan needs me.

Fear pulses through my veins. Thoughts rocket through my head. Not thoughts. Fragments. Images. Mum's mouth moving but no words. Jabbering in the background, a voice telling me I've done this to myself. Gasping for air, for hope and life.

I know what this is. Panic. *Shit, don't panic.*

"The gun is Andrew's," Renata says. "Fitting, don't you think?"

She means Andrew Scarparolo. He had a gun and she brought it over from Melbourne. Is that what she's saying?

I force myself to listen, to focus, concentrate. My life depends on it.

Her eyes narrow. "I asked you a question, bitch."

"You knew him?"

"He loved me." She shouts the words, her voice a desperate snarl. "And I loved him."

I nod.

"Everyone has one great love in their lives." Calmer now. "Andrew was mine, whereas your *great love* was screwing around with someone else." She pauses. "Wasn't he?"

I nod.

"He didn't love you. That wasn't *love*." She says it like it's a dirty word. "It's not love when you're not woman enough for him, when he has a baby with someone else, and now there's a little Charlie running around on the other side of the country." Her lips spread to an ugly grin. "And you didn't even have a clue."

She stares at me, waits.

"No, I didn't," I say in a small voice.

"You don't know much." The tendons in her neck are straining. On edge. Nervy. "I've been fucking with you this whole time. Julia's such a blabbermouth, she told me how Charlie used to call you his precious and how you use your brother's birthday as your code. It was too easy to get into your house. Then there was the best bit when she told me how upset you were after the flowers and the photo. Distraught. Because you still weren't over Charlie's death. You're fuckwits, both of you."

Forget the flowers and the photo and Esmeralda and everything that's come before. Think about now.

This woman knows what she's doing. She's keeping the gun at a good distance, not miles away and not right up against me. If she's up close, I could try a disarm. Fifty-fifty chance it might work. Fear grips my gut. Who am I kidding? I'm not that good.

She doesn't take her eyes off me as she shifts the gun to my mother. "Now you're going to find out how it feels to watch someone you love die."

"But I…" My voice sounds small, pathetic. I clear my throat. "Haven't I already done that?"

She laughs. "No, that wasn't love. You only thought it was. But this, your mother, you definitely love her. There's no other explanation when she's such a cow to you. Don't worry, she's told me all about it, the way you keep coming back, like a little puppy that's been kicked runs back to its owner. Oh, you might not like her but you love her. And now she's going to die because of *you*. Because you killed Andrew. He was the one good thing in my life, and now he's gone."

A rivulet of sweat drips down the side of my face. "Guns are loud. The neighbours will hear."

"Over all that racket? What do I care anyway? I'll be out of here. I jumped the other neighbour's fence and came in round the back. No one saw me. I'll disappear. I don't exist."

"There'll be forensics, evidence, witnesses, someone will have seen something. You don't have to do this. There's always another way."

"You sly young slag."

Her smile sends a chill up my spine. I'm not young. I'm not sly. I'm not anything.

She points the gun at my belly, then raises it again. *She knows*. Of course she does.

"You didn't even tell Julia you had a boyfriend," Renata says. "Or was he just some random root? Not that there's anything wrong with that, but getting yourself pregnant, now that's another matter. Was that some sort of belated revenge against Charlie, or do you really not understand how contraception works, you stupid, stupid bitch?"

She grins. I have to get closer. I can't run so there's no other option. I try to go through a gun disarm in my head but I don't know the drill and, hell, that was only a drill, and my head is a mess of electrical activity and I can't think, can't move or function. Shit. Fuck. I can't take this anymore.

And I can't stand here like this. My hands still up, I take a small step forward.

Renata's eyes narrow as she shifts the gun to my mother and shoots. Loud, so loud. A bullet rips through Mum's shoulder. She screams, her moan muffled by the gag.

Renata turns to me, the gun pointed at my head. My ears ringing, I'm a ball of fear and scrunched-up muscles, whereas she looks like she could stand there all day, her shoulders relaxed, her demeanour poised.

"See, I don't care about the noise," she says. "If anyone comes in, I'll shoot them."

Glancing at Mum, I let out a whimper. For her, for myself, for my baby.

"Don't worry, she's not dead yet." Renata's voice is a snarl again.

She steps closer. I flinch. And gasp. Her eyes glimmer with appreciation. She's enjoying my fear.

I let her savour it. Her guard is slipping. She's coming closer, moving in slow motion, drawing the moment out. Maybe she doesn't know what she's doing, after all. Maybe this is my chance. I look into those eyes of a woman who's getting everything she wants, and I wonder, what chance?

Renata grips the gun in both hands as she presses the barrel to my chest. She watches, loving every moment.

"I'm going to kill your mother first," she says. "So you can watch. Then I'll put a bullet in your belly. It'll take you a long time to bleed out, but don't worry, I'll shoot you in the head before that happens."

No deep breaths, no thinking, no deliberating. I do it.

I parry her arm to one side. I step off and get my body the hell out of the way of her line of fire. The gun goes off. My eardrums are ready to explode. *Don't stop.* I slam my palm in her face. Distraction. We're shoulder to shoulder. I reach for the barrel of the gun, so hot it burns. I hold on through the pain.

She won't let go. She's strong. We struggle. Shit, I've done this all wrong. I take a moment. I headbutt her. Another distraction. I keep her gun hand close to my body and grip for dear life as I pivot and twist the gun out of her hands, then slam the pistol grip into her face, once, twice, again. She cowers, hunched over. Blood drips down her face. And I see what I have to do.

I keep hold of the gun, as I clinch my hands around the back of Renata's neck. Her head is already down. Asking for it. I have to drop her and make sure she doesn't get up. I've got the gun, but I don't want to shoot her dead, no matter what she's done. So I slam in my knees, one after another. Hammer fist to the back of the head. There's no thud as she drops to the floor in a heap. Why is there no thud?

White noise fills my head. There's no *doof doof* either, only the racket in my mind. I can see Mum rocking in her chair but I can't hear her moaning. Am I deaf?

I look around for my bag, for a phone, for the next steps.

It's over. I'm alive. And so is my baby.

Chapter Fifty-Seven

Ryan moves in to look after me. Apparently, I'm stubborn and refuse to move into his place because then he'll think I've moved in for good. He makes me pace myself, forces me to follow doctor's orders, stops me from going back to work too soon.

Recuperate. Take care of yourself. Take your time. My mantra. Time passes because that's what it does.

We go to the fourteen-week ultrasound together, of course, because we're a couple. We're happy. We're going to be parents.

The ultrasound is amazing. The technology is awesome. Our baby is the most beautiful thing I've ever seen.

It's miracle after miracle. Our baby has a little heart, four chambers, the requisite number, and that little heart is pumping. The head's not so little. Huge, I'd say. Two hemispheres of brain, also the requisite number. Eyes, a nose, a mouth, such a gorgeous face. I can almost see my baby. It's all so clear.

There are two arms, two legs, little fingers, lungs, a spine, a bladder, the wonder never-ending. And a penis. We're having a boy.

My mother has been home from hospital for weeks and on the road to recovery. I've been told. Now that I know she's alive, she's dead to me, which may be ironic but I can't let her keep dragging me down. I still love her and always will because, as Laura explained to me, we're wired to love our parents. That's what makes this so hard and why I feel this ache inside.

It's also why I have to try so hard to fill my life with beautiful things and appreciate every moment. I savour my morning coffee. I make the most of my time with Laura and my chats with Amy who calls every few days. Goes without saying that I love every moment with Ryan. I enjoy the sunshine as I walk to the shops. The rain too. I see layers of green in the garden and skinks darting around and the other day I spotted a praying mantis, every moment a joy. In the evening, I think of three things I loved during the day, and I say them out loud.

Don't get me wrong, things still get very dark and though I'm trying to look at the positive side, I'm forcing myself every step of the way. Luckily, I've found the right psychologist for me, an acquaintance of Laura's, a mature woman who gets me. She tells me this sort of new-found appreciation of life after a traumatic event is normal. Normal takes many forms. I don't think I'm normal, not yet, but I will be one day. That's what the psychologist is for.

There's also yoga. Yoga is a gift.

I didn't know trauma-focused yoga was a thing, until the psychologist told me about it. Yoga makes me focus in a way I didn't know was possible.

Yoga is also the first step on my way back to Krav. Because

as soon as I'm ready, I'll be back at the dojo. Martial arts and training gave me fitness and resilience and determination and the skills that were with me when I needed them the most. Krav saved my life.

And now yoga is saving my life in a different way. The instructor is amazing. I hold each position and focus on my breathing. I'm not used to holding positions. I'm used to smashing and throwing and choking. Now I think only of my breathing. I focus. One breath in, one breath out. I notice the tension and discomfort and I breathe through it. I feel it. I recognise it. I stay in the present. I can't breathe in the future or the past. There is only now. Then there's the next position, the next sensation and the awareness that comes with it.

I come out of the studio, my yoga mat tucked under my arm, bag slung over my shoulder. I take a moment to enjoy the sunshine and the depth of blue of the sky and the high-pitched squeak of a baby bird. I look around and, sure enough, there's a nest in the gum tree on this Subiaco street. Not a magpie, luckily, because I don't want to get swooped. The other trees on the street are London planes, the sun shining through their young leaves that are pretty and perfect until they're hit by the heat of summer in a couple of months.

As I get closer to my car parked a short way down the street, I pick up the pace. Shit. The Mini. Someone has keyed the side of my car, the immaculate red paint job ruined.

I stop and sigh, looking around. Domenic Scarparolo is leaning against a plane tree on the other side of the road, his arms crossed, a smug expression on his face.

Anger courses through me. I recognise the emotion. I love my car. How dare he? Why doesn't he piss off out of my life?

I remember how the police told me afterwards that Andrew Scarparolo had an ex-girlfriend who was in a mental hospital in Melbourne when he attacked me and Charlie, which is why I'd never heard of her. 'Renata' then had another few months to simmer and formulate a plan before she was released. For a nutcase, she had some pretty impressive planning skills and she showed great patience in moving to Perth and ingratiating herself with my mother.

I remember my anger at the police because it was a bit bloody late telling me all of that now, also my anger at my mother who befriended Renata and thought she was eloquent and amazing. *Don't think about it.*

Breathing through it, I let it roll over me. I focus. I can do this. I can do anything.

Scarparolo cups his hands around his mouth. "Goodbye darlin'."

Goodbye is good. Goodbye is fabulous. I might be wrong but I'm hoping he's pissed off out of my life.

Chapter Fifty-Eight

A normal day, where nothing is normal. And where Ryan is awesome.

"You need to take it easy," he says.

I glance up from the KitchenAid because of course Joel would only buy the best. The mixer is good, I have to admit. It does what it's supposed to do. It mixes. I smile and pretend I can't hear Ryan over the noise.

He comes around and switches the machine off.

I still haven't committed to moving in with Ryan. I've told him I have a responsibility to Joel to continue housesitting, but that's only an excuse and I know where this is headed. I like where it's headed, if I'm going to be honest, but there's something holding me back.

"You're getting all manic again," Ryan says. "Like you used to with your exercise. You need to hang back."

"I'm making a cake."

Laura has invited us over for dinner and I don't want to turn up empty-handed. Also, I happen to know her kids love chocolate cake, and mine is superb if I do say so myself.

Ryan places his hand on my lower back. "Why don't you sit down and I'll take over?"

"I'm pregnant, not incapacitated. I'm taking care of myself and the baby." I place a hand on my stomach even though it's not exactly huge. "I'm not going crazy with the exercise."

"You're doing too much."

He's right. I hate it when he's right.

"You shouldn't overbeat a cake mix," I say, as if this is a delicate operation and no one other than me can handle it.

"Kate, I've designed buildings and done house renovations. Trust me, I can bake a cake."

"Okay, I trust you."

It hits me that I do. And I need to trust him even more. I need to tell him. Everything.

I sit at the table while Ryan finishes mixing the cake. I've already lined the cake tin with buttered wax paper so the mixture doesn't stick, ready for the next step.

A picture of Renata flashes in my mind. I didn't kill her or beat her to oblivion. I knew exactly where that line was, and I didn't cross it, not that time. She's where she belongs, back in a mental institution, and I hope she stays there. I don't want revenge or complete annihilation or for her to rot in jail for the rest of her life. Sure, she might get let out one day and I'll worry about that when it happens. I have enough to worry about now.

I did the right thing with Renata. I couldn't bear to have another life on my hands. It's been hard enough to live with myself as it is.

Ryan is clattering around in the kitchen. I hear the sounds, the scraping of plastic in the mixing bowl, the soft gloop-gloop as he tips the mixture in the tin, the oven opening, Ryan's voice as he chats, yet somehow it's not registering properly.

I have to get this over and done with. Air, I need air.

"Can we go outside for a sec?" I say.

"Sure."

"I want to show you something."

We step onto the deck and I lead Ryan to the spot where he buried Esmeralda.

"I bought a climbing rose." I point to the potted plant sitting on the garden bed ready for me to plant.

"That's perfect for Esmeralda."

I raise my eyebrows. "You think so?"

"Absolutely."

"I only hope Joel approves of my plant selection."

The sun on my back warms me and despite the fact the heat isn't exactly searing, I pull my sleeves up. Ryan has seen my scars many times before so it's no big deal, that's what I tell myself. It's also good practice for summer when I may actually get back to wearing sleeveless tops.

I'm procrastinating, distracting myself with other thoughts. I don't know where to start, or how. Not only am I a procrastinator, I'm something much worse, a murderer. Whereas Ryan is a good man. As the father of my child, he should know everything I've done and the kind of person I am.

"Are you okay?" he asks.

Perspiration beads on my forehead. My heart is thumping like crazy. My lips part. *Talk, woman.*

The eternal torture. I want to forgive myself for killing a man but I can't let go of it. Can't even speak the words. I have to.

I take a deep breath. "I've told you about the night Charlie and I were attacked."

Ryan nods.

"I killed a man," I say.

"I know."

"I didn't have to kill him."

"It was self-defence." Ryan's eyebrows go up in the middle,

his expression softening, and I wonder if he'll look at me this same way afterwards.

"I've always said it was self-defence," I say. "But that doesn't quite cover it. I'm not who you think I am."

He gives me a look like he doesn't believe me.

"You know most of what happened," I say. "Charlie had been stabbed. He was done for. Then Scarparolo went for me with the knife. It was frantic, stabbing, slashing, in and out, the knife slicing through like I was butter. Then we ended up on the ground. I lied to the police, Ryan, I lied to everyone."

He waits for me to continue.

"I told the cops I didn't know how it happened, that I must've landed with my elbow at Scarparolo's throat, that it was bad luck." I swallow. "Luck had nothing to do with it."

Ryan nods. "Go on."

"By that time, the knife was gone. I remember feeling it underfoot and the sound as it slid away across the concrete. And I thought, *He doesn't have the knife anymore.* Somehow I landed on top of him. I got in quick and hammered him across the face. One good shot that made the back of his head slam into the concrete. And I knew how easily this could have gone the other way. I kept hitting. Saw his eyes roll back. He was out. Probably. I jammed my thumbs in his eyes and started to get up."

"Kate, you did what you had to do. I have no doubt of that."

"Andrew Scarparolo wasn't moving. I'd straightened my arm, and I had a moment, not much time, just a moment when I could think about my choices. Run, maim, scream, stay, give up, get up and get the knife. I saw his throat was exposed. I took it all in. I knew what could happen and how dangerous this was. Lethal even."

Even under all that stress, part of me knew there was the moment before and then there would be the moment after.

Ryan takes my hands into his. "Oh, Kate."

"I knew. And I did it anyway. I slammed my elbow into his throat, dropped my full weight on him, knowing exactly how devastating that strike would be and that it would probably kill him. I didn't have to do it. So is that murder? Or is that self-defence?"

That's the big question I didn't want answered by police or the court or anyone else because one thing I know from talking to Laura is that the law isn't about what's fair. The law is only about the law.

And I killed a man. Acted with a singular aim. Sounds a lot like murder to me.

I remember the look in Andrew Scarparolo's eyes earlier that night, the ordinariness in his expression, how he had the look of a man going about his business. That's what scared me the most, other than the knife, of course. And although I didn't have a mirror and I'll never know for sure, I'm pretty sure that's the same look I had when I finished him off. Just going about my business. Job done.

"You know what else?" I say. "I whispered the words *Die, motherfucker* like he was a cockroach, like something out of a lame movie or like he was nothing." I drop my head into my hands. "I'm not so innocent after all."

There. I've finally told someone.

Ryan pulls me into his arms and holds me. I used to think Charlie's hugs were the best but they're nothing compared to Ryan's, because he has so much more strength and integrity. I couldn't bear it if this was the last time he'd hold me in his arms and I couldn't stand it if he looked at me with disgust and despair because now I was a lesser being.

He breaks off the hug, cradling my jaw in both hands, and gazes into my eyes. He's not letting me go. He's hanging on.

"No one should have to go what you went through," he says. "You made the right decision."

I nod, though I'm not sure what was right or wrong, only that I'm alive and that's got to be a good thing.

"You haven't told anyone, have you? Not Laura?"

I shake my head. "No."

"Good. Look, from my point of view, I think you did nothing wrong, but the courts might say it was unreasonable force against someone who wasn't armed at the time. Or they might not. Point is, you don't want to go there. There's too much at stake. I don't want you to…"

To end up in jail. He doesn't need to finish the sentence.

I nod. "It's why I haven't said anything before."

"We don't need to find out what other people or the courts would think. You don't need to go through that again, like you did in Melbourne. And we don't need to talk about it anymore. Unless you want to. I'll go with whatever you want, Kate."

I want to have a healthy baby and a normal boring life doing lots of normal boring things. And I want Ryan.

"You don't want to back out?" I ask. "You're not afraid of living with someone like me?"

"I'm not scared of you, Kate. I'm in love with you." He smiles. "And I'll feel pretty safe walking around with you at night anywhere, any time, any place."

I take his hand. "Let's go inside."

He pulls me closer. "I'm glad you told me. But remember, I'm not a cockroach."

"I'll remember."

"Because you're pretty scary when there's a cockroach around."

"Lucky you're not a cockroach, then."

"Thanks. That's some compliment."

I give him a gentle nudge. "Wouldn't want you to get a swollen head."

THE END

Acknowledgements

My biggest thanks goes to James who is my best buddy, my biggest fan and also my first reader. I wouldn't be who I am today without you. It took me years to come out of the closet and say I wanted to be a writer and since then, you've believed in my books completely. No one understands me the way you do.

Thanks also to my talented son Louis and Tyra, the newest member of the family, for all your support. I remember some years ago when you said you had better things to do than *read* on your school holidays. I'll be quizzing you about this book.

A big shout-out to Michelle Kelly for being a good friend, for answering my cat questions and for being living proof that not all cat ladies are childless. You might notice that the place in Laura's laundry where the kitty sleeps is remarkably similar to yours.

Sally Smith and Una Couper were a great help with legal matters and the concepts around self-defence. I didn't know how to apply for a restraining order before but I do now. Our book club is indeed a group of accomplished women. Among other things, we're very good at discussing topical issues, devouring a cheeseboard and drinking wine.

Thanks to Noah Greenstone for sharing your fifty years of Krav Maga, self-defence and other training, and for running an awesome dojo. I'm honoured and inspired every time I go to training. And exhausted when I leave.

I recently found the opening chapters of an earlier version of *Under the Skin,* which was completely unrecogniseable.

Thanks to my fabulous writing friends who've been with me all the way and who provided feedback on that early version: in no particular order, Lorraine Mauvais, Claire Boston, Teena Raffa-Mulligan, Juanita Kees and Anna Jacobs. And a big thanks to Teena for her initial proofing.

I've got to thank Michael Cain for many years of friendship and for being more excited about my book deal than I was. I can be a bit slow sometimes but I'm definitely excited now.

Which leads me to the fabulous team at Bloodhound who believed in me. Thanks to Rachel Tyrer for picking up *Under the Skin*, Betsy Reavley and Tara Lyons for all your work, Ian Skewis for your thoughtful editing, and thanks also to the rest of the team. I have a horrible feeling I may have missed someone because I'm still getting a handle on what you all do.

And thanks to YOU of course for reading my book.

About the Author

A former librarian, Susanna Rogers has an honours degree in philosophy with cognate studies in English. She lives on a leafy street in sunny Perth, Western Australia. By day, she works in a sensible position as a copywriter but the rest of the time, she doesn't have to be sensible. Instead she writes psychological thrillers featuring kick-butt heroines and trains in kickboxing and Krav Maga. Because life's too short to be a grown-up.

A note from the publisher

Thank you for reading this book. If you enjoyed it please do consider leaving a review on Amazon to help others find it too.

We hate typos. All of our books have been rigorously edited and proofread, but sometimes mistakes do slip through. If you have spotted a typo, please do let us know and we can get it amended within hours.

info@bloodhoundbooks.com